ORDER OF FEAR

LISA CAVINESS

Dream Theory Publishing

For Mr. America and our three ducklings.

Chapter 1

By the end of this day I will no longer be a bride about to marry.

Marveling at the majestic mountain scenery, Marissa climbed aboard the hotel's airport shuttle and sank into the only vacant seat. She glanced out at Salt Lake City's early morning crisp blue sky, gripped the straps of her purse, and inhaled. Despite the reputation of smelly air from the bacteria decay in the Great Salt Lake, Marissa's lungs escaped putrid intrusion. The kinetic scene—vibrant and hopeful—stood in total contrast to her mood.

My day begins surrounded by the beauty of the Wasatch Mountains and will end in the demise of a four-year relationship.

Calling off her wedding triggered a lengthy list of decisions and activities. Three items competed for the top spot on Marissa's unavoidable to do list: grieving the death of her relationship, chiding her stupidity in falling for David in the first place, and finding a new place to live. Her heart rattled in response to the immense change. Home would no longer be her "can't wait to get to" place.

Sighing, Marissa settled her laptop bag in between her feet and tossed away thoughts of a cancelled wedding and broken engagement, just for a little longer. Instead, she considered her trip. The meeting with her firm's newest client had gone well. As an accountant, she'd been thrilled with their prepared and organized portfolio, which spoke well for the working relationship she'd encounter with the company, Royce Electronics. After her meeting yesterday, she'd relayed her excitement to her boss, Bernie Dunbar. His faith in her ability to handle this multi million-dollar account had placed Marissa on par for partnership in the corporate accounting firm.

She smiled. Marissa Nash, CPA and partner in the accounting firm of Van Buren and Dunbar, would be a dream realized. Perhaps there *was* a bright spot in her life right now.

The driver stored the last of the luggage in the back, turned his navy Utah Jazz cap—visor portion to the back—and started the engine.

As the bus jerked forward, Marissa's shifted in her seat, thoughts of her life altering plans caused a wrinkle of panic. Now that her business trip had concluded she had no more excuses. She'd accepted the last minute business trip in hopes of getting a break from the wedding preparations and more importantly to think about her future. No luck forgetting the wedding plans. Constant calls from her mother wouldn't allow for any neglect. She couldn't blame her mother but Marissa needed this trip to come to terms with what she already knew she had to do. Measured and circumspect were great attributes for an accountant and those qualities carried over into all parts of her life. She rarely made a rash decision.

"Who takes a business trip so close to her wedding?" her mother had complained before she left.

A bride whose groom had other female interests, Marissa had wanted to say.

"Excuse me." An elderly lady sitting across from her smiled.

Marissa turned toward the woman. "Yes?" Bright, inquisitive eyes belied a wrinkled, tanned face, her posture erect and regal.

"You have a beautiful engagement ring. When is the wedding?" The woman nodded toward her sparkling one-carat diamond.

"Next week." Marissa's ring finger began to itch, as if the circular band constricted her digit. The square-cut rock sparkled, but did nothing to calm the distress raging inside. For the first time since she'd made her decision, she considered the ramifications. The gorgeous ring would be the first of many casualties. Sadness stabbed at her heart as she stared at the piece of jewelry, which should have made her insides flutter.

Her fiancé, David Seybold, had been ecstatic to present her with the bauble, but the proposal was a long time ago, and circumstances had changed. She spun the diamond, and the rock disappeared under her finger like the moon in an eclipse.

"I'm in Utah to visit my first great grandchild." The elderly woman opened her wallet, and pulled out a picture of a pink-faced baby swaddled in a yellow blanket.

Marissa ignored the bolt of pain slashing through Marissa's stomach. "She's beautiful. My best friend has a six-month old. When I held him for the first time he had me hooked."

The woman smiled, slipping the photo back into her purse. "Babies can melt your heart in seconds. Her parents live two hours away, so I had them bring me to the hotel yesterday. I didn't want them getting up at the crack of dawn to drive two hours, especially with a newborn." She turned to Marissa. "You remind me of my grand niece. You both share exotic green eyes and beautiful brown hair." She smiled. "You will make a stunning bride. Enjoy this time."

Marissa nodded. "Yes, ma'am." Could strangers tell something she lacked enthusiasm for her own wedding? Turning from the woman, she extracted her phone from her purse to check the flight's status. Perhaps bad weather back in Virginia would delay her arrival. A few seconds later, with mixed emotions, she noted the flight's on time departure. She should be back in Virginia by early afternoon. A ripple of panic flowed through her. A delayed flight might not be such rotten luck.

The elderly lady cleared her throat. "I'm Stella Richey, from Ohio. My daughter is always scolding me about striking up conversations with strangers but if I introduce myself we're no longer strangers." She smiled, her brown eyes crinkling at the corners.

Marissa returned the smile. "Marissa Nash. I'm on my way home to Virginia." The mention of home tugged at her heart again.

Ten minutes later as they pulled into the airport, Marissa could still spot the mountain range in the distance, tempting her to miss her flight and hide out in a ski lodge. She sighed. No use putting off the unpleasant mission any longer.

The driver slammed on the brakes and jumped out of his seat. He sprinted to the rear luggage area and tossed bags onto the curb.

Marissa gathered her purse and laptop bag and made her way to the front. Cars, buses, and taxicabs mixed with people milling about or rushing inside the terminal. She rounded the back of the shuttle, holding her breath as noxious exhaust fumes puffed out. Spotting her blue hardtop bag, she pulled the luggage onto the curb.

Mrs. Richey stood on the sidewalk, fumbling through her purse. "Where did I put that ticket?"

In the rush of passengers scooping up their bags Mrs. Richey lost her balance, sending her purse flying. Medicine bottles, keys, a wallet, and coins scattered across the pavement.

Marissa left her bags on the curb and rushed to help.

"Thank you, honey." As Marissa retrieved the errant items, Mrs. Richey tossed them into her purse.

"You're welcome." Marissa returned her wallet and then bent to retrieve a medicine bottle. In her periphery, a cab pulled up to the curb several feet away.

As Marissa stood, she spotted a blonde woman jump out of the back seat. A shiny pendant, hanging around the woman's neck, flashed in the sun. In an instant the woman flew behind Marissa, knocking her further into the street at the same time the cab accelerated.

The impact sent her flying. Screams from nearby people and the cab's screeching brakes registered in her mind. She crashed to the ground, her back slamming into the concrete. Pain seared through her body. Her vision narrowed and fuzzy flickers of lights sparked in her periphery, like thousands of tiny fireflies emanating their luminescent glow. As she lay on the ground, she saw the hazy fire dim to black.

Chapter 2

Marissa stared at blurred white ceiling tiles and grimaced as pain trampled across her head.

"Can you tell me your name?" A man leaned over her, his watery blue eyes pierced and focused.

"Marissa Nash," she croaked out. With splayed hands against a narrow bed, she struggled to a sitting position. A large collar encircled her neck and made moving difficult.

Strong hands held her in place. "Whoa. Let's not sit up yet." He waved a bright light in front of her eyes several times and nodded. "I'm Dr. Rigsbee. Can you tell me what happened?"

Marissa blinked at the offending light and another bolt of pain shot through her head. "I was hit by a cab at the airport. I arrived by ambulance at this hospital somewhere in Salt Lake City. I had a flight back home to Virginia." *There. I couldn't have been clearer.* She'd already been asked these questions in the ambulance.

She stared up at the doctor. His hair, as white as his lab jacket, and his pale blue eyes reminded her of the brilliant Utah sky above snowcapped mountains.

Dr. Rigsbee chuckled. "Okay, that sums it up." He continued to examine her, his warm hands gentle against her goose bumped skin.

"You have a few cuts and bruises. I don't anticipate any broken bones, but I'd like to get a head computerized tomography scan, a CT scan, just to make sure there's nothing more serious."

After completion of the CT scan, which showed no further injury, Marissa winced as Dr. Rigsbee removed the cervical collar. Grasping the bed's side rails, and with the help of the doctor, Marissa sat up. Immediately, the room spun like an out-of-control planet on a tilted axis. She blinked several times as her vision stabilized.

Dr. Rigsbee straightened. "You have a mild concussion and likely will have a bad headache and some dizziness, which should dissipate within twenty four hours. It's best to take it easy for a few days and see your doctor for a follow up exam."

Marissa offered a weak smile. "Thank you. I can rest when I get home. I need my phone so I can arrange for a cab to the airport. Hopefully, not driven by the same insane driver who hit me."

"Air travel isn't ideal and can exacerbate the symptoms of a concussion." He clasped his hands together in front of him as if preparing to lecture a student.

"I really need to get back home today. Is there a pill or something I could take?" Marissa shifted on the bed and lifted her hand. She surveyed red cuts on her palm she assumed occurred from a hard landing in the street.

"I can give you something for the headache but if you won't consider delaying your plans for another day, I'd at least like to observe you for a couple of hours. As a precaution." He patted her arm, smiled, and left the room.

A nurse made her comfortable with a cup of water and a warm blanket.

Marissa glanced around the room. "Where are my purse, luggage, and laptop?"

"Your purse and luggage are under the bed but you didn't come in with a laptop." The nurse checked under the bed again, shook her head, and handed Marissa her purse.

Marissa gasped. Her heart fluttered and another dagger of pain lanced through her head. "I have sensitive work information on that computer. Even password protected, a skilled IT person can get in." Thoughts of client fallout from leaked sensitive financial information ramped up her pulse. All her hard work to achieve senior accountant status headed toward partnership wavered at the thought of admitting to a stolen laptop.

"Try to stay calm. I'll check with the EMTs." The nurse exited the room.

Marissa closed her eyes. *What a nightmare.* Her boss would be concerned about her, but theft of a company computer her firm considered a major issue.

A few minutes later, the nurse returned and informed her the EMTs didn't have her laptop, nor had they noticed a bag anywhere around her at the scene. She could try the airport to see if someone turned in a laptop, and if not, make a police report.

One more problem.

David would be expecting her—maybe. By the time she departed for Utah, she hadn't seen him in three days. She finally spoke with him before leaving the hotel that morning. He'd been distant and preoccupied, which wasn't anything new. She'd made the intentional decision not to announce her desire to discuss their future, for fear he'd disappear again. Claiming work demands, he'd already pushed their honeymoon back by a couple of days. In addition, he'd canceled wedding-related meetings, neglected dinners, and his increased irritability were only a few examples of his out-of-character behavior of late. Before her trip, she'd discovered the reason—a trampy big bosom woman with a penchant for sexting.

She pulled her cell phone from her purse to see four messages from her mother. She played the first one, but clicked off before finishing. Ava Nash's latest panic button point—hors d'oeuvres. She didn't want to alarm her mother with news of her accident, which would then cause her father to worry, and then her bossy sister, Vanessa, would get involved.

She couldn't bring herself to call David. Instead, she picked up her phone and called her best friend, Kelly.

"Are you home already?" Kelly didn't bother with a hello, thanks to caller ID.

"No, I had an accident. I'm fine, though. Some idiot taxi driver hit me at the airport. I have a mild concussion, but I will be heading home as soon as I can get another flight."

"Are you sure you're okay? I can catch a flight out and help you get back home."

The concern in Kelly's voice warmed Marissa's heart. "Thanks, but I'll be fine. Just don't tell my mom. She's in wedding mode, and this trip has already sent her over the edge."

"She's called me twice today," Kelly groaned. "Something about hors d'oeuvres."

The baby gurgled in the background.

"Is that Gavin?" Kelly and her husband, Craig, became parents six months ago and had named Marissa as godmother. Although she could never replace Kelly, she'd been honored at the important role in his life and couldn't help thinking how her own life would be with a baby.

"Yes. He's teething, so he's a bit cranky." Kelly calmed the baby, and then said, "David must be worried sick."

"I didn't call him, so I'd appreciate if you wouldn't either." Marissa didn't want to talk to David.

"Have you made any decisions?" Kelly and Marissa had a three hour-long phone conversation last night about her plans. At the time, Marissa hadn't been completely sure of her next move but with the morning came new perspective.

"Yes, but Kel, the nurse is here. I'll text you with my flight details." Marissa ended the call and leaned back against the pillow. She hated lying, but she couldn't talk about her decision yet. The next few days would be torture. Running away to a ski lodge appeared even more inviting.

Two hours after another exam and promising to see her doctor when she got home, Marissa settled into a cab on her way back to the airport. She'd managed to get a direct flight out, arriving in Virginia by five. Traffic would be horrendous, but at least she'd be home.

She darted into the terminal without being run over and headed to the airline's counter. Her laptop hadn't been turned in, but a representative filed a report and promised to contact her if the computer was located. *Fat chance.* Marissa also filed a report with the Salt Lake City police. Her stomach growled, alerting her she hadn't eaten all day, but the thought of food didn't sit well. Ignoring hunger pains, she bought a bottle of water to appease her appetite.

When she reached the gate, she collapsed into a seat. The medicine the doctor had given her hadn't touched the ringing in her head. Disregarding the pain, she fished a pad of paper from her purse and made a list of items to address with her wedding planner.

The plane landed a few hours later, and her mother greeted her first with a phone call.

Marissa explained her flight had been delayed and she was bone tired. She promised to come over for breakfast in the morning and discuss wedding details, which mollified her mother. Marissa slid into her SUV, which had been baking in the long-term lot of Dulles International Airport under unseasonably scorching early June temperatures.

The stop-and-go traffic into Virginia lasted over an hour and ramped up her stress level and headache. When she pulled into the condo's two-car garage beside David's silver BMW, she wished only to curl up with her dog, a Hungarian Kuvasz, named Halo, and take a nap. Part of her hoped David wasn't home, but postponing the inevitable would be cruel.

Before she could get out of the car, Marissa heard Halo's deep bark. Like a mother knows her baby's cries, Marissa recognized the barks coming from inside weren't happy or playful.

Unlocking the kitchen door, she stepped into a dark room. *Odd.* The kitchen blinds were usually open during the day. David must have forgotten. She took a tentative step forward pulling her bag inside. As she deposited her bag and purse just inside the door, Halo jumped on her from somewhere to her left. The 100-pound ivory-colored canine licked her face.

"I missed you, too. What are you doing in the dark? Where's David?" Marissa rubbed his head.

Halo nudged at her and barked a few more times.

"What's wrong with you, Halo?" The stale odor of sweat prickled her nose as she reached for the light switch and called out, "David!"

With a click, the lights illuminated the destruction of the room.

In shock, Marissa stared at the mess. *We've been robbed?*

Her breath caught.

Kitchen drawers were pulled out, their contents strewn about. Smashed dishes were scattered across the floor.

Halo nudged at her again.

Marissa pulled him close and backed toward the garage door. She turned ready to bolt. Then something caught her attention.

The quickening of her heart and the prickling of her skin rendered her motionless.

Red stains smeared Halo's cream-colored coat. "Are you hurt?" She ran her hands over his fur but found no injury. "We need to get out of here." As she turned she glanced through the kitchen and into the den, noting a crumpled mass on the floor. For a moment she assumed her vision had blurred due to the concussion. She blinked but the mass remained.

A step closer and her heart dropped.

"David?" Marissa jumped over broken plates, ignoring the possibility the intruders could still be inside. "David!"

He remained still.

"David, wake up. Please wake up!" She tapped his blood-caked shirt and then shook him.

His head rolled to the side, and he stared in wide-eyed horror.

Marissa scuttled back, slamming into an overturned coffee table. *This can't be happening.*

She crawled closer and placed her ear on his chest in search of a heartbeat, even though deep down she didn't expect to detect a sound. Marissa gasped and pulled away. "David!" Tears blurred her vision. She screamed.

Halo joined her in a howl of his own.

She stumbled back and ran to the kitchen. Ruffling through the disorder, she found a kitchen knife to use as a weapon and rushed toward the door. Scooping up the purse she'd dropped, she ran through the door and into the garage. "David is dead!" Breathless like she'd just sprinted a mile, her heart drummed. The knife slipped from her hand as she fumbled through her purse and found her cell phone. When she heard the operator pick up the call, Marissa screamed, "Please help me. My fiancé is dead!" After several prompts from the operator, Marissa managed to relay her address.

Halo barked and jumped around her causing her to drop the phone. She could hear the operator talking in muffled tones but her heart beating in her ears dominated.

Maybe he wasn't dead. She eyed the door. *Should I go back inside?* He needed help.

She picked up the knife and peered inside at the destruction. He hadn't moved. Tiptoeing inside with Halo next to her, Marissa kneeled at David's side.

His lips were blue, almost black, and his mouth drooped open.

She struggled to catch her breath. For a moment Halo had quieted and the erratic huffing of her own breath dominated the room. Her vision tilted and she had the sensation of being in a room sucked free of air, taken over by death.

She shivered as droplets of perspiration erupted on her skin. With a shaking hand, she touched the side of David's face.

The quarter-sized hole in the middle of his forehead, now caked with dried blood represented the bullet's deadly entry into his skull. The bullet's explosive exit annihilated half of the back of David's head.

Ignoring the condition of David's body, she cradled his head. "David, David," she chanted. The sticky sensation of his blood coated her hands. This wasn't supposed to happen. She'd been ready to tell David she couldn't marry him. Maybe they could have worked through their problems, or maybe they could have parted as friends, but now they'd never get a chance. Anger and preoccupation would no longer alienate them. The easy humor and quick laugh, absent in recent weeks, would never return.

Halo stood next to her, his warm fur plastered against her damp arm.

Surrounded by blood, she glanced at one wall of the kitchen. Her stomach roiled as she studied the brain matter splattered on the wall like abstract art. The wall, once tan in color, had been stained a ghastly shade of red.

Marissa blinked several times, hoping to erase the sick scene, but the reality remained. David was dead.

The last few weeks she'd been embroiled in romantic, tranquil colors. Soft peach hued roses. Elegant gray candles. Delicate swirls of ruffled silver icing on a too-pretty-to-eat wedding cake. A snowy white wedding dress.

Now her world was blood red.

Chapter 3

This best man responsibility included a lot more than Dr. Justin Tanner had anticipated. A best man needed to organize the bachelor party, stand next to the groom at the wedding, and make a toast at the reception. He'd been running errands and had been recruited to pick up wedding guests at the airport later in the week.

Now he understood the difference between getting married and having a wedding. Getting married involved a license and a name change. Having a wedding meant a huge, stressful production. At the moment, Justin wanted no part of either.

He considered a twelve-hour marathon nap like winning the lottery, but sleep would be an elusive beast today. He'd been called in earlier to perform emergency surgery on a car accident victim. Five hours and a successful case later, Justin emerged from the catacombs of Highland Memorial Hospital.

As he climbed into his blistering Toyota Land Cruiser, he sighed, mustering the energy to keep going for the next hour. First stop, an overdue haircut. The light brown hair skating an inch below his collar required a trim to meet best man standards. David and Marissa's wedding pictures shouldn't be sullied by his straggly appearance.

Thirty minutes later, with a fresh haircut, he climbed back in the Toyota. As he pulled out of the parking lot, he heard his cell phone ring. A quick glance at the screen indicated another call from the jewelry store. The jewelers couldn't locate David, and Marissa hadn't answered their calls. Justin had been the next authorized person to pick up the rings. He didn't even know jewelry stores authorized people to pick up rings, but apparently, as the best man, he'd been designated. After ending the call with the jewelers, he punched the button for David's cell on his car panel and, for the third day in a row, received no answer. Justin huffed out a breath. Second stop, jewelry store.

Once home, tired and still grumbling about David being MIA, he took a shower and collapsed into bed. He got two full hours of sleep before his pager went off again, summoning him back to the hospital after his patient experienced complications. After another exam and altering the patient's medication, Justin scooted up to the computer at the nurses' station to check labs on his other patients. He wrapped up his charting and double-checked coverage for all of his upcoming vacation days.

"Dr. Tanner, thanks for coming back in. Mr. Collier's blood pressure is stabilizing," said Carol, one of the nurses.

"I reviewed his latest labs. Much better." Justin logged off the computer and moved to the other side of the nurses' station. "While I'm here, I'll check on a few other patients, but I'll examine Mr. Collier again before I leave." Justin glanced at his watch. "Oh, and please call his daughter with an update. She had to go home to relieve the babysitter."

"Will do." Carol nodded.

"Thanks." Justin smiled. "Keep my patients alive while I'm on vacation."

Carol chuckled. "Like I said to my kids when they were young, don't make me come after you."

Justin laughed. He enjoyed working with Carol and found her no-nonsense approach with doctors refreshing. Justin understood how arrogant and demanding some of the doctors could be, so he appreciated Carol having the guts to stand up to them.

Most of his colleagues hadn't seen a lick of military training and didn't share the spirit of camaraderie and brotherhood, which existed as the backbone of military life, particularly in a war hospital. Over five years ago, he had fought for the lives of his fellow soldiers alongside nurses and techs. They were all equal team members, and they shared an internal ache when they couldn't save an injured soldier. Here in this civilian hospital, doctors were doctors, the top chiefs on the totem pole, while nurses fell somewhere beneath. Carol appeared oblivious to the unwritten hierarchy, despite her twenty-year nursing career.

She grinned and peered over the rims of the half-moon glasses perched on the tip of her thin nose. "Are you out of town for Army Reserve activities, or to spend time with someone special?"

Carol had been after him to settle down, but a relationship didn't figure into his priorities now. "No Reserve duties until next month. I'm the best man at a friend's wedding, and then I'm heading to my aunt and uncle's for homemade apple pie, fishing, and sleep. Not necessarily in that order."

"Maybe some nice girls will be at the wedding. Keep your eyes open." She winked and patted him on the shoulder before retreating into the private office to call Mr. Collier's daughter.

Yes, at least one nice girl would be there, but she'd be wearing a big, white dress. He'd stand beside David, recite a clever toast, and then get the hell out of Dodge.

After two surgical consults and a quick perforated ulcer case, Justin glided through the automatic doors. Steamy heat slammed into him. He slid into his SUV, cranked up the air conditioner, and pulled out his cell phone. Once again, he got no answer on David's cell. He had already called the condo several times and left messages. Marissa was out of town, and he hadn't heard from David in days. David always returned a call within a day.

Fifteen minutes later, Justin pulled up to the GT Training and Rehab Center, a plain two-story concrete building. David and Justin often worked out at the center. Maybe David had needed to work off some pre-wedding stress. Justin scanned the parking lot for David's BMW and, although he didn't see the silver sedan, he pulled into a slot and jogged inside.

"Hey, Chopper." Gabe, the front desk attendant, hopped off his stool and sauntered to the counter. Separated from the Army several years now, Gabe had lost a leg to an IED in Iraq. Humor and an upbeat attitude carried him through the dangerous health scare.

Justin grinned, unsure if Gabe knew his real name. The guy gave nicknames to everyone. The name Chopper, an ode to Gabe's impression he chopped up people to put them back together, had stuck, and now everyone around the center called him by the moniker.

"Hey, Gabe. Have you seen Dave today?" He scanned the facility but didn't see David.

"Nope. Don't tell me Data is skipping out on the wedding. He flashed a picture of his fiancée a few months ago. Lucky bastard." Gabe beamed, showing off his trademark toothy grin.

"You're right. I've been calling him for the last couple days. I thought he might have stopped in."

"I haven't seen him in over a week, and I've been in every day but one." Gabe rested his elbows on the counter.

"Thanks. Hey, how's your new prosthetic?"

"I've been upstairs working with it all week. I'll be ready for the Olympics any day now."

In addition to the gym facilities, the center also specialized in rehabbing veterans who'd lost limbs or simply needed a safe haven. Private ownership eased some of the government bureaucracy. Gym memberships helped offset costs, along with healthy donations from many generous supporters. The center had been open for almost four years, and so far, the General Tanner Training and Rehab Center rated as a raging success.

"Great news, Gabe. No time for a workout now, but I'll be back. Give me a call if you see that idiot come in." Justin took a last look before leaving. Back inside his SUV, he consulted his phone again.

No texts or missed calls from David. He pulled out of the parking lot and headed for David and Marissa's condo.

Where was David? He wanted to tell him the rings had been picked up, but more than that, he wanted to ensure David hadn't done something stupid. With David's family coming in tonight and all the wedding activities ramping up in a few days, Justin felt a duty to the groom. So why was the groom AWOL?

The last time he'd seen David they were in the private room at a golf and tennis club for his bachelor party, over a week ago. With scheduling difficulties for many of the guys, Justin decided to have the bachelor party a couple weeks before the wedding. The party had included an un-serious round of golf and a huge steak dinner topped off with a raucous game of poker. The typical all-male party included the obligatory female entertainment. With his fun-guy party personality, David should have been in his element, but he'd been jumpy and sullen. Numerous times Justin witnessed David not only glancing at his cell phone, as if expecting a call, but also checking the club's windows and locking the door of their private party room.

Judging by David's weird behavior of late, Justin feared what he would find. As he turned into David and Marissa's neighborhood, he recalled the last private conversation he'd had with him. They'd met for lunch three weeks ago, and David arrived late.

The entire time he scanned the restaurant and insisted they move to another table with a clear view of the kitchen and exits.

Justin had thought his actions were paranoid, and said as much.

David shrugged off concern, accusing Justin of being the paranoid one.

Now, as he got closer to the condo, Justin's senses perked with dread. The same familiar inkling he'd had moments before his own world had been turned upside down. When he pulled in front of the condo, Justin stared at the house. With the garage door raised, he spotted both cars inside. He jumped out of the SUV sprinted a few feet, then turned back to the vehicle, drawing his gun from the case under the seat.

Instead of going to the front door, Justin went in through the garage. Screams from inside sent him sprinting toward the door while pulling his gun.

Marissa.

He drew his gun, bursting through the door and into complete destruction. In the middle of the destruction Marissa sat on the floor, her back to him.

Halo, standing next to Marissa, growled and flashed his teeth.

"Halo, it's me." Justin held out his hand in a show of friendliness. The dog knew him but appeared agitated and startled at his intrusion.

After a second, Halo flapped his tail and allowed Justin to move closer.

Justin's gaze swept the room as he jumped over upturned furniture.

Then he saw David, and his pulse notched up. "What happened?"

Blood caked over a dark hole in his friend's forehead as Marissa shook and cradled his dead body.

Justin moved to face Marissa. "I need to call the police. But I'm right here, okay?"

She nodded. "I think I called them."

He pulled his phone from his pocket and punched in 911 as he kneeled next to Marissa. "Are you hurt?" Justin didn't spot any outward signs of injury but the blank stare indicated she was in shock.

Marissa moaned and rocked. "I-I came in and he looked like this. Everything destroyed. He's dead." Marissa stared blankly at Justin.

As the 911 operator announced herself, Justin performed a quick check for vitals on David's blood-covered body confirming what he already knew—his friend was dead. Based on his condition, he'd probably been dead at least a few hours.

After giving the operator the address, he informed her of the deceased victim. He remained on the line as instructed and moved closer to Marissa. "The police are on their way. I need to make sure no one else is here, okay?" His heart pounded in his ears as he placed a hand on Marissa's arm. "Let me take you outside."

She shook her head. "I shouldn't leave him."

Justin skimmed the room for signs the intruder remained on the premises but he didn't detect noise or movement. "I'll be right back." He jumped over debris and ran from room to room with gun raised, making sure not to touch anything. The rage flowing through him would be more than enough to take on an intruder—even without a weapon. His military training kicked in as he scanned each ransacked room. After finding no one, he rushed back to the kitchen.

Justin tucked his gun away and knelt beside Marissa. Gingerly, he touched her arm. "Are you hurt?" he asked again.

"No, but David is dead. How can he be dead?" Marissa pulled David's lifeless body closer.

Justin stared at the familiar bluish-gray pallor and the wide-open eyes no longer registering life. Even as a physician, he never got used to the presence of death as it consumed another person he cared for. However, the bastard who blasted David's brain matter on the wall put this death in a different category.

The dog moaned and nudged at Marissa as they both hovered over David's body.

"We needed to talk," she whispered.

Marissa continued to cradle David's body.

"Who the hell did this?" he whispered through clenched teeth.

Halo knew Justin, but eyed him as he stood watch over Marissa and David.

In the distance, sirens screamed.

"Marissa, the police will be here any minute. We've got to let him go. Let the police do their work." He gently moved David from her lap and wrapped an arm around her.

She leaned into him, sobbing.

When sirens wailed outside the condo, he disconnected from the dispatcher.

"I'm going to open the door. I'll be right back," Justin said. A few seconds later, he returned with two uniformed police officers.

Halo stood and began to growl.

"You'll have to get the dog out of here, sir," one of the officers said.

"Halo." Justin pulled the dog closer. "Marissa, the police are here." He knelt beside her. "Let me take you and Halo outside."

Marissa nodded and stood. David's blood coated her clothes, hands, face, and the tips of her hair. She swayed and her legs crumpled beneath her.

Justin caught her before she hit the floor. "I've got you."

Chapter 4

The Virginia Blue Ridge Mountains made the perfect backdrop as Vivian stood beside the fence and watched Titan gallop past. The raw strength of the horse, combined with the steadfast mountain range, mimicked the force of her own power.

Sired by Chappell's Ice, a prize-winning racehorse, and Nyx, an extraordinary black mare, Titan's exquisite chestnut-colored form exhibited the regal nature of his heritage down to the star-shaped marking in the middle of his sloped nose.

Before Titan's birth, Chappell had developed an esophageal obstruction and had been put down. Nyx, Titan's mother, died during his birth. Vivian witnessed the birth and hadn't bothered to have the blood stained barn stall cleaned. The agony Nyx had suffered remained cemented in her memory. Wild black eyes had bored into Vivian's as if Nyx understood her death neared and wanted Vivian to carry on. Vivian, too, had understood the pain of childbirth and the agony of death. They had been kindred spirits, and although she cared for the horse, in order for Vivian to grow more powerful, Nyx's death became inevitable. The horse had understood, and passed her perceptive powers on to Titan.

Titan had experienced his one and only foray into the horseracing world last year. He had been entered into a small race with five other horses. During the race, a horse named Can't Buy Happiness had cut off Titan as he came around the backstretch. The horse had taken the lead and Titan placed second. After the race, Titan had appeared angry and agitated, stomping his feet. When Vivian had peered into his eyes, she understood. A week later, Can't Buy Happiness's remains had been found scattered in pieces over his owner's farm.

Now, Titan sauntered up to the fence and nudged Vivian.

She placed her hand on his neck, and his strong muscular cords pulsed under her touch. "Can't Buy Happiness is fertilizer. Power is so energizing," she said to the horse.

He whinnied and stomped his left hoof.

His response fueled her, and she moved her hand over his star marking. "Yes, you know, don't you? We don't need clichéd races to prove ourselves."

The horse nodded and stomped again.

"We have both inherited magnificent intelligence and supremacy from our fathers, but I call on Nyx's power today." She caressed the star marking and closed her eyes as the horse remained still. After several seconds, she removed her hand and Titan galloped away.

The gravel behind her crunched and Vivian turned to see her assistant approach.

Edward squinted his razor-sharp aquamarine eyes. He folded his thin fingers together, his fitted, all black suit juxtaposed to the earthy scene. Despite a few strands of his dark hair whirling about his face in with the wind, he remained still. "Ms. Sinclair, your guest is here."

Vivian nodded. "I'll be along in a minute."

"As you wish." Edward returned to the parked golf cart, ready to drive Vivian back to the house.

Fifteen minutes later, Vivian entered her study through the back door. She slipped inside her bathroom to wash her hands. When she emerged, she accepted a warm towel from Edward, then she took her seat behind the behemoth mahogany desk. "Let him wait." Vivian's jaw firm and set as she wiped her hands and passed off the towel.

Edward nodded. "While your guest is waiting, Roy Bane is on line one. He says he'll be passing through the gates in twenty minutes." He left the room, thick carpet muffling the sound of his footsteps.

Vivian clicked a button on her phone. "Give me an update."

She still didn't know how much David Seybold knew about her organizations. According to Bane, the condo search hadn't turned up anything. Mr. Seybold had been eliminated, but the threat of his actions prior to death remained. Harold Silva, CEO of Skies International, confirmed the data breach at Skies. Had Seybold shared his findings with his fiancée? Did she know where he had hidden the data? Perhaps he chose to confide in his best friend, the doctor. She pursed her lips considering this unacceptable situation. She'd deal with those two later, but now a more pressing matter must be handled.

She ended the call and tapped her nails on the desk. After a few minutes, Vivian picked up the black-and-white picture on the credenza behind her desk. Seven black-suited men bearing stern expressions surrounded one man seated in the middle—Russell Sinclair. Vivian stared at the handwritten caption—*My Chairman and Council of Six*. Even the bold strokes of Russell's handwriting suggested power.

Vivian studied her father. Dueling emotions of anger and awe surfaced within her. Russell Sinclair—even in death—never failed to ignite Vivian's passions.

Russell had ruled The Order with an iron fist. He'd demanded, and received, absolute loyalty. Those straying from his edicts were dealt severe punishments. Through him, Vivian learned the rules of governing and decision-making. As the only offspring of Russell Sinclair, Grand Commander, she acknowledged inheriting his title wasn't automatic or assured. She was a woman, after all. Only after Russell's intense scrutiny and proving worthy through sacrifice, had he granted her the title of Grand Commander. Proud her father, upon his death, found her suitable to assume his role, she vowed to continue his objectives.

After replacing the picture, she pulled a five-inch knife from her desk drawer. The blade's pointed tip glinted off the sun streaming in through the window behind her. A gift on the day he named her Grand Commander. As a teenager Russell had stolen the knife, a family heirloom, from his father when he ran away from home. His father, a Scottish immigrant, had inherited the hunting knife from his father. Gripping the wooden handle, she placed the cold blade against her cheek. This knife her ancestors once used to provide food for the family now provided power and control.

"Penance is the ultimate price for sins against The Order. Father, Grand Commander, please accept my offer. *Ordo Ortus*," Vivian whispered.

She placed the knife inside her desk and called Edward.

Seconds later, Edward opened her office's main door and led in Harold Silva.

"Vivian! You look ravishing, as usual." Harold's gaze darted around the office as he approached. He embraced her and then stepped away.

Vivian waited for Edward to vacate. Once they were alone, she turned to Harold. "Thank you for coming again on such short notice. I know you had a long drive."

"Anything for you."

Offering a curt smile, she gestured to the chair in front of her desk. While she reclaimed her seat, she noted he hesitated. "Harold, we are dealing with a serious situation. My men, thus far, have been unable to ascertain the extent of the security breach. We know the culprit to be David Seybold, but we don't know if he shared the stolen data."

Harold's smile faded, and his wrinkled mouth shifted into a scowl.

"Your hesitance is a sign of weakness, which is unbecoming of an executive in my organization."

Harold cleared his throat. "I've had my security team working on this matter."

"Is this paltry report all your security people have identified in the last few days?" Vivian held up one sheet of paper before training her gaze on Harold. One time she cared for him, now she held only contempt.

He shifted in his chair and then scratched his ear. "This type of analysis takes time, Vivian. Rest assured, I am doing everything in my power to ensure our assets and data are secured. As stated during our earlier meeting, I have implemented background checks on every employee, and the process continues as we speak." He nodded and crossed his spindly legs.

Surely, he doesn't think I'm satisfied. "I'm not worried about your future plans. I'm concerned about what's happened and who may have their hands on sensitive information." She pursed her lips as she paused. "My father started this organization, and I built it into an empire. I took earnings from adequate to astronomical."

Harold reached into his jacket pocket and pulled out a bleached white handkerchief, his initials embroidered at one corner, and dabbed sweat from his baldhead. With a click of his teeth, he slipped the handkerchief back into the inner breast pocket. "You have done an extraordinary job. Russell would be proud, but he ruled as Grand Commander of The Order, not a mega conglomerate. If I can speak openly..." He licked his lips and adjusted in his seat, then continued. "I'm not sure he would agree with all of your capitalist pursuits."

Her chin jerked up, matching his gaze with a flaming stare as she leaned forward on her desk. "I've put us on the fast track to ensure my father's goals will come to fruition. I have high-level government leaders and important business contacts at my disposal. The power I've amassed is beyond your comprehension and represents the dominance my father only dreamed of."

"What are the goals, Vivian? You forget I once served as a council member, under your father's reign, before you disbanded the body. I understood your father." He extended a crooked finger and pointed to the picture sitting behind her desk. "Russell wanted respect and order.

"What the hell does that mean, Harold?" She pounded her fist on the desk. "He wanted The Order to lead a one-world government. Simple as that."

Harold laughed, throwing back his head. "Every third-rate dictator and American president has the same desires. Amazing a smart woman like you could actually buy into such drivel. Your father was a great leader, but his advisors saw the real world. We listened to his talk of sacrifice and banal one world domination but we kept him focused."

"You might have been there, but you have no understanding about my father's wishes. I have set the course to achieve greatness even beyond Russell's imagination. You have no appreciation for sacrifice. I gave up my child in order to pay penance to my father, the Grand Commander, and now *I* hold the title." She crossed her arms and flashed a cold smile.

"No, you didn't give up your child, you killed *our* child."

Vivian leaned back in her chair, her gaze focused on Harold. With her right hand, she opened the desk drawer and gripped the knife. Rage coursed through her body like a high-speed train. *Nyx understood sacrifice and had more courage than this pitiful man will ever have.* She released the knife to keep her from plunging the blade into Harold's pathetic heart. "I did what was necessary."

"Your father said motherhood channeled the downfall of an ambitious woman. Common sense and thirst for success evaporate as soon as a woman's womb is full. A mother can't see beyond her child to make the necessary decisions for the good of all." With another swipe of his handkerchief across his forehead, Harold relaxed against his chair.

"I don't recall you objecting." Vivian tilted her head and flashed an icy smile "You were all too thrilled to have me. A man fifteen years my senior. I was just a girl. Eager to please. And I did please you, didn't I, Harold?" She glared at the worthless blob before her.

His sallow skin flushed red. "Vivian, we have gotten off subject. What's in the past needs to stay there."

"But the past has a way of squirming back into the present." She clasped her hands together. "I am not only my father's daughter but, also a student. Eventually, the student becomes the teacher." She pressed a button under the desk.

The door opened, and Roy Bane entered carrying a large duffel bag. He towered over six feet tall, resembling a large oak tree with solid limbs and swelled muscles. Stepping to the side of the door, he dropped the bag and stood silent, his beady black eyes focused ahead.

Harold didn't turn. Instead, he slumped in his chair.

"You knew why I sent for you. Why did you come? I would have had more respect had you attempted to flee." Vivian cocked her head. Pity. He had such potential. She placed her hands in her lap, waiting for a response.

"My life ended long before now. I know all about penance. I know all about the damn garden. I know too much. I stayed with the organization because I had nowhere else to go. I made a lot of money and, as long as I remained above water, I had no worries."

"Ahh, the money. You had a wife and child to support. Did you ever tell her about our tryst? I bet not."

"She died without ever knowing that piece of ugly truth."

"A car accident, right? Your lovely wife, your very young wife I might add, and daughter, lost together. Pity." Vivian pulled the knife from the drawer and placed it on her desk.

Harold's eyes bulged as he focused on the knife. Pulling his gaze, he turned back to Vivian. "You know damn well your father had them killed. They did nothing wrong!" He moved to stand.

Roy moved to his side in seconds, grabbing his arms. With one hand, Roy laid out a large section of plastic under the chair before slamming him back into the seat.

Harold's glasses were thrown astray, and he grimaced as Roy tied his limbs to the chair.

Harold hung his head, in apparent surrender.

"Oh, Harold. You've had all these years to figure me out. I really thought you were more intelligent." Vivian paused. "I didn't like seeing you so happy. You knew too much about the organization, and I couldn't have you trotting off into the sunset with Jessica Rabbit." She stood and crossed the room to the far bookcase. With the press of a few buttons, the music of Max Bruch filled the room. Eyes closed, Vivian listened to her father's favorite classical piece, "Scottish Fantasy", for a few seconds before pulling a lab jacket off a nearby coat rack along with a pair of rubber gloves. She returned to her desk and slipped on the gloves.

"You! How could you? Nora did nothing, and Chelsea was only four years old." Tears filled his eyes.

Vivian clenched her gloved hands. "And my child was an infant! My mother a young woman. We all have to pay penance." She grabbed the knife. With a quick nod, she glared at Harold as Roy held Harold's hand, pulling his wedding ring up past his knuckle.

Vivian stood over Harold and smiled. *Ordo Ortus*. With several hard strokes, she sawed off his ring finger.

Harold screamed and struggled against the restraints. Blood spurted and, finally, the digit severed from his body.

Vivian picked up the finger and smeared the blood across her right cheek.

"You didn't have to kill them." Harold's breath grew shallow, and sweat streaked down his face. "I shouldn't have put them in danger." His voice softened, defeated.

"Penance must be paid. Your usefulness has been exhausted."

"If there is one good thing—our baby escaped growing up with a monster like you." Harold slumped over farther in the chair.

Vivian shrugged. "To think as a young girl I could have loved such a weak fool." She tossed the knife onto the plastic and removed the gloves and lab jacket, dropping them on top of the knife. With one last glance at Harold, she stepped back and nodded to Roy.

The sound of the gunshot reverberated through the room.

Harold's head leaned at an odd angle, blood oozed from the hole in the center of his skull.

Edward rushed in with a jar of clear liquid and opened the lid.

Vivian dropped the severed finger inside. She stared out at the Black Garden, the dark-poppies in full bloom. The statue of Russell Sinclair stood in the middle, looming over his entombed inhabitants, ready to welcome another.

Ordo Ortus. Order Rising.

Chapter 5

Justin carried a shaking and pale Marissa away from the bloody scene. He wanted to grab a blanket, but the officers wouldn't allow him to remove anything from the condo.

A tall, middle-aged officer with a thin ribbon of hair around the base of his otherwise balding skull glared at Justin from across the kitchen floor.

Justin understood the officer had to, at least at the onset, consider both he and Marissa as potential suspects, but he hoped suspicion wouldn't last long.

Once they were outside Marissa stood, leaning on him. Justin quieted Halo's barking, as he told the officers what little information he knew—he'd arrived at the condo, heard Marissa screaming, and found David. Who wanted David dead? Was the killer someone David knew or could this be a simple robbery gone badly? Based on the amount of high-ticket items destroyed or remaining in the condo, theft appeared a stretch.

David, what were you involved in?

Marissa, in clipped, monotone sentences, managed to tell the officer her name. She indicated she'd come home to find David on the floor.

A young officer with a nameplate reading Cooper escorted them to a police car. "The dog has blood evidence on him. Animal control and crime scene techs are on their way. Until then, we'll have to put the dog in the back of my patrol car."

Halo barked and bared his teeth sending the officer scooting out of reach. "Can either of you get him in my cruiser? Try not to handle the dog more than necessary."

"He knows me. Halo, come." Justin stood in front of the dog, waiting for him to obey.

Halo continued to bark and eyed the officer.

Marissa moved into Halo's field of vision. "Halo."

The dog stopped barking.

Justin clicked his teeth. "Let's go, boy."

Halo licked Marissa's hand and then moved toward Justin. After a few seconds of persuasion, the dog hopped into the car. His large body engulfed the back seat as he stood and sniffed through the cracked window.

Marissa leaned in toward the car window. "It's okay." Tears coursed down her face and Justin slid an arm around her.

The dog stared back at her and appeared to nod.

Justin loved animals, but his hectic schedule at the hospital wouldn't allow him to give a pet the proper attention. He recognized the special nature of the dog, and he guessed the animal would lay down his life for its owner. The bomb dogs Justin had seen in Iraq were obedient and smart. Halo reminded him of those dogs and just earned high marks in his book.

The heat raged on, despite the onset of dusk peeking at the horizon. One large elm tree in the center of the yard provided the only hope of shade but stood too far away to offer any protection.

Justin pulled Marissa closer, her body shaking. "I think we need the EMTs."

Cooper nodded and led them to the ambulance.

Justin helped Marissa sit in the back of the ambulance then turned to an EMT. "I'm a doctor, she's had a huge shock and the heat isn't helping. Can you get a vitals check on her?"

The EMT pulled out a blood pressure cuff and squatted in front of Marissa.

A few seconds later, the EMT reported a slightly elevated BP.

"Do you want to transport her to the hospital?" Cooper said.

Marissa's eyes bulged and she shook her head.

"As long as she's stable, we'll hold off," Justin said to Cooper and the EMT. As the EMT handed Marissa a bottle of water, Justin nodded. "Water will help."

She glanced at the bottle as if the new data required in-depth analyzing. Finally, she took a small sip.

Although the officer remained close by, Justin expected he and Marissa would soon have to separate in order for the detectives to get their statements. He rubbed the bridge of his nose. Although Justin understood a murder must be solved, the idea he and Marissa would be investigated unnerved him.

Shell-shocked eyes stared past him, and Marissa's cold hands continued to shake.

His chest tightened at the familiar expression. They'd both just landed in a different kind of war. "We'll get through this together." Even though Marissa nodded, Justin questioned if she comprehended.

"Have you called anyone else to be with you?" He glanced at the cell phone in her hand.

She shook her head. "I couldn't bring myself to say the words."

Justin had been trained to deliver bad news. The task never got easier and he empathized with the grieving family, but training taught him to let the death go. Internalizing the death of every patient wouldn't serve him well.

But, this was different.

David's death struck him as personal and painful as hell. He swallowed against the lump in his throat. "Let me have your phone."

Marissa gave Justin her phone, her hand making brief contact with his. "Thanks, Justin."

After punching a number from her contact list, Mr. Nash answered, and Justin inhaled before delivering the news. The brief conversation ended with Mr. Nash promising to be at the condo within fifteen minutes.

Next, he phoned the Seybolds. They'd already arrived from Florida and had been staying with Mrs. Seybold's sister who lived forty minutes away. The news of David's death bought confusion from David's father and a moan of grief and shock from his mother.

He made the last call to Marissa's best friend, Kelly. She responded with concern for Marissa and told Justin she and Craig would drop off the baby before coming to the condo.

Justin wasn't sure if Marissa heard any of his conversations.

She continued to stare at the grass. "How could this happen?" she whispered.

Justin couldn't attempt to explain something he didn't understand. He spotted two authority type figures approaching and assumed they were the detectives. He prayed they'd have some quick answers.

A lanky brown-skinned man with large brown eyes stopped in front of them. His baldhead gleamed with perspiration. The sleeves of his pale blue dress shirt were rolled up, giving the appearance of hard work, and led up to darkened crescent shaped shadows under his arms.

With a grim face, a thin woman with an athletic build stood next to him. She appeared to be in her early thirties and wore her blonde hair pulled back into a long ponytail giving her a girl-next-door vibe.

"I'm Detective Ron Streeter." He hiked his head to the side. "This is Detective April Kearns. We'll be working on this case." He extended his hand to Justin and then bent to shake Marissa's hand. "First, can you both identify yourselves?"

Marissa and Justin obliged, then waited for the detective to continue.

"Ms. Nash, I'm sorry about your loss." Detective Kearns knelt in front of Marissa and placed a hand on her back. "You have my promise I will do everything I can to find the person who killed your fiancé."

Marissa nodded. "Thank you."

"We'll talk briefly about what happened today, and then we need to take your clothes. They contain blood evidence. You can change in your powder room."

Justin studied Marissa as confusion swept over her face. With dried blood smeared across the front of her shirt and caked on her jeans, she resembled someone who'd waded through a slaughterhouse.

Marissa rubbed a hand across her jeans and gasped.

Justin wanted to scoop her into his arms but such a show of affection would be inappropriate. Instead, he placed a hand on her shoulder.

A female police officer appeared with a new set of clothes Justin assumed were from Marissa's closet.

Marissa followed Detective Kearns and the police officer back into the house.

"You were the one who called this in?" Streeter asked, a small notebook in his hand.

"Yes." Justin told Detective Streeter everything he did from the time he arrived at the condo.

The detective handed over his card and explained he and Marissa would need to make a formal statement at the police station later that evening.

"David was my best friend and about to be married. Please, find who did this."

Streeter nodded and headed back into the condo.

The life of two people he cared about had been irrevocably changed. David had been killed, and Marissa would need all the support she could get.

He'd promised to help Marissa manage the painful events to come, but delivering on that promise might cause him to open wounds he'd hoped would remain closed.

Chapter 6

Marisa stood on the sidewalk and stared at the condo awash in the flashing lights of law enforcement vehicles. She'd spent twenty minutes with Detective Kearns answering questions about how she found David's body.

Perspiration snaked down her back and her heart rumbled like a runaway locomotive in her chest. She rubbed her hands together as she waited on an update about Halo. The animal control officers had arrived to aid the crime scene technicians in collecting evidence from her pet. Marissa stared at the van. Could Halo have witnessed the murder? She was thankful the murderer spared Halo but all the people and lights ramped up his agitation.

She'd assumed Detective Streeter had completed his interview with Justin as both men approached.

"Are you okay?" Justin asked, taking her hand.

She nodded and turned to Detective Streeter.

"Ms. Nash. Your dog is in the back of the animal control van." Streeter pointed to the white van behind him. "The crime scene tech retrieved a sample of his fur but your dog is still quite agitated. We had to sedate him to get a cheek swab. The dog may have bitten the intruder, giving us a chance to obtain a DNA sample."

"There's no other way?" Marissa blinked against the flashing lights.

"No, but the mild sedative will wear off quickly and you can take him with you." Streeter held up a finger and moved away to consult with an approaching officer. When the officer retreated, Streeter turned to Marissa. "Your family is here. They may come as far as the police tape."

Marissa nodded and hurried toward her parents. John and Ava Nash, alighted from their car and Marissa ducked under the police tape to meet them.

Ava pulled Marissa into her arms. "Oh, honey. I'm so sorry. Are you hurt?" She pulled back to look her over.

"No, Mom. I'm okay." She closed her eyes for a second, her body numb.

"Marissa, are you sure?" John gathered her into a fatherly hug.

She nodded and glanced for the first time at the clothing the officer had chosen. The ratty red T-shirt and gray sweatpants with a tiny hole in the knee had been on the third shelf in the back of the closet. They'd been earmarked for donation to the local women's shelter, but she'd debated whether they were too shabby. Now the old clothes proved a tangible reminder her old life had been obliterated.

Her father released her. "Justin explained you need to give a statement at the police station. I'm calling Andy to go with you."

"Dad, I don't..."

"Just a precaution. Andy advises in situations like this, no one should speak to the police without an attorney present." He paused and adjusted his rectangular-framed glasses. A retired mechanical engineer, John Nash valued preparation. "No one could think you had anything to do with this, but we need to be prepared."

Marissa turned to Justin as he stepped forward.

Justin placed a hand on her arm. "Your dad is right. You should have an attorney present."

Marissa's eyes grew wide as the enormity of the situation dawned.

David had been murdered and by her parents' lack of questions, they already knew what happened. Her family and friends would never believe she had anything to do with David's death, but the police didn't know her. She bit her lip as her stomach tumbled again.

Her head pounded, and the flashing lights of the police cars added to the queasiness threatening her stomach. She closed her eyes, wishing she were anywhere but here.

She opened her eyes as commotion rumbled within the growing horde of onlookers. Within seconds Vanessa pushed through the crowd, announcing her connection to the victim. She dashed forward and embraced Marissa.

Eli, her husband, followed close behind.

Now she had to deal with her domineering sister and passive brother-in-law. *What a circus.*

Vanessa patted her arm. "This is such a tragedy. Right before your wedding. Of course, you will stay with Mom and Dad. Did the police allow you to get some of your belongings?"

The idea she would no longer live there hadn't crossed her mind, much less assembling an overnight bag. "I don't know."

"Honey, it's okay." She turned to her husband. "Eli, go find out if we can pack an overnight bag for Marissa."

Eli nodded and trotted off to find an officer.

Marissa groaned.

A few minutes later, Kelly and Craig arrived. Kelly raced toward Marissa, her long brown hair whipping in the wind. She scooped Marissa into a hug. "I'm so sorry."

Craig gave her a hug. "What can we do?"

Marissa shrugged. "Take Halo home with you. I can't take him to my parent's house because my mom is allergic."

Kelly held Marissa's hand. "We'll take care of him. Don't worry."

David's family arrived next. His parents, Roger and Linda, stood grief-stricken and in shock.

Marissa knew they had a right to be there and were devastated like she, but she longed for an escape.

LATER IN THE EVENING, Marissa's horror continued at the police station. She stood in the lobby, preparing to endure more in-depth questioning from the detectives. Although she had initially resisted her father's insistence on a lawyer, she was now grateful not to have to brave the session alone.

Andy Tolbert gave Marissa a hug, his full head of salt-and-pepper hair brushing her cheek. "I'm so sorry, honey. I know this is upsetting." He released her and met her gaze. "I'll be with you throughout the interview."

Andy, a close family friend, had been in Marissa's life for as long as she could remember. After Andy's wife died of cancer several years ago, the event brought him even closer to the Nash family. Marissa trusted him like she would a close uncle.

Andy coached her to be clear and concise. "You're not a suspect. They need as much information as you can provide so they can find David's killer."

Her father waved Justin over. "Andy, please meet Justin. As David's best man and best friend, he's feeling the loss, too."

The men shook hands.

Marissa could sense Justin's support as his warm brown gaze swept over her. She offered a slight nod in hopes of conveying something akin to thanks. Thank you didn't seem appropriate. Thanks for helping me through the shock of finding my fiancé's cold, lifeless body? Was that the sentiment one should convey? She sure as hell had never seen it on a Hallmark card.

"Take care of her," John called as Andy and Marissa made their way down the hall.

Marissa stopped Andy when they were out of earshot of her father. "Before we start, I need to ask you something." She wrung her damp hands as she informed Andy of her intention to call the wedding off. After briefly explaining how she discovered David's infidelity and her plan to confront him, she asked Andy if she should disclose the information to the detectives.

"You need to tell them everything. This woman could be important to the investigation. Be open and honest. I'll stop the questioning if something is wrong." He placed his hands on her shoulders and gave them a squeeze.

Detective April Kearns greeted Marissa and Andy. She led them to a door labeled "Interview Room". The small room contained a round table with four chairs. "Can I get you or Mr. Tolbert a cup of coffee or a bottle of water?"

Andy pulled out a chair for Marissa. "Nothing for me, thank you."

Marissa shook her head.

Detective Kearns smiled and slid into a chair next to Marissa. "I know this has been an overwhelming day but in order to find David's murderer we need to know as much as possible about him."

Marissa settled into the chair and swallowed the lump in her throat.

"Ms. Nash, how long have you known David Seybold?"

"I've known David for four years."

"You were due to marry in a little over a week?"

"Yes, umm..." She hesitated, unsure how to disclose her cancellation plans. Could his girlfriend have anything to do with this murder?

Kearns adjusted in her seat. "Can I call you Marissa?"

Marissa nodded.

"I sense there's something going on here. How was your relationship with David?" Kearns leaned forward.

Marissa glanced at Andy.

He nodded.

"I intended to call off the wedding. I'd been in Salt Lake City on a business trip and returned this afternoon. I went straight from the airport to the condo, but I never got the chance to tell him."

"Why were you canceling your wedding, only a few days away?"

Marissa swallowed, now wishing she'd accepted the water. "Before leaving on my trip, I discovered David had been seeing another woman."

Kearns's blue eyes softened. "That must have been difficult."

Marissa nodded and straightened in her chair. "David wasn't ready for marriage."

"How did you discover David's infidelity?" Kearns's voice, soft and soothing, gave Marissa the impression she was talking to a friend.

Marissa provided as much information as she could, but only knew the woman as Tiffany based on the series of texts she'd discovered. She explained how she came across the messages by accident. David had been in the shower and his phone continued to chirp, signaling receipt of text messages. The phone chirped so much she thought there'd been an emergency so she glanced at the posts. Several sexy messages from Tiffany, describing her body, stared back at her.

"Did you and David argue about your finding?"

Marissa shook her head. "You'd think. He calmly denied everything, but when I questioned him about those messages, he eventually admitted to the affair. Then he accused me of snooping and stormed out. He didn't answer any of my calls and didn't try to contact me. I didn't see him for the next three days, and then I left on my business trip." Tears fell as she sniffled. "I knew I couldn't marry him, but at the same time, I thought maybe we could work out our problems. During my time in Utah, I decided I had to call off the wedding."

Her father's insistence upon having Andy, a criminal attorney, with her struck a chord. While Andy provided some comfort, the need for his presence, other than her well being, frightened her. What would happen if they thought she killed David? Time of death would be important. She'd been on a plane, but if he were killed shortly before she got home, would become a suspect? The image of David's body flashed in her mind. The room spun, forcing her to place her hands on the table for support. Sweat erupted from her forehead as her head pounded.

"Are you okay?" Andy placed a hand on her shoulder.

Detective Kearns jumped up and returned quickly with a bottle of water.

"Thanks." Marissa took two big gulps and closed her eyes. She concentrated on the hum of the air conditioner as she inhaled and exhaled. Several seconds later, her nerves stabilized. "Sorry."

Andy's watery gray eyes gazed at her. "Shall we continue?"

"Yes, please." She wanted to get this over with as soon as possible.

Kearns hesitated. "If you need a break, let me know." She paused then continued. "Do you know of anyone who would want to hurt or kill David?"

Marissa contemplated an answer. Her mind raced through David's friends and acquaintances, but she drew a blank. "No, I can't think of anyone. I can't believe David is dead." Her voice broke.

Kearns pushed a box of tissues across the table. "What about business contacts?"

Marissa pulled her emotions together. "David didn't tell me a lot about his work because of client confidentiality. I learned long ago not to ask."

"Were there any financial concerns?"

"Not that I'm aware of. Both our names are on the loan for the condo." Her mind spooled back to happier times. During the first three-fourths of their relationship, David had been attentive, loving, and funny. She'd loved their times together, and when they moved into the condo, their relationship deepened. What happened during the last fourth of their relationship to push him to a point he needed another woman?

Kearns cleared her throat. "Marissa? Anything else?"

Lost in memories, she jolted. "I'm sorry." She inhaled and continued. "I insisted on contributing to the mortgage, so we opened an account for the payments. We both transfer money into the account. Otherwise, we have separate accounts and split the bills. He bought a new car recently and is constantly buying clothes, so I don't think finances were a worry."

The room tilted again as she noted referencing David in the present tense. For the past four years, he'd been a part of her life, and now he lay dead.

The questioning went on and on. They covered what she knew of David's life previous to their relationship, and their lives together up until her horrifying discovery. Kearns walked her through every nuance of the day; from the time she awoke until finding David's corpse.

David's final moments must have been terrifying. Despite their last interaction, she cared and certainly didn't wish him dead. As flashes of his bloodied body lit her mind, she tried to push them away in order to maintain her composure. "Detective, what will happen with David's body? Do you think he experienced any pain?" Her thoughts ran like a cheetah through her mind.

Kearns placed her hands on the table. "His body has been taken to the morgue and an autopsy will be performed. I can't answer your question on whether he experienced pain. We may be able to provide an answer later. I can assure you his body will be treated with dignity."

Marissa nodded and sat straighter. *Don't cry.* "I don't understand this...if I'd have come home earlier, maybe..."

With a shake of her head, Kearns leaned across the table, her intense blue eyes drilling into Marissa's. "If you'd have come home earlier, you likely would have been killed, too."

Andy placed his hand on Marissa's. "She's right."

Marissa inhaled. "But his parents, his family...clients need to be notified. All of his friends."

Andy patted her hand. "One thing at a time. You have lots of people around to help."

When the interview ended, Andy and Kearns discussed the next steps as Marissa's thoughts floated from one topic to another.

She and David had planned to redecorate the living room after the wedding. She couldn't decide on tan or a tranquil ocean blue paint color. Either would match their furniture. As she pondered paint hues, she muted the voices in the room. She drifted, focusing on a memory of silent jellyfish jettisoning through the water.

She considered the fluorescent jellyfish. They probably would have seen a few on their honeymoon to Fiji. Pictures of the island she'd viewed on the Internet were exquisite. For months, Marissa had been looking forward to their trip. A tropical island, her hot husband,

and a week of relaxation sounded like paradise. Now she'd have to shed all thoughts of tropical vacations.

What was she thinking? If David were alive right now, they'd be discussing their breakup, or at least the postponement of their wedding. Perhaps their lives were destined to change on this day.

After the three-hour interview, Andy drove her back to her parents' home. The familiar setting should have been comforting, but she dreaded the nonstop attention. She craved privacy and peace to process what had occurred.

Imaginary weights rested heavily upon her, like her entire body had been pounded into quicksand. Her eyes fluttered in response to the grittiness of the day. Sleep would be a gift, but as she stepped inside the house, her family and Justin quickly surrounded her.

Vanessa talked incessantly about preparing her old room, and her mother discussed the breakfast menu.

Mr. and Mrs. Seybold arrived and embraced her.

"We'll always think of you as a daughter-in-law," Mrs. Seybold said.

Mr. Seybold patted her arm. "We'd like you to help make the arrangements."

Marissa nodded and thanked them. She wanted to say more but couldn't find the words.

At some point, Kelly texted her to let her know Halo was asleep in their bedroom. Kelly also informed her she would purchase whatever clothes Marissa needed and bring them by in the morning.

At least Halo will get some sleep tonight.

Her father spoke in hushed tones to Andy. Did the police find something? What if her discovery of David's affair put her at the top of the suspect list? Didn't all the crime shows say the people closest to the victim were always considered possible culprits? Did David know his killer? Who could do this? And why? What if...her mind stalled, unable to proceed with more horrifying thoughts.

Breathe.

As everyone left, Marissa asked Justin to stay behind. Once they were in her room and seated on her bed, Marissa stared at her clasped hands. "Thank you for today. I know I was in shock. Everyone is so focused on me, but I want you to know how sorry I am. David was your best friend."

"I've known David a long time." Justin sighed. "I hate his life came to an end this way."

"What am I supposed to do? My brain feels like mush, and there are a million questions with no answers." Marissa rubbed her temples.

"I know you'd like to have some answers, so would I, but we'll have to accept the fact answers will take time."

She nodded. "You don't have any idea who did this either?"

"No. For the last several weeks, I've been unable to connect with David and neither could the jewelry store." He paused. "The rings are in my car. Do you want them now?" His voice softened.

"No." Marissa chewed her bottom lip. "I hope I don't sound callous. I just can't deal with that now. I have to call Pam, my wedding coordinator, and cancel the venues. We've already started getting wedding presents, so those will have to be returned." She began forming a list in her head of all the things she needed to handle. In seconds, the list expanded into a daunting catalog of activities she knew wasn't nearly complete.

Justin placed a hand on her shoulder. "You don't have to handle this alone. Your parents, Vanessa, and Kelly will help. And I'll do whatever I can." He smiled.

"I came home to a nightmare. What kind of person does this? So much blood. She placed her hand over her mouth, ran to her en suite bathroom, and vomited into the toilet.

Justin approached and handed her a towel.

She wiped her mouth and leaned against the counter, expecting tears but her eyes remained dry. When she glanced up, Justin stood behind her, his tall muscular stature dominating the room. "I-I don't know what to do."

He pulled her into his embrace. "Marissa, you're still in shock. You're pale, cold, and shaking like a leaf. You have every right to feel what you feel. Believe me, you will go through every emotion you've ever known, and probably some you didn't know existed. Your family and friends will want to take care of you. Let them if you want, or don't. It's up to you, but always know, I will be right here for you."

She couldn't get warm despite the heat from his body. "Thank you."

"I will stay as long as you need. He held her a few minutes longer before pulling back. "Do you need anything to sleep? I can prescribe some sleeping meds."

"No, I'll be fine."

He led her out of the bathroom. "How about I come by for breakfast? Your mother already invited me."

"I'd like that."

After Justin left, Marissa stood in the center of the room and surveyed her childhood space. She hadn't lived in this room for any length of time since high school. The soft lavender walls and matching bedding appeared soothing, but didn't deliver tonight.

A knock on the door startled her.

Her father peeked in. "I don't usually advocate drinking, but would you like something strong? Sometimes alcohol can take the edge off."

Marissa shook her head. "No, Dad, I'm fine. A hot shower and my bed will do."

Her father stepped into the room and kissed her forehead, patted her arm, and left.

As much as she appreciated everyone's concern, she needed to be alone. She padded into the bathroom and caught a glimpse of herself in the mirror. She focused on her light brown hair, the tips matted with dried blood. Another reminder of the horror she'd witnessed tonight. Turning from her blank stare, she removed her clothes, climbed into the shower, and allowed hot beads of water to pummel her body. Flashes of scenes from the night beat through her mind. Images of David, shot and bloodied on the floor, popped out at her. Bone, blood, and indistinguishable parts of David's brain littered the wall. Halo's howls echoed in her memory, followed by David's mother crying hysterically, slumped into her husband's arms.

Scrubbing at her body and hair, she wanted to be clean, to somehow wash away the entire night. Hot steam swirled around her, and she gasped in an attempt to control her breathing. She braced her hand against the shower wall, counting to slow her breaths. Earlier, Justin's embrace had soothed her. She'd sensed he'd become a friend she could trust.

After a few minutes, her breathing normalized. She shivered as she stepped out of the shower and wrapped herself in a towel. She crossed into her bedroom and riffled through her dresser. After pulling out an oversized T-shirt and sliding the garment over her wet hair, Marissa climbed into bed.

Had she been so selfish that on David's last day of life she'd wanted to throw him a curve ball? She'd been determined to postpone the wedding. Would he have understood or argued?

The darkened room and the warmth of a thick blanket failed to bring her comfort. She waited for tears to flow, but they remained locked away. Her mind swirled with images all leading her back to why.

The last kiss they shared, prior to her discovering his affair, had been wooden and unemotional. Could his lack of passion been due to his affair, or something more?

Most of David's friends were either current or ex-military, and based on the ones she knew, there didn't seem to be any animosity. Perhaps this woman hadn't known David had a fiancée. Could she have something to do with his murder?

David had always been guarded about his job. He started Seybold Consulting five years ago, and to her limited knowledge, his client list and net profits had both tracked on an upward trajectory. He'd been an intelligence expert in Army Special Operations and used his military training and computer knowledge as a security consultant. She understood the need for confidentiality—her job required discretion, as well—so she had no issues with him being close-lipped.

Would a client kill due to unsatisfactory results? The notion appeared extreme, but she realized how little she knew about David's world.

The detectives had pressed her for anything she could recall to help the investigation. She could point to nothing. Closing her eyes, she tried to remember anything, a conversation or some weird event but nothing materialized.

As David's closest friend, did Justin know something? Maybe David shared things with Justin he hadn't shared with her. Would Justin tell her if he knew anything?

With a sliver of moonlight coming in through the window, Marissa could make out the poster of her ballerina grandmother, Valentina Estrada, *en pointe* in her pink tutu. She'd been five years old when she took her first ballet class and would try to emulate her grandmother's pose in the picture. Her mother recognized Marissa's keen interest in dance and had the picture enlarged and placed in her room. Marissa loved listening to grandmother's adventures as one of the first Hispanic prima ballerinas to grace the stage of the Royal Ballet Company in England.

What would my life have been like had I pursued ballet as a career? She stroked the ballet shoe necklace, a gift from her grandmother on the momentous occasion of her first pair of pointe shoes. Glancing at the pendant, Marissa pondered the familiar question of what could have been, even though she loved her job as an accountant. If she'd found success in ballet would she even have known David, much less have time for a relationship? They'd met at a party. If she'd been with a dance company she probably wouldn't have been out that night.

Dance, particularly ballet, had always been a stress reliever and now as a teacher and co-owner of her grandmother's dance studio, she could work through her frustration any time on the dance floor. Were her father not such a light sleeper, she would have jumped in the car and driven to the studio to dance. Instead, she tiptoed outside.

The clock on her phone read 1:09 in the morning. Her long T-shirt hung loose, fluttering against her legs in the light, warm wind.

She leaned against the railing of the wraparound porch and stared up at the night sky. Once again, she considered how much her world had changed in one day. Many decisions loomed and she would be meeting with the Seybolds later today to discuss funeral plans.

A cat crept into her visual field bringing her out of her musings. With stealthy and unassuming moves, the gray cat ambled through the neighbor's yard and moved toward the street. As Marissa hurried to the corner of the patio to get a better view of the feline, she saw a large black SUV drive toward the house.

The vehicle slowed on approach, the driver shielded by dark-tinted windows.

She peered closer and could have sworn a face stared back. Her breath caught and her skin prickled. For what felt like several minutes but was more likely a couple of seconds, she had the sensation of being watched. She shivered as the SUV picked up speed and moved out of view.

Her heart continued to pound. Had her imagination ignited, or had someone really been staring at her? She closed her eyes and focused on slowing her heartbeat. *Probably someone looking for an address or maybe a lost pet. Nothing to get concerned about.*

The day had been long and terrifying, her nerves were on high alert with her brain likely feeding her inaccurate information.

She glanced at the street and observed the cat disappearing into another hedge. As she shivered, she pulled her shirt down even though it hovered around her knees. Once again a quiet calm blanketed the street, but she couldn't shake the belief watchful eyes were still close.

Chapter 7

The sparse crowd at Quigley's Bar gave Justin a quiet place away from people to think. The stop-for-a-drink-after-work-crowd had long dissipated, saving the establishment for the down-on-their-luck crew to assume the bent over the bar position as they sipped their chosen alcoholic panacea. He found a booth in the back, avoiding patrons and the potential for conversation.

A busty waitress approached.

He ordered a scotch and soda, on the brink of ending his five-year sobriety. He rubbed a hand across his chin stubble and clenched his hands. Admitting to being an alcoholic had been a huge deal, potentially ending his sobriety an even bigger one. After he watched the waitress retreat, he leaned against the back of the booth.

Quigley's, located a few miles from Highland Memorial Hospital, had once been a familiar playground. As Justin stepped through the door, he inhaled the scent of stale beer and fried foods. In an instant Justin's memory transported him back to times spent drinking away his hurt. The dark paneled walls bound with various sized televisions, the vintage jukebox with Vegas style flashing lights, tall barstools hugging the worn wooden bar as tables and black leathered booths occupied the remainder of the room, all sent him back to a painful time in his life. He moved past the bar, spotting the familiar pool tables, pinball machines, and dartboards, which once rounded out his bar experience.

Tonight, sports and bar games didn't make the list of reasons for his patronage.

He hadn't been in Quigley's since he gave up drinking. The years of gore and agony had been hard to get a handle on. Watching young soldiers die under his hands had been agonizing, but the last day of his final war deployment unfolded like nothing he'd ever experienced. Like most post-war veterans, assimilation had been difficult. During that time, to ease his pain, Justin had begun drinking. A drink here or there to relax enough to sleep without flashes of people being blown to bits, morphed into a habit. He never drank on duty, or within twenty-four hours of going on duty, but on his days off, freedom allowed him to imbibe.

Then his sister noticed.

After the waitress slid the drink in front of him, he stared into the amber liquid, inhaling the smoky cork aroma. Six years ago, he would have downed the drink without a single thought. Now, the small, innocent glass stood like a huge formidable python ready to snap him up into a world he'd fought to be free of.

Blinking tired, gritty eyes, Justin moved the glass away a few inches. He considered calling his sponsor, but decided against it, as he pulled a bronze sobriety chip from his pocket. Flipping the coin over and over in his hand, Justin eyed the glass, half the Quigley's logo peeled off. He sighed and pushed the drink up against the wall of the booth, out of his line of sight.

The image of David's body surfaced, and he reflected on what the police might know but weren't revealing to him or Marissa. Justin wasn't worried about being a suspect. He could account for every moment of the day, plus surveillance footage from the hospital and his after work errands in addition to people at the hospital, would back him up. With closed eyes, Justin recalled Marissa's shocked expression. He didn't think the police considered Marissa a serious suspect and he hoped she had an adequate footprint of her where-abouts. Instead, he worried about David's recent activities.

His interview with Detective Streeter hadn't clued him in to what the police were thinking, which he surmised would have been counter-intuitive to such an interrogation. An attorney he'd used for several personal business functions recommended a colleague to advise him during the interview.

Justin had known David since their undergraduate days at Notre Dame University and had half a lifetime of memories, good and bad.

Many stories about David filled his memory, but could any of them help find the killer? What, if at all, did his past play in his murder? He didn't know how much Marissa knew about David's past, and up until now, he hadn't felt responsible for telling her. If David were any kind of man, he would have told his wife-to-be about his checkered background. Did she find out about David's affairs? Guilt dripped through him for briefly questioning if Marissa could have shot David. Granted he didn't know her well, but Marissa wasn't a killer. Maybe one of his many women or even a jealous husband caught up to David.

The detective took him back to their college days and then through their respective military careers. Justin could only provide a cursory overview of David's role in Special Forces. Many of David's missions were classified, and they never discussed work. While they were both Army officers, their paths rarely crossed.

Justin told Streeter all he knew about his friend, from his gambling and drug problems in college ending with his discharge from the Army. An honorable discharge had been David's good luck. He hadn't deserved leniency, and Justin told him as much at the time. Having an affair with your commanding officer's wife, after being caught several months earlier with another officer's wife, weren't honorable grounds in Justin's book. David caught a huge break when the officer in charge of the inquiry felt he had bigger fish to fry and turned a blind eye to David's slimy conduct.

Having satisfied their military obligations, even though Justin remained in the Reserves, neither had discussed much of their past military lives.

Justin told the detective of David's recent uncharacteristic behavior and the somewhat sketchy phone message he left a few days ago. He hadn't left any indication about what he wanted but ended the message with the phrase "DEFCON Two".

Justin understood the military readiness levels from DEFCON Five, the lowest level of alert, to DEFCON One, the highest level of alert meaning war was eminent. DEFCON Two indicated increased caution and one step below all out war. David had initiated the terminology during their college years to alert Justin to his level of trouble. DEFCON One meant drop everything as he was in dire danger. When Justin received David's phone call he'd been in surgery, and after a long day, he hadn't returned the call until much later.

David never answered Justin's calls.

At the time, Justin presumed his message had regarded a last-minute wedding detail or errand, as the DEFCON meanings since their college days had been reduced to watered down emergencies like, can't do lunch, work crisis, drunk, or need a ride home. David's strained voice during the message now took on a different meaning, perhaps this time he'd made a serious call for help. As Justin considered the possible meanings behind the cryptic message, he noted how David always assumed Justin would come to his rescue whenever called.

Justin's cell phone buzzed on the booth's table. He glanced at the screen and sighed. He'd already spoken to his sister, Wendy Hinton. She knew about David's murder, but he wasn't ready to go home and certainly not ready for her well-meaning advice. He let the call roll over to voice mail.

His jaw tightened, and he crushed the napkin he'd been holding. *Who killed David?* Based on bits and pieces he could catch from the detectives, Justin thought they believed the whole scene and manner of kill appeared professional. Although the condo had been ransacked, a clear pattern emerged; nothing of value had been taken. Flat screen televisions, jewelry, and all the usual items stolen in break-ins remained. A wad of cash, probably reserved for their honeymoon, remained untouched. Everything other than the computer.

Had David returned to his old tricks? Justin sighed.

One clean shot to the head. His years of trauma surgery gave him a lot of experience with intentional hits versus random heat-of-battle wounds. An autopsy would reveal more, but Justin, just as the police, surmised this had been a professional hit.

His cell phone jangled again. *Wendy.*

She wouldn't stop calling until she spoke to him. Justin inhaled and jabbed at the button on his phone to answer. "Wendy. I'm fine."

"Don't give me that. Your best friend is dead. You are *not* fine." She paused, and then her tone softened. "Where are you?"

Justin grimaced as he eyed the full glass of alcohol.

He and his older sister by two years were close, and he'd never lied before. Upfront and honest had been the cornerstone of getting through some tough times together. He couldn't start a bad habit now. "I'm at Quigley's." Justin hung his head low, as if he'd already fallen off the wagon.

"I'm calling someone to watch Sam. I'll be right there."

"No!" Justin inhaled and ran a hand through his hair.

The busty waitress glanced at him, but the other patrons didn't appear to notice his outburst.

He lowered his voice. "I don't need a babysitter."

"I'm afraid for you. You've come so far. Don't do it."

"It's not about me right now."

"Do the police have any idea who killed him?"

"No, I don't think so but it looks like a professional hit. I don't know what the hell happened."

"The police will figure that out. How is Marissa?"

"In shock. She looked like the walking wounded I saw in Iraq. Still able to move and talk, but totally broken." Justin picked up the glass and swirled the liquid, staring at the amber substance catching the light from the fixture above his booth.

"She is lucky you were there. I'm sure you both will benefit having each other to lean on." Wendy paused. "Don't let this be the catalyst to destroy yourself again. Just like Laura…"

"Don't. Thanks for listening, sis. I'll be home in half an hour. Love you." Justin punched the button to end the call. He set the glass back on the table.

"You haven't even touched your drink, sugar. Can I get you something else?" Busty sidled up to the table, her dark hair piled in sloppy cascades on top of her head.

"No, I'm good." Her intense eye makeup had Justin pondering how much time she spent in front of a mirror.

"You look like you have a lot on your mind."

"Yeah, tough day." Justin rubbed his tired eyes as she walked off.

His mind wandered back to why and what happens next. The perpetrators were obviously looking for something. Had David been in the way, or did his death result from a planned attack? They had to know Marissa lived there. If they didn't find what they were looking for, Marissa could be in danger.

I'll be there for you, he'd promised. Taking a chance, he punched in her number. The phone clicked after the first ring. "Marissa, it's me, Justin. Did I wake you?"

"No, I couldn't sleep. I went outside to get some air and …" her voiced trailed off.

Justin straightened in his seat. "What's wrong?"

"I don't even know if I saw what I thought I saw. And even if I did, it probably means nothing."

"What did you see?" Justin's muscles tensed and, without thinking, he pushed aside the drink.

"I saw a black SUV drive at a low speed down the street. The windows were tinted, but through the front windshield I thought I saw someone." She paused. "I could swear I saw someone looking at me."

Justin clenched and unclenched his fists as he considered her story. He feared the murderer or murderers believed Marissa knew something about whatever they were looking for and would come after her. "Are you inside now?"

"Yes, and the security system is on."

"Good. Try to get some sleep, I'll come by first thing, and we'll go talk to the detectives."

"Okay. Umm..." She hesitated. "How well did you know David? I've been trying to remember anything that might help."

Justin paused, and then told her about the voicemail David had left for him three days ago. "Might have been nothing, or something about the wedding. I just don't know."

Silence followed and then Marissa whispered, "I'm scared."

He wanted to assure her safety, but he'd learned early on in his medical training not to make assurances he couldn't guarantee. "I'll be heading home in a few so I'll drive by the house. Call me anytime you need, and don't be afraid to call the police if you hear even the slightest disturbance. I'll be there first thing tomorrow,"

She sighed. "Thanks, Justin. I appreciate all you've done tonight."

"Get some sleep." After disconnecting the call, he signaled for the waitress. While waiting for the check, he recalled Marissa clinging to him as if he were her lifeline. He vowed to be with her every step of the torturous journey ahead—a journey he knew all too well.

He'd been doing great. Great practice. Great home. Lately, however, he'd been concerned for Marissa. David wasn't himself, which likely meant he'd been involved in something troublesome. Now this. *Damn it, David.* Concern from afar was one thing, but Justin had no clue how he would help her. If David had sunk to his old ways, then they both needed to strap in for a rough ride.

Justin rushed out of Quigley's, leaving a tip and an untouched drink.

Chapter 8

In the brief seconds after opening her eyes, Marissa thought she'd awakened in her condo's bedroom. A glance at her surroundings sparked a harsh reminder she'd slept in her childhood room and ignited fresh memories of the horrifying circumstances which found her here. She rubbed her eyes, trying to ground out bloody images.

Marissa sat up in bed eyeing a stack of extra wedding invitations on her desk. Her heart hitched. Had she not been set to postpone the wedding, she would have married a man capable of cheating, and maybe much more, pledging to stand by him in sickness and health. The realization stung.

David wanted to postpone their honeymoon. What had been so important?

In addition to her wedding planning business, her wedding planner, Pat, also maintained a small travel agency to help her couples plan the perfect honeymoon.

Marissa washed her face, brushed her teeth and hair. She dressed in the jeans and T-shirt left by Vanessa or Kelly and hit Pat's speed dial button on her phone. Pat's warm voice greeted her.

"Marissa, honey, I'm devastated to hear about David."

"I'm struggling to believe any of this is really happening."

"Don't you worry. I will take care of everything on this end."

"A few weeks ago, did David call you about postponing our honeymoon?" Marissa squeezed the phone and concentrated on keeping her voice steady.

"Yes. Many couples decide to wait a few days because the wedding day can be very tiring."

"Did he tell you why he wanted to postpone?" Marissa didn't believe for a moment David delayed their trip out of concern for their energy level. He had to be motivated by another reason, which she believed led to his death.

"Well, no, but I just assumed you two spoke about the decision and agreed to delay your departure date. He did mention something about a work issue." Pat cleared her throat. "Is something wrong?"

"No, no, Pat. I'm reviewing the last few weeks. Thanks."

"I'll cancel everything, and considering the circumstances, I'm sure I'll recoup a percentage of your deposits."

Marissa leaned against the wall and stared out at the street. No creepy black SUVs in sight. Had David exposed her to danger? Could he be so callous as to not tell her that her life, and possibly lives of those she cared about, had been in jeopardy?

"Is there anything else?" Pat asked.

Marissa turned away from the window. "Don't cancel the reception venue or the caterer yet. I'll get back to you with more details." She'd accepted David's proposal. Didn't she owe him a proper goodbye?

Five minutes later, she stepped into the kitchen and all gazes turned to her. Her parents, Vanessa, Eli, and Justin were seated around the table. Marissa steeled her spine, determined to lock up her emotions for another time.

As the shock of David's death settled in, she believed the time had arrived to start making plans. First up, a visit to the police station. She would not have her family put in danger. Now, she'd have to get through breakfast.

"Hi everyone." Marissa tried to make her voice light. She didn't need her mother and sister insisting she returned to bed for more rest.

Justin stood and embraced her, giving her arm and extra squeeze before he pulled out the last remaining chair. "I just got here and your mom has this huge spread."

Marissa smiled. "Mom never disappoints when it comes to food."

"You look so much better but you need to eat." Her mother jumped out of her chair. "I have fresh fruit, bacon, eggs, toast, waffles, coffee, and juice. Whatever you want." She stopped and waited for an answer.

Marissa hugged her father, who already had a full plate.

He patted her hand and smiled.

Her parents had completed remodeling the kitchen about a month ago, and Ava now stood in front of a gleaming stainless steel gas stove. She enjoyed cooking, and her father joked he enjoyed eating, so they made a perfect match. They'd used her upcoming wedding as a reason for the remodel with all the family and friends around.

The notion her designation no longer included "engaged to be married" shook her. Marissa's future would now take a different path. "I'll have coffee and some toast." She grabbed a mug from the cabinet. As she poured the steaming, brown liquid into her mug, she sensed gazes boring into her back. She wanted to scream, but instead slid into a chair between Justin and the chair her mother just vacated.

"Hmm." Her mother piled two strips of bacon, a scoop of eggs, and half a syrup-covered waffle onto the plate she placed in front of Marissa. "You need your strength."

Arguing was pointless, so she cut a section of waffle and slipped a small piece into her mouth. Her mother always made perfect waffles and she assumed today was no exception, but the morsel tasted like a lump of play dough rolling down her throat.

Justin squeezed her other hand under the table before turning to Ava. "You're a great cook. Thanks for breakfast, Mrs. Nash."

Ava grinned.

John rolled his eyes. "Son, you are welcome anytime and for any meal, but you just opened a can of worms. She loves new people to test her recipes." He laughed.

"Vanessa sure didn't inherit the cooking gene," Eli chimed in. Vanessa glared, and in response he added, "Oh, she does just fine in the kitchen, but I have to say Mom delivers on another level."

"Eli, what do you do for a living?" Justin took a bite of his bacon.

Marissa smiled, thankful the attention had shifted from her.

"I'm an engineer, like Dad. My specialty is electrical, though. The work pays the bills and keeps Vanessa happy in designer clothes—somewhat." Eli laughed.

"Vanessa's hobby is filling up closets." Ava slid into her chair next to Marissa.

"There's nothing wrong with wanting to dress well." Vanessa took a sip of her coffee.

Justin placed his napkin on the table and turned to Marissa. "After breakfast, why don't I drive you over to see Halo? Early this morning, I went over and took him to the groomers. We could take him for a walk. I'm sure he misses you."

"Sure." Relief swept over her. Justin understood she wanted to speak with the detectives first before she alerted her family to any potential danger.

Ava kissed Marissa on the forehead. "Don't forget we're having dinner here tonight—the whole family, along with David's. Justin, we expect you here, too."

Once they were in Justin's car, he turned toward her. "I assumed you hadn't told your family about the suspicious SUV."

Marissa shook her head. "You've seen them, they are watching over me like hawks. I love them, but I won't pile on more misery when I don't know for sure what I saw."

Justin nodded. "I didn't spot anything out of norm but let's make a report."

WITHIN THIRTY MINUTES, they were inside the police station. Detective Kearns was out, but they were informed Streeter would see them. After a brief wait, they were shown to a private office. Marissa let out a held breath as she sat. This room resembled a standard office, much less bland and intimidating than the previous night's interview room.

"Detective, thanks for seeing us. I'm concerned I'm being watched." Marissa gave a full description of what she'd seen and felt.

The detective cocked his head. "Are you sure this is what you saw? Maybe the driver was lost."

Marissa scooted to the edge of her chair and shook her head. "No, I don't think so. He wasn't outside the vehicle calling for Scruffy."

Streeter smiled, and then turned his gaze back to his notes. "Ms. Nash, you are just as much a victim of a violent crime as your fiancé. Oftentimes, the imagination can do wild things especially after such a disturbing experience."

"I don't believe the creepy SUV was just my imagination." She folded her hands in her lap.

Streeter wrinkled his forehead. "Didn't you indicate the SUV had dark tinted windows?"

Marissa nodded. "Yes. The SUV drove by my parents' house, and I'm certain the person looked at me." She leaned across the desk toward the detective. "Have you ever had the feeling you were being watched? Little hairs on the back of your neck stand up." Marissa barely recognized the pleading tone of her own voice. Why wasn't this man listening?

Streeter rubbed his chin. "I understand the feeling, Ms. Nash, but at this point in the investigation, nothing indicates the perpetrator, or perpetrators, would come after you. Besides, based on the quick and methodical nature of the crime, these people know what they're doing. If they wanted to hurt you, they would have."

Justin placed a hand on Marissa's. "Detective, do you have any suspects in the murder?"

Streeter adjusted papers on his desk. "I can't comment on an open investigation. We'll let you know when we have something concrete."

Justin continued. "You're the professional here, but with all due respect, how can you conclude Marissa is or isn't in danger when you don't know who killed David?"

Scratching his neck, Streeter blew out a breath. "Honestly, I can't." Streeter rolled his chair back and rounded the desk to sit on the edge. "Dr. Tanner, did you see this SUV, as well?"

"No." Justin paused. "We can't be sure if there is any threat right now, but we can't discount the possibility either."

Marissa jumped up. "My family's safety is at stake and…"

The detective held up his hand. "I understand, Ms. Nash, and I'll put in a request for patrol cars to monitor your street. They won't be camped out in front of your door, but they'll do a couple of sweeps, more if they're having a slow night."

Marissa batted away a stay hair from her face. She'd have to accept an occasional drive by as good enough for now. "Thank you."

"Stay vigilant and observant," Streeter said. "Feel free to call me. We're still working through everything, but chances are we'll need you both for more questions."

Marissa nodded. "One last thing. When will David's body be released? We need to begin making arrangements."

"Usually they release bodies within twenty-four to forty-eight hours. The ME is scheduled to perform an autopsy in a few hours." He patted her shoulder. "I'll call you and the Seybolds when I know more."

Within minutes they were back in the car. "I don't think he believed me." Marissa leaned her head against the seat.

"We're less than twenty-four hours after you found David. The police are still trying to determine what happened."

Marissa rubbed her eyes. "I *was* tired, but I know what I saw."

Justin nodded. "I believe you." He turned out of the parking lot. "Let's go see your dog."

Chapter 9

Justin gripped the steering wheel and stole a quick glance at Marissa, whose eyes were trained straight ahead, unblinking. Worry slithered through his veins.

The numbing pain of losing Laura had sent him on his own dark journey with grief soaked so far inside him despair flowed through his bloodstream and into his bones. Misery parked itself within his soul and left him devastated, unable to move. He hoped Marissa's journey took a brighter turn.

Twenty minutes later, Justin pulled into his driveway.

"Where are we?" she asked.

"My house." Justin slid out and jogged around to her side of the car.

"This is your house?" Marissa followed as he held open the door. "It's beautiful."

"Thanks. I didn't set out to buy such a big house, but after my last deployment I..." Justin paused. "Let's just say I needed a bit of normalcy, and this place reminded me of the house I grew up in before my parents died."

The large yellow colonial had multiple dormers and light brick accents. The leaded glass in the front door allowed light to shine in and a window-filled solarium jutted out from the side. The yard reminded him of his mother and he could picture her sitting on the lush green grass while tending the flowerbeds.

Marissa shielded her eyes from the sun, meeting his gaze. "I'm sorry about your parents. I remember David telling me they died in a plane accident."

"Long time ago." He didn't want to get into old wounds. Even though the accident had been years ago, his parents now lived in a sacred part of his heart he wasn't quick to share.

Wendy opened the front door and Halo bounded out of the house at full speed, straight for Marissa.

With a gasp, Marissa bent down to hug the dog.

He greeted her with his tail flapping in excitement and a lick to her face.

"Halo, I missed you," Marissa buried her head in his white fur. She scratched behind his ears and glanced at Justin. "Thanks. I needed to get away. My family means well and I love them, but sometimes..."

"I understand. It's nice to breathe."

They were quiet for a few minutes. Halo calmed and sat close to Marissa as she continued to stroke his head.

Justin's heart ached for her. In the bleak days after Laura's death, he'd needed help but refused aid. The road back had been long and riddled with potholes. Marissa faced a similar battle, and he vowed to help her.

But could he?

Damn, I feel like I'm just skating by, even though my life is great right now. Who am I to think I can really help her? Something inside told him to try.

He turned, fighting the urge to bring her close. Shoving his hands into his pockets, he no longer trusted himself not to reach for her. He had no clue how to define his attraction, but he wanted no part of this type of soul-searching, at least not now.

David's death had been a blow to his gut. He cared about his friend, but he'd also helped David through some dark times, most of which David himself had been responsible for. Justin hated complex emotions. Delving into someone's body to fix a broken or damaged part was within his wheelhouse, but analyzing emotions were tasks he'd rather not handle.

"You could have let him stay with Kelly and Craig a while longer. I'm sure they wouldn't have minded." Marissa continued to pet Halo.

Justin turned at the sound of her voice and cleared the lump in his throat. "I dropped by Kelly and Craig's to check on Halo this morning. Kelly needed to take Gavin to the pediatrician and Craig had an important meeting so rather than leave Halo alone I took him to the groomers and brought him back here." He gave Halo a pat on his head. "He's a great dog."

"Thank you." She scraped her teeth across her bottom lip. "As much time as David spent in Halo's presence the two never really bonded." She stroked Halo's head. "I think they mutually tolerated each other."

Justin shrugged. "David didn't care much for animals, but Halo is hard not to like."

Marissa bent again and took Halo's face in her hands. "What did you see?"

Halo flapped his tail and peered at her. "I can't imagine what David went through." Her voice caught as she buried her face in his fur.

Halo licked the side of her face and nudged her.

"I'm glad Halo is okay." Justin crossed his arms. Why hadn't the murderer killed such an imposing dog, especially if Halo turned aggressive?

She drew a deep breath. "Do you happen to have a leash? I'm still not allowed back home, and I never thought to get one."

"I picked up one while at the groomers. Which reminds me, is Halo overly attached to his collar?"

"No, why?"

"He wouldn't let the groomer remove it. They did their best to clean the collar, but I thought maybe you'd like a new one. Just a thought."

"David bought him that collar. His way of appeasing me, I think." Marissa touched the collar around Halo's neck.

Justin stared down at the black collar with silver and crystal studs. He remembered David telling him about buying the expensive accessory. Crap. He didn't want Marissa thinking he had intentions of erasing David's gesture.

"Thanks for your kindness. The collar is special to me, and obviously to Halo so I think I'll keep it on a while longer."

Suddenly, the door to the house opened again, and Sam came flying down the stairs, followed by Wendy.

"Is that your dog?" Sam's brunette curls blew in the light wind as she stopped a few feet away.

"Yes. My name is Marissa."

"This is my niece, Samantha, and her mother is my sister, Wendy."

Justin placed his hands on Samantha's shoulders. He hadn't been sure about bringing Marissa here, but a distraction might be what she needed.

Marissa shook Sam's hand, and then turned to Wendy. "Nice to meet you both."

"I helped take care of Halo today." Sam beamed.

"Thank you." Marissa scratched Halo's head.

"What kind of dog is he?" Sam's small hand caressed Halo.

Marissa bent next to Halo and Sam. "He's a Kuvasz. The breed is from the country of Hungary. His instinct is to guard livestock and protect them from danger. He learned as a puppy to protect his human family. Usually he can pick out the good people from the bad."

Halo gave Sam an enthusiastic lick on the face.

She giggled in return. "I think he likes me. He didn't bite me or anything." Once again, Sam sunk her small hand into Halo's wavy fur.

"He'd better not. Halo is usually a very good dog," Marissa said.

"He just laid around for awhile when he first got here. He seemed really sad. Why?" Sam patted his head in gentle motions.

Justin stared at the dog. He had appeared sad. Sam had an amazing awareness of people and apparently dogs. She kept him on his toes with insightful questions only a six year old dared ask.

"Samantha, enough questions, sweetheart. Halo probably missed Marissa, that's all." Wendy gave Marissa an apologetic look. "She's at the age where questions have no limits."

"She can depose a person like a seasoned attorney," Justin added.

Marissa smiled and turned to the girl. "Do you like to be called Samantha, or Sam?"

The girl put her finger on her chin. "I like them both. My mom did a good job naming me. I think I like Sam 'cause that's what Uncle Justin calls me."

"Can I call you Sam, too?" Marissa asked.

The girl nodded.

"Well, Sam, I teach ballet to girls, some of them about your age, and I always like to tell them the truth." Marissa glanced at the dog. "Halo and I are very sad because a good friend of ours went away."

"Oh, I'm sorry. My friend Carmen went away. Her mom and dad moved to Florida. She's lucky, 'cause Mom said she gets to live near Mickey Mouse." Sam smiled. "Did your friend go there, too?"

Marissa shook her head. "No, honey, he didn't."

"Sam, why don't we let Marissa and Halo have some time?" Wendy took Sam's hand.

"Wendy, can Sam help me take Halo for a walk?" Marissa held on to Halo's collar.

"Please, Mom? I promise I won't ask Ms. Marissa too many questions, and I'll be real good." Sam bounced on her toes as she pleaded with her mother. "I never got to walk a dog before 'cause we don't have one. But I think I'll ask Santa for one, and being with Halo is real good practice."

Wendy smiled. "Okay, be good."

"Sam, why don't you go get Halo's new leash? It's in the kitchen." Justin watched her run off.

Once the child moved out of earshot, Wendy turned to Marissa.

"I'm sorry about your loss. If there is anything I can do, please let me know."

"Thanks. Your brother has been a lifesaver."

Wendy glanced at Justin and sighed. "Justin is a really great guy, but he's very good at hiding his feelings and focusing on others. Don't get me wrong, he's not selfish and he never does anything half-heartedly but he takes everything in, good or bad, and it stays there."

Justin crinkled his face. "Okay, enough pop psychology."

"I hope Halo wasn't too much trouble," Marissa said.

"Sam fell in love at first sight. She took him to her room and they both napped." Wendy pulled out her cell phone and showed Marissa the picture she'd snapped of Sam and Halo underneath a pink blanket.

"Adorable." Marissa curled her lips and looked away.

"Oh, I'm so sorry." Wendy patted her arm.

"No, I'm fine." She exhaled, and then added, "No worries."

Justin placed his arm around her shoulders. "Would you like some water, or to sit for awhile?"

"Nope, and I promise to keep it together with Sam. We'll just walk down to the corner. We won't be long."

"I got the leash, and I'm ready to go." Sam ran toward them.

Halo jumped up at the sight of the leash.

Justin leaned toward Marissa. "You sure you're up for this?"

"Yes, Sam and I will be fine." Marissa clipped the leash onto Halo's collar and turned to Sam. "Which way?"

"Bye, Mommy and Uncle Justin!" The girl called. "This way!"

Justin kept an eye on the trio as they left the driveway. He'd been on notice for lurkers or shady people trailing her. No suspicious black SUVs in sight, however, they were dealing with professionals, so he couldn't be sure. He didn't want to alarm Marissa by attempting to get her to change her mind about walking Halo, but he didn't want to take any chances either. *Damn, how will I keep her safe while not freaking her out?*

"You care about her, don't you?"

Justin turned to Wendy before glancing back at Marissa and Sam.

"She's a friend, and she's in trouble. Finding David's dead body sent her into shock."

"I'm sure. I'm glad she has you, but I don't see you looking at her as a friend." Wendy cocked her head and smiled then glanced toward Marissa and Sam. The girl had taken hold of Marissa's hand as they walked. "Cute." Wendy took her cellphone from her pocket and snapped a quick shot. She punched at the phone. "I'm sending this picture to you. Marissa has more than one fan in the family."

Justin sighed and stalked to the end of the driveway. Over his shoulder, he said, "I don't want to have this conversation." He loved his sister and would do anything for her and Sam, but she could be smothering at times.

After their parents' death, they'd bonded in a way only tragedy can spur. Then, after her jerk of a husband cheated on her when Sam was only a couple months old, Wendy divorced Brad. Justin had been in Iraq and the house sat empty, so he suggested Wendy move in. The partnership suited them both. When Justin returned, he and Sam became inseparable, and with Brad's nonexistent presence, Justin, with happiness, assumed the alpha male role in her life.

Wendy followed. "Okay, I'll drop it—for now. I'm sorry about David, but I'm worried. You were at Quigley's last night. You had a major shock. You *are* allowed to be rocked." She shielded her eyes and followed Justin's gaze. "Why are we watching them?"

Justin placed his hand on his hips and scanned the street. The hum of Mr. Payne's lawn mower across the street and the far off roar of an airplane were the only sounds resonating on the street. No idling SUVs or strange people skulking down the sidewalk. Justin turned back to Marissa and Sam, calculating the distance from his house to the corner. With the wide expanse of each lot's frontage and the distance in between houses, he estimated the length at about a half-mile, give or take a few yards. He could get to them easy.

Justin turned back to Wendy. "I've been clean for five years. I'm not screwing up my sobriety. I admit to a moment of weakness, but I rose above it." He resigned himself to having this conversation with

Wendy. She wouldn't let up when concern took hold and Justin loved her for such devotion.

Wendy crossed her arms. "You lost your best friend and now you're taking care of his fiancée. What about you?"

"Thanks for caring, but I'm fine." Justin sighed. "I won't lie, losing Dave hurts like hell, but I'm not in the same place I was before." He recalled the last veteran's group session he attended a few weeks ago at the GT Training Center and their discussion about ways to cope with the horrors of war, including the death of close friends.

"This has to bring up memories of Laura." Kicking a pile of rocks Sam and her friend recently used to highlight their sidewalk chalk artwork of flowers, rainbows and indistinguishable animals, Wendy pushed the stones to the edge of the driveway. She returned to Justin's side.

Justin stared at the innocent pictures on the pavement. He hoped Sam and Wendy's life would always be happy, safe from the dangers of the world. Shifting his gaze ahead as Marissa, Sam, and Halo headed back toward the house, he huffed out a sigh "The scene was bad, gory but not the worst I've seen. I'm good. I got it covered."

This time, someone else had deeper wounds. He hoped his and Marissa's shared grief would bring them both through this much stronger.

Wendy nodded. "I wouldn't be the pain-in-the-ass sister if I didn't say something."

Justin smiled. "Just like Mom."

Wendy chuckled. "I miss her and Dad, especially as Sam gets older. They would have loved having a granddaughter."

General Phillip Tanner and his wife Connie died in an airplane crash five months into Justin's sophomore year at Notre Dame. Wendy was a senior at Northwestern in Chicago. A horrendous time, but their Aunt Iris and Uncle Lou served as surrogate parents.

Although a huge hole remained in his heart, Sam brightened his life. "I can picture Dad taking Sam fishing. You remember when he took you, the ultimate girly girl? You screamed like a banshee just putting bait on your line." Justin chuckled as he simulated holding a worm with his thumb and forefinger.

Wendy grinned. "Dad was a general long before he actually got the title. He yelled at me to put the damn worm on the hook, and the thing just wouldn't stop wiggling."

They laughed and grew quiet. Justin interrupted the silence a moment later. "Will you be okay traveling with Sam?" Ever since their parents' deaths, Wendy had been leery of planes.

"I got it covered." She smiled and turned back toward the house. "I'm going to dig out a juice box for Sam."

When Marissa, Sam, and Halo approached the driveway, Justin ushered them inside. "How was the walk?" He held the door open for them.

Justin noted Marissa's faced flushed crimson and her hands shook. His heart lurched. Something had happened.

"Great. Sam made a perfect assistant." Marissa diverted her gaze from Justin.

"Halo is a really good dog. He can even do tricks. I love him." Sam kneeled at the door to hug the dog.

"I'm glad you have a new friend but can we avoid inviting every fly in Virginia inside the kitchen, Sam?" Wendy stood with her hands on her hips.

"Okay, Mommy but can I please have a dog like Halo? I promise I will take him for walks just like Marissa did. Pleeeease!"

"I'm sorry." Marissa mouthed.

Wendy shrugged and set a juice box on the counter. "Samantha, remember we are going on a big plane to visit Aunt Debbie in California so we don't have time for a dog right now."

Sam offered a pout then within seconds perked up. "I know, we can get one when we get back." She took a sip from the juice box and returned it to the counter.

"Must be nice to have everything figured out." Justin kissed Sam on top of her head.

"Yep!" she said skipping around Halo, who sat with his tail flapping against the wooden planks of the kitchen.

"Would you like to stay for dinner, Marissa? I'm making lasagna." Wendy retrieved two eggs from the refrigerator.

Marissa glanced at Justin. "I wish but my mother is having a dinner and David's family will be there to discuss arrangements."

"I'll be back late." Justin bent down to pet Halo.

"Sam, thanks for helping me walk Halo. Do you think you could take care of him another night, if your mom agrees?" Marissa kneeled and put her arm around the dog.

"Can I Mom, please?"

"Sure. Halo's no trouble at all."

After spirited goodbyes and a few whines from Halo, Marissa and Justin climbed back into his SUV. As soon as they turned the corner, Justin pulled over in front of the park. "What's wrong?"

Marissa inhaled. "I think I saw them again—the black SUV. Down the street at the corner. I was scared to death to have Sam with me."

Justin scanned the street. No black SUV.

"Could you see anyone inside?"

"Not in any detail but other than the driver there may have been another person. I'm sorry for putting Sam in potential danger. We should go back and talk to Wendy." Her eyes were wide and her hands trembled

"I'll talk to Wendy."

"Do you think I'm crazy? There's no one here now but I know what I saw."

Justin swiped a hand through his hair. "We'll figure something out. Are you okay about this dinner with your family?"

She shrugged. "It will be difficult but..."

Justin gripped the steering to keep from touching her. "I don't want to overstep boundaries so just tell me to back off if you need space. Believe me I get it."

Marissa shook her head. "You've been a bright spot for me. If it isn't too much trouble I'd really like you come tonight but first make sure Wendy and Sam are okay."

He nodded.

"David was lucky to have a friend like you."

"I'm not doing this for David." He paused, considering his next words. "Losing someone you care about in such a tragic and unexpected manner is a harsh blow. I hope I can help."

Marissa stared out at the park before she glanced at him. "What do you think they want? I don't know anything." She laughed a low throaty chuckle. "I could have married someone I didn't even know." She stared for a second at the huge diamond engagement ring. "Did David confide in you?" Her green eyes narrowed, pleading with him for understanding.

Justin shifted in his seat as he angled himself toward her. "No, the last few months he seemed...different. Like I've already told you he called me a few days ago. I didn't think much of the call then, but now I wonder."

He hadn't been sure whether he should tell Marissa about the phone call but erred on the side of honesty. She deserved that. He'd mentioned the phone call to the police but he couldn't be certain if the detective considered the information important. Justin knew otherwise. Whatever David wanted to talk about had to be connected to his murder. A distress call wouldn't have been the first time David summoned Justin to help him out of a jam.

In time he'd tell Marissa about the real David.

THE FAMILY MEETING EXHAUSTED HER. The Seybolds were supportive, and Marissa appreciate their kind gestures, but the haunted, broken appearance of David's parents shattered the last remnants of her heart. She faced an uproar upon announcing she'd decided to use the wedding reception venue for the funeral luncheon.

"Marissa, are you insane?" Vanessa jumped up from her seat. "You don't have to be a martyr."

Marissa leaned her head back against the sofa. "I already told Pat not to cancel the venue. I can't do anything more for David, but I have this wonderful place and all this food so why not?"

Ava clasped her hand around Marissa's. "Honey, are you sure? You don't think it would be too much?"

"No, Mom. I'm sure."

David's parents were touched, but wanted to make sure she'd be comfortable.

Her father offered to pay her for any lost costs, but her decision hadn't been about money.

She wanted to run. Her life had spiraled out of control. The police made her look like a neurotic alarmist, afraid of her own shadow and seeing nonexistent surveillance SUVs. Now her family thought she'd lost her mind for daring to suggest using the reception venue for David's funeral.

Marissa spent twenty minutes calming their concerns before they agreed.

Justin, who'd parked himself near the foyer, had stayed out of the fray. Instead, he made intermittent jaunts to the door, probably on the lookout for the SUV.

His presence gave her a sense of safety, a feeling she'd lost well before David's death. David's lack of interest in her and their relationship had bothered her for some time. Not until her business trip had she gained perspective and recognized what she needed to do.

After more discussion, Marissa's headache had reached a new level.

Her mother had been relentless in making her eat and every few minutes offered her a plate of food.

David's sister, Amanda, burst into tears every time she glanced at Marissa, and Vanessa's overbearing nature took center stage as usual. Marissa had been mortified when Vanessa, out loud, in front of everyone, gave her permission to cry.

She caught Justin's glances a number of times. At first, the attention reassured her, but then she'd become uncomfortable with everyone waiting for signs of boiling over, catching fire, or melting down like she'd assumed the role of subject in their science experiment. At an opportune time with everyone engaged in conversation,

Marissa escaped to her room and called Kelly, begging her to come pick her up.

Fifteen minutes later, after leaving a note stating she'd be at the studio, Marissa scrambled out the back door and crept around to the front of the house. She slipped inside Kelly's car. "Go, go!"

Kelly's mouth dropped open as she stared at Marissa. "What's going on?"

"Just go!" Marissa glanced back at the house as Kelly gunned the car down the street.

"Would you like to tell me why I'm speeding down the street in a getaway car?"

"They are driving me insane. They all mean well, but I just couldn't take the pity stares or sadness. I'm sad, too, but they are making me feel like a defective doorbell that just won't ring right."

Kelly glanced over. "Okay, I get it. It's hard to know what to do. This is such an unexpected tragedy."

"Would an expected tragedy be better?" Marissa glanced out the back window again to see if any strange SUVs were behind them, and then back to her friend. "Sorry. I appreciate everything everyone has been doing, including you. I just needed a moment."

Kelly nodded. "Where to?"

A half-hour later, she climbed into the rental car and sighed. *Alone and feeling like a grown up again.*

She hugged Kelly and told her she needed to be alone for a little while.

Kelly made her promise to call in the morning, or sooner, if necessary.

After taking a roundabout route, in hopes of fooling the stalkers, she pulled into the studio parking lot. With key in hand, she darted into the studio and locked the door behind her. All of her tail-dodging abilities came courtesy of the movies, so she had no idea if her zigzag route and NASCAR driving skills were useful in outsmarting a guy in a creepy SUV.

The studio loomed dark and empty. Relief swept over her as she flipped the light switch of her office. The older girls sometimes had class or rehearsed late into the evening, but tonight she had the studio to herself. She changed in the small office she shared with two other teachers, glad she kept spare dance attire and *pointe* shoes on hand. With her hair rolled into a familiar ballet bun, she entered a large mirrored room, cued the music, and began her warm-up routine.

Her favorite Mozart compilation wafted through the speakers. For several seconds, Marissa closed her eyes as she grasped the *barre*. She opened her eyes and, with her lean legs supported on the *barre*, she bent back to stretch as she moved through *pliés* and *tendues* to ready her limbs.

Once she warmed up, she moved into a favorite routine. She performed several *fouettes*, *grande jetes*, and *pirouettes*. Her movements took on a life of their own as she glided across the floor on *pointe*.

The piece, Sleeping Beauty, had been Grandmother Valentina's favorite, and one Marissa had been set to perform for her Juilliard audition. She curled her lips. Juilliard was a long time ago.

Once ballet reclaimed an important role in her life, she enjoyed the soothing effects dance evoked. Now, as part owner of Estrada Dance Academy, she couldn't picture life without dance. She enjoyed the occasional performance, but her pride soared seeing her young students embrace their lessons.

As the music died and her performance came to an end, she once again stood at the *barre*, her breath making a small circle of fog on the mirror in front of her.

Grandmother Valentina knew the freeing feeling of expressing emotions on stage, of feeling the music pull you in until you were as much a part of melody as the notes. Valentina Estrada recognized innate talent in her granddaughter and mentored her up to the point of her being weeks away from a Juilliard audition.

Marissa had disappointed her grandmother when she chose a business degree over a career in dance, but in the end, she made the right move. She allowed her thoughts to wander to the "what if". What if she had attended her Juilliard tryout? What if she had been accepted? Would she have danced with a major ballet company?

She'd wanted to please her grandmother, but after the accident, her life spun in another direction. On her way to rehearse for her senior winter ballet performance, someone pulled out in front of her. She slammed on her brakes and another car plowed into her. She broke her ankle, and with a Juilliard audition two weeks away, she'd been unable to dance.

At first, she'd wallowed in her bad luck. Juilliard only accepted a handful of new students a year. Heartbroken, she decided to apply to other colleges. She excelled at math and after speaking with her teacher, Marissa decided to major in Accounting. Several months later, she received a huge scholarship from University of Virginia.

Turning from the mirror, Marissa switched the music to a more contemporary tune and began a complicated routine. Ten minutes later, again out of breath, she turned to grab a towel.

Then an explosion rocked the building and the room went dark.

Chapter 10

Strong arms enveloped her as she struggled against a vice-like grip. Rough facial hair brushed against her cheek. She wanted to scream, but a hand clamped down across her mouth.

A flash of fire from the front reception area lit up the darkness. Her heart roared inside her ribcage.

He's going to kill me! She writhed and struggled against the stranger.

Her brain fired on all circuits. She needed a weapon.

My pointe shoes.

"Marissa, it's me!" a voice screamed.

Ignoring the call, she raised her leg and slammed down the box of her *pointe* shoe on the attacker's foot.

"Ow!" He released her.

As soon as his grip loosened, she raced for the back of the studio. The back door exit sign, illuminated in the darkness, loomed ahead like the beam of a lighthouse calling her to safety. A quick glance over her shoulder confirmed the orange light from the fire in the front of the studio had grown brighter. She reached for the door.

Massive hands swooped down and clamped around her waist.

She screamed and flailed as the attacker picked her up.

"Marissa! It's me, Justin." He relaxed his grip, allowing her to whip around to face him.

She turned and stared at him. "You scared me half to death!" Her muscles quivered as her pulse raced.

"We need to get out of here." Justin scooped up her dance bag and threw the strap onto his shoulder. He pulled his gun as he opened the back door and peered out.

They ran out the back exit and rounded to the front of the studio.

Marissa pulled up and stared at the dwindling fire in the front reception area of the studio. She stepped closer and gawked through a shattered window at the blaze, limited for the moment to the sofa. "What happened?" Marissa blinked as smoke streamed out the broken window. The automatic overhead sprinkler system had engaged, dousing some of the flames. Smoke swirled in the air burning her nose and eyes.

"Someone tossed a firebomb through the window." Justin holstered his gun and pulled his cell phone from his pocket. "I'll call for fire. You call Streeter or Kearns."

Marissa continued to stare at her studio. *A bomb?* She fished her cell phone from her bag and hit Detective Kearns's number. The detective informed her she was on her way.

"Someone bombed my studio?" From a distance, she surveyed the broken window in front of the sofa. What if students had been inside? Her heart slammed against her chest as the wail of fire trucks screamed from a distance.

"The Molotov cocktail came from a black SUV." Justin scanned the parking lot and street.

Fear snaked up her spine. "You mean *the* black SUV?"

Justin placed his arm around her. "They took off. You're safe now."

A fire truck barreled into the parking lot and firefighters jumped out, dispersing in a flurry of activity.

One of the firefighters approached. "Are you two hurt?"

Justin crossed his arms. "No. The fire is limited to the sofa and the sprinklers took care of the flames."

"Is there anyone else in the building?"

"There's no one else inside," Marissa said, pulling at her lip.

The firefighter instructed them to stay well away from the building while they assessed the fire and checked for further danger.

Five minutes later, Streeter pulled up in an unmarked car, followed by another police vehicle. Streeter and a police officer jumped out of their cars and approached a firefighter. They held a brief conversation before Streeter jogged toward Justin and Marissa.

"I was close by and saw the fire trucks. Are either of you hurt?" Streeter placed a hand on his hip as he gazed at the studio.

"No, we're fine." Justin clamped his jaw tight.

A few seconds later Kearns drove into the parking lot. She ran up to the group, her ponytail swinging from side to side. "What happened?"

Justin wiped sweat off his forehead. "I was outside in the parking lot when I saw a man in a black SUV throw a lit bottle into the studio window. The vehicle slowed for a second and took off in that direction." Justin pointed to the empty street inhabited by small businesses and restaurants. Justin pulled Marissa closer.

She trembled. The leotard and tiny shorts offered little warmth for her sweaty skin against the sudden cold breeze. Marissa caught a prolonged stare from Kearns.

"I have a blanket in my car, if you're cold." Kearns nodded toward her vehicle.

"No thanks." Marissa rubbed her arms.

Kearns stared at the reception area now doused with even more water at the hands of the firefighters. "Did you get a license plate or a good look at the perpetrators?"

"No, my first thoughts involved getting to Marissa. I jumped through the broken window and shut off the lights in case they doubled back," Justin said.

Justin's body heat stopped her shivering. A few minutes ago, his strong arms had enveloped her. She'd been in fear of her life but now she appreciated his strength. She stole a quick glance. Massive pectoral muscles strained against his blue V-neck T-shirt. Bulging biceps flexed when he moved his arms. When Marissa followed Justin's hands as he anchored them on his hips, her gaze traveled to his well-developed legs filling out his jeans.

Why hadn't she noticed Justin's killer body before? She blinked and shook her head. *What the hell am I doing? I could have been killed, and I'm ogling him like a rock band groupie.*

"Ms. Nash, did you notice any strange vehicles in the parking lot?" Streeter peered at her.

"No, I didn't see anyone and I didn't think I'd been followed." Her need to dance tonight could have gotten her killed. She stifled a scream.

Streeter held up his index finger. "Just a second." He and Kearns went inside to confer with the firefighters.

"Are you okay?" Justin eyed her.

Aside from feeling stupid. She nodded. "How did you know where to find me?"

"I saw you get into Kelly's car. I followed you from the car rental agency to the studio. I had no intention of bothering you, but I wanted to make sure you were safe, so I sat in the parking lot across the street."

Marissa's gaze met his. "You followed me?"

"Yes, and I won't apologize for trailing you. I lost you at one point. I'm assuming you intended to take the most out of the way route, but I had a feeling you were coming here." Justin huffed out a sigh. "For now, going off on your own is a bad idea." He released her hand and stood in front of her.

She lifted her chin. "I needed to get away." Rubbing her temples, she attempted to massage away the growing headache. "If the people in SUV from the other night did this, why damage my studio? I have absolutely no idea about David's business dealings or clandestine affairs."

"Unfortunately, they don't know that. Consider this attempt tonight a warning shot, probably not even a serious effort. Tossing a Molotov cocktail seems...juvenile."

"You mean they were just playing with me?" Marissa twirled and pointed to the broken window. "I don't look at my damaged studio and think child's play."

A frown shadowed his face. "They want you to be scared."

Kearns and Streeter returned as the firefighters continued trekking through the studio's reception area.

"The fire investigator is on his way," Kearns said. "I believe we know what started the fire, but we need the official ruling. I understand this is nerve-wracking and slow, but we will get to the bottom of this."

"Ms. Nash, you were inside the studio while Dr. Tanner waited outside in the parking lot?" Streeter glanced from Marissa to Justin.

Marissa inhaled. "I made a mistake going off on my own but I had no idea they'd come here."

"You were lucky Dr. Tanner decided to watch the studio from the parking lot. These guys are dangerous, although we can't confirm yet if this is connected to your fiancé's murder." Kearns pushed a stray hair behind her ear as she moved away to take a phone call.

After getting permission to go back inside the building, Marissa surveyed the reception area. The sofa and reception area of the studio sustained fire, smoke, and water damage. She'd have to cancel classes for the next several weeks. Without the kids here she'd feel better knowing they wouldn't be in danger.

She made a beeline to the studio. Grasping the smooth wooden *barre,* she stared into the mirror. From her peripheral vision, she spotted Justin coming up beside her. "I feel awful about taking off tonight."

"Up to now you didn't know the extent of the danger. Despite what the detectives say, we need to operate like these guys have targeted you." Justin stepped closer. "Come stay with me. Wendy and Sam are leaving for California at the end of the week, and I'm probably already on the bad guy's radar."

Marissa shook her head and turned to face him. "I can't put my family or yours in danger. After tonight, I don't know what these people might do. Since the police will now be monitoring my parents' house, I'll stay there."

"For how long? We don't know when this threat will be eliminated." Justin placed both hands on her arms.

She tapped the heel of her foot against the mirror. "I just wanted to dance—forget all this for a few minutes. Is that selfish?" Self-doubt invaded. What if she caused someone else to get hurt or killed?

"No, you're not selfish, it's called surviving. The human brain can only take so much before it shuts down. In medicine, we often tell people with concussions to avoid as much stimuli as possible in order to help the brain recover. Patients are urged to avoid computers or phones, and sometimes even sit in a dark, quiet room for periods of time. This keeps the patient from engaging in other things while the brain heals. That's what you did tonight."

Marissa met his gaze. "The doctor in Utah said the same." The talk of concussions had her recalling her injury via an out of control cab. The doctor had advised her to relax and see her own doctor when she got back in town. She'd never made an appointment but here she stood taking advice from another doctor. Not a good track record.

"What happened in Utah?" Justin leaned one arm on the *barre*.

Marissa waved him off. "Just a stupid accident at the airport. I went to the hospital with a slight concussion." She stared at him, unable to keep her gaze from his muscular chest.

"A concussion is nothing to treat lightly. If this doctor was worth his salt he'd have advised you not to fly." Justin straightened. "Are you sure you're okay?"

Marissa nodded. "He did and I'm fine." Her voice caught as Justin's brown eyes bored into hers. She bent to slip off her *pointe* shoes.

Justin reached for a shoe. "So this is what slammed into my foot." He examined the shoe. "This is barbaric. How do you dance in this thing?"

Marissa laughed. "It takes a while for your foot to get accustomed. Trust me, ballerinas don't have pretty feet."

Kearns opened the door to the studio. "We have a situation across town so I can't guarantee when the patrols will start in your neighborhood. You have our numbers if you need us." She began to shut the door before adding, "The fire investigator is here, and we'll have someone come by and board up the window."

After Kearns shut the door, Justin scooped up her dance bag. "When we're done here I'd like to show you something. Are you game?"

An hour later and after a quick call to check in with her parents, Marissa stared at a large, concrete building. A sign read: GT Training and Rehabilitation Center. She'd never heard of the facility. A glance at her watch told her the time neared 10:00 at night. "Kind of late to see a patient, isn't it?"

He jumped out of the car, jogged to her side, opened the rear door, and grabbed her dance bag he'd deposited in back. "We're not here for a patient."

Marissa accepted his hand noting he had her dance bag. Her gaze shuttled from the dance bag to Justin's hand. The warmth of his grip traveled up through her arm and spread like wildfire through her body. She shook off the feeling. Everything was off. The constant headaches, her inability to handle her family's help, and now her faux attraction to Justin were all symptoms of the horrible way she'd been handling David's death. *Get a grip.*

"Hey, Gabe, you're still here." Justin grinned as they entered and approached a huge man with a full beard.

The man limped over to them at the reception counter and slapped hands with Justin. "Hey, Chopper! Arlo had a bad day so I said what the hell, I got a few free hours." He glanced at his watch. "For the next two hours anyway." His gaze left Justin and moved to survey Marissa. "And who do we have here?"

"Watch it, Gabe. This is Marissa. She was David's fiancée."

The first time she'd been introduced as David's fiancée in the past tense unsettled her. Hadn't she wanted to at least place a temporary halt on her escalation from fiancée to wife?

Gabe leaned on the counter. "I'm sorry about David. He was one of us, which makes you one of us. If there's anything I can do, just holler." He gave her a wink.

The sincerity in his eyes made his wink more of a show of support than anything sexual.

Marissa smiled and thanked him. As Gabe, with an unsteady gait, sauntered to the other side of the reception desk, Marissa caught sight of his prosthetic leg extending from his khaki shorts.

"Anybody over in rehab?" Justin took her hand and moved past the reception desk.

"I think a few people are still up there." Gabe sank onto a stool.

Justin and Marissa snaked their way through the rows of weight machines, passing men and women working out, some with observable prosthetic limbs. Many of the gym-goers yelled out hellos to Justin.

Once they cleared the weight room, she followed Justin down a wide hall adorned with pictures of military members. Marissa noted each picture featured soldiers with lost limbs mountain climbing, running, swimming, or simply smiling with their families. She slowed to examine each photo. "What kind of place is this?"

Justin cocked his head, pushed open a wide door, and waited for her to enter. "This place keeps me sane. The GT Training and Rehab Center is a place especially for military, but we welcome anyone. Some come here just to use the gym facilities, but others come here to rehab missing limbs."

A woman dressed in black athletic pants and a bright blue shirt, emblazoned with the letters GT, yelled across the room. "Hey, boss!"

Justin responded with a wave, and then ushered Marissa along. He gave her a tour through the facilities. In addition to the rehab area, the facility included a fitness area, swimming pool, hot tubs, sauna, basketball courts, massage services, childcare services, group therapy rooms, and open studios for classes. He described how they handled rehab, a combination of individual, family, and group centered activities. They even gave their clients the opportunity to connect with a mentor, someone a little further along in their therapy. All military members had their services paid for by donations.

When many of these soldiers returned with missing limbs they faced treatment, which could be a solitary journey, except for those lucky enough to have involved families. Even then, many family members couldn't understand military life, especially after a deployment.

Both the facility and Justin impressed her. Once the tour ended, Marissa leaned toward him. "Did she call you boss?"

"I kind-of own this place." He flashed a sheepish grin.

"What? I never knew." Marissa took in the surroundings. The facility included state-of-the-art equipment. Everywhere she turned, she noticed patrons and staff greet Justin with happy smiles.

"I don't go around broadcasting I own this place because the facility is about serving the needs of current military and veterans. Anybody, for that matter—we don't discriminate."

"Justin, this is huge." She stared at him with new appreciation.

"My father invested well and after his death I had a decent chunk of money, so I took a chance." He shrugged "We've been open for almost two years now. Wendy is my business manager."

"This is a really...special." Marissa spun in awe. "What does GT stand for?" she asked as they entered another room similar to one of her studios.

Justin glanced at his feet before reestablishing eye contact. "GT means General Tanner."

"After your father?"

He nodded. "Thanks for seeing this place the way I do. We have a unique vibe here, but the spirit of the people makes this place special."

"Amazing. Why didn't David ever say anything about this place?" Marissa paused. "I'm finding out he didn't say much about a lot of things."

"He was here a lot, so I assumed he told you about the facility. Something you said earlier made me suspect the contrary."

"Thank you for invading my privacy and following me." She smiled. "I'm glad you were there." She paused and stared. His brown eyes shone and his smile had grown since they entered the building. "Who are you? You have this place that does so much good, and you've been my lifesaver."

Justin shrugged. "That's me, a real lifesaver."

Something about his tone told Marissa his comment meant a lot more.

"Now, show me how these weapons of dance work." Justin handed her the dance bag.

"You mean here?" She hiked her eyebrows and glanced around the room.

"Will this floor work?"

"Sure." Marissa relented and pulled off her sweatpants, revealing her shorts. After lacing up her shoes she showed him how to stand on *pointe* and even performed a brief routine.

"Wow. You're a great dancer."

Marissa shrugged and placed her hands on her hips. "Would you really know an adequate dancer from a great one?"

Justin laughed. "Okay, I don't know crap about dancing, but it looked pretty good." He rose from his sitting position on the floor. "Why accounting instead of dance?"

"I considered a professional career once." Marissa removed her shoes. "It's a long story and doesn't matter anymore. I like accounting." She didn't want to talk about why she hadn't pursued a professional dance career. While she didn't regret choosing a business degree, she was plagued by the what-ifs.

Justin pursed his lips. "I understand wanting to keep painful things locked away."

Marissa considered his words. "What about your dark secrets?" She wrapped the pink ribbons around her *pointe* shoes and placed them back in her dance bag.

"Some things are best kept on that shelf." He moved toward the door. "I do a lot of weightlifting, and I always thought of dancing as pretty benign in providing any level of fitness benefit, but I was wrong."

She decided to go with his change of topic. "People don't give dancers enough credit. Dancing is a complete workout, probably harder than lifting."

Justin clicked off the light.

Marissa flipped it back on. "I think that's a challenge." She placed her hands on her hips and sauntered to the middle of the floor. "Dr. Tanner, welcome to your first dance class." She curtsied. "Change your clothes. You're gonna sweat."

For the next thirty minutes, Marissa led Justin through a sequence of ballet warm ups, rudimentary dance positions, and even an uncomplicated sequence.

By the time he'd finished, sweat streamed down his face and he collapsed on the floor.

"Ballet is painful," he said. "My body is not meant to contort that way. You broke me."

Marissa laughed and sat beside him. "Fun, huh?"

"In a torturous kind of way." After a couple of minutes, he unfolded himself. "My turn."

They lifted, squatted, pushed, and pulled weights for over thirty minutes. Justin guided her through a series of exercises, standing by her through each one to ensure she could lift the weight.

"Okay, maybe we should call it a draw." She flopped down on the floor.

Justin joined her as they both panted and wiped sweat from their faces. "Combining the two activities made for a crazy combination. Maybe I should consider offering a ballet-weight lifting class. I'm sure the trend will go over well with our military studs." He chuckled as he rose to pull two bottles of water from a large refrigerator housed in the hall. He handed her a bottle then resumed his place beside her.

"David and I never worked out together." Marissa sipped her water.

"I asked him once why he never brought you here. He said this wasn't your kind of thing."

Marissa lifted her eyebrows. Over the years, she'd asked David several times to work out with her, but he always had an excuse. "Did he ever bring anyone else here?" She understood she might be placing Justin in an uncomfortable position, but she had to know.

Justin shook his head. "He always came in alone." He downed half the bottled water.

She let the subject drop. "Thanks for this distraction. I needed to do something physical."

They were silent for a few seconds, and then Justin rose. He offered his hand and pulled her up. "There's one more thing I need to do." They crossed the weight room and headed toward the locker rooms. When they got to the men's side, Justin asked her to wait. Two minutes later, he returned with a black gym bag. "This is David's. I didn't look inside, but I thought you might want it." He held out the bag.

Marissa glared at the bag. With their condo still considered a crime scene, she had none of David's personal belongings. Gazing at the bag, she wasn't sure she wanted it. She had absolutely no idea who David Seybold was, but finding out was long overdue.

Chapter 11

Gunfire exploded over his head. Justin leaned over and shielded his patient from the bits of glass and drywall before drawing a sheet over the injured soldier. A sheet would do little to stop a big projectile or a direct hit, but it was the best he could do. He glanced at the damaged facility. Conditions would only get worse.

Another explosion rocked the facility. Stabilizing the soldier was no longer an option.

The patient's bloodied body shook in response. Where was the nurse? Come on, soldier, stay with me! He packed ragged wounds, half a missing left arm and shrapnel lacerations from head to toe. In another setting, Justin could have saved the patient, but now he only hoped he could get him to a transport helicopter.

As the medical facility took another direct hit, surgical instruments and unoccupied gurneys crashed to the floor.

Justin unlocked the soldier's gurney and rolled toward the exit. The intense firefight made rescue difficult, but not impossible, for a transport helicopter to land long enough to pick them up. He pushed toward the rally point, glancing at the person on the gurney. The closer he got, the more nervous he became the helicopter wouldn't arrive. Hell, even if the helicopter arrived, flying back out would be another feat altogether.

Reverberations from another round of rockets slamming into the earth had him bracing his arm against the gurney's rails.

The back half of the medical structure went up in flames. For the first time, Justin heard other patients moaning. He stopped the gurney and ran back, pushing more injured soldiers toward the door. Where were the other doctors and nurses?

Another explosion intensified the fire. The flames were too high. He couldn't save the others. The unmistakable flapping of a helicopter approached. Justin sprinted back to his original patient, ready to usher the soldier to possible safety.

Then the sky erupted.

He jolted awake. Sweat covering his body, his breathing ragged. Justin stared ahead for several minutes. He hated the nightmares and hadn't experienced one like this in years.

Grimacing, he slowly sat up in bed and massaged the knot in his neck. When the nightmares were plentiful, he learned to practice a deep breathing method called foursquare breathing to settle the whirlwind inside. He moved to the side of the bed and focused on a photo of a red space nebula on his bedroom wall as he breathed in, held his breath and then released air, each step four seconds long. Repeating this breathing technique five times centered his thoughts as the memories faded.

He ambled into his bathroom and splashed water on his face. Exiting the bathroom, he scooped up his phone, charging on the nightstand. The screen indicated early morning. Just as well—he was used to getting up at 6:00 in the morning. Creeping past rooms occupied by Wendy and Sam, he padded into the kitchen. After starting a pot of coffee, he performed a quick perimeter check of the house, and then inspected the locks on every door. Back in the kitchen, he approached the alarm panel. A steady red light indicated an engaged system ready to alert. Satisfied, he sat at a kitchen barstool and waited for the jolt of caffeine.

Although his body could have used a few more hours of sleep, his mind operated in alert mode. He slept in his SUV outside the Nash house last night. The police were supposed to do extra patrols, but he only spotted one cruiser drive by. The police probably didn't consider checking on Marissa a high priority and if they were called away on more important runs, she'd be forgotten. Justin hadn't noted any mysterious vehicles on the street, but just in case he inspected the outer perimeter of the house several times to ensure no incendiary devices or bad guys were evident. By 4:00 in the morning, he decided to go home and sleep in his own bed.

The rhythmic drip of the coffeemaker stopped. Justin retrieved his Duke Medical School mug, filled it with coffee and a splash of skim milk. The hot java soothed his body as the liquid slid down his throat, but did nothing to stop the onslaught of images of Marissa in shorts, dancing combinations, and pumping iron. He marveled at her dancing talent, passion about her work, and much more than her beautiful face. The more he got to know her, the more incredible he found her. He huffed a breath. Hands-off. Going after his friend's fiancée seemed a smarmy move, especially when David hadn't even been buried.

Something she'd said stuck in his mind. Marissa hadn't known about the training facility, which meant David never told her where he worked out. He worked out at GT on a regular basis. Why couldn't he tell Marissa this one simple fact? Justin got the feeling Marissa remained in the dark about a lot more.

Shuffling on the back stairs alerted him to Wendy coming down, wrapped in her favorite fuzzy blue robe, her hair up in a messy ponytail. "You are off work this week. Why on earth are you up this early?"

"I couldn't sleep, so I made coffee." Justin got up and filled a second mug. "Did you check on Sam?"

Wendy nodded. "She's sound asleep. Halo is right next to her. He opened his eyes when I peeked in, but he didn't move."

"Good." Justin patted the stool next to him. "Since you're up, have a seat."

Wendy accepted the mug and peered over the rim as she sat. "Okay, what's up? Why did you call and remind me to turn on the security system last night?"

Justin blew into his mug as he pondered his next words. He

settled on straight and to the point. "Someone threw a Molotov cocktail into Marissa's dance studio last night."

Wendy jerked her head around and gave a quick inhale.

Justin placed a hand on her arm. "She was inside but she's fine. The detectives are putting a guard at the Nash house, hopefully sometime today."

"Sounds like she needs to protection. I'm glad she's okay. She must be worried and scared." Wendy shook her head, and then sipped her coffee.

"I waited in the parking lot and saw the incident. It has to be the same people she saw at her house the other night and yesterday just outside."

"You mean outside of our house?" Wendy's eyes shot wide.

"Not exactly." Justin winced. "Down the street. Marissa saw them when she and Sam took Halo out for a walk."

"What! They were that close to Sam?" Wendy jumped off her chair, sloshing hot coffee on her hand. "Damn!"

Justin retrieved a paper towel, dabbed at her hand, and then cleaned up the mess. "You and Sam are not the targets. Marissa is the one they are interested in. I don't want to alarm you, but to be safe I want you and Sam to leave for California earlier than you planned. I'll pay for the change in your tickets."

Frowning, Wendy placed her mug on the counter. "I agree we have to get Sam away from here, but Debbie called me last night. Her mother is sick, so I rescheduled our trip for next month."

Justin rubbed his eyes. "Then you both can go to Uncle Lou and Aunt Iris's for at least a week. They would love to have you, and they adore Sam. Consider it a vacation."

Wendy ran her finger around the rim of her mug. "I need to finish up some paperwork at GT. I have some orders to complete, and three people coming in for interviews over the next few days. I'll call Uncle Lou and see if they can take Sam this morning. I'll join her in a couple of days."

"Both of you need to be out of this house ASAP but as long as Sam is away I won't give you a hard time if you check in periodically.

Marissa is scared her family is in danger, so she may stay here for a few days as long as you and Sam are off the premises."

"Okay, we have a plan." Wendy studied him. "You've been checking on her during the night, haven't you?"

"The police were supposed to do periodic checks on the house until a guard can be placed. I couldn't be sure they actually would, so I slept outside the house." Justin stared into his coffee, hoping Wendy wouldn't delve further.

"And you just happened to be in the parking lot of her dance studio?" Wendy went to the refrigerator and retrieved four eggs.

"Okay. I followed her." Justin tensed his jaw. As the words tumbled from his mouth, he comprehended the appearance of his actions. "I had a feeling these guys might try something. I knew she needed time alone, but she would have been a sitting duck so I stayed in the parking lot." He liked Marissa, a lot, and by the way Wendy glared at him, she understood his feelings.

Wendy smiled. "I like her, too, but Justin, her fiancé was just murdered. Not exactly the time to start a romance."

"Did I say anything about a romance?" He spread his arms and cocked his head. "David was my best friend, and she is, or was, his fiancée. I need to make sure nothing happens. It's the least I can do."

The sound of Wendy cracking eggs sliced through the otherwise silent kitchen. As she prepared two omelets, several seconds passed before she smiled. "Okay."

After breakfast, Wendy went upstairs to pack Sam's belongings while Justin retreated into his study. He turned on his computer and leaned back in the chair. After the computer initiated, he searched through his emails. The week of David's death had been hectic at the hospital. Several times, he'd been called into emergency surgery, and he had another five patients who were in their immediate post-op phase, one requiring a return to the OR to correct a severe complication. Justin crashed at the hospital a couple of nights, surviving on stale coffee and reminders of his time as a resident where days and nights couldn't be distinguished under the OR lights. As he sorted David's emails, he skimmed David's subject lines. Justin spotted everything from Hey Bro to Need a Favor but zeroed in on David's most recent email entitled, "Urgent".

With a deep sigh, Justin opened the email, dated three days before his death.

J, Need to talk ASAP. Very important. Call me. DEFCON Two.

Justin leaned back in his chair.

DEFCON Two.

He pulled out his cell phone and punched a button. In seconds, David's baritone voice filled the room. Did he know his days were numbered? As the brief message concluded, David ended with a simple phrase: DEFCON One. The drop everything plea for help. What trouble had warranted this call two days before his death? Justin replayed the message. David's tone, rushed and serious, didn't appear congruent with a man, days away from marrying the love of his life.

What happened to up his plea to DEFCON One?

Since receiving David's messages, repeated attempts to contact him were unsuccessful. Was David already dead? The autopsy results hadn't been delivered but Justin recalled seeing dark sticky blood pooled under David's body, which meant David might have been dead for a few hours.

Justin checked his phone for an emergency text he might have missed and didn't find one. Why only one email message and one phone message? David understood his life as a surgeon. If he'd been in desperate need, why not phone him again or call the hospital and have him paged? Justin pulled up the contact information for Streeter and Kearns. He forwarded David's last email to the detectives.

On a whim, he checked David's company webpage listing some of his clients. He scanned the page, recognizing some of the companies, but none hit as being out of place.

Justin selected a command and the printer behind him spat out a page of companies David claimed to have performed consultation services for. He stared at the paper in the printer tray. Justin had no proof, not even a hint, but his gut told him David had been involved in something torrid.

Justin logged off his laptop and stared out at puffy gray clouds. Rain loomed on the horizon but, if he hurried, he could get in a run before the weather turned. Justin sprinted upstairs to change. On his way down, he peeked in Sam's room. The girl lay asleep as Wendy tiptoed about the room placing her belongings in a purple and white dotted suitcase.

Halo's head popped up and his tail flopped up and down.

"Come on boy," Justin whispered. "Going for a run," he said as Wendy nodded.

Five minutes later, Justin and Halo matched pace as they ran along trails at a nearby park. Halo had lots of energy and Justin enjoyed having the animal with him. Maybe when things calmed he'd get a dog. Sam would love a puppy and Halo made him appreciate the companionship.

By the time Justin returned, fed Halo, and showered the usual morning activities were well underway. Sam watched cartoons on the kitchen television as she picked at her breakfast while Wendy, as per the normal morning dialogue with her daughter, urged Sam to eat her meal.

Now what? His thoughts doubled back to David's email. Would Marissa know what the DEFCON reference meant? He doubted David would have discussed this with her. David and Marissa had been one week away from becoming husband and wife, and she had no clue who she'd been about to marry. *She deserves better.* Justin grabbed his cell and hit the button he'd designated for Marissa's cell.

Marissa clicked on within a couple seconds and uttered a weary hello.

"How are you?" Justin gave her high praise for how she'd been handling the horror of the last few days.

She let out a big sigh. "Which version do you want? The truth, or the polite I'm-hanging-in-there?"

"I'll come by later this afternoon. Maybe we can get away for a run. Halo is a great partner and I wouldn't mind another go, if the weather cooperates." Images of her in shorts jogged through his mind. He paused, searching for the perfect way to broach the topic of

David's past. "I found an email from David, sent a few days before his death. I had a helluva schedule with several surgeries so I didn't notice it right away. The email only indicated he needed to speak with me ASAP and was signed DEFCON One."

"DEFCON One?"

Justin hadn't expected her to know. "It's a military term but David started using the phrase as an emergency call for help. There are varying degrees from one to five. The first time David used DEFCON One he intended the plea as a joke. You know, 'help me, there's a girl I'm not interested in clinging to me'. Harmless stuff."

"I'm assuming this last time wasn't a joke. He was in trouble."

"Appears so."

"This is a nightmare. In a few days we'll bury David, but all of this will continue."

Justin stared out the window, hoping he could ease the awful week she had ahead but feared her situation would only get worse.

Chapter 12

The Virginia sun burst from the horizon with a mixture of orange and yellow hues. Marissa had been up for hours, and although she'd witnessed night morphing into day, she couldn't recall actually seeing the transformation. The last several days had been a whirlwind of people in and out of her parents' house, bringing casseroles, desserts, hams, and anything else they decided mourners should eat.

Clanging of dishes and the nutty aroma of coffee signaled her mother preparing another mammoth breakfast. Although her stomach growled, the thought of food sickened her.

She sighed wishing she could hide under the covers for the day. Marissa dreaded the funeral in a few hours. The thought of the services almost had her bolting back to Utah. Instead, she headed for the shower.

As water sluiced over her, she considered the future. Because of the wedding, she'd already taken two weeks of vacation. Marissa had pondered returning to work early but paled at facing her colleagues. New life motivation for the day—avoid people. Of course, she couldn't dodge people and most meant well, but she loathed feeling like a drama-charged soap opera character with everyone waiting for her to flip out.

Okay, keep the vacation time, then what? Stepping out of the shower, she wrapped herself in a towel, then rummaged through her purse. She pulled out a small notebook, hoping her mind settled by making a list.

Sliding into her familiar oversized chair, Marissa opened the notebook. The number one task—selling the condo—a no brainer. She'd have to manage the mortgage until the property sold. Running through the numbers of her bank account gave her conclusive proof she could swing the mortgage for at least a year before her finances took a hit. Thanks to discipline and expert financial knowledge, she'd managed her money well.

Finding a place for her and Halo numbered two on her list. The daunting job of moving and going through anything left of their belongings caused her head to pound.

She shoved the notebook into her purse and stood. Facing the closet, Marissa dreaded the day ahead, but she couldn't put off the inevitable any longer.

Her wedding dress hung in full display in the center of the closet.

Vanessa wanted to pack away all wedding paraphernalia, but Marissa insisted on keeping the gown visible a while longer. Over a week ago, she'd decided to postpone or cancel the wedding. She had planned what she would say to David, but if presented with the opportunity, would she have broken up with him?

She stepped into her closet and studied the dress. Caressing the lace bodice, she waited for a reaction. *Nothing.* Shouldn't a bride have a connection to her dress? A lack of bridal enthusiasm should have been a red flag. Excitement about wedding gown shopping never surfaced.

Marissa traced the old world texture of the white lace bodice down to the tulle skirt, reminiscent of her ballet tutus. Her gaze traveled to the photo of her grandparents on their wedding day, tacked to the wall of the closet for inspiration.

Her grandparents married in Valentina's hometown of Valencia,

Venezuela. Marissa's wedding gown contained all the elements she'd wanted, matching her grandmother's style with a modern twist.

Marissa knew the dress would have pleased her *abuela*. The daily pang of disappointing her grandmother rattled her heart. A wedding dress could never take the place of going to Juilliard and dancing as a professional, but Marissa hoped her grandmother would have been pleased with this choice.

Grandmother Valentina made her own hard choices. When she met her husband, Edmund Estrada, she said goodbye to professional ballet and welcomed motherhood. Valentina and Edmund had three children: Robert, Ava, and Sylvia. None of her children displayed an interest in dance. By the time she welcomed granddaughter Marissa, Valentina had her own ballet school in Virginia, and Edmund had been dead for over ten years.

Valentina's death nine years ago devastated Marissa. Grandmother never had a chance to meet David. *Would abuela have liked him?* An uneasy answer surfaced. With a lurch of her heart, Marissa turned away. The dress was perfect, but the relationship far from flawless.

Instead of a white dress, she would be wearing a blue one today. Her heart shuddered as she slipped into the dark blue column-style frock. Her hands shook as she pulled the zipper. Now this was familiar. Even before death, David fared better at evoking sadness in her than anything close to giddiness.

A light knock sounded.

"Marissa, honey, are you awake?" her mother whispered, opening the door. "I thought you'd be up. I wanted to talk before the flurry of activity begins. I can't say I know how you feel. The man of my dreams is snoring up a storm in the next room. If I know you well enough, you are plotting a mad escape, but there's no rush." Ava crossed the room. "Your father and I are here for you."

Marissa smiled. Just like her mother to read her mind. "I'm so thankful for you and Dad. I don't know what I would have done without you, but I need to find a place for me and Halo."

"You will, in time."

"Thanks, Mom. I just want to get through the day without being pitied. I'll be okay and I'll get on with my life."

Ava pulled her into a hug. "I know you will. I love you, my darling. Don't worry about what others see. Today is a day to be selfish."

A few hours later, Marissa stood, staring at David's body, her last view of him before the service started. Although she'd been given the opportunity to view his body earlier, she remained unnerved at the shocking sight of David lying in a casket. His ashen face appeared out of sorts, despite claims from others he "looked like himself". She viewed this David as plastic and unnatural.

Next to the casket stood a large candid picture of David in his Army fatigues, his dark hair in the mandatory crew cut. His mother's favorite picture displayed his dimpled grin and mischievous eyes.

Marisa and David had some great times. They took vacations and spent quiet evenings watching movies or sharing a bottle of wine. Yet, their relationship hadn't been enough. She hadn't been enough. Could Tiffany be here? She fought the desire to turn and scan the packed church. Since she'd learned about Tiffany, she believed there could be others. *I shouldn't think such thoughts.* As their last year together rolled past in her mind, most of her memories were of David's indifference, rejection, and bad-tempered moods. She stared at his body and asked herself the same question she'd been asking for almost a year—what happened to you?

She leaned toward the casket and whispered, "My feelings for you were real. I loved you." She couldn't say out loud that maybe she hadn't loved him in the way she should have, for a woman about to marry. Maybe he didn't, either. Perhaps, if given the chance, they would have discovered their lack of deep feelings for one another.

She took one last look and caressed his cold hand. As she pulled away, she spotted something jutting out from under his back. She moved closer. A green patch had been placed inside the casket. She steadied herself on the wooden edge. The emblem on the patch didn't look familiar. Had someone from the funeral home mistakenly dropped this?

Vanessa approached, touching Marissa's elbow. "We need to

begin soon."

Marissa nodded and when Vanessa turned, she slid the patch further under his back. She'd think of a way to grab it later.

Marissa followed Vanessa back to the pew. Quick glances from Vanessa and Kelly, seated behind her, emanated concern. They had appointed themselves sentries on the lookout, waiting for her to dissolve into a hysterical mound of unbridled tears.

As she sat between her parents and David's, Marissa prayed her emotions would remain stoic. Sad eyes on her made her uncomfortable.

Justin moved up to the shiny mahogany casket next. He spent a few minutes staring at the body, patted David's arm, and then embraced both sets of grieving parents and David's siblings. Marissa stood and Justin gathered her into his arms. "I'll always be here for you." He brushed a light kiss on her cheek.

Her body reacted like she'd been zapped with electricity.

After they pulled apart, he held her gaze as warmth and understanding flowed between them.

Had he seen the suspicious patch? She broke his gaze. Not the time or place to discuss a likely meaningless item.

As the service started, Mrs. Seybold's sniffles grew into uncontrolled weeping. Marissa placed her arm around the woman and tried to console her, even though there was little she could say.

When her sobs subsided, Mrs. Seybold whispered, "You would have made David a good wife."

Mr. Seybold, almost as emotional as his wife, had David's brother scooting closer to take his father's hand.

As Marissa stared ahead, unable to concentrate on the service, she noted how much the scene appeared opposite of what might have been. The sweet aroma of flower arrangements permeated her nose. Instead of blush roses and delicate white calla lilies adorning the church, the flowers were maudlin attempts at reverent masculine arrangements in blue and red tones. David's casket sat in the center aisle in front of the altar, the very location they would have exchanged vows.

Just before the ceremony ended, Marissa whispered to her father she'd like a few minutes with David before the pallbearers transported the casket out of the church, and she wanted the closed casket opened again.

Her father hesitated for moment, but nodded and went off to speak with the funeral director and pastor. The sanctuary emptied and the funeral director opened the casket. Her father patted her arm and told her they'd be waiting outside.

Justin nodded and followed her father out.

She approached the casket, gripping her purse so tight her knuckles blanched. With shaking hands, Marissa reached in the casket and retrieved the green patch. As she glanced at the circular patch, she had the overwhelming feeling the item held significance. Without studying the text and artwork in detail, she slipped the patch into her purse.

Just as she turned to leave, she came face-to-face with a woman dressed head-to-toe in black, a thick veil concealing her face. Ramrod straight, the woman remained still, as if frozen, reminding Marissa of someone who'd just gazed at Medusa.

"Such a tragedy. We'll all be there one day," the woman said, her voice thick and raspy. "Death isn't only for the old."

Marissa stared at the woman. She didn't recognize the voice. "How did you know David?"

After an exaggerated silence, the woman spoke. "The tradition of surrounding the deceased with flowers is quite sad, a mockery of sorts. Flowers are beautiful, but when cut, separated from their roots, torn from the life-giving earth, they die." She remained focused on David.

Marissa considered the veiled woman insane or a person coming to terms with her own mortality. Perhaps she enjoyed crashing funerals and interacting with bereaved family members.

The woman cleared her throat and continued. "Such cruel irony. We shower the deceased with something so full of life, killing the living to celebrate death. I'm sure people will comment about the beautiful flowers, not recognizing their sacrifice. How noble of the flowers, but then again, they didn't have a choice. When death speaks..." Her voice trailed off as her gaze locked on the cross mounted on the far wall of the sanctuary.

Marissa glanced around the empty church. Her stomach tensed as she stepped back. "Nice of you to come." She turned to leave.

"I'm an old friend," the woman whispered.

Marissa turned back.

The woman adjusted her hat, and her black-gloved hand crossed the veil revealing a large emerald ring.

A sudden cold breeze blew through the church. Marissa shivered as the veiled woman glided past her and slipped through a side door, taking the draft with her.

After a short ride to the cemetery, Marissa sat in front of David's casket again. A voluminous spray of red roses splayed across the closed casket. Instead of concentrating on her last goodbye, she stared at the flowers. The woman's words replayed in her mind. Those flowers *would* die alongside David.

At the conclusion of the twenty-minute service, everyone descended upon Marissa and the Seybold family.

Marissa greeted everyone she could. Most were business associates and former military colleagues. Gabe and others she recognized from the training center attended. Fellow teachers and students from the dance studio surrounded her, plying her with hugs and kisses. Even a group of her co-workers offered their condolences.

Wendy gave her a hearty hug and pressed a photo into her hand. "I snapped a picture of you and Sam walking Halo." She paused, closed her purse, and slid the strap onto her shoulder. "I thought the cute picture might help."

Marissa's heart lurched as she hugged the picture to her chest. "Thank you. I'd like to come by and thank Sam for taking such good care of Halo, if I can get away later."

"Sam would love that, but I took her to my aunt and uncle's." Wendy hesitated then added, "We didn't want Sam in the house."

Marissa nodded. Wendy appeared as if she wanted to say more but when she didn't, Marissa placed a hand on her arm. "I understand. You and Justin made the right decision to send Sam away." She chewed her lip, hating her presence in their lives could put them in danger. "I'm so sorry. I had no idea..."

"Sam is safe so please don't worry. I hope they catch them soon." Wendy gave her another hug then hurried toward the parking lot.

As the crowd thinned, a tall woman in her twenties approached. She wore a lot of makeup unnecessary for her pretty face but highlighting bright brown eyes and full lips many women paid for. With a buxom chest, long dark brown hair, and a tight-fitting black and white dress, she marched over to Marissa, her sky-high heels digging holes in the grass. "I'm sorry about your loss." She spoke with a slight Southern accent.

Marissa shook her hand. "Thanks. How did you know David?"

"Umm, the company I work for hired him to do some consulting. I'm an assistant there. He was so funny and cute." Her smile dropped into a serious expression. "I'm going to miss him."

Marissa nodded, observing the woman's sudden somber expression. "And you are?"

"Tiffany Clover." She flashed another smile.

Marissa's heart thundered. Even though she'd never found a picture of the woman David had been seeing, something told her this was the Tiffany starring in his sexy texts. "I appreciate you taking the time to be here."

Tiffany nodded. "My momma always told me friendship never dies. It's the least I could do." She touched Marissa's arm, and then pulled away. "Well, I gotta get back to work." She pulled car keys from a brown leather purse with fringe jutting from the bottom. Keys jangling, she plodded away, blending into the crowd heading toward their cars.

Marissa pulled at her lip. Somehow, seeing this woman didn't anger her. Tiffany had enough respect to come to the funeral and even offer her sympathy. She didn't get the feeling the woman carried a vindictive vibe. She probably didn't know until recently David had a fiancée, but even so, Marissa couldn't muster any sort of jealousy.

Kelly interrupted her thoughts by shoving a flower into her hand.

With a warm arm across her shoulders, she asked, "Can I get you anything?"

Marissa shook her head and, for the first time, glimpsed a flawless day. A few wispy clouds occupied an otherwise bright blue sky. Gentle winds offered a perfect touch to cool the warm day. They would have had a beautiful wedding. She turned her gaze to the flower in hand and gasped. Once again, the words of the old woman came roaring back.

We kill the living to celebrate death.

Marissa stared at the single red rose with curled petals tinged a faint brown, signaling an imminent demise. She let the dying flower fall to the ground.

JUSTIN COULDN'T COUNT the number of funerals he had attended. Too many. Now, every funeral reminded him of his last deployment. Flashes of exploding IEDs, soldiers groaning in pain, and dead bodies resembling broken toys all parading like a movie trailer through his mind. The pain of the grief-stricken family remained constant at every funeral, but this time death hadn't been caused by war. Or had it?

At the cemetery, Justin stood off to one side of the funeral tent. Muffled, whimpering cries from David's mother and sister cut through the pastor's reverent words. He glanced at Marissa. The pain and devastation on her face wrenched at his heart. Her tearless face a barrier to the turmoil and confusion he assumed were churning inside.

He promised he would be there for her, but could he really keep her safe when he had no idea who, or what, they were up against? Tugging at his tie and pulling on the cuffs of his jacket, he scanned the crowd. No one appeared suspicious or ready to attack.

Detectives Kearns and Streeter stood under a tree off in the distance. They were probably scanning the crowd for suspicious people, too. With no suspects in the murder and no apparent evidence of a break-in, Justin believed David's killers were people he knew, or at least didn't initially fear.

After the services concluded, Justin spoke to a number of friends and associates as he moved toward the edge of the crowd. He spotted a brunette woman talking to Marissa and when she moved toward the parking lot, with a few long strides, Justin caught up. He knew a lot of David's friends, but had never met her. "Excuse me." He stepped into her path.

The woman smiled. "Yes?" Her mouth dropped open, and she took a step back. "You must be the doctor."

"Should I know you?"

"No." She laughed and splayed brilliant purple-tipped nails across her chest. "I knew David very well. He mentioned you, and I guessed. He said you were a good guy and a really smart doctor. Plus, he showed me a picture." A wind gust blew her hair across her face and, with an exaggerated response, she shook her head to shift the strands from her eyes. "Tiffany Clover."

"Justin Tanner." He extended his hand. "How did you meet David?"

She explained they met when he arrived to consult with her company.

Seconds later, Justin surmised this woman was David's latest dalliance. He took her elbow and moved her away from a small group of soldiers gathered nearby. "I don't mean to be crass, but did you and David maybe go out for lunch, or meet for dinner sometime? If you know what I mean."

Tiffany glanced at her hands before meeting his gaze. "Well, yeah. He put in a lot of time at my office. One night, we went out for dinner and kind-of started seeing each other from there." She paused and glanced around. "You look cool, so please don't tell his fiancée. I didn't know about her until recently."

Justin nodded and softened his voice. "Water under the bridge now. When did you see him last?"

"About two weeks ago, but we exchanged emails two or three days before he died."

"Do you mind me asking what those emails were about?" He hoped David opened up to this woman about his plans.

She shrugged. "Nothing serious. Sexy talk. Know what I mean?"

"Yeah, I get it." Justin nodded. "Was he ever upset or angry?"

"David? He was always upbeat, and sooo funny. He told me he'd buy me a car because he'd soon have a lot of money. I drive an old Honda." She shifted her gaze to her green painted toenails, peeping out of her shoes and kicked at a blade of grass. "I didn't find out about his engagement until a few weeks ago, but he told me he wanted to be with me."

How could David want this girl and Marissa at the same time? Tiffany had a cute, overt sex appeal, but Marissa took gorgeous, interesting, and intelligent to another level. They were two different kinds of women, but David always enjoyed the challenge of multiple relationships. "Thanks for your time."

"I'm not in trouble, am I? My boss frowns on having a "relationship" with a consultant." She put relationship in air quotes.

"No, I think you're okay. Has a detective or police officer contacted you?"

Gasping, she nodded. "I got a call from a detective yesterday but I haven't had time to call back. Should I worry?"

"No, but you can do me a favor. Actually, do David a favor and talk to the detectives investigating his murder. They may want to know the time frame of your last conversations."

Her heavily made-up eyes grew large.

"Don't worry, everything is confidential." Justin dug into his jacket pocket and handed her the detectives' business cards.

She stared at each card and slipped them into her purse. "I really am sorry he died." She turned to leave.

Justin touched her arm. "Tiffany, what company do you work for?"

"Skies International." She smiled again and trotted off.

Skies International. Why did that sound familiar?

Chapter 13

Marissa observed the dwindling crowd, sure she had shaken hands with or hugged everyone at the funeral.

"Are you okay?" Kelly asked, coming up behind her.

Marissa nodded. "Just anxious for this to be over. I think David would have been pleased with the service."

Kelly took her hand. "I'm sure he would have." She paused. "Your sister and mother are worried because you didn't shed a single tear during the funeral. They think you may be heading for a major breakdown. I can't deny being a little worried, too."

"I'm sorry I can't muster up some big fat crocodile tears. Don't get me wrong, David's death has been horrifying, but..."

"I understand. Lots of mixed emotion." Kelly smiled and hugged her.

Marissa loathed feeling the fool for trusting David. Tiffany couldn't have been the only one. Admitting she'd been dead wrong about David, plus all of the months of waffling about calling off the wedding made her seem fickle but Kelly understood. Her dad had advised Marissa against moving in with him. He never indicated he distrusted David but perhaps he sensed her boyfriend couldn't be trusted. Maybe if she hadn't ignored his advice she would have detected David's penchant for women and dishonesty without the intimacy of playing house.

"I wished David had talked to me. Maybe we could have..." Her voice trailed off. If David had been open with her would the end result have been different?

"You need time." Kelly hugged her again, and then stepped back. "I told Mrs. Seybold I would make sure all the flower arrangements find a home. I'll be close if you need me." She squeezed Marissa's hand and ran off to find the funeral director.

"Marissa, you remember Neal and Susan Wingate." She turned to see Justin approach with two people in tow. "Neal, David, and I were once roommates at Notre Dame. This is his wife, Susan."

Neal removed his designer sunglasses and reached for her hand. "I'm sorry for your loss. David and I had a lot of good times."

Marissa stood five foot five inches and Neal, just a couple inches taller, puffed his chest. His mousy brown hair, neat and trimmed as if fresh from the barber's chair, framed his pale, pointed face. Dark brown eyes focused on her like he considered her of ultimate importance. The expensive gray suit matched a crisp white shirt embroidered with his initials at the cuff. Despite his stiff, polished appearance, he flashed a warm smile.

"Of course, I remember. Nice of you to come. David valued your friendship."

Susan moved a strand of short blond hair from her eyes. "So shocking to hear about his death. We will both miss him terribly."

Marissa nodded.

Susan sparkled in every sense. Her blonde hair shone with almost white highlights while her bright teeth could only be achieved through chemical aid. Dazzling pink diamond earrings adorned her lobes, a huge diamond ring glimmered on her finger, and what looked to be a shiny emerald pendant peeked out from her black dress.

Neal shook his head. "We had some good times, didn't we Doctor?"

Justin nodded. "Sure, we had a blast, but those days are long gone and presumably everyone grew up."

Marissa glanced at Justin as she contemplated his dry, tense tenor. David always spoke with fondness about Neal but Justin didn't appear to share the emotion. *What happened?*

Neal threw his head back in laughter. "Always the Boy Scout."

Justin shifted closer to Marissa. "We don't want to lose sight of why we're here, Congressman. David was our friend and it's a damn shame he lost his life so young."

Susan cleared her throat. "He *was* a special person."

"That's soon to be Senator. But, yeah, Dave was special all right. I wonder what new secrets he died with." Neal glanced back at the casket.

Marissa followed Neal's gaze. *What secrets did Neal know?* How close had Neal and David been lately?

Justin's pager buzzed. "I'm on vacation so this better be something serious." He pulled out the device and studied the information. He turned to Marissa. "I need to go, but I'll check in with you later."

Marissa nodded and hugged Justin. "Thanks for everything."

"We need to shove off, too. Marissa, again our deepest condolences." Neal grasped her hands in his.

Marissa's eyes were gritty and tired but she smiled through her exhaustion. "I'm honored you would take time to be here. David would be moved."

Neal leaned toward Marissa. "This is a loss for us all. If there is anything you need, just call, even if we're out campaigning. Here's my private cell." He handed her his card.

"Thank you." Marissa slid the card into her purse. "Good luck with your upcoming election."

As Neal and Susan headed for their limo and Justin rushed off to his SUV, Marissa questioned what other secrets David had and just how much his friends knew.

Hours later, Marissa entered her room and collapsed on the bed. Curbing her emotions proved a tiring feat. David deserved a decent funeral but now her obligation had been completed. As she lay staring up at the ceiling, deep remorse draped over her but not for David. The heartache displayed for David reminded her of another much more personal loss, one never mourned in public. Sorrow and grief rained down for the baby she'd lost to a miscarriage—David's baby. Along with her grief, anger arose, not because of David's affair or her missed wedding, but for his disregard and abandonment of her after the miscarriage. Even more, her anger grew at his disinterest in their baby. He placed his feelings above anyone else's. Marissa arose from the bed and admired the piece of jewelry on her finger. The ring had ceased to have any meaning.

Memories of David's proposal flooded to the forefront. He'd bought Halo the collar in order to bring the dog into their special moment. The pouch, which hung a few inches from the collar, carried her engagement ring. Incorporating Halo into the marriage proposal had warmed her heart but now the gesture seemed a lifetime ago.

She pulled the engagement ring from her finger and dropped the meaningless bauble into her purse.

Chapter 14

The bullet had entered the patient's chest cavity and lodged near her heart.

Justin fought through six hours of surgery to keep the woman alive. As he began to close the wound, his expectations of her survival grew.

Jan Lambert, a wife and mother of two on her way home from work, stopped to buy milk. Two masked men burst into the convenience store demanding money. One of the men brandished a gun. According to eyewitnesses, the clerk complied, but someone knocked a can off the shelf, and the nervous gunman started firing.

The masked robbers took off, leaving Mrs. Lambert bleeding on the convenience store floor. Police and EMTs arrived within minutes. Their quick actions likely gave Mrs. Lambert a chance to get to the hospital; Justin's actions offered her a chance at the rest of her life.

Justin pulled off his surgical mask and stepped outside the OR. *What a long night.* He'd been called in after another surgeon had a personal emergency. Once his patient stabilized, he worked through the night to save her. Even after a lengthy surgery, Justin often experienced a high when a case went well and a life had been spared. Today, however, exhaustion crept up on him. He trudged into the waiting room and delivered the good news to her family.

Mrs. Lambert's experience brought to mind the memory of Laura, her mangled body dead in the war zone half way across the world. He recalled the smile she'd given him just before the attack. They'd been joking about who would triumph in their never-ending chess battle. Laura beat him the previous time, and Justin had been determined to make a comeback. Then the room exploded.

Pushing away thoughts of her, he tapped the button to open the recovery room doors.

After checking on Mrs. Lambert and speaking with her husband, he informed the staff he would be in an on-call room. These rooms were like mini hotel rooms with a bed, a computer workstation, and a bathroom. Outside the rooms were refrigerators, microwaves, vending machines, and just down the hall a small fitness center.

Justin entered the room and flopped on the bed, fatigue washing over him. He closed his eyes, allowing thoughts of Marissa to overtake him. Under normal circumstances, responding to an emergency call didn't bother him, but he longed to be with Marissa, especially today.

He sighed, locking away his emotions. All romantic notions of Marissa were off limits, he reminded himself for the thousandth time. He couldn't afford to muck up their congenial relationship by confusing grief with romantic feelings. *Shake it off, man.*

Less than an hour later, Justin awoke and headed into the recovery room. After another hour, Mrs. Lambert had progressed enough he discharged her from recovery to a room of her own. As he updated the family, Justin observed the worry and exhaustion on the faces of Mr. Lambert and the children.

Mr. Lambert informed him the family only recently moved to town, and the kids weren't comfortable with the neighbors yet. Mrs. Lambert's parents were on their way to the hospital but lived eight hours away.

Justin sympathized with the father and offered the children his on-call room. Although the gesture stood out from normal practice, he recognized the kids were exhausted and could use a real bed. Before going home, Justin bought the family sandwiches, beverages, and brownies from the hospital cafeteria, which bucked the trend by having great food.

The twelve-year-old girl hugged him and thanked him for saving her mother.

Better than any paycheck.

On his way home, Justin turned on his cell phone. Within seconds, a ring-tone chimed. The screen in his car told him Wendy had called. She'd texted him a couple times since he last saw her at the funeral informing him she remained safe and Sam loved all the attention she'd been receiving at Uncle Lou's. Justin punched a button on the car's display panel to return Wendy's call.

"Justin, where are you?" Wendy's voice intoned breathless and strained.

"I'm almost home. What's wrong?" Justin gripped the steering wheel.

"The house has been burglarized." Her voice caught. "It's a mess. The police are here."

"I'm ten minutes out." He tossed the phone onto the passenger seat. Justin made every light and blew through a couple of stop signs before pulling up to the flashing lights of police cars. Unable to reach the driveway, he parked on the street, grabbed his phone, and sprinted toward the house. He spotted Wendy standing on the sidewalk. Relief swept over him to see her unhurt. "Are you okay?"

"Yes. I forgot a file I needed for work and came home to find the place trashed. I got out of there as soon as I saw the mess and called 911."

He released a breath and embraced her. "You did the right thing."

"I'm so glad we got Sam out." Her voice quivered as she stared at the commotion surrounding the house.

Justin nodded. "Stay here."

Wendy pulled his arm. "I had to call Marissa. Halo is hurt."

"Where is she?" As soon as he stepped away, he spotted Marissa running toward the house.

"Wendy called me. Is everyone okay?" Marissa scanned the yard. "What happened?"

"Everyone is okay." He took her hand, but before he could say anything more, Detective Kearns and Streeter approached.

Kearns cleared her throat. "Crime Scene Investigators are going through the house. After they have completed their work, I need you and your sister to go in and see if anything is missing."

Streeter turned to Marissa. "Your dog has been hurt. He's in back."

Marissa froze, her eyes wide.

Justin and Marissa raced around the house.

A mound of white fur lay on the deck. Halo's eyes were open, and his stomach moved in a jerky rhythm.

Marissa slid to the floor of the deck. "Halo? I'm here, buddy." She leaned in close to his head.

His eyes, although they looked tired and afraid, brightened.

She cradled his head and chanted, "Please be all right, please be all right."

Justin's heart broke at the scene, so similar to how he'd found Marissa with David's body. Justin zeroed in on the vomit near Halo. A quick search on his phone, confirmed to Justin a location of an emergency veterinary clinic fifteen minutes away.

"I can't lose him, too." Marissa's eyes were wide with fear. "He has to be okay."

The police allowed Justin to bring his SUV to the back of the house.

The dog weighed about a hundred pounds, but Justin easily hoisted him into the back. Justin shut the rear hatch and darted back to the driver's seat. He grabbed an empty paper cup once containing a soft drink and scooped up a portion of Halo's vomit. Before leaving, Justin asked Wendy to work with the police and promised he'd check in as soon as he could.

Screaming sirens and flaring lights of a police cruiser accompanied Justin and Marissa to the veterinary clinic. Justin glanced at her.

Face ashen, she stared straight ahead.

"Think positive thoughts. He's breathing and that's good." After arriving at the veterinary clinic, Justin jumped out and rounded the SUV to the back.

Marissa followed Justin and held the door open as he picked up the dog. A veterinary technician approached and led them to the exam room.

After they were ushered out of the room, he and Marissa collapsed into chairs in the waiting room.

Marissa's hands shook as she completed the clinic's forms. "I can't believe they hurt him. What did Halo have to do with anything?" Her green eyes blazed. "I guess the situation could have been worse—they could have shot him. Of course, if he dies what's the difference?"

"He's a strong dog." Justin placed his hand over her trembling one. He prayed they got him to the clinic in time. Losing Halo would send Marissa over the edge, and he wasn't sure he could bring her back. He'd lived there, and that kind of darkness was difficult to swim out of.

"I'm glad you're here." Marissa continued to stare straight ahead.

While they waited, Justin called Wendy.

She informed him nothing appeared missing except for his computer.

"You need to go to Uncle Lou and Aunt Iris's tonight."

"I need to finish up a few things at work, so I'll stay with a friend tonight," Wendy said.

Justin swiped his hand through his hair. "I'm not thrilled with the idea, but I'm in no mood to argue."

"How is Halo?" Wendy asked.

"We still don't know. I'll call you back. Be careful." Justin's mind whirled with plans. He considered beefing up security at the Training Center, but discarded the idea with the number of combat trained active and retired military using the facility.

When he had the chance, he'd call Uncle Lou. As a retired Army general, Uncle Lou would understand Justin's concerns about the safety of everyone. With Sam tucked away with his aunt and uncle and Wendy on her way there soon, Justin could concentrate on Marissa. She had to be the real target.

Almost an hour later, an assistant called them into the exam room.

Lying on his side on the table, Halo's eyes were open but he didn't move. An IV line snaked into his foreleg.

The attending vet, a short man with round glasses, thick, wiry hair, and huge jowls, huddled over Halo. The doctor reminded Justin of a sleepy basset hound.

"I'm Dr. Morton." He jerked his head up. "I understand Halo might have been given some type of poison, so we ran a battery of tests which came back positive for arsenic."

"Will he survive?" Marissa clutched Justin's hand.

"I believe we got to him in time. The arsenic level in his system is high, but not to a level I would anticipate he couldn't survive. Arsenic can affect the kidneys, but Halo's kidney function is normal. We performed a gastric lavage to clean out his stomach contents and as you can see, we've started IV fluids to flush out the remainder of the poison. All in all, you were lucky. He'll be fine." He picked up a chart and studied the file. "Thank you, Dr. Tanner for the sample of his emesis. The sample helped make a faster diagnosis. We also collected a blood sample for the police investigation."

Marissa sighed and placed her hand on Halo's neck. His gaze tracked her and his tail slapped the table once. "You'll be okay. Love you, boy." Marissa kissed the top of his head and his tail flopped again.

"Will you keep him, or can we take him home later?" Justin rubbed Halo's head.

"I'd like to observe him overnight. If he looks good in the morning, he can go home, but be prepared, as he may need another night here. He will be lethargic, so he'll likely sleep the rest of the night, but if anything should change, we'll call." Dr. Morton ran a hand down Halo's back. "He's a good dog, very healthy."

"Thank you, Doctor. I appreciate all you've done." Marissa smiled. "He's my lifeline." She said a goodbye to her dog.

Justin shook the doctor's hand and he escorted Marissa out of the exam room. In the lobby, he headed for the check out area to pay for the services.

Marissa caught up to him. "No. I will not allow you to pay for Halo. He's my dog. I've spent too long allowing David to run parts of my life but I appreciate your generosity." Marissa dug into her purse and slapped her credit card on the desk.

Justin nodded and stepped back.

Once they were in the car, Marissa leaned her head back. "I just want to go to sleep, wake up, and pretend none of this is happening."

"How do you think your family will react to this latest development?"

Marissa turned her gaze to him. "By totally freaking out. They will want to keep me under lock and key. I really need to find my own place. I want my dog back, and I'd like to find my new normal."

Justin stared out the front window. "Having so many emotions flooding you is tough at the same time your future is up in the air."

Marissa turned to him. "You sound like you speak from experience."

He shrugged. "As a doctor, I see death all the time. I'm trained to distance myself, but sometimes the casualties back up on you. Like wading through sludge."

"I don't know what I'm doing. Last night I did some research on my Dad's computer. Five stages of grief, Maslow's Hierarchy of Needs. I remember most of this from my Intro to Psych class."

Justin grinned. "It's great, intellectually. These geniuses have wrapped everything in one nice, neat diagram. These theories have a place and can be helpful, but when you're grappling for a lifeline, knowing you are in the denial stage of grief isn't much help."

"I feel like my life is out of control and that scares me." Marissa wrung her hands.

The urge to wrap her in his arms grew, but Justin tamped down the desire. Instead, he placed a hand over hers. "There are no shortcuts through this. You're sad, scared, and angry, but you're not alone."

Chapter 15

"What a thrilling funeral." Vivian waltzed into her private dining room, followed by Edward. With sparkling eyes, she beamed at her assistant. "You know my mother once told me to stop playing with my food. I never paid attention. It's so fun to toy with their menial lives before I devour them. Mother was such a dribbling idiot." She paused and placed a finger on her pale jaw. "Father was right to kill her."

Edward nodded and placed a saucer followed by a cup of hot tea on the shiny maple dining table. He presented her usual breakfast of lox, one sliced whole-wheat bagel, five strawberries, and three melon wedges on a blue Wedgwood plate.

Vivian stared at the plate before turning to Edward. "Take this back to the kitchen. Tell the cook I'd like strawberry crêpes today." She smiled and waved him away. Time to do something different. Celebrate.

Edward nodded, seized the plate, and disappeared through a side door into the kitchen.

Vivian stood at the French doors and stared out toward the stables and empty corral.

Her smile dissolved, replaced by a firm-set mouth and narrowed eyes. She glanced at her watch. With creased brows and pursed lips, she picked up the nearby house phone and connected with the stables.

When one of the assistants picked up, with a stern voice, Vivian said, "It is now four minutes after eight. My expectation has always been to have Titan in the corral every morning at 8:00. I don't want any excuses. If my horse isn't in the corral in exactly three minutes, the entire stable staff will be fired." She slammed the phone into the cradle and started the countdown clock on her cell phone.

Just past the two-minute mark, Titan sauntered into the corral.

She stared at the horse for the next fifteen minutes, turning away when Edward entered with her new breakfast.

Once Edward placed her plate on the table, she shooed him away and sat to enjoy her crêpes. The flavorful pastry melted in her mouth as the strawberries added a touch of sweetness. If she wanted to be hospitable, she would have complimented the chef, but appetizing food shouldn't be an exceptional by-product from a professional cook. On most occasions, Vivian shunned rich, calorie-laden food, preferring to keep her waistline and health in check, but today she enjoyed the decadent pastry.

As she placed a napkin over a third of the crêpe she'd left uneaten, she considered her latest target. Getting into Marissa's head during the funeral had been a brilliant move. The beautiful woman appeared even more attractive with the strained look of torment and terror in her eyes. Vivian had contemplated sending a bouquet of dead flowers but discarded the plan, believing the idea unimaginative.

Years had passed since she'd played this cat-and-mouse game, and she'd matured in her tactics. Harold's wife, Nora, had been the last recipient of this kind of fun. Sending her dead flowers had been an amusing act, but the dead rats she planted in Nora's closet made Vivian almost squeal in delight. With her breakfast completed, she retreated to her office to call Roy Bane.

He answered right away.

Vivian cleared her throat. "Is it done?"

"Yes, we found one laptop. The sister probably has one, based on the power cord we found in her room, but likely had the computer with her. Want us to grab that one, too?"

"No, the sister wouldn't have anything. Did you find any other useful bits of information inside the house?" Vivian leaned back in her chair. She'd already performed her research on Dr. Justin Tanner, including his sister and her kid. Power came from knowing your opponent's weaknesses.

"Zogby and I searched the house. That's a negative," Bane replied.

"Very good. Did you take the pictures I asked for?"

"Yes, ma'am. They're uploaded and sent via secured connection to your computer."

"Good. What about the dog?"

"Our surveillance over the last couple of days showed someone would let the dog out midmorning. We had his food laced and ready to go. He gobbled it up then later collapsed on the back porch. Per your directive, I gave him enough poison to make him sick for a few days, not kill him."

"Excellent. Continue surveillance on the girl and the doctor. Do not move on them until I give you the go-ahead." Vivian clicked off the call. Killing the dog would ramp up the girl's emotion and destroy the fun. Waiting for the climax proved almost as thrilling. She turned to her computer, and pulled up the pictures.

Bane and his partner, Carl Zogby, had done a thorough job of documenting the inside of the house.

Vivian flipped through each picture, but stopped when she came to the doctor's desk. Two pictures sat on his desk. The photo of a middle-aged couple included a man in an Army uniform, his stars signifying general status, and a smiling woman in a stylish red dress. Vivian knew the doctor's parents were dead, so she moved on to the other photo of a pig-tailed brown haired girl grinning brightly, exhibiting two missing teeth and wearing a soccer uniform. This must be the doctor's niece.

The next image taken by her men lay beside the laptop. The

picture, a shot of Marissa, the little girl, and the dog, made her smile. "Hmm." She caressed the little girl's image on the screen and whispered, "Hello, my pretty."

Chapter 16

Justin awoke in the on-call quarters at the hospital. His gaze skirted the room, taking a minute to recognize his surroundings. The police worked late into the night processing the burglary at his house, and with the enormous mess, he decided to crash at the hospital. Mr. and Mrs. Nash offered their guest room when he escorted Marissa home, but he rejected the offer, citing a need to be at the hospital.

He'd been worried about Marissa, but had relaxed when he spotted a police car making a slow pass in front of the Nash house. At least the police had a presence on the street.

Justin stretched before crawling out of bed. He picked up his cell phone and checked for messages. With nothing urgent to attend to regarding his patients, he called Detective Kearns.

"So far we haven't picked up any useful fingerprints from your house." She groaned. "The perpetrators circumvented your security system with apparent ease leading us to believe once again we're dealing with professionals. Based on you and your sister's assessment, the only thing stolen was your laptop so we're working with a similar MO."

"Can I start the clean up process?" Justin crossed the room and stared out at the parking lot below.

"Yes. The techs are done. By the way, the lab is running tests on the dog's food. We've been in contact with the vet and we're pretty sure he ingested poisoned laced food."

"Have you been able to make anything of David's email I forwarded?"

"Still working on it."

Justin hadn't anticipated much coming from the email. He'd informed the detectives regarding David's DEFCON terminology but with no context around the plea, deciphering the source of trouble appeared impossible without more information.

After he ended the call, Justin huffed out a sigh. The police were no closer to finding who killed David or determining the source of the latest crimes against he and Marissa.

Justin phoned Wendy. "Are you okay?"

"Yes. I stayed with Becca last night," Wendy said.

"Great. I'm at the hospital." Justin yawned and rolled his neck.

"You're supposed to be on vacation."

"Couldn't be helped. How's Sam?"

"Aunt Iris is spoiling her rotten. She took her shopping yesterday, and they came back with several new outfits. She's disappointed about Halo."

"Me too. The vet said he was poisoned." Justin reached into the refrigerator and pulled out a bottle of water. "Looks like the intruders gave Halo arsenic-laced food."

"Marissa must be out of her mind."

"She's holding up and Halo should recover."

Wendy had late afternoon meetings and promised to help with the clean up later. Justin hoped she would head off to Uncle Lou and Aunt Iris's, but he didn't argue.

Ending the call with Wendy, Justin ambled back to the window. Once again he questioned if David had reverted to his old ways. During their Notre Dame days, Justin had a pinpoint focus on grades and getting into medical school while David and Neal embraced the social perks of college life. Neal could handle the heavy party scene but David spiraled out of control. Justin thought rock bottom came when David informed him he'd gotten over his head with gambling debts. Justin bailed him out with an $800 loan. For the next two semesters, David focused on school and even joined ROTC. Justin hoped David stayed on the straight and narrow, but the peaceful times didn't last long.

Justin grabbed a quick shower and ran across the street to a bakery frequented by hospital staff. He bought muffins, hot chocolate, and coffee for Mrs. Lambert's family. Something about the kids reminded Justin of the moment he knew his own parents were hurt. At the time, he couldn't fathom anything worse. If he could use his abilities, he wouldn't allow another kid to experience such pain.

In the waiting room, the children hugged him, and the father expressed his gratitude both for the food and the care provided to his wife.

Justin performed another exam on Mrs. Lambert. Her vital signs were stable and her breath sounds were clear. When her eyes popped open and she glanced at him, Justin engaged her in a brief, lucid conversation. He informed her she'd been shot, had surgery, and her family waited outside. Caution prevented him from guaranteeing she'd make a full recovery, but based on experience, Justin remained optimistic she'd rejoin her life soon.

Satisfied with Mrs. Lambert's progress, Justin headed to see Marissa. When he pulled into the driveway twenty minutes later, he spotted a police officer in his cruiser outside of the Nash house.

After greeting everyone, he slid into a kitchen chair for breakfast with John, Ava, and Marissa. They discussed the break-in and Halo's health.

Marissa had called the clinic earlier and got the good news Halo could be released.

His reaction to Halo's poisoning surprised him. Somewhere during the short time they'd spent together, he'd fallen in love with the dog. He looked forward to coming home to Halo, taking him along on his runs, or having the dog's presence in the house.

He glanced over at Marissa. With her brown hair swept up in a ponytail, she wore jeans and a University of Virginia T-shirt. *Sexy as hell.* A beautiful woman dressed in jeans could take his breath away but this one stopped his heart. Pulling his attention back, he focused on his cup of coffee. He hated having to remind himself not to stare. 'Hands off Marissa' proved to be a difficult directive. "I need to get home to begin the clean up." Justin wiped his mouth with a napkin. "Thank you for breakfast, Mrs. Nash." He turned to Marissa. "Are you still up for this?"

"Let us help you," John said.

"Thanks, sir, but I've got it covered."

Justin and Marissa cleared the table.

"We're picking up Halo, and I'll help Justin clean the house. I'm looking forward to keeping busy," Marissa said.

John nodded and turned to Justin. "Marissa tells us you lost your parents a while ago. I'm sure they are proud of the man you became." He rose from the table and patted Justin on the shoulder.

At the mention of his parents, Justin's heart tightened. A quick flash of the crash site surged in his memory. The ugly scene had a permanent home just below the surface. He pushed away the scene and replaced it with a happy memory of his parents at his high school graduation, his go-to image.

"Don't worry about cleaning up. You guys get going." Ava turned to Justin. "You are always welcome here, so feel free to come back for dinner, or anytime. If you need a place to stay tonight, there's a room available." She hugged Justin and kissed Marissa on the cheek as they exited the kitchen.

Once they were in the car, Justin turned to her. "Any black SUV sightings last night? I noticed a police patrol on your street."

Marissa shrugged. "I'm thankful the police have been patrolling the street but for some reason their presence hasn't eased my concern."

"I want this solved and the people responsible put away as soon as possible. Too many people I care about are in danger." He pulled out into the street.

They rode in silence for a few miles. Marissa appeared preoccupied. He spotted dark circles shadowing her eyes, before she turned her head toward the window.

"Are you okay?" Justin asked.

Marissa inhaled. "I'm fine." She paused. "No, I'm not. I have my phone but I'd like to use a computer. My family hovers and I need to research something. Can we stop someplace?"

"The intruders swiped my laptop. How about we stop at the hospital? You can use the computer in my office while I check on a couple of patients."

Fifteen minutes later, they stepped off the elevator onto the eighth floor. As soon as they rounded to the ICU, they came face-to-face with a flurry of activity.

One of the nurses spotted Justin. "Dr. Tanner, Mrs. Lambert is coding."

"This is Marissa. Get one of the aides to take her to my office. Let her use my computer," Justin yelled as he raced down the hall.

A young woman nodded and waved for Marissa to follow. She wore dark blue scrubs, her red hair wound into a loose bun. The woman peered at her periodically on the short walk to Justin's office.

Marissa straightened her shirt and smoothed her hair, now self-conscious. *Did she have toilet paper on her shoe?* She resisted the urge to check as the woman swung open the office door.

"Dr. Tanner said you needed to use the computer?" She cocked her head to the side, hands on hips.

"Yes, thank you." Marissa glanced around the small office.

"Dr. Tanner allows a few of the residents to use his office when their area is crowded. He's really nice." She bent over, punched in a password, and the computer came to life. "I haven't seen you around here. Are you a resident?"

"No, just a friend." Justin never mentioned dating anyone. For the first time, Marissa questioned if he had an active dating life or even a girlfriend, although she didn't recall Justin having a plus one for the wedding. By the way this woman spoke of him, she had stars in her eyes for Justin.

"Your name is Marissa? I'm Emily, a nursing student, but I also work here." She scanned the office before facing Marissa. Emily leaned in, and whispered, "He's so hot—the hottest doctor I've ever seen. A lot of people around here have crushes on him. If you're his girlfriend, watch out."

Marissa chewed her lip. Not hard to believe Justin claimed the title—hospital stud. Based on her limited knowledge of him and all the time he'd spent with her over the last week either a girlfriend didn't exist or she was the most understanding, patient woman ever.

"Nice to meet you, Emily, but Justin and I are just friends."

"He never brings a woman here," Emily said, as if to challenge her claim. "I think he's interested." She nodded and smiled. "You seem nice, so I'll try to keep the nasty witches around here from trashing you."

"Thanks. We just walked in, so who would even know about me?"

Emily sighed and shook her head. "You definitely don't work in a hospital, because if you did, you'd know how fast news flows. You might as well have announced your arrival over the hospital loud-speaker."

"Well, you can tell everyone we're just friends."

"Uh huh." Emily rolled her eyes. "Okay, you're all set with the computer. There is a small fridge in the corner if you want a drink." She crossed the room and patted the top of the waist high refrigera-tor. "I'm sure Justin won't mind his *friend* taking something." She winked, then closed the door.

Marissa shrugged. She hadn't convinced Emily of her friend status in Justin's life. She'd have to alert Justin to brace for rumors. Would a rumor about her and Justin as hot and heavy lovers be such a bad thing? She shook her head. *Don't be stupid.*

Sliding into the desk chair, Marissa surveyed Justin's office. A bookshelf on one wall displayed medical journals, and three file cabi-nets occupied the adjacent wall. A wide window at waist-height inhabited the area in front of the desk. Marissa smiled at the photo of Sam and Justin, both wearing baseball caps and grinning ear-to-ear. Justin cared deeply for his niece and would make a great father. Her stomach clenched at the idea of David as a father.

Marissa inhaled and turned to the computer. Ever since David's funeral, she grappled with even more unknowns. She'd met the woman he'd been trading sexy messages with, and while she wanted to hate her, Tiffany appeared to be a naïve, but decent, person. Despite Marissa's observations, could Tiffany be involved in David's murder? What about the mysterious veiled woman with her creepy dead flowers talk? The woman hadn't said how she knew David, but could she be part of his secret life?

Now, the patch she'd grabbed from the casket nagged at her. She pulled the item from her purse and inspected it. The patch, with seven sides in the shape of a heptagon, contained the phrase *Ordo Ortus* and the year 1953 in the center. The phrase appeared to be in Latin. Maybe the patch belonged to the funeral home, or the casket manufacturer. She pulled up the website of the funeral home and found nothing resembling the phrase or the insignia. Next, she pulled up the company website for the casket manufacturer. Again, nothing.

Studying the phrase again, she entered the words into the search box. In an instant, results populated the screen. The Latin phrase translated, meant Order Rising but she didn't find an organization or a business using the phrase.

She entered the English phrase into the search box. Information about The Order of the Rising Sun popped up. She read through the text and didn't see any connection between the green patch and an honor bestowed from the Japanese government to exemplary individuals. Another top search result concerned the New World Order, but the concept seemed farfetched. Order Rising could pass for some evil, villainous group looking to take over the world, but she doubted the patch represented an organization run by Superman's archenemy. She giggled a sarcastic laugh. *This is crazy.*

Marissa slammed the patch on the desk, cursing her waste of

time. *Probably means nothing.* She searched David's name, something she had never done before. Before she could scan the results, she rubbed her head, an imaginary jackhammer pounded away on her skull. Marissa scanned the desk for a bottle of pain reliever. *No luck.* With the pain intensifying, Marissa dropped the patch into her purse and headed out of the office in search of the elevators to take her to the first-floor gift shop. They were certain to sell pain relievers. She could ask Emily or one of the nurses, but they had their hands full and she didn't want to get in the way.

She took two turns and ended up in the ICU waiting room. She spotted the elevators on the other side of the chairs. As she crossed the floor, she saw Justin emerge from a door on the opposite side of the room.

He approached an elderly couple and a man with two young children. Pulling aside the man, Justin, who towered over him, bent close. The children, a girl who looked to be about twelve and a boy about ten, huddled close to the older couple. After a few minutes, the man lost his footing, and Justin grabbed his arm and led him to a chair.

Marissa turned from the scene, not wanting to intrude on a private, and obviously devastating, moment. *Those poor children.* She stepped into the elevator and rode down to the first floor. A wrong turn caused her to end up near the loading dock area. She glanced through a window just in time to see a black SUV speeding by. Shocked, she pressed herself against the wall and peered out again. The SUV turned the corner a few seconds later, but the chill invading her body told her the enemy had been near. She turned, hurrying back to ICU. The doors opened, and she stepped off the elevator, still thinking about what she'd seen.

Justin rushed up to her with a grim expression and a set jaw. "Where were you?"

"I went down to find the gift shop." She paused and moved closer. "Are you okay?"

"I just lost a patient, a wife and mother who shouldn't have died. This morning, her condition had improved. I can't figure out what happened." Justin rubbed the dark stubble on his face.

"Could she have suffered a set back?"

"Possibly, but I examined her earlier. She'd improved. I hated having to tell her husband and kids she won't be coming home." He pounded his fist against the wall.

"Justin, I'm so sorry." She placed her hand on his arm.

"Let's go." He punched the elevator button.

The doors pinged open, but Emily yelled for them to wait.

They turned as she ran toward them.

"Dr. Tanner, I think something fell out of your pocket in the patient's room." She handed him a green patch.

Justin accepted the patch and shook his head. "This isn't mine."

Emily cocked her head sideways. "Maybe it belongs to those two guys I saw leaving the patient's room just before she coded."

Marissa took the patch from Justin. She stared at the same patch matching the one inside her purse. With shaky fingers she turned the patch over. Written in black ink on the back was the word "penance".

Chapter 17

Once inside the SUV, Justin exhaled. "I apologize for my mood. I hate losing a patient, especially needless-ly." He met Marissa's gaze. "She went to the store for milk. A simple errand, and now those kids don't have their mother. I operated on her last night, and I knew she'd pull through. In fact, this morning everything appeared on track." He swiped his hand through his hair. "I don't see how this happened."

"I'm sorry about your patient and agree she didn't have to die." Marissa opened her purse. "I need to show you something."

Justin started the car and flipped on the air conditioner.

Marissa pulled the green patch from her purse. "Have you seen this patch before?"

"Yes, that's the patch Emily had a few minutes ago." Justin hadn't paid much attention to the patch.

"This particular patch is the one Emily found, but I found the same one inside David's casket. At first, I thought maybe the funeral home or the casket manufacturer left marketing information, but after an online search, I didn't find any connection."

Moving closer, Justin reached for the patch from the casket. He studied the patch, the phrase *Ordo Ortus, 1953* in the middle of a heptagon. "What does this mean?" Something knocked within him.

"According to my research, the phrase is Latin and means Order Rising." She paused, and glanced around the parking lot. "Justin, your patient died at the hands of these people." Marissa flipped the patch from Emily and handed it to Justin. "Look."

Justin straightened in his seat and studied the patch. "Penance?" He paused. "Damn it! Why kill an innocent wife and mother?" He sighed. "Who the hell are these people?" They were dealing with not only professional murderers but also people intent on terrorizing them. He rubbed his eyes and then dug his phone from his pocket. Both Kearns and Streeter weren't available so he left a voice mail message to contact him immediately.

"To my knowledge, my patient had nothing to do with David. They think we know something. Killing this innocent woman just upped the ante."

"What do you think they did to her?" Marissa shuddered.

With a tight jaw, Justin stared at the patch as his mind whirled in every direction. "No obvious signs of strangulation, no marks around her neck. She was breathing on her own. The only thing I can think of is they injected something into her IV line. An autopsy and blood screen will indicate anything unexpected in her system."

Marissa touched his arm. "At the hospital, on my way to the gift shop, I took a wrong turn. I ended up near the loading dock. I happened to turn and see a black SUV leaving the area."

Justin jerked around. "You saw these guys, here at the hospital?" He stared at Marissa. "They walked into my patient's room, killed her, and strolled out of the hospital." What if more of his patients were targets? His mind ticked off possible vulnerabilities. Operating on instinct, Justin called the ICU and requested the room not be cleaned. Emily told him the patient had been prepped and moved to the morgue and housekeeping had almost finished with the room. Justin sighed. Most of the evidence had probably been destroyed. He placed the patch on the console.

His phone buzzed. The display indicated Kearns was on the line.

He put the phone on speaker so Marissa could hear. Justin explained the discovery of the two patches and his patient's mysterious death.

"Doctor, you're the expert, but if this woman sustained a shot to the chest wouldn't she be at risk?" Kearns replied in a bored manner.

Once again, he ran down the health status of Mrs. Lambert emphasizing her improving progress.

Kearns let a loud sigh escape. "I'll see what I can do." She clicked off before he could say anything else.

"She didn't sound invested in pursuing the possibility your patient was murdered," Marissa said.

"If the police didn't give any credence to my theory the chief of staff surely won't shell out money for more security." Shoving the phone into his pocket, Justin paused a second, and then pulled the phone out again. He called the hospital's chief medical officer to request the staff be on the lookout for suspicious visitors.. Justin provided what little details he had and ended the call unconvinced the hospital would ramp up security. He stuffed one of the patches into his pocket, then punched another button on his phone. A few seconds later, he connected. "I need a favor."

GRAY CLOUD-COVERED SKIES darkened Justin's house. He flipped on a light illuminating the destruction inside. Justin and Marissa stood side by side staring at the mess.

Halo tiptoed through the clutter until he found a clear spot and settled into a corner of the living room. They'd picked him up after leaving the hospital. The veterinary assistant explained Halo would be somewhat sluggish for another day or so, but should be back to normal soon.

Marissa knelt in front of Halo. "I'm thankful they didn't kill him."

Justin picked up broken pieces of a coffee table and placed the wood in a pile. He stepped across books and Sam's toys, before bending to pet Halo. "Me too."

The dog's tail thumped at the attention.

Marissa and Justin worked for over an hour.

"Justin, do you have any more of this cleaner?" Marissa held up an empty bottle, an hour later. She had been wiping down shelves before replacing the books, marveling the bookshelf had been left intact.

"No, but I can go to the store to get more."

"Thanks, I'll press on."

Justin hesitated. "Maybe you should come with me."

"I'll be fine here. Besides, I don't want to leave Halo alone." She glimpsed Halo resting next to the bag of items from the vet.

At the mention of his name, Halo sauntered over and settled at her feet. His tail flapped against the wood floor as he gawked at her.

"All right, but lock the doors after I leave. I'll pick up lunch on the way back."

After Justin left, Marissa continued re-shelving the books. She worked for a few minutes, then collected the bag and headed into the kitchen. "Time for your medication." The vet had given her medication to help Halo continue to flush out the poison. Digging into the bag, she searched for the bottle and spotted Halo's bloodstained collar. Divots were dug out of the leather by crime scene investigators where drops of David's blood had been. She'd been surprised they didn't confiscate the whole collar.

Halo, who'd ambled in behind her, regarded her with sad eyes.

Marissa glanced at the dog. "I know. This is crazy. I should just get rid of the collar."

Halo nudged her and sat.

Her chest tightened as tears blurred her vision. Halo's collar represented a morsel of goodness within David, tenderness she'd come to know he had in short supply. The proposal using Halo's collar as a delivery system for her ring had been wonderful but now the collar only induced anger. She pulled out Halo's medication and shut the bag. She'd keep the collar for now as a reminder to never let anyone make a fool of her again.

She gave Halo his medication. As she placed the bottle back in the bag, she heard her cell phone ring.

Detective Streeter inquired about Halo and explained he expected preliminary lab results on the dog food soon.

"I'm a little shaken. I keep looking over my shoulder, expecting the bad guys to be there." She and Halo strolled back into the living room. Marissa added one more book to the shelf and then sat next to Halo. "I'm at Justin's house now. Could you have police cruisers perform extra patrols in this neighborhood?"

"We're not in the business of personal protection, Ms. Nash. We had an officer at your parents' house for the day but we can't justify continuous patrols."

Marissa shook her head. "Never mind. Sorry for asking." Streeter may be a great detective but he had a gruff exterior.

"I'll see what I can do." He sighed. "I have four kids, two of them are college-aged girls. Having ambition ain't cheap. I don't make enough to get tipsy on the weekends so I've had to be creative to keep my wife and kids from knocking me off for insurance money. In addition to reminding my kids they aren't the spawn of millionaires, I tell them to learn to take care of themselves. Like I advise them, be self-sufficient. Learn to defend yourself. Can't always count on the police to get there in time."

The room darkened as the black clouds expanded. Marissa shivered. "I see."

Streeter huffed an obscenity. "Dr. Tanner is there with you so you should be fine."

Marissa caressed Halo's back. "Actually, he's not. Justin had a couple errands to run."

"Remain alert and call us if you see anything suspicious."

Marissa thanked him, placed the phone on the table, and resumed cleaning. The wind picked up outside, slapping tree branches against the north side of the house. Up until today the weather had been perfect, but storms were on the horizon. A metaphor for her life. Life had been going along pretty well, then suddenly everything imploded and now she found herself in a new reality, one she had not been prepared for.

A loud crack permeated the silence. Marissa jumped, and her heart pumped faster.

Halo rose slowly and blinked his eyes.

"I know. Calm down." She peeked out the window, spotting a nearby tree branch splintered and waving by a tendon of wood in the wind.

As the sky darkened, the house appeared to grow shadows. A loud crackle exploded like a lion tamer snapping a whip.

She jumped again. *Only lightning.*

Marissa clicked on another light, the illumination casting eerie shadows on the destruction.

The gray sky opened up, and the pounding rain beat down with fury. She hurried across the room to close an open window. Rushing through the ground floor with Halo trotting along beside her, she shut all open windows. Cursing, she darted upstairs. A rain-soaked mess wouldn't help their cleanup process.

She entered the guest bedroom and shivered in the breeze as the wind flapped through the wavering curtains. The lights flickered, and Marissa stopped, a wrinkle of alarm twisting through her.

Just the wind. Don't be a baby.

She ran to the window, fought the wind-ruffled curtain, and glanced at the street. Was a black SUV parked two houses down and across the street? If the rain weren't obscuring her vision, she could tell if the vehicle met the description of the mysterious SUV. The vehicle could have been blue for all she could tell.

She rubbed her eyes. *I can't go through life afraid of every black SUV.*

A creak echoed through the house. Fear burrowed into her rational thoughts, and a knot settled in her stomach. She twisted away from the window and came face-to-face with a masked intruder.

A hand clamped over her mouth, cutting off her scream.

Chapter 18

The man held her against his hard chest, the soft, damp leather gloves pressed into her face as a musky aroma floated around her nose. Her mind shrieked, making attempts at sensible thought ineffective.

"Don't move and don't scream." He strengthened his hold.

Marissa nodded as a pointed object jammed into her back. *A gun.* Her pulse raced in response.

"Where is the flash drive?" The man removed his hand from her mouth and turned her to face him, but he kept a tight grip on her arms.

She stared up at the black ski-masked man, his voice deep and gruff, like he needed to clear his throat. "I don't know anything about a flash drive," she whispered.

Halo stepped into the room, growling and baring his teeth.

"Call off the dog, or I'll shoot him." The man rotated the gun between Halo and Marissa.

"Don't hurt him." Marissa wanted to move next to Halo, but the man continued to immobilize her. If the poison hadn't weakened Halo, he would have attacked the man already.

Halo moved closer. Large canine teeth flashed as his gaze focused on the intruder.

The man raised the gun and fired into the ceiling.

The explosive bang reverberated against Marissa's chest.

Halo stood his ground and continued to growl.

"Halo, down." Shaking, Marissa eyed the dog and prayed he'd obey. She didn't doubt the man would kill him.

"Your boyfriend stashed a large amount of data on a flash drive." The intruder yanked her closer, whipping back her head. "I want it back." Black obsidian eyes glowered through the slits in the ski mask. Evil eyes.

Marissa's heart beat as if she'd just run a marathon at full speed. She knew nothing about a flash drive, but this man wouldn't believe her.

He reared back and slapped her hard across the face.

The blow knocked her off balance and she collided with the floor. Her head spun as pain bolted through her. The metallic taste of her own blood verified her lip had been busted. Unsure of whether to rise, she turned and stared up at the man.

"Look, bitch, this isn't a game." He bent closer. "Where is the flash drive?"

His breath held a hint of mint—toothpaste or candy. "I don't know. David never told me."

He trained the gun on her. "Then what good are you?"

Halo pounced. The man yelled as the dog clamped onto his leg.

The masked man flipped around and aimed the gun at Halo.

She levered her legs in front of her and kicked his wrist, sending the gun flying across the room. Scrambling, she got onto her hands and knees.

He grabbed her leg and, with violent force, pulled her close. He kicked at Halo, jabbing him in the nose.

Halo yelped and backed away.

Marissa fell, her back slamming hard against the floor.

The masked man jumped on top of her, rage burning in his eyes.

Marissa writhed and kicked, trying to loosen his hold, but the more she fought, the stronger he held her.

He encircled her neck with his hands and squeezed.

Is this how I will die?

As he squeezed his hands tighter, his black-eyed gaze drilled into her face. Through clenched teeth, he grunted, "Where is the data?"

Marissa tried to shake her head, but his grasp on her neck held her in place. The sensation of floating, drifting away, blanketed her. As her eyes fluttered, she glimpsed Halo's second attack.

He clamped the man's leg in his jaws.

Once again the man howled in pain, and the pressure around her neck released.

The dog tore at the intruder's legs as the man attempted to rise. With Halo's jaw still clamped around his ankle, the intruder punched the dog away.

Halo, still lethargic from the poisoning, yelped as he fell on his side. His paws scraped the wooden floor as he fought for traction.

Marissa coughed and gasped for air as wind and rain battered the room through the screen of the opened window. She searched for Evil Eyes through the stormy haze. "Halo!" The dog would do his best to protect her.

Within seconds, Halo stood at her side, his gaze focused on the man just out of reach. He growled and readied to attack again.

Evil Eyes scanned the room for the gun, but whipped his head toward the hall as the hum of the garage door opening below interrupted his task. In one quick move, he leaped across the room. Snatching up the gun near the bed, he bolted through the window.

Marissa shot up and stumbled to the window. Fear turned to anger. "You kicked my dog!" She crawled out of the window, still eyeing the man scurrying across the roof to the lowest hanging eave. Perhaps the man would remove his mask, or she could get the license plate number of the SUV. Anything she could give the police to go on.

He hung in the air a second, gripping a secure section of the gutter, and then landed on the ground with stealth, like a jungle cat.

Halo barked from the open window, but Marissa ignored his apparent warnings.

Although the rain came down at a steady rate, she hadn't anticipated the roof being so slippery and lost her footing. Grasping at roof tiles, she slid toward the edge of the two-story house. She screamed as she dug in her fingers and beat her feet against the tiles to stop her momentum.

"Marissa!" Justin shouted from the open bedroom window. "Hang on!" He disappeared into the house.

"Justin!" Her feet slipped again, sending her even closer to the edge. She grappled at the wet roof, trying to slow her skid. *Don't look down.* Her efforts were futile. She tumbled off the roof but managed to hang on to the gutter.

"Hold on." Justin, now on the ground below her, propped a tall ladder against the house.

"My hands are slippery. I can't hold on much longer!"

With a calm voice, Justin said, "I'm almost there. Hold tight."

Driving rain pelted her. Wet palms scraped against the gutter as Marissa fought to hold her position. Tires squealing on wet asphalt brought Marissa's attention back to the street below. The SUV barreled away, eliminating any chance of getting their license plate numbers.

Justin climbed the ladder, and Halo barked below.

A second later, Justin's arms were around her waist. "I've got you." He held her tight as he positioned her on the ladder. "Slow." He led her down the ladder as the rain continued to bombard them.

Once they were on solid ground, she turned and wrapped her arms around his neck. "Thank you," she whispered.

Chapter 19

Justin and Marissa sprinted for the house. Once inside the kitchen, Justin placed his hands on Marissa's face, brushing back wet hair plastered to her head "Are you hurt?" He ignored the water running down his own face.

Marissa shivered, wrapping her arms around her middle. "He strangled me, but I think I'm okay." Her raspy voice shook.

He pulled out his phone and called 911, requesting police and ambulance assistance.

Marissa bent and hugged Halo. "He could have killed you." She released him and once again wrapped her arms around her midsection.

Halo bounced around them, agitated and on edge.

"Halo, sit," Justin said.

The dog stopped, and then obeyed.

Justin tilted her head with his hands and gently touched the ugly red marks encircling her neck. "You'll have some nasty bruising. I don't think you sustained any damage to your trachea, but to be on the safe side, you need to go to the hospital." He moved her closer to the light in the kitchen, noting her reddened eyes, typical of strangulation survivors. "Are you having any trouble swallowing?" He examined her neck again and checked her pupils.

Marissa shivered again and gulped. "No. I'm okay. No hospital, please."

"I'm not arguing. You're going, if for no other reason than to placate me." Justin touched the other set of red marks on her face. "Did he hit you, too?"

Eyes wide, she nodded. "He was in the upstairs bedroom. When you came home, he heard the garage door open." She shivered even more.

Afraid she was going into shock, Justin ran to the closet and searched for a blanket usually kept inside, but with all the disarray he gave up. Instead, he rushed to his SUV and pulled out a blanket from the back. When he returned, he observed her standing in the same spot.

Noting her blank expression, he felt anger roil through his stomach, along with the intense desire to rip apart those responsible. He led her into the living room and gently lowered her onto the couch. He wrapped the blanket around her shoulders and then pulled her into his arms. She could have been killed. Tossing aside his off-limits rule, he accepted he wanted her in his life. When her shaking eased, he pulled away and stared. "Tell me what happened."

She explained she'd been upstairs in the guest bedroom closing the window and the man appeared. "He asked me for the flash drive. I don't know anything about a flash drive, but he didn't believe me."

"Did you recognize him?"

She shook her head, and then jerked as wailing sirens neared.

"You're safe now." He pulled her closer. The perfect way she fit into the crook of his arm made his protective nature surge even more. "He dragged you out on the roof?"

"No, I ran after him." Marissa straightened and met his gaze.

Justin drew in a breath. "What the hell were you thinking?" He jumped up. "You could have been killed!"

"I know." Marissa nodded. "I thought if I could get a look at their license plate, I'd have something to give the police."

Justin sat again and pulled her into his arms. "These people are dangerous. Don't become an easy target." Horrible possibilities played through his mind.

She wiped away a wet strand of hair. "I understand, but I wanted to do something. I feel sick your patient may have been killed because of this when I don't even know what "this" is." Her raspy voice intoned thick with frustration.

Sirens screamed outside the house now.

Justin released her and moved to open the door.

AN HOUR LATER, Marissa sat upright on the hospital gurney, anxious to be released but thankful all tests revealed no damage to her throat, larynx, or vocal cords. She'd have some bruising, but the discoloration would fade in time.

Justin had called Kelly and Craig to take Halo back to their house while he accompanied her to the hospital.

"Are you sure everything is okay? Your lurking is making me nervous." Marissa rubbed the ballet shoe charm on her necklace.

Justin stopped pacing and approached her, tossing a gym bag onto a nearby chair. "You're fine but he could have killed you." He began pacing again, and then stopped in front of her. "I thought you might want to freshen up. Here's your bag, left in the car from the other night."

Before she could say more, Streeter and Kearns entered the room.

Marissa relayed the details of her encounter with the intruder.

Holding a pen and pad, Streeter leaned forward in his chair. "Did you get a look at this guy?"

"No, he wore a mask."

"What type of mask?" Streeter glanced up from his notes.

Marissa swallowed, grimacing slightly from the pain. "He wore a black ski mask. I didn't see any tattoos or marks. He had a deep voice and stood about six feet tall. I couldn't distinguish his race, but he had very dark eyes. He was strong, and if not for Halo and Justin..."

She explained how she went out the window to try to get a license plate number.

Justin handed her a bottle of water. "Small sips."

She nodded and frowned as the water slid through her injured throat.

"Good thing Dr. Tanner came home when he did, and your dog protected you," Kearns said. "Now, let's go back to this flash drive. Are you sure David never said anything about obtaining data, even illegally?"

"No, not at all." Her hands clenched. "Communication became a problem—he never talked to me. Always sullen and moody, but I never thought in a million years he could be involved in something illegal or something that would get him killed." She paused and pulled up the sheet, suddenly chilled. "We need answers."

Streeter nodded and rose. "We're doing all we can."

Silence blanketed the room for a few seconds, and then Justin spoke. "Do you have any information regarding the death of my patient? I spoke with Detective Kearns about my concerns."

"What?" Confusion slid across Streeter's face as he turned to Kearns.

Justin glared at Kearns.

"Things got hectic, and I didn't get a chance to discuss Dr. Tanner's *theory* about his patient being killed by the same people." Kearns placed a hand on her hip.

Justin explained to Streeter how Mrs. Lambert's condition took an unexpected plummet.

"Don't mean to sound crass, but couldn't her condition simply have worsened?" Streeter shifted his stance.

"Of course, but a nurse found this near her body." Justin fished the patch from his pocket and handed it to Streeter.

"Okay." Streeter bent close to read the text before handing it to Kearns. "A lot of organizations make their own patches. It's advertising."

Kearns glanced at the patch. "I don't know Latin. What does this mean and how does this indicate your patient was murdered?"

"Turn it over," Justin said.

"Penance." Streeter stared at the word. "What the hell does this mean?"

Justin rubbed his eyes. "We're hoping you could tell us."

"I saw a similar one inside David's casket, only it was blank on the back." Marissa reached for her purse and pulled out the identical patch.

Kearns cleared her throat. "I'll investigate."

Justin crossed his arms and with a terse voice, uttered, "Thanks."

Kearns angled her head. "I thought you surgeons were unfeeling machines. A death should be par for the course."

Justin glared at Kearns. "I haven't met one physician unaffected in some way by a patient's death. For the sake of the next patient, you learn what you can and move on. I had a hard job of looking a father in the eye and telling him the person he loves, the mother of his children, will never come home. You must know the feeling."

"Absolutely, but sometimes things look worse than they are when you're under lots of stress." Streeter offered a slight smile.

Kearns placed her hands on her hips, displaying her gun holstered to her side. "My advice to you both is to check into a hotel —at least for the night, maybe two."

Kearns' blue eyes gave off an air of pity.

"What about my parents? I'm concerned about their safety." Marissa's gaze shifted between the detectives.

With an exaggerated sigh, Kearns nodded. "We'll try to have the street units increase patrols by both houses."

"We don't have a lot to go on, but crime scene investigators have processed your house, Dr. Tanner, and we hope to pull some prints. We also found blood droplets, probably from the dog bite, so we're processing the evidence for DNA." Streeter placed his notepad in his pocket.

Justin shifted closer to Marissa. His body blazed hot next to hers, and she shivered from the temperature differential.

"I agree staying in a hotel for a few days is a good idea, but that's a temporary solution," Justin said. "What about two weeks from now, or a month?"

"The investigation is moving." Streeter spoke up. "This is not like a *CSI* episode, we can't wrap everything up in a nice package in one hour."

"Marissa, what is your middle name?" Kearns asked.

Marissa wrinkled her forehead. "Elizabeth."

Kearns typed the information into her smartphone. "And your mother's maiden name?"

"Estrada."

"Check into the hotel under the name Elizabeth Estrada. Dr. Tanner, what about you?"

"Michael Raines."

Kearns nodded. "Get a trusted friend to make a reservation in their name. You will have to show ID but tell the front desk clerk not to use your real names if someone should call or come in and ask for you. If you have any difficulty, call me."

Streeter placed a hand on Marissa's shoulder. "We're doing all we can to find these guys. Don't tell anyone where you're staying—of course the friend who makes your reservation will know, but don't text, email, or call anyone with your location"

Marissa nodded, and a shiver ran through her. *Now we're forced to flee.* What about Halo? What about her family? "How long do we need to stay away?" Despite her efforts, Marissa's voice shook.

Justin covered her hand with his and squeezed.

"Let's take it day by day." Streeter's voice held a calm, soothing tone.

As Kearns collected the patches and stepped toward the opening of the ER bay, she turned. "Keep your eyes open, your hotel door locked at all times, and forgo housekeeping for a few days. When you get to a hotel, call one of us to let us know where you are. Just in case."

Once they were gone and she'd been discharged, Marissa asked for privacy to get dressed.

Justin assured her he'd be right down the hall and then left her alone.

She hopped off the bed and picked up the bag. She peered closer. *David's*. She stared at his black gym bag. For reasons she couldn't fathom, her heart thundered. Seconds ticked by. She inhaled and opened the bag. Maybe she'd find his special face wash she sometimes borrowed. Rooting through the bag, she came across soap, shower shoes, deodorant, and a toothbrush. She opened the zipper pouch inside the bag and spotted a familiar container. She extracted the aloe-based face wash and a yellow piece of paper floated through the air.

Marissa bent to pick up the slip of paper and examined the words. Even with the chill in the room, tiny beads of sweat erupted on her forehead. She stared at the note. Could this be a clue to David's secretive past?

Chapter 20

Wet kisses shellacked her face as Marissa knelt in front of Halo. She couldn't leave without seeing him.

They'd arrived at Kelly and Craig's house late in the evening. Justin took a roundabout route, but they reached the suburban house without spying a black SUV. During the drive, he'd spoken to Craig about making hotel reservations for he and Marissa.

Once again, she had to say goodbye to Halo. Some hotels accepted dogs but a huge white dog tagging along would draw attention. Kelly had the bag containing all of Halo's medications, shampoo, dog treats, and the collar. Marissa explained his treatment regime and nodded toward the bag. "Halo's old collar is still inside, just leave it."

Kelly nodded and placed a hand on her arm. "I'm so worried about you. Are you sure you're okay?"

"I just need a good night's rest." Marissa smiled.

Justin cleared his throat. "Thanks, Craig, for making the hotel reservation. Please keep our location secret."

Craig bounced Gavin in his arms, as the baby reached for Halo. "Glad to help. Do you need anything else?"

Halo stood and licked the baby's heel reducing Gavin to excited giggles.

"We'll be fine." Justin glanced at Halo. "These two should have a good time."

Kelly grinned. "Halo has always been gentle with Gavin. I never worry about having him here." Kelly placed an arm around Marissa. "It's you I'm worried about."

Marissa gave a weak smile. "At least I'm not alone." She met Justin's gaze and felt a warm sensation settle inside.

After a quick but emotional goodbye, they drove to the Nash house. Marissa hated having to tell her parents about the attack, but she couldn't lie.

Her mother cried and pulled Marissa into an embrace.

John placed a hand on her shoulder. "Take my gun. Do you remember what I taught you?"

She nodded. During high school John taught her and Vanessa what he considered essentials for living. He instructed them how to change a tire, light home repairs, budgeting, and how to handle and shoot a gun. "Dad, I don't want to take your gun." She bit her lip. He might need the weapon.

Justin stepped forward. "Sir, I have a gun permit, and I will have my weapon at the ready."

John nodded and shook his hand.

Marissa packed what few items she had and said another goodbye.

Two hours later, they checked into a hotel in Washington D.C.

Marissa collapsed on the couch and glanced over at the large bed. Sleep sounded inviting, but her throat ached, and a ramped up anxiety level made relaxation impossible. She picked up the hotel phone and left a message for Streeter naming their location. Next, she placed the "do not disturb" sign on the door.

The soothing forest green-and-cream colors made her want to burrow under the covers and sleep until next year. The image of sleeping in Justin's arms jolted her, along with the knock on the adjoining door.

"I'm starving. How about I call room service for a late snack?" Justin stood in the doorway.

Marissa found the room service menu on the desk. "I'd love a glass of wine. How about you?"

Justin gave her a prolonged stare. "No, I'm fine."

"Are you sure? Then maybe a beer?"

"No, just water for me." Justin stepped into the room.

After placing their order, she opened her mouth to speak and then clamped it shut. She needed to talk to Justin but apprehension kept her quiet. The more she thought about the note, the more suspicious the contents became. Did she want to know?

"Kearns and Streeter didn't indicate the patches meant anything. They also didn't give much credence to your patient being murdered." At the window, Marissa gazed at the Washington Monument off in the distance. Her throat still burned, and while she wanted the soothing effects of a glass of wine, the hot tea she ordered would comfort her more.

"I don't have a shred of evidence to prove murder, except for the patch." Justin moved next to her. "There's a guy in the lab who got a blood sample from Mrs. Lambert. I'll check in with him soon."

"I don't know how you do it. Dealing with death, I mean." She ambled away from the window and sank into a nearby chair.

He slid into the chair across from her. "I try to focus on the good outcomes—the people I've saved."

"I admire your ability to handle a crisis. "Were you born knowing what to do or did you learn through the Army and medical school?" She studied the dark and light green patterns on the chair before turning her focus to him.

He shrugged. "A combination of everything, I guess. As a young kid, my dad always drilled into me how to handle emergencies especially since he traveled so much. Sometimes my mother, Wendy, and I went with him, but many times we stayed behind. He wanted me to be able to take care of the family. Wendy, too." He paused and ran a hand over the stubble forming on his chin. "Of course, the Army trains everyone, even the medical corps. During medical school, we're trained to manage the medical aspect, but the humans on your table have families and a life. My goal is to return every patient to their life, but sometimes things don't work." He shuffled his Nikes along the brown carpet. "We're taught to compartmentalize. When I'm in surgery, nothing else matters but my skill, my hands, and the patient. When I lose a patient, I'm supposed to handle the situation and move on." He uttered a bitter laugh. "The thing is, you only have so many compartments, so many rooms, and you lose your way to the one just for you."

Silence draped the room. The palpable pain in his voice, thick with feeling, struck her as a new emotion from him. Suddenly, he wasn't Dr. Tanner, the hunky wonder doc, or Justin, the dependable rock, but a man with layers. She took a chance in peeling back one of those layers. "The death of your parents is locked up in one of those rooms."

Justin met her gaze. "I guess so." He raked a hand through his short-cropped hair.

His gesture, Marissa now recognized, signaled him thinking through his next move. She grew quiet and waited for him to expand.

"I was a sophomore in college at Notre Dame. Wendy was a senior up at Northwestern in Chicago. My parents were flying in to spend the weekend with me." He smiled. "My mom liked flea markets. She could spend hours looking at old furniture or artwork. She loved those jars. What do you call them?"

"Mason jars?" Marissa tucked both feet under her.

Justin nodded. "I never knew Mason jars could be so captivating. Anyway, Mom wanted to go to the flea market near town. Dad liked to think of himself as a serious Army general, and he was, but with my mom, he became just another sucker hooked by a beautiful woman."

Thinking of her own parents, Marissa smiled.

"My mother hated flying, but endured every flight Dad coaxed her on. A close friend of our family owned his own plane and volunteered to bring my parents to Indiana." Justin paused, his jaw rigid and his gaze focused on the patterned carpet. "I arrived at the airport in time to witness the plane go down and burst into flames. I remember charging down the runway. Being stopped by either the police or the firefighters. I don't know which. My first thought was maybe I could help them, start CPR...something. In one instant, they were all gone, and I couldn't do a thing to help them."

"How horrifying. I'm sorry." Marissa wanted to climb into Justin's lap and kiss away the pain. Or at least try. "Crazy how life changes in a second."

A knock sounded on the door.

Justin crossed the room and squinted through the peephole before opening the door to room service. Once the attendant left, he took a big gulp of water.

She sipped her tea, the warm liquid soothing her throat.

"You didn't have to order tea just because I'm not drinking."

"I don't like drinking alone." She hadn't been in the mood for anything heavy, so she'd ordered a yogurt parfait. She dipped a spoon into the mixture and stirred the yogurt, granola, and fruit.

"You're not alone." Justin sliced his turkey sandwich in half and took a bite.

She smiled. "I guess not. You're not a drinker?"

He put down his sandwich. "David didn't tell you? I'm a recovering alcoholic."

She paused, her spoon in midair. "I didn't know. The best man is supposed to give a toast. I would have ensured we had non-alcoholic champagne." Justin appeared so put together. She couldn't imagine him losing control of himself to such a degree.

"My affair with alcohol had been brief, but intense. Right after my last deployment, a bottle of scotch seemed a better friend than anything human. I broke up with that friend five years, three months, and four days ago."

"Did you find quitting hard?"

"Not as hard as you'd think." He dug into his pocket and flashed a bronze sobriety chip. "Wendy went ballistic. She's more motherly to me since our parents are gone. One day, I realized how pathetic I was, so I put away the bottle. I needed to be there for Sam. I love that little girl, and she didn't deserve another absent man. Her father had already exited her life."

Marissa stared at Justin, her opinion of him on an upward slope. She reflected on the two men who'd called themselves friends. To her knowledge, David hadn't confided in Justin about his activities or expressed any concern for his life. Yet, David made him best man. She slammed down her spoon, the clanging of china more pronounced in the quiet room. "I feel like I don't know anything."

They lapsed into another period of silence.

"Can I ask you something?"

Justin nodded.

"Where was David at the time of your parents' death?"

"Around somewhere."

"I mean, what did he do?"

Justin shook his head. "Marissa, I don't think..."

"I'd really like to know. Please."

"I didn't see him for over a week. I left him a message, but he had hooked up with a girl he met at a party and didn't return my message right away."

"When you did see him, what did he say?"

Justin pursed his lips. "He said, sorry about your bad luck."

"Like you spun the wheel and got parents' death on unlucky number thirteen?" Her voice dripped with bitterness, but David's unfeeling behavior no longer surprised her. She'd seen the ugly side of him before. "How could you still maintain a friendship?"

Justin sighed and placed his sandwich back on the plate. "David doesn't mean to be a complete asshole all the time. He lost his way, and all the crap he got involved in had been his way of finding something to believe in, something he could win at. Something was missing in his life."

"At the risk of others he claimed to love?" she asked with an incredulous tone, throwing up her hands. "How could he have been an effective Army officer with such a selfish outlook? You both were in at the same time, how did he perform as an officer?" Marissa leaned toward him.

He ran a hand through his hair, his biceps protruding as his arm flexed. "He received an honorable discharge, but we were in different units with different jobs."

"That's a safe answer. You were his best friend." She waited for him to offer her more. When nothing came, she continued. "You served in Iraq, too. You put your life on the line to care for the injured. Why didn't David have the officer and gentleman demeanor?" Her body tensed.

"Marissa, everyone in the military isn't the same. We may dress the same and follow orders, but in the end, we're all different people."

She studied him, sure he held something back. "What's a deployment like? Maybe David had issues. A lot of soldiers come back different, right? What about your re-entry?"

Justin stood, took two big steps toward the window, and stared out. "What no one ever says is once you are in battle, training is important, but luck determines whether you walk out or are carried out. One step to the left, and your life could be over. The understanding of the slim line you're life is balanced on plays with your mind. Everyone coming back has a pretty hefty adjustment period. Dealing with re-entry is all individual, and for some, very private."

Was he warning her not to delve further? The pain in his voice told her something had happened. Once again, she wanted to comfort him, but something kept her glued to her seat. Was Justin's attitude due to his own issues, or did he know something more about David? Perhaps his reaction contained a little of both, but she didn't want to push him.

"I thought I knew David before, but now I realize he never believed in me. In us. At some point, maybe he wanted to, but when I..." Her voice trailed off. Some subjects were off limits. Like Justin, she had a private room, too. She inhaled, letting the air out through pursed lips and decided on a different route. "I found out about Tiffany before I left for Utah. I wanted to hate her, but then I met her at the funeral and couldn't. She seemed nice, but David used her. I don't know the real David Seybold." She stood, opened her purse, and pulled out the note. "Take a look at this."

~

"Where did you find this?" Justin asked, scanning the note's contents.

They sat side by side on the bed as they viewed the note. His respect for Marissa tripled after learning she'd been about to call off the wedding. She deserved better than David, better than him. Her willingness to talk about her issues with David deepened their bond, but he sensed she held something back. He admitted to being an alcoholic, he admitted to the pain of losing his parents, but he couldn't quite admit his failure in Iraq. The deaths of so many people, especially Laura, settled in uneasy fashion on his conscience. Harboring deep anxieties seemed a common trait between him and Marissa.

"I found this note in the bag from his gym locker. Do you know what it means?" She read the note aloud.

June 20, 1323 hrs

BL 299.9 (Brix)

Re: Skies Falling

Defcon 1

He read over the cryptic note. "Not all of it. You know the DEFCON reference. 1323 is 1:23 p.m. in military time."

"David moved our honeymoon back to June 21. I wonder if this had anything to do with his decision?" Marissa stared at the note. "Whatever this is."

Justin recalled David's behavior when he got involved with gambling and drugs—absent for days at a time, and either wanting to borrow small amounts of cash, or flashing large wads of money. The toxicology screen results would take weeks to come back but based on the lack of high value items remaining in Marissa and David's condo, he believed the intruders probably weren't drug dealers interested in collecting on a debt. Plus, Justin hadn't seen any physical signs of drug addiction in David in years.

The detectives had reviewed David's bank account and credit card activity, and so far hadn't asked any follow-up questions nor had they mentioned finding financial issues, so gambling might be a dead end. If David were in financial trouble, he would have come to Justin, like he had in the past. The guy didn't have any qualms about asking for money.

Marissa hadn't said anything about financial problems either. Adding to her feelings of being duped didn't interest him, so he rejected the idea of telling her right now about David's gambling problem. He returned his attention to the note. "Did David talk about any meetings or new clients?"

Marissa gave him an 'are you kidding' look.

"Sorry." He turned over the note in his hand. No other markings were on the printed paper, eliminating the opportunity to recognize if David had written the note.

"Do you know what 'Skies Falling' means?" Marissa finished off the last of her tea and placed the mug on the bedside table.

"No." The hum of the air conditioner resonated with the hum of Justin's brain as he tried to make some connection to the words on the note. He re-read the note, zeroing in on the word "Skies".

"Skies Falling." Justin paused and then jerked his head up. "Skies International. That's the company Tiffany works for." Justin pulled out his phone and, within seconds, he located a website. "Skies International is a company based in New York and here in D.C. They have divisions covering energy, health, finance, commercial real estate, and agriculture."

"Hmm, what does DEFCON One have to do with a company like Skies International?" Marissa touched her neck and winced at the flash of pain.

The military took DEFCON One as a critical situation, so what could David's version mean? He'd been discharged from active duty, so the note probably had no relation to an actual military operation. Justin jumped off the bed and crossed the room. Staring out of the window into the inky blackness of nightfall, he let the darkness penetrate his thoughts. Laura loved D.C. at night, but she'd never see this sight again. He shook away the thought, moved his gaze lower, and the lights of the city brightened the night. "We can assume this note was meant for David since you found it in his bag, but who wrote it?"

Marissa pointed to a spot on the paper "Does BL 299.9 mean anything to you?"

Justin shook his head. "Nothing." He turned from the window and threw the note on the table. "We also have to accept the possibility this note means nothing, at least in terms of David's murder."

"You don't believe that, do you?"

Justin tried to mask his surprise. Sure, anyone could come to the same conclusion regarding his opinion about this note, but he perceived her assumptions to be much deeper, more visceral, although he couldn't pinpoint why. He scratched his head. *Stupid. Now, I'm some love struck teenager who is positive I have this deep connection with her.*

"We're getting nowhere and it's almost midnight. Why don't you get some rest?" He moved toward the adjoining door. "Knock if you need anything."

After placing the "do not disturb" sign on his door, he slid onto the bed and leaned against a pillow propped up on the headboard. Unable to get the mysterious note or the attack on Marissa off his mind, he flipped on the television. Finding an episode of *Star Trek*, he recalled a recurring debate with David on the best Starfleet captain, Kirk or Picard. Justin appreciated Kirk's leadership but questioned his reliability. A sexy alien could easily sidetrack Kirk. Picard, the stable, dependable leader, would go down with the ship. David maintained team Kirk status, proclaiming even alien women loved him, like sex appeal equated to great leadership.

Ten minutes later, a knock on the adjoining door interrupted his musings. After he opened the door, he tried to keep his gaze on Marissa's face but his efforts were in vain—he couldn't keep his eyes off her sensuous body. Judging by her wet hair, she'd taken a shower, and although she wore a T-shirt and shorts, the outfit had to be the sexiest he'd ever seen.

"I'm sorry to bother you, but can we keep this door slightly open?

I'm not usually one for nightlights or anything, but I don't want to feel like I'm alone."

"Ah, sure. No problem." *In fact, I can come in and keep you company. Wait, now I'm playing the role of Kirk. Great.*

She paused, biting her lip. "Thanks for talking to me. David couldn't manage much in the way of conversation the last few months." She scrunched her nose. "Sorry, I can't keep my bitterness in check. Not attractive."

"No problem." He paused. "I don't have a carry permit in D.C., but I have my weapon and I'll use it if I have to."

She nodded and placed her hand on the door, inches from his. With her slight movement, he inhaled a whiff of her fresh lavender scent. He fought the urge to pull her into his arms.

"Goodnight, Justin." She moved the door a couple inches closer to the jamb and retreated further into her room.

She was beautiful. He'd do anything to keep her safe. The question was: could he?

Chapter 21

Dawn broke over Washington, D.C., bathing the city in the soft hue of the new morning sun. The city yawned to life with a few early risers out for a run and a trickle of pre-rush hour traffic.

Sipping his coffee, Justin stared at the country's power nucleus and speculated about whom David had angered. People here usually didn't forgive and forget. One had to have thick skin and a strong heart to deal with the sharks in this town.

His thoughts drifted to Marissa. The image of her standing at the door last night remained. Her simple request to leave the door open had him wanting to pound the masked guy who'd assaulted her.

A light knock on the door shook aside his thoughts.

"Can I come in?" Marissa asked. She stood in the doorway, dressed in a pair of jeans, a light jacket opened to reveal a yellow tank top peeking out.

He couldn't help appreciating her curves. Although he doubted she intended to look sexy, she was. Her brown hair, tousled in a mass of soft waves, hung past her shoulders. Justin found himself in awe. Looking away, he answered, "Yes." Then added, "I didn't know what you wanted, so I ordered coffee, bagels, and yogurt. What do you normally eat in the mornings?"

"Usually just a strawberry smoothie, but coffee sounds great." Closing the adjoining door, she crossed to the small round table and sat. "I thought we could discuss the note again after breakfast." She tossed her purse on a chair and picked up the mug. Blowing across the top of the liquid, she took a sip and winced.

"I thought you might like the yogurt, since your throat is probably still sore."

Despite her sexy appearance, her pale face and the nasty bruises on her neck reminded him of the horror she'd endured.

Marissa nodded and tore open the top of the strawberry yogurt cup.

Justin sensed a change in her quiet attitude. *Did she have a bad night?*

Her hands shook as she stirred the yogurt.

When he connected with her gaze, he saw apparent anger burning in her green eyes. "What's wrong?"

She placed the yogurt on the table. "You were in college with David and remained friends afterward. You *have* to know more about him."

How do I explain David had so many vices he probably did something to get himself killed? David had been a good guy a long time ago, and the memory of that David kept the friendship going from Justin's end. They had fun as guys, and Justin could count on him. Then things changed. Snippets of the old David remained, but a new darkness had invaded him. "You're right, I knew a lot about David. I even knew about Tiffany."

"You and David just let me go on looking like a fool?" She jumped up, knocking the chair back. "Planning a wedding, enduring my mother's endless calls about flowers and cake? I'm such an idiot." Her gaze bored into his.

"So I should have popped in and informed you your fiancé was cheating? What would you have said?"

Frowning, she chewed her lip.

"Marissa, I know all this is a huge shock and your life is upside down, but I promise you, I have no idea why David got himself killed. If that's the theory we're going with."

"I just don't know who to trust. I keep asking myself: what else don't I know? What other surprise is around the corner? I need to go back to my room." She marched to the adjoining door.

Justin grabbed her hand. "Don't go." The minute he touched her, he felt her tense. He let go. "I have a meeting with Neal Wingate this morning. He and David were very close. I'm convinced he knows something." He paused. "I want you to trust me." He stepped closer. "I care about you."

The best man title had been both an honor and a curse. He'd wanted to tell Marissa marrying David would lead to heartache, and not because he selfishly wanted her for his own, but because he understood David, a narcissistic prick with women. However, best man duties certainly didn't include breaking up the couple.

Justin cursed himself. Alarm bells rang inside his head. Do not get involved, do not allow yourself to fall. She almost married his dead best friend. Warning bells be damned, he wasn't about to let her walk out. His first priority remained keeping her safe, so he should shove aside his feelings. But just this once…

He drew her into his arms.

He had failed Laura and wouldn't make the same mistake with Marissa. He couldn't.

He wanted to keep her close, bury himself in her, but he let go, almost taking his breath with her.

Standing inches apart, he stared into her captivating green eyes, unsure if he'd exhaled or not. The curve of her lips transfixed him, and he wanted to touch them. He wanted to feel her skin on his again. "I'm sorry."

"Justin…"

Scuffling sounded from Marissa's room.

He pulled her away from the door, thankful she'd closed the adjoining door when she entered the room.

"Did you remove the "do not disturb" sign?" Justin whispered, grabbing his cell phone from its charger and his gun from the bedside table.

Her gaze fixated on the gun. "No, the sign is still on the door."

Justin crossed the room and pressed his ear to the door. The slamming of drawers confirmed his suspicions. "Someone's in there."

Marissa's eyes widened. She picked up her purse and slung the strap across her body as he grabbed her hand.

After opening his room door, he peered down the hallway, gun pointed outward.

All clear.

"Let's go!"

THEY WERE HALFWAY DOWN the corridor when the hall door to Marissa's room burst open.

She turned back, and for a brief moment, her gaze locked with the intruder.

Obsidian eyes stared back. Evil eyes.

"Justin, it's him!" Marissa's heart galloped in her chest.

The man didn't wear a mask, but the chill down her spine told her the gun toting man had been the intruder who attacked her in Justin's house. She'd never forget those black eyes.

Evil Eyes bore down on them, along with another man she'd never seen. The thundering of their shoes boomed in her ears.

Justin tightened his grip on her hand and tugged her along.

Evil Eyes and his partner were now fully alerted, like bloodhounds tracking a scent.

Marissa stumbled.

Justin caught her. "Don't look back!"

As they rounded a bend in the hall, she heard a pop. The whistling bullet sailed past their heads, lodging in the wall. The faint odor of smoke tapped at her nose. If they didn't find a way out of this narrow hallway, they would surely be shot.

Justin pulled her even faster, his long strides outmatching hers until her legs almost couldn't keep up.

Don't fall.

Justin turned and fired.

After the ringing from the explosive gunshots subsided in her ears, Marissa heard heavy footsteps behind them. The bullets missed them and the pursuit continued.

A bank of elevators loomed ahead. *Please open, please open.*

Another bullet zipped past them, exploding a vase on a nearby table.

Marissa screamed.

They were fifty feet from the elevators. A door leading to the stairwell nearby presented another possible way out. If they took the stairs, they would be slowed by having to navigate the steps. The two goons would catch them.

Just then, an older man stepped out of his room.

"Get back inside!" Justin yelled to the startled man.

The old man jumped back into his room.

The elevator doors remained closed. The panel above the elevator ticked off the floors as the car rose. Two more floors. As they got closer, so did the pounding feet.

"What do we do?"

"Keep moving!" He slowed their pace and pushed her behind him into a recessed door opening. Turning, he aimed his gun at the two men. He shot twice, causing them to scramble and duck.

Marissa glanced at the elevator panel. *One more floor.*

They were a few feet from the elevator. With a ding, the door opened. Scrambling the remaining distance, they leapt in as the doors closed at a painfully slow rate. Unaware the elevator had been occupied, Marissa turned to see a young woman, eyes wide, sitting on the floor.

Just as the doors were almost closed, Evil Eyes barreled toward them, his friend close behind. With narrowed eyes almost like slits, Evil Eyes gripped the gun and aimed.

A chill slithered up Marissa's spine. She could almost feel his determination to kill her. His partner pulled up beside him and trained his gun their way, too. Marissa dove to the other side of the elevator.

Another shot fired toward them.

The woman screamed.

Justin slumped against Marissa as the elevator door slid shut.

Chapter 22

"Justin!" Marissa screamed. "Are you all right?"

Leaning on the side of the elevator, he stood and grimaced. "The bullet just grazed me." Blood seeped from his shoulder through his light gray shirt, turning the fabric stormy, but the injury would have to wait. He glanced at the elevator panel. They were going down and would be in the lobby in seconds. They needed a plan. He turned to Marissa. "Are you all right?" He stood and reached down to help her up.

"I'm fine."

Justin tucked the gun in the waistband of his pants, and then turned to the hysterical woman curled up a few feet away. "I won't hurt you. Those were the bad guys." He nodded toward the now-closed elevator doors.

She stared at him through big, weepy eyes and nodded.

Scattered papers were strewn across the elevator floor, ejected from an open briefcase lying on its side next to the woman.

Marissa bent to help her collect the papers, dropping as many as she picked up. "I'm just as scared as you, but he really is a good guy." With shaky hands, Marissa succeeded in grasping a few of the papers, handing them to the woman.

The woman stuffed the papers into her briefcase in haphazard fashion. Her voice wavered as she mumbled a "thank you".

Justin helped the woman stand. "Ma'am, call the police and let them know what happened."

"Th-those men had guns." The woman's eyes were large and she clutched her briefcase against her chest.

Justin stood in front of her. "I know. Those men are not after you. It's us they want. When we get to the lobby, I want you to head directly to the front desk."

She nodded, her chest moving in rapid motion.

"Ma'am, control your breathing—in and out." Justin demonstrated the breathing technique and she followed suit.

"Good." Justin glanced at Marissa. "Are you okay?" Losing control at this point would be justified but they couldn't afford to deal with emotion yet. He enfolded his hand in hers, giving a gentle squeeze.

When the elevator doors swooshed open, Justin pointed the woman toward the front desk.

As she stumbled away, Justin pulled Marissa closer. "Stay next to me."

The crowd, most of whom were heading in the direction of conference signs, didn't appear aware of what had occurred several floors above. However, a quick glance at the frantic activity of hotel security guards and staff told him reports of gunshots had been made.

No sign of the gunmen, but to be on the safe side, Justin sidled up to a wall near the elevators and with a quick swipe, pulled the red lever of the fire alarm. Lights blinked and sirens wailed as hotel guests stood shocked for a moment before moving toward the exit doors. As Justin expected, more people poured out of the stairwells and into the lobby. In seconds, more activity spread through the lobby, as people rushed for the exits and hotel staff urged others, milling about in apparent disregard of the alarm, to evacuate.

Making their way through the growing crowd, Justin continued searching for the gunmen.

They were halfway to the door when Marissa pulled on his arm. "I think I see them. Near the front doors."

The men were up ahead. *Did they plan on grabbing them in front of all these people?* Bold move, but the men were well trained and probably knew how to capture them even in the presence of a crowd. He and Marissa had not been spotted yet, so he changed course and pulled her perpendicular to the flow of the crowd. They entered the restaurant and exited through another door leading to the conference wing. Throngs of people were moving toward another side exit. They joined this crowd.

When they were outside the hotel, Justin didn't let down his guard. These guys could be anywhere.

As he rounded the corner, he saw three fire trucks pulling up to the front of the hotel, sirens blaring. Fire fighters jumped off the truck and ran into the building. Police cruisers parked close in slanted arrangements, and several officers entered the hotel while others tried controlling the crowd. Justin hated disrupting the guests and his role in the swarm of police and firefighters descending upon the hotel, but these guys meant business.

He and Marissa kept up with the crowd and moved away from the hotel.

"Should we go back and talk to the police? Or call Kearns and Streeter?" Heavy, labored breaths escaped Marissa as she scanned the street.

Justin shook his head. "I'm not convinced who to trust anymore. Let's keep moving." Four blocks away, he scooted them into a breakfast diner.

He chose a booth in the back, facing the majority of the restaurant. "We're safe now."

"Are we? These guys just burst into my room. They shot at us." Marissa downed a huge sip of water the waitress had plopped in front of them when they arrived.

Unlike earlier, her hands were steady as she drank half the glass. Even in the face of danger, she'd managed to keep it together. Some of the most seasoned soldiers could go to pieces in the heat of battle. Once again, his respect for her notched up.

"What about you?" She reached across the table and laid two fingers on his injured shoulder. "You're not bleeding as much but you need to get to a hospital."

"The bullet grazed me. I doubt I'll even need stitches, but after we get our bearings, we'll find a drug store."

"Does it hurt?" Her eyes were soft with concern.

"The sting will wear off."

She rooted through her purse. "I have some pain reliever." Finding the small bottle, she shook out three pills.

He popped them into his mouth and followed with a big gulp of water.

The waitress returned, and they ordered coffee.

She glanced at Justin's bloody shirt. "Are you okay, honey?"

"A cab kicked up a rock while we were walking down the street. It's really nothing." Justin shook his head and smiled.

She reached into her pocket and pulled out a Winnie the Pooh bandage. "Sorry, that's all I've got. My two boys are always in need of a bandage, so I'm used to carrying them."

"Thanks." Justin grinned again, accepted the bandage, and waited for the waitress to leave the table.

Although they were seated well away from the window, Justin continued to scan the restaurant for the two men. "How the hell did they know where we were?" he asked through gritted teeth.

"No one knows we were at that hotel except for Streeter." Marissa's head swiveled toward Justin. Her mouth dropped open. "You don't think..."

"I don't know. When the detectives hear about the shooting at the hotel, they may suspect we were involved. The gunman could have trailed us to the hotel. Somehow, they could have traced our phones or put a tracker on my SUV. I mean, we don't know who these people are, or how powerful."

"We checked in under assumed names. Of all the hotels in D.C.

how could they know to pick this one?" Marissa scrunched the napkin in her hand.

Justin sighed. "We didn't check in with our credit cards so they couldn't have tracked us by a transaction. Unless they've studied everyone in our lives." He finished his water. "That leaves the police. You left one message for Streeter?"

Marissa nodded as the waitress returned with two cups of coffee. Once she moved away from the table, Marissa said, "I didn't call anyone else."

"Let's assume Streeter informed Kearns, so the two detectives are the only ones who knew our location. They could have told someone else."

"Maybe. We've called them every time something has happened. Are you ready to chalk them up as bad guys?" Marissa locked on to his gaze.

"These guys knew where we were, down to the room number. Unless they've got trackers on us, someone is working with them." Justin sipped his coffee. Maybe the infusion of caffeine would spark insight as to the trustworthiness of the detectives.

Marissa placed her cup on the table. "I spoke to Streeter minutes before being attacked at your house. He knew I was alone."

Justin tapped his finger on the table. "Could be a coincidence but I don't like the odds." He paused then inhaled. "Since Halo is staying with Kelly and Craig, I'm assuming you trust them." He hated to implicate her friends but Craig made the hotel reservation.

Marissa's eyes widened. "No. Neither Kelly nor Craig would ever intentionally put my life in danger."

The waitress returned. "Do you want to order breakfast?"

Justin glanced at her. "We're fine with coffee."

"Let me know if you change your mind." The waitress moved on to another table.

Justin overruled eliminating anyone yet but would avoid voicing unsupported suspicions of her friends for now. "I had to ask. I have a meeting with Neal in an hour. I'm hoping he can offer something more about David's recent activities."

"Do you trust him?" Marissa stirred her coffee.

"No. We have known Neal since college. David and Neal had a much closer relationship than Neal and I ever had." Justin sipped his coffee. "Let's just say politics suits Neal. He's arrogant and loves a captive audience. I'll get him talking and hopefully he'll spill some secrets."

"What's our game plan?"

"In the lobby of Neal's office building is a bookstore. I want you to hang out there while I'm with him. Don't leave the store, and stay within sight of other people." *Here I am giving orders.* "I don't mean to be domineering."

Marissa crinkled her forehead. "I've never been in a situation like this. You obviously know how to handle a gun and it's been awhile for me, so I'll yield to you on this one." She smiled.

He grimaced as he reached across the table and took her hand. His wound stung, but he'd survive. "We'll get through this."

Marissa whispered. "We're being hunted."

Chapter 23

After finding a drugstore, dressing his wound, and darting into a men's store for a new shirt, Justin and Marissa entered the lobby of Neal's office building. Justin stepped into the elevator and waved as the doors slid shut.

Marissa wandered into the bookstore. She strolled through the aisles, unable to concentrate on the books as her eyes remained on the doors, windows, and various store patrons. After ten minutes of aimless meandering, she forced herself to control her breathing and resemble a normal person browsing through a bookstore. She didn't want to draw attention, so she searched for shelves containing books on ballet. *Maybe this will calm my nerves.* She picked up a thick book on the history of dance and flipped through the pages. Fifteen minutes later, Marissa shut the book and glanced at her surroundings.

A mother chasing two young kids bound for the shiny toys of the kids' section whipped past her. An older man, deep in a history book, sat close by, and a young woman with multiple piercings pulled several books off the Art History shelf.

All appeared normal, but her life had rocketed into something unrecognizable. She'd landed in a world where everyone carried a badge of suspicion. How long would this feeling dominate her life? Would she always need to look over her shoulder and wonder if Evil Eyes and his partner lurked around the next corner?

She moved to the travel section where a glossy pictorial on Virginia caught her eye. The book detailed various towns in Virginia. Included in the pictorial were photos of Virginia Beach, the state-house in Richmond, majestic scenes of the Blue Ridge Mountains, the farmlands of the Shenandoah Valley region, Historic Jamestown, and interesting trivia of small towns around the state. A chapter on a haunted library in Fauquier County caught her attention. The ghost of Civil War hero Colonel William Chapman was said to haunt the Edgehill Farm, belonging to his wife's descendants.

Something about the story sparked a thought. She stared at the book

"Such a frightening tale," a woman said in an English accent.

Marissa jumped.

Dressed head-to-toe in red, the woman stood a few inches shorter than her, and wore a large, wide-brimmed hat covering most of her face. The woman kept her gaze directed at the bookshelves.

"I suppose so." Something appeared familiar about the woman, but Marissa couldn't pinpoint how she knew her.

"Ghosts are a curious phenomena. I've heard our departed loved ones check in on us from time to time. They could be standing beside us right now. I suppose some may be more restless than others, perhaps those who have made enemies here." She drew out the word 'here' so it sounded more like a hiss. The old woman ran a gloved finger along a thick animal encyclopedia.

A chill slithered up Marissa's spine. She took a step away. "I need to get going."

"Animals are exceptional beings," the old woman continued. "They can carry special power, the ability to connect with humans, to sense danger. Amazing creatures."

"Yes, they are."

"I had a dog once, when I was a young girl, a pup. You know how puppies are, they chew and get into things. One day, this puppy chewed a pair of my father's shoes. Black-and-white Stacey Adams. He was furious. He shot the dog right in front of me. I hated my father, but later I learned." She paused and continued caressing the book. "Actions have consequences. The stupid dog sealed his fate. He had to die."

Stale air swooshed down on Marissa, yet beads of sweat erupted on her face. Her breath caught as she closed her eyes. The woman seemed to suck the air from the room. Marissa placed her hand on the bookshelf to steady herself. When she opened her eyes and turned the woman had vanished.

Marissa raced out of the bookstore. She scanned the lobby. No woman in red. Marissa turned and bumped into a man. As she glanced up her heart shuddered. "Craig, what are you doing here?"

THE SLICK, contemporary offices matched the occupant. Neal Wingate sat behind his large glass desk and leaned back in his chair. He cradled the phone in the crook of his neck as he flipped through the papers stacked in front of him. A gray suit jacket hung on a coat rack in the corner next to a glass wet bar. Two white leather sofas, adorned with yellow and orange pillows, sat at an angle partially facing floor-to-ceiling windows offering a view of the Capitol from the ninth floor perch.

An assistant shut the door after offering Justin a beverage, which he declined.

Neal waved him to a gray fabric chair in front of his desk. He held up a finger and mouthed he'd be finished in a second.

Justin expected to see a picture of his wife, Susan, on the corner of his desk. Instead, the only pictures in the office were of Neal—and sometimes Susan standing next to him in the supporting spousal role —with various VIPs. Justin spotted world leaders, important business heads, celebrities, along with the current and two former US presidents.

"I don't care about the polling, I need that district. Set up some face-to-face interviews. ASAP." Neal slammed down the phone then his expression erupted into a wide grin. "What the hell brings the mighty Dr. Justin Tanner into my lair of deceit and corruption?"

Justin returned the smile. "Time to see how the other half lives." He surveyed the office and raised an eyebrow. "Not bad."

"Who would have thought a schmuck like me would end up in an office like this, and a few months from having the title Senator in front of my name?"

"You're awfully confident." Justin wanted to punch the grin off his smug face.

"The right attitude is half the battle." Neal rose, slapped a polished handshake on Justin, and strolled over to the bar. "Water? Anything?" he asked, pouring juice into a small glass.

"No, thanks. Juice is pretty tame for you. Losing your edge?"

Neal threw his head back and laughed. "I never touch booze before noon." He took a long sip of juice and turned to Justin. "I hear you're a teetotaler now. Some guys just can't handle the hard stuff."

Justin shrugged. "Couldn't afford to fog my vision. Besides, alcohol puts on the pounds." He made a show of glancing at the slight paunch of Neal's stomach.

Neal's expression clouded before he reeled his emotion back. The consummate politician wouldn't be caught allowing a jab to penetrate.

"So, are you here to make a donation?" Neal returned to his desk and placed the glass onto a coaster with his photo.

"I gave on the way in." Justin ran his hand across his chin stubble. "You're a busy man, I'll get to the point. In addition to killing David, the murder also took his computer."

"Weird. What is the status of the investigation?" Neal took a sip of his juice.

Justin shrugged. "No real leads. Probably a professional kill."

Neal held the glass in midair. "A professional hit? Geesh. What was he up to?"

Justin straightened in his chair. "I thought I'd ask you. I never got a chance to talk to David in the days before he died but maybe you did."

Neal placed the glass back on the coaster and exhaled. "I've been embroiled in a campaign so I have no idea about Dave's recent deeds or misdeeds."

"When did you talk to him last?"

Neal scratched his ear, glancing away at the floor. "What are you moonlighting as a detective? Aren't there enough sick people?" He chuckled.

Justin smiled and crossed his legs. "By the stall tactic I gather you had spoken to him recently."

Neal pursed his lips then blew out a breath. "Dave called me about six months ago. He complained about the wedding and the cost of getting married. Said Marissa would probably want kids soon and they would be another drain on his money. I told him to hold firm and nix the kid. She's hot with a banging body so we both agreed he should stay with her, for now. You know reap the benefits." Neal grinned.

Justin clenched his fists. If he'd heard this from dribble from David he'd have gotten great pleasure out of pounding his friend's face in. Perspiration erupted on his forehead as he adjusted in his seat. He needed Neal to continue so he inhaled and clamped his jaw shut. Justin nodded. "He called you to gripe?"

Neal shrugged. "In a word, but he also asked me to introduce him to some heavy hitters in town to propel his business to the next level. I invited him to a campaign party."

Justin rested his elbows on the arms of the chair. "Did he get any bites?"

Neal laughed. "Bro, I don't know. My gig, my crowd. I focused my attention on the donors, i.e. the money." He paused as he stared off in space for a couple of seconds. "I met this beautiful woman who happened to be interested in my senatorial career. She gets off being around the power set. I left the party fairly early to go, you know...talk more policy with her." He waggled his eyebrows and grinned.

"You gotta do what you gotta do. How does Susan feel about

sharing you with your constituents and backers?" Justin crossed his arms to keep them from throttling the bloviating windbag.

Neal grinned. "She knows I'm a busy man." He paused before adding, "Plus, I scored a huge donation."

"Great for you she was in a charitable mood." Justin didn't think Neal caught his sarcastic tone.

"Oh, absolutely. I love this town. I got tired of the K Street lobbying game. Time to move up." He gulped the remainder of his juice. "Even with his own consulting firm, Dave wanted more."

Justin nodded. "Nice of you to help?"

"I know a lot of important people so I made a few introductions." Neal paused and stared at the ceiling. "I believe I introduced him to Todd Wenger, CEO of Wenger and Associates, Harold Silva, CEO of Skies International, and a few others."

Justin straightened in his chair. Skies International. *There's that name again.* Definitely not a coincidence. "Did anything materialize after those introductions?"

Neal made a show of checking his Rolex watch. "I'm not his flunky. I don't know. He called me a few weeks back and said he had something big going on. I didn't ask questions but he said he'd be contributing some major dough to my campaign. Too bad, he will never achieve top-dog status, but shit happens, right?"

Justin clamped his jaw. "Easy to say while you're still breathing."

"Oh, I miss the guy. We were planning this insane victory party after my win. We used to have some great times." Neal grinned.

"Yeah, you did."

"We partied hard back at ND, but I never thought Dave would end up like this." He paused. "I remember when I arrived on campus from the hills of Kentucky, a face full of acne and skittish as hell. I didn't come from money, my father was out of the picture, and my mother drifted in and out of relationships. I felt out of place being at such a prestigious university, but Dave didn't seem to care. When you and Dave arrived on campus and treated me like one of the guys, I'll admit I went a little overboard."

Justin hiked his eyebrows. "A little overboard? Maybe you've forgotten how many times I had to rescue you and David. Walked you home in a drunken stupor, slipped you past dorm monitors, supplied you with coffee to sober up, and prodded you awake for classes."

Neal shrugged. "Okay, you were a Boy Scout. Thanks, man. But I had the time of my life, and I have to think those experiences were priming me for all this. I never would have had the balls to enter politics, but my first win in student government hooked me. I'll admit politics are like a drug."

"We both know what happens when you're hooked—you'll do anything to catch the next high." Justin reined in his disgust. How could he have such disdain for this man when he had his own demons? At least he could say he constantly worked to conquer his, but Neal wore his like a badge of honor. The man's sliminess fit politics perfectly. On more than one occasion, Justin had witnessed Neal's penchant for going after his opponents. From drumming up phony marital affairs to making minor issues into major scandals, his anything-goes approach had no limits.

Neal grinned. "Nothing better than sparring with your opponent. The key is to make sure he's the dirty one, and you come out looking like Mr. Clean. Politics has no Boy Scouts, at least not for long. It's a nasty business, but a lucrative one in power and dollars, and I'm following the golden trail straight to 1600 Pennsylvania."

David had once been entangled with some shady characters, but had he continued on the same path from his college days? Aside from gambling, David had also stepped into the illicit world of drugs. At first it started off as recreational then moved to a predictable routine.

"A pity you were relegated to cleanup man. Too busy studying to go out and play."

Justin shrugged. "I had a thankless job—keeping you two out of jail. You're welcome."

Neal leaned back and laughed. "Touché." He got up from his chair and rounded the desk. "I'm sorry about David. Why don't you leave the murder investigation to the professionals and go back to sewing up people? Oh, and coming to the aid of poor damsels in distress. She's gorgeous, but a bit crass on your end, going after Dave's girl, especially from someone as principled as you."

Justin jumped up and moved his hands to his side, willing his fists to refrain from damaging Neal's face. "As usual, you have no idea what the hell you're talking about." Squaring his shoulders, he stepped back. "Say hi to Susan for me. Thanks for your time. Senator."

Chapter 24

The hour ride back to the compound didn't tamp down the high. Vivian hadn't stretched her acting chops in some time. *How exhilarating.*

"Edward, I'd like some tea." Vivian breezed into her office and stripped off her large red hat and gloves. What a wonderful day. Punching in her code, she opened the safe, extracted the emerald ring from a blue velvet case and slid the ring on to the third finger of her left hand. The ring would have been a sure giveaway, and she wanted Marissa to remain in the dark a while longer. "I could have been an Academy Award-winning actress. The English accent had been a brilliant move."

Edward nodded and stood at the door. "Congratulations on a successful operation."

"Yes, very exciting. Although, the time is nearing when I have to give up these games and allow Bane to pounce." She clasped her hands together. "I'm having such fun."

"Will there be anything else, ma'am?"

"Get Bane on the phone. And hurry with my tea." Vivian turned on her computer to check her email and review the pulse of her employees. Although she wasn't a big fan of computers, she recognized their necessity. "Stupid people," she said as she read through a number of comments on the Skies Intranet about Harold. Idiots were worried the old man had dementia and wandered off. Even some of her board members were questioning his whereabouts. She had put safeguards in place to keep her identity unknown to the employees but board members were bound by contract to keep her identity secret. When she communicated with the employees, she forwarded her messages to one of the board members to disseminate under their name.

With a sigh, Vivian straightened in her chair. She typed a short email message to announce Harold Silva had decided to retire. The stress of the position had become too much. Vivian indicated he had decided to move to an undisclosed location for much-needed rest and relaxation, and would appreciate privacy. A new CEO would be announced at a later date. She finished the email. *That should satisfy the buffoons.* Their beloved Harold had definitely been retired. She glanced out toward the Black Garden and smiled.

Her desk phone beeped. Edward informed her Bane waited on the line and he would forward her email cloaked as one of the board members.

Vivian punched the blinking button. "Good work today. I only wanted to scare them."

"We didn't expect the doctor to shoot back, but we were prepared."

"I'm sure he believes he's a worthy opponent. Pull back for now. I have big plans for them, but I want them to relax their guard a little. The next surprise will be much sweeter. The girl told you she didn't know about the data. When I'm finished, she'll know exactly what data you were referring." She disconnected from Bane and turned toward the rattling of china.

Edward arrived with her Darjeeling tea. He placed the silver tray on the corner of her desk, gently set the elegant cup and saucer in front of her, and quietly left the room.

Vivian inhaled the floral aroma of the hot beverage before taking a sip. Again, she picked up the phone. A few seconds later, she reached her head of security. "Are the facilities ready?"

"Almost. We are doing final checks on cell integrity. Several months have passed since we've hosted a visitor," Bill Williams replied.

"Just get it done." Vivian hung up.

Her private phone rang. The day had turned into a flurry of activity, but she needed to ensure all pieces were in order. "Yes," she said into the phone, the small screen alerting her to the identity of the caller.

"I see you got the information on their whereabouts."

Vivian stood and walked to the window. "Yes, I'm pleased I can count on your continued cooperation."

"Of course. I'm looking forward to this last test and my subsequent induction," the voice said.

"Well, let's take this one step at a time. I'm delighted with your eagerness and enthusiasm. I recall my induction ceremony." She closed her eyes, remembering the thrill of gushing blood. The intense red of newly spilled blood. The metallic scent. The sticky pull when exposed to the elements. Beautiful.

"I'm excited to one day take the helms of the organization."

"Your actions indicate so, but don't get ahead of yourself. The final task is fast approaching."

She ended the call and punched a button to connect another.

"Vivian, it's good to hear from you. How can I be of service?"

"Your zeal is both endearing and stupid." Vivian chuckled and then turned serious. "Never show your desperation." She mentally placed a black mark next to the name of the speaker. Her successor must never display weakness.

Silenced ensued, and then the sound of someone clearing a throat. "I won't apologize for my commitment to you and The Order, but I accept your advice."

Vivian nodded. "Better. Now, I'd like an update."

"Certainly. The doctor just left the offices with Marissa. She appeared shaken, very pale and nervous. They got into a cab and headed west past the building."

"The girl reacted just as I expected. Good work. You know your next assignment."

"Yes. I'm prepared."

Vivian disconnected, but continued to hold the phone. The night of her induction had been special in more ways than one. She caressed her belly. The lifeblood had flowed from her body. If she had allowed herself to feel, she would have grieved, but the outcome made her a better leader.

Penance proved a harsh lesson. Women and children were often spared from the perils of war or danger, like precious pearls exempt from the stain of blood on their white veneer. Vivian had learned the price of greatness often meant sacrifice, which didn't exclude women and children. Or even puppies.

Her father had no hesitation exerting his power over his own wife. He held loyalty in high regard. When he saw Mary smile at one of his board members, he enacted penance. She'd been beaten severely, and then a few years later killed and buried in the Black Garden.

Vivian, only nine years old at the time of her mother's death, carried contempt for her father for many years. However, as she got older and studied the principles of The Order, she understood. She'd not only admired her father for his tough choices, but she also came to recognize his weakness.

Russell made demands, but he didn't always ensure they were carried through. Russell Sinclair, Grand Commander of The Order, wasn't so smart.

Vivian smiled and rubbed her belly. Penance could be exacted on others, but she stood above reparation. She'd defied her father's decree. She proved *she* maintained control, and made a far more powerful Grand Commander than he could ever have been.

Whoever thought someone as powerful as me could also be a mother?

Chapter 25

When Justin emerged into the lobby from the elevator, he spotted Marissa in conversation with a well-dressed man. As he approached the duo, he recognized the man. What was Craig doing here? He searched his memory for Craig's occupation but came up empty. Could he have been responsible for leaking their location? Marissa had been certain he would never place her in harm's way.

"Craig." Justin extended his hand. "Weird seeing you here."

Craig pumped Justin's hand and smiled. "I finished a meeting up on the fourth floor and I ran into Marissa." He paused and stepped closer to Justin. "Are you guys okay? She told me what happened at the hotel."

Justin kept his expression neutral. "We're both fine. You didn't mention where we were to anyone, did you?"

"Absolutely not. If anything happened to Marissa, Kelly and I would be devastated." He placed an arm around Marissa, giving her a quick squeeze before releasing her.

"Please keep our location confidential." Marissa chewed her lip.

"Sure. Anything I can do, just call." Craig shifted the laptop case in his hand. "What are you guys doing here?" He leaned closer to

Justin and Marissa. "I thought you two were supposed to be in seclusion."

Justin met his gaze. "I met with Neal Wingate upstairs."

Craig nodded. "I didn't know Neal had an office in this building. Seems like a good guy."

Justin studied Craig. Could he be trusted? "What do you do for living?" Justin asked.

"Construction management." Craig pumped his thumb upward. "One of the building tenants is considering new offices. It's a huge contract so wish me luck."

Justin nodded. "We better get going. Thanks again for your help and good luck with your contract."

Marissa hugged him. "Take care of my two guys and tell Kelly I'll call soon."

After hailing a cab, Marissa and Justin headed away from Neal's office. Justin asked the driver to take them toward Reagan National Airport.

"What's wrong?" Justin sensed something had happened.

She gripped her phone as she gave him a brief rundown of the odd lady in red.

Justin pulled his phone from his pocket and then took hold of hers. As they rounded a corner, he rolled down the window and tossed both phones out.

"What are you doing?" Marissa turned to see her phone splintered in pieces.

"Our phones can be tracked. I'm not taking any chances."

Marissa stared out of the window for most of the way but continued to hold on to Justin's hand.

He didn't dare move for fear she'd retract her hand. Having her close made him want more. On impulse, he pulled her closer.

She gave him a quick glance before she laid her head on his shoulder.

When those green eyes bored into his... *Ah, how am I supposed to resist?*

As they neared the airport, Justin had the driver drop them off at a bank. Once the cab drove away, he explained they couldn't return to his SUV parked in the hotel garage. Instead of renting a car and enduring the hassle of paying by cash, he'd take this last chance and pull a chunk of money from his bank account to buy a used car. From now on, they would have to survive without credit cards.

"Justin, I can't ask you to do this." Marissa clutched his hand.

"You're not asking me." He marched into the bank. "We're in this together."

She caught up to him and spoke in a low voice. "Then let me raid my bank account, too."

"No time, unless you have an account here."

She shook her head.

An hour later, they were inside a six-year-old Jeep SUV. As he drove off the car lot, Justin glanced over at Marissa. Concern lapped over him. They'd been shot at and barely escaped with their lives. Events weren't adding up, and he wouldn't let Marissa pay the price for ignoring his gut.

He drove an hour away from the bank and car dealership. If they were tracked based on their activity, he didn't want to be anywhere in the vicinity of their latest financial transactions. With Marissa's hand in his during the entire drive, he hoped she'd relax a little.

He'd spent years working in a war zone. The military war hospital in Iraq regularly took on enemy fire. Exploding bombs and warning sirens were part of daily life, and although he never took the warnings for granted, he grew accustomed to donning his Kevlar vest and helmet. All the while he understood the enemy didn't care who he was, only that he wore an American flag on his uniform. The war he and Marissa found themselves took a much more personal slant.

After picking up burner phones, more clothes, and essentials at a nearby mall, Justin pulled into the parking lot of a Mexican restaurant beginning to swell with the lunchtime crowd. Safety in numbers, he hoped, as they were seated in a booth.

A petite waitress with a bright smile took their order and deposited a bowl of salsa with a basket of tortilla chips on the table.

Once they were alone, Justin said, "Tell me more about the woman in the bookstore."

"Creepy, in a word. She talked about ghosts, and actions having consequences." Marissa paused as the waitress returned with their beverages. She took a gulp of water and continued. "She wore red, head-to-toe. I couldn't see her face because of the large red hat, but I'm positive this person was the same woman from David's funeral."

"Why?" Justin leaned against the table's edge.

Marissa shrugged. "Both wore gloves, but the woman from the funeral had a large emerald ring. This last woman didn't, and she spoke with an English accent when the woman at the funeral didn't. There's just something...She spoke without much movement or emotion. The same way the other woman did. Both women were the same height and frame."

Justin crumpled his napkin as he pondered the event. "If the book store woman and the woman at the funeral are in fact the *same*, who is she and why does she keep popping up? Are you sure you've never met this woman before?"

"No, I would remember someone so disturbing." Shivering, she took a sip of water. "She seemed to materialize, and then poof, gone."

"Did she mention David?"

Marissa shook her head.

Justin pumped his straw up and down in his glass. "Did you see where she went when she left the bookstore?"

"No. I should have followed her."

"No, you shouldn't have." Justin leaned across the table. "We don't know anything about this woman, or who might have accompanied her. I don't want you taking unnecessary chances. We had enough with the close call on the roof of my house. Your dad would kill me if I let anything happen to you." Justin scooped up salsa on a tortilla chip and took a bite.

She gave the restaurant a sweeping gaze before turning back to him. "Did you learn anything from Neal?"

"He is a jerk and on the path to become a more powerful jerk. He claimed not to know anything, but he invited David to a big donor party to make business contacts. Maybe he angered someone at the party, and they were out for revenge. Hard to tell."

Marissa twirled her napkin. "When was this party? Is this where David met Tiffany?"

"Within the last six months." Justin took a sip of his lemonade. "I don't know if Tiffany attended but Neal introduced David to a couple of CEOs. One of them was Harold Silva of Skies International." Justin swiped a napkin across his mouth. "Recently, David told Neal he had something huge going on. We need to investigate these CEOs, especially this Silva guy."

Marissa nodded. "Worth a try."

Justin picked up another chip. "Okay, no more splitting up. We stay together." He paused and met her gaze. "Something has been bothering me about the note. Tiffany works for Skies International. What if she's somehow involved in this?"

"Do you think she wrote the note?"

"Possibly, but I don't get the sense she would be entangled in something so clandestine. More likely, she'd pass the note, rather than create it. But, I could be wrong."

They paused the conversation to allow the waitress to deliver a platter of fajitas for Justin and veggie quesadillas for Marissa. The savory aroma wafted up Justin's nose, and his stomach gurgled in anticipation. Dodging bullets and dealing with a narcissistic politician hadn't left much time for food.

The events of the day also had him concerned about Marissa. The pallor of her face and dark circles under her eyes led him to conclude fear and sleep deprivation had taken hold. He knew just where they would sleep tonight, and prayed they'd be safe.

After a few minutes of eating in silence, Marissa wiped her mouth. "The date on the note is set for tomorrow. I think I've figured out the exact meeting location."

"What?" Justin lowered his fork with a clang. "Why didn't you say anything earlier?"

"I needed to think it through before I said anything." She pulled the note from her purse and spread the paper on the table. "I believe

BL and Brix means the Brixton Library and 299.9 is a book call number." She tapped the table. "The meeting is at the library."

"You might have a future in detective work, Ms. Nash," Justin said, smiling.

"Only if I'm right."

"How about we keep the appointment and see what happens?"

THE SMALL TOWN OF KEESPORT, Virginia reminded Marissa of the quaint towns from the photography book she'd read at the bookstore. They passed a baseball field, a fruit stand advertising fresh peaches, an ice cream and yogurt shop, and several antique stores.

Justin turned onto Main Street, drove through the town center, circling around a large statue of the town's founder. A stone-faced Oliver Keesport, dressed in traditional cutaway coat and top hat, watched over his town, incorporated in 1894.

As they drove past the Keesport police station, Marissa pondered the trustworthiness of the small-town police department. Would they be helpful?

They headed away from the town center. Marissa, ignoring the air conditioner, which in the older car wasn't as cool as she'd like, lowered the car window. A humid breeze smacked her face while she inhaled the sweet aroma of passing cornfields. Turning from the scenery, Marissa studied Justin. "Do you think this is a good idea? I don't want to endanger your family any more than I already have."

Justin nodded and glanced in the rear-view mirror. "I won't abandon you. We'll be fine for the night, but we'll move tomorrow."

She brushed a strand of hair away from her face. "Are you sure your family is onboard with me staying?"

He turned onto another road, passing a small white church. "We'll be okay. I'm a doctor, and I don't make grand proclamations without good data. Believe me, Uncle Lou is very security-minded. In fact, if we ever get separated, I want you to find your way back here."

Justin spoke with such conviction she gleaned the man represented more than just an uncle. She pulled out her new phone and entered the address and phone number Justin rattled off. Her heart pounded being so near him. She considered his strong profile, his chocolate brown eyes focused on the road. "Okay, one night, and we leave."

"Deal." He nodded.

Five minutes later, they pulled up to the gated entrance of a two-story white colonial house with green shutters, a well-tended lawn, and vibrant roses in full bloom at the front porch. Purple roses on an arched trellis marked a colorful entrance to the backyard.

An older man waved them through the open gate directing them to follow the driveway curving toward the back of the house. Once they were a several yards down the driveway, he jogged over and locked the gate.

Justin parked in front of the four-car garage, hidden from the road.

The back door flew open, and Sam and an older woman stepped out.

Sam bounded down the stairs and jumped into Justin's arms as he got out of the SUV. "Uncle Justin! You got a new car! Guess what? Aunt Iris let me help her make chocolate chip cookies."

"My favorite." Justin hugged the girl and turned to the woman. "Aunt Iris, you have your hands full." He hugged her.

Sam wriggled out of his arms and hugged Marissa. "I'm glad you're here."

Marissa smiled. "Me too."

Slim, with bright white hair and flawless skin, Aunt Iris displayed timeless beauty. A smile lit her face making the skin around her clear brown eyes crinkle at the corners. "I love having my house full of youth."

The man approached and hugged Justin. The tall gentleman had a balding head but, despite being older, his muscles bulged as evidence he took care of himself. His deep voice, both soothing and authoritative, held a warm quality.

"Aunt Iris, Uncle Lou, this is Marissa Nash."

Aunt Iris hugged her in a strong embrace. "You poor thing. We are sorry about your loss." She pulled back and held Marissa's hands. "Such a pretty girl. Lou and I met David for the first time when he and Justin visited from Notre Dame."

"Such a tragedy." Lou embraced Marissa, and then Justin again. "You did the right thing getting everyone out of there. What is the plan for you two?"

"I'm working on it. The police have been less than reliable in keeping her protected, and after today I think we're on our own." Justin took her hand.

A shiver shook her body. Like a lightning rod, Justin's hand sent a jolt of electricity through her. The air grew thick, and the humidity closed in. His strong, muscled chest rippled under his T-shirt. With his busy schedule, she marveled at how he found time for exercise. Keeping up his physique had to take lots of training. As a dancer, she appreciated the hard work, dedication, and pain required to sculpt a body to Adonis-like proportions. With an effort, Marissa shifted her attention from Justin and turned to his aunt and uncle. "Thank you for allowing me to stay here."

"Oh, honey, we're glad to have you both. Justin is always busy, so when we get him, we hold on." Aunt Iris gave him a motherly caress across the cheek.

Wendy joined them. "Are you two okay?" Concern blanketed her face as she gave Marissa's arm a gentle squeeze.

"We're fine." Justin embraced his sister. He glanced at Sam peering into the window of the SUV.

Wendy pulled up her sunglasses and stepped closer to the group of adults, out of earshot of her daughter. "I heard about the intruder. How frightening."

"I'm just happy Justin came home when he did." Marissa glanced his way. For a brief instant, she pictured her and Justin standing there with their children. He'd make a great father. Her gaze moved downward. *Stop with the silly thoughts.*

Plans for her future were a big black hole of unknown. After this threat had ended, then what? She and Justin shared an attraction but where would it lead? Should she even remain in Virginia? With stellar recommendations she could probably land a good job anywhere. But first she'd have to survive.

Sam tugged on Marissa's arm. "Did you bring Halo? Mommy said he went to the doggie hospital."

"No, honey, he's not with us." She stroked the girl's hair. "He was sick, but now he's better and staying with my friends. I'll make sure you two get back together very soon."

"She's been going on and on about Halo," Wendy said, with a shake of her head.

"Uncle Lou and Aunt Iris have a little dog, but he doesn't play with me like Halo does."

Uncle Lou chuckled. "Ernie is old and doesn't have much energy."

"Let's go inside. I've got a roast in the oven for later." Aunt Iris squeezed Marissa's hand as she turned to head back inside.

Sam ran ahead with Wendy and Aunt Iris.

Uncle Lou hung back until Justin nodded, then the older man turned and climbed the stairs with strong, capable strides, disappearing through the back door.

Marissa scanned the surroundings. The house stood on a large plot of land with a dense tree line bordering the property. The mammoth trees and the closed driveway gate offered her some sense of security.

Justin pulled their belongings from the car and set the bags on the ground. "Uncle Lou is also General Lou, retired. No matter the circumstances, you're welcome here."

"Your father and his brother were both generals?" She leaned against the car, the warm sun coating her face.

"Yep. Lou is Air Force and Dad was Army. Lou and Iris don't have children. My parents happily shared Wendy and I. Medicine was a little outside the family business, but I saved face by joining the medical corps. My decision made Lou proud, and I have to think Dad smiled down, too."

She stared at one of the open garage bays with a small metallic purple bike, balls, and sidewalk chalk stored against the wall. She assumed the toys were Sam's. Marissa's heart lurched at the simplicity of a child's toys and the love surrounding Sam. Her child may not have had an involved father but he or she would have had an abundance of love. Marissa's belly fluttered.

Justin shut the SUV door. "Are you ready to go inside?"

She stared at him. This man painted an impressive picture, important to a lot of people. "Justin, if anything happens..."

He pushed a stray tendril away from her face, his hand lingering on her cheek. "I know this is scary, but we're in this together."

She floated toward his massive chest as his large arms encircled her. She rested her head on his muscular pectorals. Warmth and comfort greeted her, making her wish she could remain there longer.

Pulling apart, they gathered their bags and went inside. For the remainder of the evening, she forced her thoughts to stay in the moment. Aunt Iris prepared a delicious dinner, and Marissa enjoyed spending a fun and light evening with the Tanners.

Justin never left her side for more than a few minutes. Several times throughout the evening he'd lean over and ask if she was okay. The gesture warmed her heart, but she couldn't resist once again comparing Justin to David. Justin cared about others. David had only cared about himself. Justin had a way of making her feel important. David had brushed off her feelings. She'd have the rest of her life to determine how she had fallen for David in the first place.

After helping Wendy and Aunt Iris clean the kitchen, they joined Lou, Justin, and Sam in the living room. The large room, decorated in blues and tans, had two oversized sofas and two chairs all facing a fireplace. Twin bookcases stood like sentinels on either side of the fireplace, and the mantel above contained various knick-knacks, family pictures, and even Sam's drawings. The homey atmosphere resembled a picture-perfect room for family gatherings.

Sam pulled Ernie close and the beagle moaned at her rough treatment.

"I miss Halo." Sam patted the dog's head as he collapsed on the floor.

As soon as Marissa sat, she made room for Sam to snuggle up to her.

Sam asked her everything about Halo, from where she got him to how much he ate. Marissa even showed her pictures of Halo she had stashed in her wallet.

After Sam yawned several times, Wendy announced bedtime.

"Ten more minutes, Mom. Please?" Sam whined.

Justin swooped in and lifted Sam. "You want ten more minutes of this?" He tossed her in the air.

"Yes!" She squealed and laughed.

Once he put her down and she gathered herself, she turned to Marissa. "Can you teach me ballet?"

Justin stared at Sam, eyes wide. "Ballet? What happened to soccer?"

"I'm going to be a soccer player-ballet dancer, and then I'm going to be a doctor just like you." Sam put her hands on her hips and cocked her head.

"And what about the Air Force, young lady?" Uncle Lou asked, giving her a frown.

"I forgot. I like the shiny medals Uncle Lou has, and he said I could earn my own if I proved myself."

Wendy laughed. "You certainly can, but you have to work hard and get some sleep." She paused. "I'll let Marissa give you a quick ballet lesson."

Marissa smiled as she stood in front of Sam and showed her first position, and explained about the five ballet positions. "Each position is the basis of more difficult ballet steps."

Sam tried to mimic Marissa's stance.

Marissa helped adjust her foot and arm positioning. "Good. Now let's try second position."

After a few minutes and more help from Marissa, Sam stood in nearly perfect form.

Marissa stood back and surveyed Sam. "You know, you are much better than your uncle at this."

"You gave Uncle Justin ballet lessons?" Sam giggled.

"I tried." Marissa laughed.

"Honey, you're very ambitious. He's all muscle and no grace." Aunt Iris laughed.

"Hey, it was late and I was tired. Besides, Tanner men don't back down from a challenge, huh, Uncle Lou?" Justin nodded and puffed out his chest.

"Come on, Uncle Justin. We can practice together." Sam pulled him up from the sofa.

Wendy pulled her feet under her in the chair. "This should be good."

Marissa guided Justin to a spot next to Sam and she took them through several ballet positions and one beginning sequence. Justin, tall and massive, next to little Sam made a hilarious sight, but when Justin missed a move and groaned as his body hunched over in an awkward position, everyone exploded in laughter.

Sam stopped laughing, and a serious expression clouded her face. "Uncle Justin, you should marry Marissa. She's lovely."

Marissa felt her face flush.

Justin stared ahead and rubbed the stubble on his chin.

Sam glanced at everyone and shook her head. "I heard that on a movie. Mommy said they were London people."

"You mean they were British," Wendy said. "And it's not our business to tell Uncle Justin and Marissa who they should marry." She mouthed "sorry" to them.

Justin bent down to make eye contact with Sam. "You're absolutely right. Marissa is lovely, but neither of us is getting married anytime soon." He kissed her forehead. "Now, go to bed."

Wendy ushered Sam out after the girl kissed everyone goodnight. Returning in fifteen minutes, Wendy resumed her place in her chair. "She's out already."

Aunt Iris had supplied everyone with a beverage while Wendy put Sam to bed.

"Detective Kearns called me this afternoon." Wendy picked up her coffee cup. "She wanted to know where you two were. I'm not sure she believed me when I said I didn't know."

"I figured they'd contact you." Justin shrugged.

Eyebrows hiking upward, Wendy held the cup in midair. "Marissa almost plunged to her death after some crazed man broke into our house. Why aren't you taking their calls?"

"Is that wise, son?" Uncle Lou asked as he leaned forward.

Justin explained the shocking death of his patient and the shootout in the hotel. "We haven't done anything wrong, but I suspect someone associated with the police leaked information about our location. I'm not positive I can trust the detectives."

Uncle Lou clasped his hands together. "Concealed carry firearms in D.C. is illegal. Did you hit either of them?"

Justin shook his head. "Couldn't be helped but I had to consider the hotel guests. There were no injuries. They grazed me, but I'm fine. I'm not sure they were actually aiming to kill us, either." He glanced at Marissa. "We're okay now, and I'll make sure we continue to be."

Uncle Lou nodded. "You're in good hands," he said to Marissa.

She got the impression Justin signaled to Lou to change the subject, so the conversation moved to Wendy and Justin's parents. Marissa enjoyed hearing the happy stories. They sounded like wonderful people, much like Uncle Lou and Aunt Iris, who made Marissa welcome in their home and treated her like one of their own.

"Are you with a ballet company?" Aunt Iris asked.

"No. I co-own a ballet studio, but I'm an accountant by day."

Wendy wrapped her hair in a loose bun. "You've got great posture. Why didn't you pursue dance, if you don't mind me asking?"

Marissa took a sip of tea. "My grandmother inspired my love for ballet and I reached a point where I prepared to audition for Juilliard. A few weeks before my audition, a car slammed into mine and I broke my ankle." She shrugged. "The recovery period gave me time to think. Ballet is beautiful, but not a sustainable long-term career. Logic won out, and I enrolled at UVA."

Justin placed his hand over hers for a brief second.

"I'm happy as an accountant, as boring as the profession might sound. I have the ballet school, perform occasionally, which I feel honors my grandmother."

"Wow, you and Justin are a lot alike. He created the GT Training Center as a tribute to our father. I'm sure you serve your students well, just like the vets and active military we assist." Wendy glanced at her brother, whose eyes blazed, and then she pursed her lips. "My brother hates accolades so I'll go to bed, too."

Aunt Iris stood. "The hour *is* getting late. Marissa, let me show you to your room."

"Once you get acclimated and if you're not too tired come back down. We need to research the men David met at Neal's campaign event," Justin said.

After getting the lay of the upstairs, Marissa closed the bedroom door. The cornflower blue-and-white furniture and accessories reminded her of a tranquil *Better Homes and Garden* photo. A family photo in an oblong dark wooden frame sat on the edge of the white dresser. Marissa picked it up and stared at Justin, Wendy, Aunt Iris, Uncle Lou, and based on earlier pictures she'd seen, General and Mrs. Tanner. The picture must have been taken about fifteen years ago, and depicted a smiling group huddled together in familial companionship. Justin's brown hair and eyes pulled her like polar ends of two magnets. The photo of the happy family added to the room's cozy ambiance. She wanted to grab the picture and snuggle underneath the puffy comforter. Instead, she placed the photo back on the dresser and changed into sweats and a T-shirt.

Twenty minutes later, she and Uncle Lou sat on either side of Justin at the kitchen table as he logged into Wendy's computer.

Justin typed in a name in the search window. Seconds later the screen filled with results. "Todd Wenger is CEO of Wenger and Associates in New York. They are wealth management group." Justin scanned the page. "Before the break in, I had printed a list of the companies recorded as clients on David's website. I don't recall seeing Wenger and Associates.

"I know them. They are huge. I met a couple of the partners at a finance conference last year." Marissa leaned over to get a better view of the screen.

Uncle Lou rose from his chair and filled a glass of water. "Anyone need anything?" When Justin and Marissa declined, he slid back into his chair. "Do you think Todd Wenger has anything to do with David?"

Justin pulled up Wenger's biography page on the company's website. "Hard to tell. Certainly appears this guy would be rolling in money but his connection to David is not apparent."

"Marissa, do you recall any of David's associates or clients?" Uncle Lou angled his chair to meet her gaze.

She shook her head. "No, he didn't discuss business with me."

After another ten minutes reviewing data on Wenger, Justin entered the second name in the search box. "Harold Silva is CEO of Skies International." Justin slapped his hand on the table. "This is where all the connections come into play. Tiffany works for Skies and the word "Skies" is mentioned in the cryptic note."

"This can't be a coincidence." Marissa stared at the face of the older, balding gentleman sitting behind a huge desk. She read his biography, noting his wife and daughter were killed in a tragic car accident many years ago. Could this man have anything to do with David's death?

Justin updated Uncle Lou on the note she'd found in David's bag and the mysterious patches.

Uncle Lou nodded and took a sip of water. "If this Silva fellow and his company are involved, they are not only dangerous but also well funded. Tread carefully."

Chapter 26

The next morning before breakfast and anyone else had awakened, Marissa crept down to the kitchen and sat at the kitchen table with a cup of coffee.

Uncle Lou soon entered the kitchen. "Coffee. You must have read my mind." He opened the cabinet, retrieved a blue mug labeled Air Force on the side, and filled the mug.

Marissa smiled. "I hope I didn't wake you. I'm an early riser. There's something about the mornings with a cup of coffee or a strawberry smoothie and a few moments of quiet before the day begins."

Uncle Lou sat across from her. "I remember mornings watching the sun rise on a Naval aircraft carrier. I was on a joint training mission with the Navy. For a moment, I could forget all the dangers in the world."

Marissa took another sip of her coffee. "I want you to know how grateful I am for Justin's help. He could have walked away and left me to deal with this alone. Although I'm scared, I feel so much better with him next to me."

Uncle Lou met her gaze. "I've known Justin almost since birth. I didn't see him for the first year of his life due to a deployment. He's smart as a whip, loyal beyond question, and feels deeply. He won't walk away."

Shifting in her chair, Marissa placed her mug on the table. "I know he has scars. I'm not asking for information. Justin has shared some but he can decide if he wants to tell me more. I don't want to make his life any more difficult." She shivered and placed her hands on the warm mug. "I don't want to endanger Justin, you, or anyone else in your family."

Patting her hand, Uncle Lou cleared his throat. "By bringing you here, Justin made you one of us. We'll take care of you."

Marissa nodded and blinked away tears. "Can I ask you for a favor?"

Ten minutes later she met Uncle Lou in the backyard, which extended for more than an acre. They moved to the far end, in a section well away from the house and bordering on a field. A shooting target with concentric black circles stood yards away.

"You've said you have shot before. I've got a gun with easy handling." Uncle Lou handed her goggles and earplugs. He prepared the gun and, with muzzle down, extended the butt end of the gun toward her. "Are you ready?"

Marissa nodded. Her heart pounded with the reality she might actually have to fire a gun to protect herself or someone else. She prepared the gun as instructed and let out a slow breath. "I'm ready."

For over an hour Uncle Lou guided her and gave her pointers in correct stance and gun handling. Marissa's comfort level rose as well as her confidence the more she handled the weapon.

After they concluded the session, Justin approached and smiled. "Didn't want to interrupt. I'm impressed." He winked as they made their way back to the house.

"I need everything in my arsenal to take care of myself and anyone else."

After eating a hearty breakfast, Justin and Marissa said their goodbyes. They stood in front of the SUV with Uncle Lou and Wendy while Aunt Iris and Sam remained in the house.

"Son, be careful." Uncle Lou pulled Justin into a strong embrace, and then whispered into his ear before letting go.

Justin nodded and turned to Wendy. "Keep your cell charged at all times. Be cognizant of everything around you. Don't let Sam out of your sight."

"Are you sure all this is necessary?" Wendy's blue-eyed gaze focused on her brother.

"No, I'm not sure, but let's err on the side of caution. No shortcuts. Okay?"

Wendy nodded, still clinging to Justin's hand.

The bond between Justin and Wendy displayed a strong sibling relationship. They exuded the utmost respect for each other and, unlike some siblings, appeared to genuinely like each other. Marissa loved her sister, but grew tired of Vanessa's overbearing nature after thirty minutes.

Just as Justin placed their belongings in the SUV, Sam raced out of the house, followed by Aunt Iris.

Aunt Iris embraced Justin and Marissa.

Sam hugged Justin extra tight before wrapping her arms around Marissa. With a proud smile, the youngster handed her a bag of cookies she had baked with Aunt Iris. "I'll miss you Marissa."

Marissa kissed the top of Sam's head. *What a special little girl.*

JUSTIN SCANNED the parking lot of the suburban Virginia library. He exhaled as he pulled the Jeep into an end slot near the lot's exit. No black SUVs. He stared up at the three-story neo-classic structure looming above them in the afternoon sun. A sign in front of the old building boasted a construction date of 1933. Four stone columns guarded the main entrance at the top of a wide staircase.

Marissa and David lived over an hour from the Brixton library and would have no reason to visit, with their local branch only fifteen minutes from their condo. Why would David come here? Of course, if this *was* a clandestine meeting, an out-of-the-way location made sense.

The gun in the holster pressed against his ribs. In addition to the borrowed holster Justin now wore, and Marissa's gun, Uncle Lou had also supplied him with more magazines and an admonition to be safe.

"If things look weird, we are out of here." Justin placed his hand under Marissa's chin and turned her to face him. "Are you with me?"

She nodded, eyes bright. "I'm anxious to see if anyone shows."

Seconds later, Justin opened the large wooden door for Marissa. He inhaled the familiar library scent, a musky mixture of old print and aging leather. In his mind, the timeworn appearance of the Brixton Library stood juxtaposed with images of the many days and nights he'd spent inside the more modern Duke Medical School library. He spotted the Brixton Library directory, and they crossed the cavernous lobby to study the layout of the building.

A woman entered the library behind them. The clickety-clack of her heels against the marble floor dissipated as she sailed past them.

Behind her, a man about his age rushed inside. Face flushed and mousy dark hair plastered to his sweaty forehead, the man gave a loud exhale. He smoothed his wrinkled shirt, but the gesture did little to change his disheveled appearance. A library badge hung from his neck, and Justin concluded he'd either arrived late for work or late returning from lunch.

According to the sign, books with call numbers in the 299 range were housed in the southeast corner of the second floor. Justin and Marissa headed for the stairwell.

"Are you okay to use the stairs?" He peered over his shoulder.

"Of course, I may have a few bruises but my legs aren't broken," Marissa replied with a frown.

"Didn't know you spoke smartass."

"One of my many talents." Marissa opened the glass door to the stairwell and started up the steps.

He caught her hand and a tingling sensation rushed up his arm. Touching her had become his favorite activity. He needed to pull back, but the attraction seemed to take on a life of its own. The compulsion to be near her and connect with some part of her body, even just a finger or a strand of her hair, simulated a drug he craved. He'd been down the road of alcoholism and the necessity to use alcohol to soothe his pain. This was different. She gave him a purpose, an uplifting spirit to want to be a better man. As corny as it sounded, Marissa, without even knowing, made him want the world to be better. His goal fueled this desire to rid her of whatever unseen enemy David had bequeathed her.

He dismissed those thoughts to focus on their current task. Opening the next door for Marissa, they followed the signs to the nonfiction area on the second floor.

Five minutes later, they found the aisle. Justin ran his fingers along the books, counting toward 299.9. He pulled *Religions, Cults, and Secret Societies* by Art Valtarian off the shelf and huddled close to Marissa as they flipped through the pages together.

"What does this mean?" she asked. "I don't see how this book has any relation to anything? David never showed any interest in this subject."

Justin shrugged. "Maybe the book has nothing to do with the note. Could be a random book selected as a meeting place." He glanced at his watch. "We have about twenty minutes before the meeting. Let's see if anyone shows." He placed the book back on the shelf. As they moved away from the aisle, he grabbed a couple more books off an adjacent shelf without looking at the titles. Justin chose a small table fifteen feet away, providing an unobstructed view of the aisle.

Marissa leaned over and whispered, "How will we know who we're looking for?"

"Pay attention to anyone who goes down that aisle. Besides, maybe this guy knows David is dead and won't show, anyway." He opened a book and pretended to flip through the pages while monitoring the aisle from the corner of his eye.

A young girl with a backpack approached, glanced at the sign indicating the call numbers within the stack, and moved on.

An older man neared the aisle ten minutes later.

Marissa nudged Justin when the man turned down the aisle.

He slowed as he approached the 299 section of the shelf, but then he continued past. After perusing several books, he sauntered farther down the aisle, turned left, and moved to another section of the library.

Justin glanced at the clock. "Ten minutes past the meeting time. Maybe no on will show, but let's wait a few more minutes."

Marissa focused on her book on drawing animated characters.

Another fifteen minutes, and no one approached the aisle. "Okay, this was a bust." Justin slid out of the chair.

As he stood, he spotted the harried library worker from downstairs crossing in front of them. "Hold on, maybe we can still get something out of this."

Justin hurried back to the aisle and pulled the book from the shelf. "I think you need help from a librarian." He handed her the book.

The librarian's dark hair resembled a tousled mass of Christmas lights with various strands jutting out here and there. A pair of round wire-framed glasses would have fit his appearance, but he wore none. He sported a bright red T-shirt with a long-sleeved yellow one underneath. His library ID indicated his name, Walker Mumfrey.

"Umm, excuse me. Can you help me with something?" Marissa glanced at Justin as she reached the waist-high, circular desk.

Justin stood within listening range at a nearby display table, feigning interest in a spread of books celebrating local connections to the Revolutionary War.

Walker glanced up from his computer screen and scratched his nose. "How can I-I help you?"

Marissa placed the book on the desk. "I need to pick up a book for my boyfriend, but I misplaced the note with the information. I believe he checked this book out a few months ago and needs it again. Is there any way you could look in your system and tell who checked this book out in the last few months?" She smiled and cocked her head to the side.

He held her gaze. "I'm-I'm not supposed to offer such information."

"Oh, but my boyfriend really needs this book. You see, he's finishing up some research, and I offered to come by and check out the book."

When he stood at full height, he almost stood even with Justin, but his slouched, curved posture made him appear much shorter.

He shifted his eyebrows upward. "What's his name?"

"His name was David Seybold." Cringing, she bit her lip.

Walker continued to stare.

Marissa placed both hands on the desk and shifted her stance. "I mean is. His name *is* David Seybold," she repeated.

He muttered something under his breath as he punched at his computer.

From his vantage point behind the librarian, Justin tried to get a look at the computer.

A few seconds later, he announced, "No record he ever checked out this book. Sorry."

With a loud sigh, she said, "Thanks for your help." The book lay between them on the desk. "I guess I don't need this, then." She pushed the book toward him.

"I'll reshelf the book." Walker swiped the book off the desk.

Justin and Marissa met in the stairwell. "I thought if the librarian could confirm David checked out the book at least we'd know the book was significant," she said, following him down the stairs.

"Me too. I don't want your name associated with that book being checked out. We can stop at a bookstore and pick up a copy, if necessary." Justin once again took her hand as they emerged from the stairwell. When they were back inside the car, he turned. "Either he used the book as a marker by which to meet his contact, or the book has some other meaning."

She leaned back against the seat. "Now what?"

"I still believe the note means something." He paused observing Marissa massaging her temples. "Let's get some coffee and decide our next move."

Around the corner from the library they found a coffee house. Past the customary lunchtime hour, the restaurant had many open tables. Marissa ordered a strawberry smoothie while Justin ordered coffee and a blueberry muffin.

"I hoped somehow to have our questions answered. The contact probably knew about David's death. To go to such lengths to construct a cryptic note suggests a concern about being discovered." Justin sipped his coffee. "One thing I learned, both in medicine and the military, is patience."

"I've never been good with patience. I couldn't wait to grow up and have a career. Thanks to David and his murderous friends now I'm running for my life."

"You deserve to be happy and live the life you want. I'm certain David's actions led to his death and our current predicament. He was my friend, but he could be damn selfish." He held her gaze before tearing away.

"I didn't like the David I saw before he died. Something was definitely off." She took a deep breath.

They were seated near the door, and a sudden breeze jostled their napkins, blowing Marissa's off the table. Justin bent to retrieve the napkin, and a shadow crossed in front of him.

He turned to see the grungy librarian had entered the coffeehouse.

With slouched shoulders, the librarian shuffled to their table. "Hello, Marissa. I think you're looking for me. I killed your fiancé."

Chapter 27

"Excuse me?" Marissa stared into the librarian's face as her lips trembled and her stomach clenched. "You killed my fiancé?"

The librarian shuffled his feet and swiveled his gaze around the sparsely populated coffee house. "Can we talk?"

"How did you know we were here?" Justin placed a hand near the concealed weapon under his shirt.

"I followed you."

Justin stood, towering over him by at least two inches. "Look, I don't know who you are, but if you killed David, then I have detectives on speed dial. They'll be interested in speaking to you."

The librarian held up his hands. "I'm Walker Mumfrey. David and I knew each other."

"And you killed him?" Marissa got the sensation she was on a merry-go-round. *What was happening?*

"Not literally." Walker scrunched his nose.

Justin scooted a chair back from their table and gestured for Walker to sit. "Okay, talk." He pushed his chair closer to Marissa.

Justin's closeness provided warmth against the sudden chill.

Walker cleared his throat and sank into the chair. "I-I met David almost a year ago. I worked a political donor party for extra money, you know as part of the wait staff. My mother isn't well, and I help to support her back in Wisconsin. David attended the event."

Marissa couldn't picture this guy being a serious threat to anyone. *He takes care of his mother and spends his days around books.* She'd learned everyone has secrets. Could this man be a killer, or at least an accessory to David's murder? Her heart banged against her chest. Could Walker Mumfrey pull out a gun and shoot them right here? Her fears were soothed, somewhat, knowing Justin had a weapon and they were in public. She'd almost forgotten she, too, carried a weapon. Shivering, she questioned if she could ever really pull the trigger on someone.

Justin took her hand.

"What happened after you met David?" Justin glared at Walker.

"We made small talk, at first. Which appetizer I recommended, how much alcohol would be served, stuff like that, and then I moved on. I had a tray of toasted brioche rounds with *crème fraiche* and caviar. Farm raised American beluga. Not French or Russian, but quite delicious." He nodded, wide-eyed.

His anticipatory expression met theirs like he expected his audience to be impressed with the caliber of appetizer selections. *No way is this guy dangerous.*

"Okay, you're walking around with a bunch of fish eggs. What else?" Justin gestured to move on with the story.

"After awhile I circled back to where David stood. He told me he and Neal Wingate were close personal friends but he'd attended the event to help his own career. I wondered why he wasted time talking to a waiter and he told me the help could often provide key details from overheard conversations."

Marissa stared at Walker, searching for signs of deception. She saw none but questioned her powers of perception. "Isn't networking and mingling the whole reason for those parties?

Walker stopped bouncing his leg and cocked his head. "To some degree. David was right. You've seen countless books from the maids, butlers, or cooks of famous people. Anyway, he told me he had his own consulting firm and then he asked me about a few CEO's he'd met earlier."

Justin glared at Walker. "Do you remember the names of those CEOs?"

Walker nodded and swept the room with his gaze. "Sure. Marvin Lennox, Harold Silva, and Todd Wenger."

Marissa shot a glance at Justin.

Harold Silva, the CEO of Skies International?

Walker tapped his fingers on the table. "The political donor parties carry the power and money theme to the extreme." He paused, picked up a napkin, and folded it in triangles. "I'm sorry about your fiancé. I truly am. Art Valtarian's *Religions, Cults, and Secret Societies* has been checked out exactly nine times in the last four years. The edition's not his best work. Mr. Valtarian is a history professor at a small college in New Hampshire, student population 6,543 as of last year. His most recent work is a comparison study of Mayan traditions and beliefs to modern-day terrorist groups." He shrugged and placed a finger on his chin. "Valtarian based his conclusions around the fact these two groups share a propensity for beheading their enemies." He nodded. "Anyway, based on your discovery of this obscure book, I'm guessing you discovered our surreptitious method of communication."

"How do you play into this?" Justin had one hand near his gun and the other enclosed around Marissa's.

"We became colleagues, of sorts. I didn't kill him but I, unknowingly, somehow exposed information, putting David's life in danger." He scratched his head. "Although I can't point to a lapse in our covert alliance." He leaned closer, his right leg popping up and down. "I want to show you something." He glanced at his watch. "The library closes in five hours, 52 minutes. The staff is usually out of the building within twenty-five minutes after closing. Can you meet me then?"

Marissa untangled her hand from Justin's and clasped her cup, allowing the condensation to coat her hand. "What do you want us to see?"

Walker continued to fold the napkin until he'd made a small, tight triangle.

"How do we know this isn't a set up?" Justin leaned back in his chair and surveyed the librarian.

Walker's eyes grew large. "You've been targeted. They think you know."

"Know what?" Marissa had grown tired of Walker's tap-dancing. She wanted to yank him by the front of his shirt and demand he spit out what he knew.

"I'll show you everything tonight." He stood.

Marissa stared at him. He had awful posture and she yearned to yell, "ramrod", like her grandmother used to when her beginning dance students slouched.

"Come to the side door on the east side of the building." Walker nodded then lumbered out of the coffee house.

Maybe they'd get some answers after all.

AFTER ALMOST TWO hours in the D.C. rush-hour traffic leading into Maryland, Justin pulled into the parking lot of a red brick, five-story apartment building. The Capitol Heights, Maryland apartment building resembled many others in similar condition in the older neighborhood. Most of the buildings included a small park-like area and a main entrance.

Marissa stretched as they got out of the car and headed toward the entrance of the Clifford Arms Apartments, specifically toward Tiffany Clover's unit.

A shower of sadness swept over her. The apartment building held a forgotten, melancholy vibe. The crumbling walkway took them past a children's area containing old playground equipment with missing swings surrounded by a wrought iron fence in desperate need of a new coat of paint. The shrubs lining the exterior of the building were overdue for pruning. In contrast, fresh landscaping surrounded the sign announcing Clifford Arms, like the budget had been limited to one area.

Her hand grazed Justin's as he held the lobby door open. She'd become comfortable with his hand in hers. A silly, romantic notion, but a vision of walking hand in hand on a windswept beach entered her thoughts. Holding hands led to kissing. Improbable, but Marissa found herself daydreaming about the Harlequin moment anyway. What would his lips on hers feel like? No. She yanked the image out of her mind. *Not happening.*

They rode the elevator to the fifth floor and followed the numbered doors, some with missing digits, to apartment 527. A quick Internet search had provided the address.

Marissa glanced around the hallway. They were alone, but she couldn't help remembering the gunfire they'd escaped in the hotel hallway the previous day. She didn't think they were followed, but she lacked know-how in spotting a tail. *A tail.* She suppressed a giggle. Now, she considered herself a seasoned spy. Although the situation wasn't funny, mental and physical exhausted had taken hold, making her a bit punch drunk.

Justin knocked on the door twice.

Marissa heard a shuffling sound followed by the door opening.

"Oh, hi." Tiffany's eyebrows arched in surprise. "Marissa, Justin."

"I'm sorry we didn't call before we came by. Do you have a minute to speak with us?" Marissa offered her a smile, hoping to appear as if they were in the neighborhood and decided to pop in for a visit.

"Oh, sure. I'm meeting some friends for dinner in about a half hour, but I'm only going across the street to the Italian restaurant." She stepped back and allowed them to enter.

The front door opened into a tiny alcove with a coat closet. The small apartment smelled of peach-scented candles. They followed the short hall into a clean living room furnished with a gray sofa and two pale green chairs. Copies of *Vogue* and *Glamour* lay fanned out on the glass coffee table. A dining room table with an adjacent galley style kitchen occupied the left side of the apartment. Another small hall jutted off the living room with two closed doors Marissa assumed led to a bathroom and a bedroom.

Tiffany showed them to the sofa and asked if she could offer them a beverage.

They declined.

"We won't take up much of your time." Justin sank onto the soft sofa.

Tiffany, dressed in jeans and a low-cut, short-sleeved sweater, took the chair opposite them.

"When we spoke last, you mentioned starting a relationship with David after meeting him at your job with Skies International." Justin's voice held a gentle and nonthreatening quality.

Tiffany shifted in her chair and shot a worried glance at Marissa.

"I know you didn't know about me. It's not your fault." Marissa couldn't help the bitterness escaping. David had made a fool of her. He'd not only wasted several years of her life, thousands of dollars in wedding fees—most of which she'd never get back—but he'd rejected their baby and now placed people she cared about in danger. "I'm actually thankful. While cleaning David's office, his computer kept alerting he had messages. There were so many, I thought maybe something serious had happened. I saw a few of your messages."

Tiffany's eyes grew wide and her cheeks blushed. "I'm so sorry. I'm not the kind of woman who is cool about fooling around with someone else's man."

Marissa leaned toward Tiffany. "If he cheated before we were married, he would have cheated after. I'm sad he's dead, but I intended to call off the wedding."

"Tiffany, did David tell you anything about his projects?" Justin shifted forward on the sofa.

"The detectives asked me the same question. He didn't talk about any other clients. He'd been thrilled to get the consulting job at Skies. I would see him all the time. I'm an assistant to Harold Silva, the CEO. Mr. Silva wanted to revamp some security procedures. David had been hired to come up with a plan."

"Did he get along with Mr. Silva?"

"As far as I know. He wouldn't have remained on the project if Mr. Silva had been dissatisfied."

"How is Mr. Silva as a boss?"

Her hand flew to her throat. "He was a nice man, very fair. I'm going to miss him."

Marissa pushed a strand of hair from her face. "Where is he going?"

Tiffany licked her lips. "He's been out for several days now, and an email circulated announcing his sudden retirement." She scrunched her nose. "Just a few weeks ago, he told me he would probably die at the job, because he wouldn't know what to do with himself in retirement. He didn't even come back to clean out his office."

"What happens to your job?" The CPA in Marissa perked up. She hoped Tiffany had a decent savings account to fall back on.

"I don't know. Two of the other vice presidents came in and went through his paperwork. Then they told me to spend the next week cleaning up his office. They assured me they would find me another position within the company."

Justin nodded. "Did David ever mention being involved in anything illegal? Or did he mention anyone being angry with him?"

Once again, Tiffany shifted in her chair. "Skies is a large, powerful company and he said this job would take him to new heights."

She knows something. Marissa clasped her hands in her lap. "Tiffany, some dangerous people intend on doing Justin and me harm, or worse. If you know something, please help us."

She pulled at her sweater and then got up from her chair. "Excuse me. I need some water." She returned a few seconds later.

"Tiffany, do you know something that might help us?" Marissa forced a pleading look into her expression.

She fiddled with the hem of her sweater. "I don't know if this is important. Several weeks after David started working for Skies, I found him in Mr. Silva's office, instead of the hotel office we have set aside for consultants. Mr. Silva had been out of the country."

"Why wasn't he in his own office? Justin asked.

"I asked him, and he kind-of snapped at me. Then he caught

himself and changed his attitude. He said he wanted to know the feeling of sitting in the CEO chair." She took a sip of water. "He'd accessed Mr. Silva's computer, a huge security breach, unless he'd been approved."

"Was he?" Marissa asked.

Tiffany took another sip. "No, I don't think so. He started telling me how much he needed this job, and all the bad things possible if he lost the contract. Then he started kissing me and confusing everything."

"Sounds like David." Justin smirked. "Do you know what kind of files he'd assessed?" He rose from the sofa and moved in front of the sliding doors leading to a small balcony just large enough for two chairs and a tiny table.

"I got a glance before he shut down the computer. I don't know how he managed, but I think he entered a restricted area. Clearance is reserved for those at the senior executive level. Assessing the restricted level is a big no-no. If you even get close, security will pay you a visit."

Justin turned to face Tiffany. "Do you think he hacked into those files, or is there any possibility he'd been granted access?"

Tiffany shook her head. "Before David started, I had to submit a request for his security clearance level. I met with Mr. Silva about the issue, and he said David, under no circumstances, should receive executive level clearance. Mr. Silva limited his access to policies and procedures and some of the limited human resources stuff."

Marissa clasped her hands together to keep them from shaking. *Is this breach what got David killed?*

Justin swiped a hand through his hair. "Did you alert security about this activity?"

She immediately reddened and dropped her gaze. "No. Part of my responsibility is to log Mr. Silva's comings and goings into a computerized system so security and IT can track any issues and know who's in-house. David flustered me with all the kissing I forgot to log the data. Later in the day I remembered, but I didn't want to get David in trouble, so I logged Mr. Silva as being in-house during the time David had used his computer."

Whatever David did on Silva's computer had to be suspect. Marissa clasped her hands together. "You said you got a glimpse of the screen. What did you see?"

"A list of names. I don't know what they were."

"Do you remember any of the names?" Justin stood at the sliding door, staring toward the parking lot.

"He shut off the screen before I could catch anything specific." Tiffany glanced at the wall clock.

Marissa rubbed her temples. Her head hurt and she wanted to sleep away this nightmare, but she had difficulty picturing life on the other side of this mess. "Tiffany, thank you for being open and honest with us. I know how tough this is." She paused and tried to swallow the lump in her throat, bracing herself for the answer. "Did David confide in you about what he'd been doing on the computer?"

In the freshman days of their relationship, David had been somewhat forthcoming and open. He shared his hopes for his life and his company. He even told her he wanted to be a father someday. Had all the talk been a big lie? Did anything real exist about their relationship?

"He told me he'd finally found the vehicle to take him where he belonged." Tiffany smoothed the front of her sweater. "I had no idea what he meant. The relationship we had remained...light, most of the time. He didn't ask me a lot of personal questions, and I only knew the basics about him."

"Did he ever mention a guy named Walker Mumfrey?" Justin moved closer to Marissa.

The strong connection flowing between her and Justin knocked Marissa's concentration. Could her perception be an illusion? Maybe she needed someone who treated her with respect and honesty? Marissa forced her attention back to Tiffany.

Tiffany shook her head. "No, never heard of him." She shrugged. "I told David I'd just gotten out of a relationship. He asked me a lot about the company and didn't seem to want to dwell on the personal stuff."

"Did he ever get angry?"

"Outside of the one time he snapped, never. He was always upbeat, even funny. He had a great personality." Blinking, Tiffany stopped and placed a hand on her mouth. "I'm so sorry."

Marissa shook her head. "I don't blame you. Thank you, Tiffany. I'm sorry he misled you." She stood and hugged her.

Tiffany followed Justin and Marissa out of the apartment and into the elevator. Everyone remained quiet on the ride down. They reached the parking lot, and Tiffany said goodbye and headed away.

Justin and Marissa hopped back into the SUV.

Marissa stared out at the street in front of her as Tiffany neared the corner. She recalled a night several months ago, a night which should have cemented in her mind how cruel David could be. After all she'd been through at the time, she now understood she'd excused David's actions. Easier to pretend her tragedy didn't happen than deal with the painful repercussions.

As she relived the painful memory of her miscarriage, she heard screams. Marissa glanced up just as Tiffany's body flew through the air and landed in the street.

A black SUV sped away into the darkening evening.

Chapter 28

"Damn it!" Justin said as he started cardiac resuscitation. He'd been careful to turn Tiffany's mangled and bloody body but he needed to start CPR. She likely had multiple broken bones, and Justin anticipated serious internal injuries. Her body had twisted in such a way suggesting spinal damage, not to mention a severe head injury. Based on his experience he doubted she would survive, yet he continued to treat her until the EMTs arrived. Marissa kneeled on the other side of Tiffany. "What can I do?"

"Stay close." Justin continued with chest compressions, sweat snaking down his face. "Come on, Tiffany," he said through gritted teeth.

"I hear sirens. Paramedics will be here any second. Will she make it?"

"Not likely." Justin hovered over Tiffany's chest with locked arms and continued pumping.

A few seconds later, police and fire arrived on the scene. The police pushed the spectators out of the way and managed the growing traffic backup while the paramedics moved in.

Justin continued CPR while introducing himself as an off duty trauma doctor and providing a quick update.

A police officer stood on the curb questioning Marissa.

Justin trusted the police, but something inside warned him to be wary of the detectives. Coincidences didn't just happen. Like the gunmen at the hotel, the fire bomb at the ballet studio, and now this hit-and-run. He'd rather be too cautious and distrust everyone.

After the EMTs put Tiffany in the ambulance, one of the officers approached Justin.

Thirty minutes later, after the officer wrapped up his questioning, he informed them Tiffany had been pronounced dead upon arrival at the hospital.

"They knew we talked to her. Tiffany is dead because of me." Marissa stared out the passenger side window as they headed towards Virginia.

"Don't put guilt on yourself. It will eat you up." *I know from experience.* "Besides, we both spoke to her." He maneuvered onto the highway heading south. "I think they had her under surveillance." He slammed his hand against the steering wheel.

"Why?" Marissa whipped her head around.

"Tiffany spoke to the detectives."

"Do you really think Kearns and Streeter killed her?"

Justin sighed. "No, but something is wrong. I have absolutely no evidence or anything concrete to point to. If I went to an attorney or the police, I'd be laughed out of the office."

Marissa nodded. "Intuition can be great, if you pay attention. I wish I'd suspected danger lurked for Tiffany. Maybe she would be having dinner with her friends right now." She rubbed her eyes.

Justin paused as traffic slowed and changed lanes. "Just before my parents were killed, I picked up the phone to tell them not to come. Absolutely no reason existed for me to call off their visit. Yeah, I had studying to do, always did, but something bothered me and I couldn't..." His voice trailed off.

On the day of the attack on their medical unit, he had awoken to a feeling of dread. The day had been weird, and Justin attributed his gloomy attitude to lack of sleep and having an off day. An off day turned into a deadly massacre, and the day he lost someone special. He pulled his mind from the familiar, sticky concoction of pain, guilt, and if-only's.

"How horrible." She turned her gaze to the window and the urban areas zooming by. Then, after a few minutes of silence, she said, "One day, about a year before things started to go bad, we were on vacation, David and I were drinking coffee. I looked over at him and something popped into my head. This man will not be your husband. I dismissed the thought. Maybe if I had paid attention, our lives would be different."

"Sometimes the deep recesses of our brains spot trouble our eyes can't see." Justin shrugged. "Sounds profound, if nothing else."

The last specks of dusk claimed the sky as night readied to take over when Justin pulled into the library parking lot. After the day's earlier events, his mood sank into somberness and he anticipated little patience in listening to Walker's extraneous facts, but if doing so led to more answers, he'd endure the monologues.

"Justin, I'm scared." Marissa wiped her tears. "Tiffany didn't have to die."

He parked the car and turned to her. "In my PTSD group, I learned there is an order to fear. First fear spawns our fight or flight mechanism, then once the danger dissipates we use fear to direct our actions going forward. We've learned to be frightened and this is where our perceptions can become skewed. The last order of fear is to conquer it. We'll get there."

He pulled her into his arms, breathed in the scent of her hair and caressed her brown locks. She was his, at least in this moment, which was all he could ask, for now. He couldn't allow himself to think beyond surviving. The future would have to wait, and his heart would have to suffer. *Give me strength.*

He pulled her closer and kissed the side of her head. "I promise I will not let anything happen to you."

"Don't you think you're taking this best man gig a little far?" Marissa cast her green eyes upward.

Justin shrugged. "I want to be here, and not out of obligation. I care about you." His voice grew thick. Blowing past all stop signs in his brain, he caressed her face.

Ah, hell.

He leaned down and kissed her. As their lips melted into each other, he didn't care about David, or loyalty, or the weirdo waiting inside the library. He only cared about touching her, connecting with her. His brain fired tiny explosions as his thumb caressed the silky skin of her jawline. She belonged here—with him.

She shifted closer and parted her lips.

Maybe Marissa knew this felt right, too. Accepting the invitation, he dug deeper. She tasted of mint, the tingling sensation meshing with the sexiness of her mouth. Years of guilt and admiration from afar splintered like a high note shattered glass.

When they parted, both were out of breath. He should have apologized, but a voiced regret would have been disingenuous. He wasn't sorry.

"Justin..." Marissa shifted her gaze to the blinking light flickering on and off at the library door.

Walker Mumfrey flashed a light in an apparent signal giving them the all clear to enter. Justin slid out of the car and jogged around to open her door. As he helped her out, he felt their tender moment slip away.

WALKER USHERED them inside the library and led them to the third floor. "This way. I have everything laid out." His voice crooned light, almost jovial. "Please, have a seat." He pointed to a long table with six chairs in the library's reference section. Marissa counted four large binders and several maps spread out on the table.

She sat at the table, but her mind wandered from the meeting. Justin's kiss lingered on her lips. She'd wanted to cling tight and revel in his arms. The hard mound of his biceps and the way his hands cupped her face offered tenderness and strength, a strange dichotomy, but one she wanted to experience over and over again.

Was she wrong to enjoy the kiss? Was she wrong to be comforted and excited by Justin's nearness? She couldn't define her feelings for him. Maybe her feelings didn't matter. Maybe the kiss had been an impulsive act on his part and meant nothing. Unable to reach clarity, she turned her attention to Walker. "Thanks for helping us."

Some part of Walker's body seemed to always be in motion. She'd observed him sitting while his legs bopped up and down, and now as he stood, he paced then stopped and drummed his fingers on the table.

Marissa liked him, despite his odd nature. She sensed his intentions were sincere, even though Justin maintained an air of distrust.

Walker paced in front of the table and spoke like a professor lecturing a class. "You have to know the background of many things before any of this will make sense. I've been involved in this research for about three years now. A friend asked me to perform some genealogy work. My research led to many discoveries, most of which provided familial insight for my friend, but a portion provided me some intriguing benefits."

Justin settled into his chair. "How does this relate to David?"

Walker stopped pacing and grinned. "I understand as a trauma surgeon you need to work fast to save patients, and this trait has probably rubbed off in other areas, but I'm getting to the crux of why you're here." He cleared his throat and commenced pacing again. "First, know I am not a threat." He paused, and glanced at them. "As my research deepened, I discovered my friend's great grandparents were born in the mid-Atlantic region. The research into his family history provided a fascinating discovery. His bloodline included a Revolutionary War hero, Captain John Shields, who led a small, but successful, Army regiment."

Justin folded his arms and stared at Walker. "Interesting, but how does..."

Walker held up a hand. "I'm getting there. I know I've digressed." He strode the length of the table before he continued. "The study of a person's genealogy involves investigating several branches of a tree, hence the term family tree. Each branch..."

Justin rubbed his forehead. "Walker, we know what the term genealogy means. Move on, please."

Walker pulled at his shirt and nodded. "My foray into one artery of a family tree ended with an organization called The Order."

"The Order." Justin leaned on the table. "I'm not familiar with that organization."

Marissa placed her hand on Justin's arm. "The patch." She turned to Walker. "Identical green patches were found in David's casket and under Justin's dead patient. The patches included the phrase *"Ordo Ortus"*. Anything to do with The Order?"

"Order Rising." Walker nodded. He stood in front of Marissa. "Definitive proof. Dr. Tanner, did your patient die suddenly or under suspicious terms?"

Justin nodded. "I suspect she received a lethal dose of a drug, but I have no proof yet."

"I'm not surprised. They are toying with you. This organization, called The Order, enjoys anonymity. Probably one of the hallmarks of their existence." Walker opened a large binder and pulled out a report several pages long. He flipped through the pages and handed the binder to Justin.

Justin scanned a report outlining various attributes of The Order. "This looks like some religious cult."

"Have you ever heard of the Illuminati, or the Freemasons?"

"Sure." Marissa leaned closer to Justin and surveyed the report. "I don't know much about the organizations."

"That's by design. Their rituals are steeped in secrecy. Over the years, this secrecy has created distrust and suspicion. Much research has been devoted to them, thereby shedding light on their traditions." Walker picked up another binder and handed it to Marissa. "To understand The Order, you must first understand its founder, Russell Sinclair." He explained how Russell ran away as a young boy, joined the Freemasons, became disillusioned enough to quit, and formed his own organization. "Over time, some of the restrictive qualities Russell loathed about the Freemasons became guiding principles of The Order. Russell appointed himself Grand Commander and ruled his small flock with an iron fist." Walker handed Marissa a photo.

She studied the stern face of Russell Sinclair in a black-and-white photo. He sat at an enormous desk devoid of any accessories other than a large knife.

Justin leaned closer to Marissa to view the picture. "What is the significance of the knife?"

Walker shook his head and pulled up a chair next to Marissa. "It is said if you cross the Grand Commander, he slices off a finger and saves the digit in a jar. Then the offender is killed and buried on the compound grounds."

"This is so melodramatic." With furrowed brows, Justin studied the picture of the knife.

"Sounds crazy, but I have good reason to believe it's true. If you flip farther along in the binder, you will find information on the sudden disappearances of several members. These people were never found. My friend suspected his uncle of being a member. I couldn't corroborate his suspicion and his uncle or his uncle's body, to date, has never been found."

Marissa gasped.

"In the interest of time, I'll skip forward several years. Russell has one daughter, Vivian. He had a wife but she's never been accounted for and no record exists of her death. On his deathbed, Russell bequeathed his title to his only daughter, and Vivian became the new Grand Commander."

"What kind of organization is The Order?" Marissa glanced up at Walker.

"The group started off as sort of a cross between traditional Christianity and Freemasonry, but along the way I believe Russell got power drunk and became more imperialistic. He imposed rules on his members. Women were not allowed to hold decision-making or leadership positions, even within their own families. Everyone vowed allegiance to Russell. If he proclaimed someone disloyal or in violation of one of his edicts he imposed harsh punishments, many times ending in death."

"Where is this cult located?" Justin said.

Walker began to pace again. "Right here in Virginia." He handed Marissa single sheet of paper. "There are seven articles of The Order which drives the organization. Take a look."

She read the information aloud.

"The Ring: The soul of The Founder will forever flourish among the emeralds.

The Scepter: As the imperial symbol of authority, the holder of the staff possesses all power.

The Knife: Custodian, guardians, and councilmen will wage war through blood and vengeance to confirm allegiance to The Order and Grand Commander.

The Coin: The Order will control the coin and thereby control the fate of the members and the world.

The Urn: Death is valued by station; those loyal to the Grand Commander are celebrated while enemies are interred below the black flower.

The Eye: Members will demand understanding and clear vision along the path of unwavering loyalty to The Order and Grand Commander.

The Map: The Grand Commander will hold the map, a key to the ultimate source."

They were silent for several seconds.

Justin sighed. "What does this mean?"

Walker dug into his pocket and pulled out several bite sized candy bars. As he popped one in his mouth, he scattered the rest on the table. "Help yourself." He tossed the wrapper into the trashcan and cleared his throat. "For clarification, there are three types of members. Custodians are the general members. They hold no authoritative power and are expected to follow orders. The guardians are the enforcement branch, the police, if you will. Councilmen are the Grand Commander's trusted confidants. When I say councilmen, they are just that. Women are not allowed to hold any positions of power, except in one case. Next to the Grand Commander, councilmen hold immense power."

Marissa gripped the table. "If Russell had such abhorrent views of women, why did he make Vivian the Grand Commander?"

"Good question," Walker said. "He put Vivian through many tasks to evaluate her resolve. The most difficult came when she became pregnant with the child of one of his councilmen. He pardoned the advisor but blamed Vivian. As punishment, he allowed her to have the child, and then he forced her to murder the baby."

"These people are sick. How do the authorities let them get away with these things?" Justin continued to study the report.

"By this point, they had friends in local government. The Order kept to themselves, so the authorities turned a blind eye."

"How could she kill her child?" Marissa couldn't fathom murdering her own child and wrapped her hand around her belly.

"She wanted power even more than her own father. Since his death, she's taken The Order to new heights. What Russell only dreamed of, Vivian is doing. She's a very dangerous woman."

"She's still alive?" Justin asked.

"Oh yes." Walker nodded. "She's in her early sixties and very much in charge."

"What does this have to do with David?" Justin closed the binder and eyed Walker.

Walker adjusted the set of binders on the table, straightening them until they lined up perfectly. "Like I said, Vivian expanded the organization in powerful ways. She has gained enormous wealth over the years through companies she's either formed or usurped. She owns the Skies International Corporation."

"The company where David consulted." Marissa edged up on her seat. "Walker, why were you meeting David?"

"He wanted the information I had, and I had a keen interest in something he had, but I never got a chance to see it."

Justin rose from his chair. "Wait a minute. How did you get all this information and why should we trust you? Maybe you're part of this organization." Justin glared at Walker.

"I've spent years amassing this data. The maps are based on public documents, which are probably not up to date. The inside information comes from a rare defector from The Order who has since passed on." Walker paused and scratched his head. "I-I understand your hesitation in trusting me. There's not m-much I could say to convince you of my sincerity. At first I wanted to challenge my research skills by hunting information on the elusive group but then the more I learned the more I had to know. This is a very dangerous group. I went to the authorities and they ignored my requests to investigate so I'm on my own."

Justin pulled at his chin and continued to study Walker. "What information did David have?"

Walker slid a map out of a cylinder. "I'm getting there. This is a map of Babylon Hall. The Order purchased several hundred acres in rural Virginia." He jabbed at the map. "Vivian lives here and runs the empire from these headquarters. The estate is an impressive facility." He pointed out various landmarks and features around the compound.

"Have you been on the property?" Marissa scanned the map, locating stables, a greenhouse, and several guest cottages.

"I've been on parts of it, but security quickly escorted me off. I pretended to be a lost hiker. The southern section is densely wooded, but her guardians are like a small army."

Marissa reached for a binder. She flipped several pages until one caught her eye. Marissa's heart galloped inside her chest. She leaned in to study the picture more closely. Despite the black-and-white photo, the large emerald ring stood out. Beads of sweat popped out on her forehead, and the room tilted.

Was Vivian Sinclair the weird old woman who had mysteriously appeared at David's funeral *and* the bookstore? "I need to find the ladies' room."

"Are you all right?" Justin's hand rested on her arm.

"I just need a bathroom break." She gave him a strained smile.

Following Walker's directions, she located the restrooms near the staircase and pushed open the arched entry door containing a frosted window glass designed with flowers and butterflies.

Marissa approached the sink and splashed water on her face. When she glanced up at the mirror, she saw a figure in black standing behind her.

Then the lights went out.

Chapter 29

"Is she dead?"

"Affirmative."

Roy Bane's voice came through the phone. "Stay on alert. Stand down on the girl and doctor until I direct otherwise. I have someone else on the scene." Vivian clicked off the phone. "How dare that little bitch think she can get away with sleeping with the enemy, talk to the police, and then talk to the girl and the doctor."

She scooped up a surveillance picture of Tiffany. The image resembled a fashion model photo shoot rather than a surveillance picture. "Well, now you know what whoring around does. You're road kill, and your mother has to bury her tramp of a daughter."

Edward stood near Vivian's desk, assembling her tea in precise movements. Two teaspoons of cream, one half teaspoon of honey, and a dash of nutmeg. "This Tiffany woman appeared naïve."

Vivian's head whipped up. "Edward, did you just speak without my asking for your opinion?"

"I'm sorry, ma'am. I don't know what got into me." Edward dipped his head in apparent remorse.

Vivian's glare lingered. "Don't let it happen again. Dismissed." She turned back to the photo as Edward scooted out of the room.

Frowning, she tossed Tiffany's picture back on her desk and picked up a photo of Marissa.

Some had labeled Vivian as pretty, in her younger days. She smiled at the memory of Harold. He had been enthralled with her, and she had to admit his attention had been flattering. Then again, she deserved to be noticed.

Her attraction to Harold not only centered around the attention he showered on her, but also the power she held over him. She'd been in control, and understood the weakness of men when a woman used her body. Women like Tiffany and Marissa, with their beautiful faces and figures, had no clue about the power they held. "Stupid bitches."

As she stared at Marissa's image, she envisioned her plans for the woman and her little friend. *No one defies me and lives. I'd die before I allowed someone else, especially another woman so far beneath me, to shake my empire.*

Playing with this woman had become dull. Donning disguises had been exhilarating at first. Seeing the confusion and terror in her pretty eyes filled Vivian with glee, but, like a child bored of a Christmas toy by January, she had grown tired of terrorizing Marissa. Time to ramp up her final plans.

She pulled the knife from her drawer, the steel blade cool against her warm skin. The sharp tip would soon find a temporary home inside Marissa. Her body shivered in response. "Soon," she whispered.

Years of planning and implementation had been threatened when Harold allowed that opportunist David Seybold to gain critical data regarding The Order, Skies, and her plans. The data had to be found, and those aware of it eradicated. She counted her latest conquests. David, terminated. Tiffany, terminated. Harold, terminated. Even a random hospital patient had to pay a price.

Once again, Harold surfaced in her memory. He represented the closest she'd ever come to love, but his disloyalty ruined all possibilities. They could have had a family—husband, wife, and children. Her father ensured that didn't happen, and he'd been right. A family would have only been a burden.

She remained free to make any decision she deemed necessary without regard for anyone else. Real men of power had discovered that eons ago. Powerful men kept emotional ties at arms' length. Women lagged behind in understanding the extent of sacrifices braved to wield ultimate power, but Vivian embraced her supremacy.

The glow of power, like electricity, follows the path of least resistance. Vivian mused over the phenomenon. She trailed her finger down the knife. *I, unlike electricity, have the power to conquer all resistance.*

I will defeat anyone who resists me. It's my destiny. Ordo Ortus.

Chapter 30

*I*s *someone in here with me?*

Marissa strained to see in the darkened room. Her heart ramped up and fear trickled down her spine. She patted the wall, blind in the darkness, as she made her way to the bathroom door.

The gun.

Plowing into her purse, she pulled out the weapon just as she felt a hand clamp over her mouth and an arm snake around her from behind.

Struggling against her unknown attacker, Marissa twisted and turned to wiggle free. A flash of Tiffany's distorted body zipped through her head. *Not me.* She reared back and slammed her foot into the attacker's knee.

Groaning in agony, the attacker released her.

Had the groan come from a woman?

Marissa turned and fired a shot but the woman dove into a stall. Sprinting out of the bathroom, Marissa slammed into the inky unknown. Disorientation took hold in the murky hall. "Justin," she screamed.

No response.

Which way back to Justin and Walker?

The bathroom door squeaked open behind her, spurring her to dart left, hoping the woman hadn't seen which way she went. She raced through the nearest set of doors.

A red exit sign in the distance offered minimal illumination. Posters of Clifford the Big Red Dog, Charlie Brown, Snoopy, and other childhood favorites adorned the walls. She'd taken a wrong turn. Justin and Walker had to be on the other side of the library. If she ventured farther into the children's area, would she circle back to them? She crouched behind a shelf and peeked between the books.

A complete hush washed over the room like she'd been closed inside a tomb. Marissa fought to control her breathing as her senses and fears crossed into overload. What if more than one attacker had invaded the library? What if they'd already gotten to Justin and Walker? Through small spaces in between the books, Marissa stared at the door.

She inched toward the end of the aisle, breathing fast and shallow, pulse racing. *I need to get back to Justin and warn him. If I can just make it across the hall.* Marissa inhaled as she reached the end of the aisle. Still no attacker in sight. She waited and listened.

Silence.

Casting aside doubts about leaving her hiding spot, she stepped from in-between the stacks and crept closer to the door. When she got to the exit, she tapped open the door and peered out. The central hall loomed dark except for a sliver of moonlight from the staircase window, piercing a section of the room like a stage spotlight.

Remaining in the shadows, Marissa crept toward the other side of the hall, gun raised. She neared the reference area, hoping her sense of direction hadn't betrayed her. Just as she reached for the door's handle, she felt a gloved hand grab her wrist.

Marissa screamed and the masked woman knocked the gun from her hand. The gun clanged to the ground. *Didn't Dad tell her and Vanessa to aim for vulnerable body spots if attacked?* She jabbed pointed fingers toward the attacker's eyes. The woman stepped to the side, avoiding her aim.

The woman, a few inches taller than her, wielded exceptional strength. In one swift action, an elbow connected with Marissa's stomach, knocking her flat. The back of her head slammed against the marble floor. Marissa cried out and clutched her head. White lights twinkled behind her eyes as waves of pain trounced through her skull. She opened her eyes to see the woman standing above her glaring through the mask's slits, a gun trained on her forehead. Moonlight glinted off the gun, casting an eerie glow around the weapon and attacker like they were one sinister being.

"Where is the data?" the woman demanded in a smoky, muted voice.

"I don't know." The woman shifted, giving Marissa a second to move. She sat upright and scuttled backwards like a crab. She scanned the area for her gun and possible escape routes. Finding neither, her mind blanked in the face of a lack of viable options.

"Penance," the woman said, advancing.

Marissa's heartbeat skipped to an all-out sprint.

Suddenly, a door swung open into the hallway and Justin barreled in, aiming his own gun at the woman. "Who are you?"

"Where's the data?" With a muffled voice behind the mask, she pointed her gun at Marissa.

"Drop your gun." Justin took a step closer.

The woman switched her aim from Marissa to Justin. In her periphery, Marissa spotted her gun on the edge of moonbeam ten feet away. A sideways scoot while the woman's attention focused on Justin brought her within arm's reach of the gun. She picked up the weapon, aimed for the woman, and squeezed the trigger just as the lights came on. Marissa jerked and squinted in the sudden light, sending the bullet on a trajectory ending in a hole in the wall.

The woman seized the opportunity and raced for the door.

"Marissa, move!" Justin hollered. Following close behind the woman, he lunged, knocking her to the floor.

The woman and her gun rolled in opposite directions. She quickly recovered and sprinted out the door.

The door slam reverberated in the library halls.

Marissa released a breath and lay back on the floor. Her beating heart hadn't comprehended the danger had dissipated.

"Are you okay?" Justin hurried over to her.

She placed an arm across her head, the cool floor a pleasant contrast to the perspiration coating her back. "My head took a hit, but otherwise I'm fine. Are you?" She rose on her elbows and searched Justin for signs of injury. "You're bleeding."

He glanced at his shoulder. "My wound opened up but it's okay."

Walker emerged from one of the doors and glanced around the room. "I heard screams and gunshots. What happened?"

Justin helped Marissa up. "Someone attacked Marissa after the lights went out."

"She grabbed me in the bathroom. I escaped, but I got disoriented and couldn't find my way back to your location."

"The lights were shut off at the main switch," Walker said.

"The attacker was a woman. She wanted to know about the data." Marissa rubbed her temple. "This data is a mystery. Must be important to someone."

Walker bent and picked up a piece of material. He turned it over and stared at the green patch. "I've seen pictures but never one this close."

Marissa rushed over for a closer inspection. "That's the same patch I found in David's casket and Justin's patient's room."

Walker rubbed the patch. "The symbol of The Order. Vivian Sinclair sent her."

"The attacker was definitely a woman, a very strong woman." Justin searched the hall, combed the stairs, and then ran back up.

"What are you looking for?" Marissa scanned the hall as Justin moved a chair.

Justin moved the bench closest to the stairs. Not finding anything, he moved to the next one. "Found it!" He straightened, clicked on the safety, and held up the gun.

Within a couple of strides, Walker caught up to Justin and motioned for the gun.

Justin took a step back and held the gun away from him but

declined to hand over the weapon.

Walker nodded and examined the gun from a distance. "Oh, no. This isn't good."

"What?" Marissa moved next to Justin.

Walker folded his hands in front of him. "This gun is a Smith & Wesson M & P 9. The weapon is a polymer-framed, short recoil, semi-automatic 9 mm pistol. The ergonomics and large capacity magazine make this weapon a good choice for LE."

"What's he talking about?" Marissa winced as pain shot through her head.

Scowling, Justin turned. "LE is law enforcement. He's saying this gun is police issued. She's a police officer, or at least has a gun carried by someone in law enforcement."

"I guess you were right." Marissa sagged against the wall."

Justin checked the magazine in the attacker's gun. "Okay, Walker, we've listened to your lecture on The Order and apparently we've fought another of their minions. You know about the data they're after. I now have two weapons I guarantee will make you talk.

Two hours later, Marissa collapsed on the bed, exhausted, but not sleepy. The bed had a few lumps but the room appeared clean. They'd checked into a small hotel off the highway and over seventy miles from the Brixton Library.

Justin stood across the room. "Are you okay with just one room?

She propped herself up on her elbows. "Actually, I'm glad. Call me a wimp, but I didn't want to be alone."

Justin moved closer to the bed as Marissa willed him to wrap her into his arms. His presence created a sense of safety and she longed to coil close to Justin and fall asleep on his chest.

"I understand. Are you sure you're not hurt anywhere?"

"I'm sore and shaken but not seriously hurt. Thank you doesn't seem to get the job done anymore."

"I can thank you as well. She would have shot me." Justin kicked off his shoes and fell onto the bed next to her. "Let me take a look at your throat."

She extended her head back as Justin, with a gentle touch, inspected her neck.

After a few seconds, he moved on to her arm. He turned her extremity, and then lowered her arm to the bed. "Your arm is okay and your neck is healing, but another attack like today and you'll be black and blue all over."

Justin hadn't wanted to stay anywhere near the library. By the time they stopped for more clothes and toiletries and then checked in, the time neared midnight.

Marissa reclined on the bed. "I can't believe David hacked into Skies International and tried to blackmail Vivian Sinclair, according to Walker." She sat up on her elbows again. "Do you believe he is telling the truth?"

Justin rested against the headboard and crossed his legs. "I don't trust Walker's motives, but with a gun in his face I think he told us the truth. David resorting to blackmail isn't hard to believe."

"Why? He didn't need money." Marissa studied Justin. Could he know more about David than he let on?

"David longed to mingle with the upper echelon, according to Neal."

"So David is working at Skies, somehow accesses a restricted area in their system, takes the data, which has to be pretty important, and blackmails Vivian Sinclair?" Marissa stared up at the ceiling, spotting a few brown stains in the corner.

"According to Walker." Justin paused and slid his burner phone from the pocket of his jeans onto the bedside table. "Awful convenient David happened to run into the one guy who had accumulated a large amount of data on the very covert organization led by the person he's trying to blackmail."

"Apparently, David had only met Harold Silva the night of Neal's party so maybe the hacking idea came after talking to Walker." Marissa shifted to face Justin. "We have to find the data."

"You're right. If they are still coming after us then they obviously don't have the data or they believe we have a copy." Justin met her gaze. "They won't kill us until we are no use to them, but at some point they'll cut their losses and come after us."

Marissa shivered. "Where would David hide something so important?" She scanned her memory for possible hiding places but came up empty.

"Your condo has been searched by the killers and the police without either coming away with the data in question. Is there any other place David would have hid something so important?" Justin turned sideways, using the palm of one hand to rest his head.

Marissa wrinkled her nose and considered the question. "I can't think of a single place."

"Just relax and try to remember conversations you had with him or special places you discussed."

In their entire four-year relationship, they took three vacations: Cabo San Lucas, Mexico, Napa Valley, California, and Key West, Florida. Each time, David had grumbled about missing work and oftentimes had to be pried away from his computer. She doubted he would have hidden the data in any of those places. The police had impounded David's car, and since he worked out of the condo he had no outside office to investigate. She scanned her memory for any clues and once again came up empty. "I've got nothing." Scooting out of bed, Marissa moved to their second story window and peered out. No black SUVs occupied the parking lot below.

"Why don't you take a shower? The warm water may relax you," Justin said.

Twenty minutes later she emerged from the shower, dried off with a thin towel, and slipped into a T-shirt and shorts. She had hoped the shower would calm her nerves, but the time alone had only escalated her worries. She'd been lucky tonight, but what about next time?

No doubt remained in her mind these people wouldn't stop until they got what they wanted. How had the woman even found them at the library? What if they never found the data? Would she and Justin spend the rest of their lives looking over their shoulders, worried about the next attack?

Pulling herself together required a little more time. When Justin announced he needed a shower Marissa exhaled, glad for a few more minutes alone.

She flipped on the television. Perhaps mindless distractions would help her nerves. A show about dogs highlighted a young family with a new puppy. She smiled at the memory of Halo as a puppy. Marissa hadn't been considering a dog the day she'd gone to a local farm to buy fresh vegetables but when she wandered past a litter of puppies, she'd been drawn to one of them. The small white furred puppy rubbed against her leg and followed her throughout the farm. She chalked the interaction up to love at first sight.

She longed for the comfort of her dog. Halo had a way of grounding her. The act of caring for another living creature, combined with the unbreakable connection they shared, gave her contentment.

"Cute dog" Justin appeared beside the bed. He wore shorts but no shirt.

For the first time, she spotted a long scar extending from Justin's collarbone to his left shoulder. Although curious about the scar, Marissa didn't ask.

She followed his gaze to the television. "Makes me miss Halo even more." She paused. "You know what else I miss? Strawberry smoothies in the morning."

"Soon all of this will be over." He flipped back the covers and rounded the bed. Pulling a chair closer, he settled in and propped his feet on the mattress.

She turned off the television and slipped between the sheets. The room blanketed her with silence as she clasped her hands on her stomach and stared at the ceiling. She glanced at Justin leaning back in the chair. "You don't have to sleep in an uncomfortable chair."

Justin chuckled. "I've slept in worse places. I'm good. Get some sleep."

Marissa nodded and closed her eyes. Maybe tomorrow would bring fresh answers—or new threats.

Chapter 31

S and swirled like a gritty tornado mixed with smoke and the putrid odor of gunpowder. The hole in the side of the war hospital allowed in the toxic mixture, which burned his eyes and throat. Fire snaked up another wall dangerously close to a row of oxygen tanks.

Justin rose from the floor after the explosion moments earlier. Pain seared through his shoulder. He glanced down to see blood spurting from a bullet wound. Ignoring his injury, he scanned the room.

Laura.

A loud moan led Justin to a crumpled body trapped beneath a gurney strapped with a wounded soldier. "Laura!" He righted the gurney. A piece of metal protruded from her leg, and blood poured from a deep gash in the right side of her head. The gash extended to her right eye, and Justin suspected she'd lost her vision. A chest wound caused labored breathing. "I need to get you on my table!" The most direct path out bisected the current gun battle. The hole in the wall created a possible escape route, but its proximity to the fire-threatened oxygen tanks made running through the hole a questionable decision.

The area he'd stood in moments earlier appeared unrecognizable. Dead soldiers and body parts were scattered about like they were staged for a horror movie.

Her left eye fluttered open. "Get the boy." She grimaced and closed her eye.

Before he could decide, he ducked as bullets whizzed past. Justin spent the next few minutes defending their position. Gunshots roared in his ears as he pivoted from one threat to another. A break in the gunfire gave Justin the opportunity to check on the boy he'd had on his operating table thirty minutes ago.

The young Iraqi boy had numerous injuries to his lower extremities but quick medical intervention had saved the boy's leg. With the boy still unconscious, Justin scooped him up and raced for the door. He passed several soldiers moaning in pain, a couple of them were part of his team. In minutes they were outside. Through the yellow murky sky he spotted the helicopter lowering toward them. After the helicopter took off with the boy, Justin ran back inside.

He encountered two of his teammates, badly injured and struggling to escape the carnage. Justin hurled one soldier over his arm and had the other lean on him. As he lowered them to the ground, he glimpsed another helicopter approaching.

He had to get Laura out but on his way he encountered more injured soldiers. He moved as many people out as he could, before making his way to Laura. Finding her still breathing, he picked her up and ran toward the door.

Just as he exited the facility an explosion erupted, hurling Justin to the ground. He stared up at the fireball engulfing the medical facility.

He scrambled to pick up Laura and darted for safety. Justin tripped over debris but managed to hold on to her. He found a clear spot and set her down.

"Laura!"

This time, no response. Her beautiful smile, frozen in lifeless amusement, stared back.

Justin stumbled backwards, falling over dead bodies as sand particles rammed his face, thick and hard.

Laura was dead. Everyone, dead. Through the sand and fire dead bodies rose and mocked him. "Useless doctor, you couldn't save us!"

With a yell, he bolted upright.

"Justin, are you okay?" Marissa tapped his shoulder.

He jumped up, sweat pouring down his face.

"It's me, Marissa."

He stared, blinked twice, and fought to comprehend. The fuzzy glow of the room slowly drifted into focus. "Damn!" He ran a hand through his hair and stalked into the bathroom, where he splashed his face with water. The cold liquid shocked his system. As he stared at his reflection, he almost didn't recognize the pained expression.

Several months had passed without incident, now two intense episodes in a matter of days. Why couldn't he move past this? He'd been prepared to deal with all the ins-and-outs of posttraumatic stress from a clinical perspective. The emotional part proved another beast. He launched into his breathing exercise. Ten minutes later, his thoughts calmer, he returned to the bedroom.

Marissa handed him a bottle of water.

"Thanks." He gulped down half the bottle. "I'm not a dangerous head case." He tried to smile.

She took a step closer. "I know." Another step, and she stood wrapped in his arms.

He snaked his arms around her and pulled her close. Inhaling her familiar lavender scent, he closed his eyes. This time, he only saw her. Minutes passed, then he pulled away and led her back to the bed. "Do you feel like hearing this now?"

She nodded as they climbed into bed and she moved close to him, showing no sign of hesitation. "What happened during your deployment?" She twisted a corner of the blanket, and then placed her hands in her lap.

Justin grimaced. "Iraq was a hellish place. We treated not only our wounded soldiers, but locals also. Kids were the toughest."

"How close to the front-line were you?"

"Not far. We were the first line of care. We stabilized the injured and shipped them out when conditions appeared safe. Since we were so close to the action, we were constantly under threat of attack, and a few times we actually were."

Marissa shivered in the cold breeze blowing from the air conditioner.

Justin pulled the covers over both of them. Her beautiful green eyes stared through the moonlit darkness of the room as she waited for him to continue.

"I met Laura, a nurse I served with Iraq. We were there for each other. I didn't love her in an intense above-no-other kind of way, but I cared deeply for her. I think we both needed the relationship to get us through."

"It was one of those days. The blasted sand gusted and cast this yellow hue to everything. I woke up, and the day felt off. You know, like something evil lived in the air."

Marissa nodded and snuggled into the crook of his arm.

He took her though the entire event.

"How devastating. I can't believe any type of training can prepare a person for those conditions."

"As doctors we're expected to heal others, but the pressure really comes from us. Most doctors, surgeons especially, demand perfection. We go into every surgery, believing we will save our patient, and the reality is like hell when we lose. The decisions are tough sometimes. We can get multiple trauma patients in the space of minutes, our immediate area frequently falls under attack, and deciding which patient to help can mean the difference between life and death. But that's my job. When I couldn't save Laura, who'd been nothing but selfless, the realization sent me over the edge." With eyes closed, he inhaled. He'd never opened up like this to anyone, even in his PTSD group sessions he maintained a guarded distance.

"What happened after the attack?"

"Unknown to me at the time, I had cuts, four cracked ribs, a fractured leg, and a gunshot wound to my shoulder. I was one of the lucky ones. I went to Ramstein, Germany for several days before I returned to the states. When I got home, everything moved the same. People went about their day without a clue about the real horror of what's happening on the other side of the world."

He stared up at the ceiling for several seconds. Pushing away the images had become a game. *How quickly could I kick them out?* "Half of my unit died in the attack. I went from funeral to funeral, saying all the right things to grieving family members, but feeling like a programmed robot. Laura's funeral was last, and after I left the cemetery, I went straight to a bar where I commenced drinking away the pain. After two months of on-and-off self-destructive behavior, Wendy gave me an ultimatum—get help, or she and Sam would be out of my life."

Marissa rose on an elbow and met his gaze.

Justin scanned her face for signs of pity but saw none. "I quit drinking and started going to AA. I will never deny being an alcoholic, but I will say giving up drinking wasn't difficult. I needed to be comatose for a while, but Wendy shocked me out of my funk. I knew the time had come to get my act together, plus the end of my medical leave neared."

"You're lucky to have Wendy."

Justin nodded. "We've shared some rough times." He paused, staring ahead before he continued. "I needed to do something positive, so with the hefty chunk of my inheritance I still had from my parents, I started the center. I made the center my mission. I had the place up and running within six months. In addition to physical therapy, we run AA and PTSD group sessions. Those meetings are the most popular services we offer. I try to attend both groups once a week. The alcohol resistance I have a good handle on, but obviously, you just witnessed me still struggling with posttraumatic stress." He paused. "I hope I didn't scare you."

"Bad dreams won't scare me away."

Justin stroked her hair while an internal debate raged. Remain neutral, or plunge forward? He didn't know how she felt and he didn't want her to think he would take advantage of this emotional time.

"Thank you. I get the feeling you aren't the kind of guy who goes around talking about this." She ran a finger down the scar on his shoulder. "Is this from the attack?

Justin nodded. "They got out the bullet and once I healed, I started a therapy program to build up my muscles again." He rubbed the scar, making contact with her hand.

"What about the boy and other soldiers?"

Justin covered her hand still splayed across his chest. He had come to know Marissa, but she still surprised him sometimes. He admired her natural way of caring about others. "I never saw the boy again. Do you remember Gabe? He lost a leg there."

Her eyes widened. "Wow. He looks great. You must get a lot of satisfaction from seeing him."

"I do, but I struggle not to take the glass-half-empty approach. I couldn't save Laura or the others, but at least Gabe and a few more soldiers are still here."

"I'm glad you're here." She smiled.

He caressed her face, heat rising within him. "You're beautiful." He moved toward her until his lips met hers.

She responded to him, her body shivering.

Parting her lips, he jumped at the chance to explore her mouth. Their tongues intertwined, and for the second time in a long time, he felt alive.

Chapter 32

Marissa opened her eyes as the sun peeked through the curtains. She yawned and detected Justin's empty spot in bed. She glanced around the small room. The bathroom door stood open. No Justin.

Closing her eyes, she savored the sweet memory of the long, passionate kiss they'd shared last night. He had opened up, and she understood how difficult it must have been. The night had deepened their bond, but what would daylight bring?

She bit her lip. All this conjecture only ended in premature guesses. They'd shared another amazing kiss but it didn't have to mean anything. Maybe Justin sensed she needed the closeness and obliged her. And oblige he did. In all the years she'd been with David, she had never experienced a kiss so soul shaking.

The hotel door opened, and Justin entered wearing jeans and a T-shirt.

For a moment, Marissa followed his stride, taking in his rippling muscles and a handsome face as he moved toward her with a beverage carrier and a bag.

"I hope I didn't wake you."

Marissa sat up and pulled the blanket over her, aware of her skimpy clothes. "No, I just woke up."

He handed her a large plastic cup and a warm whole-wheat bagel.

She peered inside the cup and took a quick sip. "You got me a smoothie?"

"You seemed like you could use a bit of normal."

"Thank you." Her voice cracked as she placed the cup on the nightstand. The simple gesture had her insides turning to mush. She couldn't stop the flow of tears.

Justin scooted next to her. "I didn't mean to upset you." With his thumb, he wiped away her tears.

Marissa shook her head as more tears flowed. "This smoothie is... special." She laughed. "Stupid, I know." She huffed out a breath. "This means a lot to me." She wanted to say more but her brain put the brakes on her awakening heart.

Justin nodded and pulled her into his arms.

The warmth of his embrace enveloped her, creating a sense of safety and trust in her crumbling world. She clung to the feeling, reality telling her the sensation couldn't last, but hope claiming a tiny spot in her heart. Marissa pulled away. "I'm a little emotional today."

The hum of the air conditioner cut through the silence, before Justin spoke. "You're entitled but understand this: we're going to survive—together."

For the first time, Marissa, with all of her heart, believed, somehow, they would. They'd survive as individuals, but could she hope for more?

Once again Justin brushed his thumb across her face, his gaze boring into hers. He smiled as he dropped his hand. Rising from the bed, he reached for the bag of bagels. After spreading his bagel with a thin layer of cream cheese he busied himself preparing his coffee. "I want to talk about what happened yesterday."

Marissa inhaled. *Did he regret kissing her?*

"I know we talked about Walker and his revelations, but what does your gut say about him?"

She didn't expect a question about Walker, but her mind whirled back to the harrowing events. "I'm not sure. He seems nice enough. I haven't had time to digest any of what he said."

Justin nodded and took a bite of his bagel. "I'm not sure I trust him. As soon as you went to the bathroom, he left, claiming he had to get a map. He didn't come back until after the attacker fled."

She raised a brow. "Do you think he's an accomplice?"

"I don't know, but I'm concerned. How did the woman know we were at the library?"

Marissa tore a piece of her bagel apart as she considered Justin's suspicions.

Walker had been working with David, so we could reasonably suspect him of holding back. What if Walker had the flash drive and planned on using the data for his own interests? Walker said he had more pictures, but they weren't with the information he presented last night. They'd made plans to speak later today so he could show them the remainder of the documents he had accumulated.

"Why haven't they killed me? They've had opportunity, and while I'd like to believe I'm lucky, I'm not sure my luck runs that deep." She twirled the straw, mixing the pink colored liquid.

Justin blew across the small opening in his cup. Steam swirled upward in thin curlicues.

"The attacker could have killed you before I got there, but she obviously still thinks you know where the data is." He got up and retrieved the gun from his gym bag. "Why did she leave this? She ran right by the gun. We've already determined this gun is used by law enforcement, so this person is probably trained, yet she didn't retrieve her gun." He paused a moment before placing the weapon back into the bag. "I think she intended for us to find her weapon."

"As a warning?"

"Exactly. I think they want us to know who they are."

Marissa rose and placed her cup on the bedside table. "I'm no threat to Vivian Sinclair or The Order." She wrapped her arms around herself. "We can't be sure what Walker is telling us is even true."

"Maybe we should do a little research on our own." Justin placed his coffee cup beside hers.

He stood in front of her, but didn't touch her, his massive chest looming like a boulder.

She wanted to touch him, but refrained. Were all these emotions real? Neither she nor Justin could afford to be distracted by romantic notions.

When Justin placed his hands on the sides of her arms, she shivered.

"Marissa, I care about you. I haven't gotten our kiss out of my mind." His jaw tightened and he glanced at the floor for a few seconds before turning back to her. "I don't want to do anything to make you uncomfortable. I'm in uncharted territory and not sure which way to go. David was my best friend, and a code exists among guys..."

Marissa's heart flipped. Once again doubt invaded. Did he regret the kiss? "I understand. I just buried my fiancé. We were both...tired." Total bull, but what else could she say? *I just experienced the most mind-blowing kiss of my life?*

"I want you to trust me." He moved closer. "I loved kissing you, but I know it's probably too soon, too much, not right..."

She nodded, unable to activate her vocal chords. Telling him they were moving too fast would have been the appropriate thing to say, yet her heart signaled her to run toward Justin, not away.

"Marissa." Voice thick, his hands moved up her arms, resting on her shoulders. Then he continued upwards to her neck before caressing her face.

"Justin..."

Unsure who moved first, she drifted toward him, until their lips met. Sensible restraint evaporated as Marissa allowed herself to fall, to feel the passion from another man.

When they parted, she stared into his brown eyes.

"Did I make a mistake?" Justin took a step back.

She smiled. "You've been here with me ever since I discovered

David's body. You've done more for me than anyone else. Maybe I *should* say this is wrong, but I can't."

"I'll admit I'm struggling with what to do. I don't want to hurt you." He sighed and pulled away, the moment evaporating into a memory. "We have time to figure this out. Let's get out of here."

An hour later, they took the stairs to the hospital basement. Justin wove a familiar route through the catacombs, passing various marked doors before coming to a stop outside a door devoid of any markings.

A young man whipped open the door and peered out. "Hey, Justin, man, come on in. You didn't have to make the trip in on your vacation. I would have emailed the results." He had an unmistakable, melodious Caribbean island accent.

"Thanks, Ben, I appreciate the favor. This is Marissa." Justin continued to hold her hand. "Marissa, meet Ben Yearwood, genius."

Ben slapped Justin on the back. "This guy is freaking Spock. He calls me and says 'I got a patient, this is what I think is going on, and what I expect to show up in their labs'. Nine times out of ten, this guy is right on the money. We even started taking bets on lab results." Ben flashed a huge grin. "Currently, I owe him a steak dinner."

Marissa returned his smile. "He is pretty awesome."

Ben raised his eyebrows and nudged Justin.

Marissa's face turned crimson.

"Have a seat, pretty lady."

Justin showed Marissa to a tall stool. A panel of glass spanning the length of the office exhibited an impressive lab. At present, three people sat working at individual stations. Justin told her he'd planned their arrival at a time most of the workers went on break. He didn't want to risk a lot of attention. "What's the verdict?"

"I got nothing, Spock. The patient, J.L., had an above-normal white blood cell count, but nothing else sticks out." Ben punched a button on the computer. A machine whizzed to life and spouted out the lab results.

Justin grabbed the paper and scanned the page. "How did they do it?" He paced the floor, and then stopped. "Did you freeze blood and urine samples?"

"Yep, just like you asked. Why?" Ben leaned on the counter next to Marissa.

"SUX."

"Yeah, it sucks but I don't know what else you were expecting on this one." Ben nodded.

"No, I mean succinylcholine."

"You think the anesthesiologist overdosed her? Wasn't she a day or two post-op?"

"If succinylcholine were present in her system, the anesthesiologist didn't administer it." Justin ran his hand through his hair.

Ben raised both hands. "Whoa, I'm not a forensic lab. I can't do that type of analysis here. I can tell you if your patient's LDLs are high, if they're having a heart attack, or have a busted thyroid."

"What's succinylcholine?" Marissa asked.

Justin stopped pacing. "Succinylcholine is a paralytic agent used in the hospital as anesthesia. We use it in small quantities and under controlled conditions. If injected into my patient, she would have died almost instantly."

Ben straightened. "Are you saying someone murdered her?"

Justin nodded. "It's the perfect murder weapon. The drug works quickly, especially if injected into her IV line, and the metabolites of this medication occur naturally in the body, making forensic detection almost impossible." He examined the lab report again. "Ben, this entire conversation stays between us. I've alerted the police about my suspicions, but I don't think they're taking me seriously."

Nodding, Ben approached a computer on a nearby counter and punched at the keyboard. "There's probably still police around, if you want to catch one, just in case."

Justin hiked his eyebrow. "What do you mean I could still catch one?"

Ben hit a button on the computer, and the screen saver popped up. He turned to Justin and Marissa. "A nursing student was shot dead in the back parking lot. She worked up in ICU. Emily..."

Marissa jumped off the stool. "Emily? I met her."

"You mean Emily Filmore?" Justin stood in a wide stance, hands on hips. His mind raced back to the day Mrs. Lambert died. Had Emily witnessed her murder?

Ben glanced at him. "I think Emily was her name. The shooter escaped."

Justin met Marissa's gaze.

"Can I use your computer?" Marissa asked.

"Sure." Ben approached another computer across the room and moved a stack of manuals. He punched in a password and the screen came to life.

Marissa sat at the computer and entered Walker Mumfrey's name in the search box.

Justin stood over her and read through the returned entries. After a few minutes, he sighed. "Nothing."

A basic search yielded information on his position as a librarian, a couple of articles he wrote regarding research organization and tools. He graduated *magna cum laude* from University of Wisconsin with a double major in psychology and library sciences. Based on his online resume, he'd been employed at a library in Wisconsin for two years before moving to Virginia and working for the Brixton library for the last three years. No criminal record or evidence of legal issues could be found. There were also no apparent ties to Skies International, Harold Silva, Vivian Sinclair, or The Order.

Next, she ran a search on The Order and found nothing significant.

Justin took Marissa's hand. "Let's go." He turned to Ben. "Keep those samples on ice."

"Okay, man." Ben waved.

Justin ushered Marissa to the door and turned to Ben. "Like I said, between us. Forget the steak dinner. I owe you."

Chapter 33

The dog nudged Marissa's hand in the bright kitchen of Kelly and Craig's house.

"I'm glad to see you, too, boy." She bent and rubbed Halo's furry head. "Thanks for taking care of him, but Craig you didn't have to rush home on our account."

They'd driven into the garage with the hope of limiting their chances of being spotted.

Craig grinned. "Just wanted to make sure you two were okay." He leaned against the counter. "Justin, do you need any help? Where are you staying tonight?"

"Not sure yet but we'll be okay. You've been a huge help. Thanks." Justin patted Halo's head.

Kelly glanced at the dog. "Gavin loved having Halo around, but I know you're happy to have him back with you. Please be safe." Kelly hugged Marissa. "Are you okay?"

Marissa shrugged.

Justin cleared his throat. "Come on Halo. Let's grab your stuff and get you in the car." He turned to Marissa. "We have a few minutes but we should leave soon." He hugged Kelly. "Thanks."

Craig pushed off the counter. "I'll go get Halo's stuff."

When the men exited the room, Kelly stared at Marissa. "What's going on?"

Marissa gave her a two-minute rundown of the past few days, from meeting Walker, learning all the harrowing things about Vivian and her organization, the deaths at the hospital, Tiffany's death, to the attack at the library."

Kelly inhaled. "Wow. That's a lot to process. Are you feeling okay?" She gently touched the ugly bruises on Marissa's neck.

"I'm better. Looks worse than I feel." She paused. "Justin and I kissed. I'm confused."

Kelly smiled. "I thought I detected something. He's a good guy. I know you're both dealing with a lot of emotion so don't put pressure on anything. Don't feel guilty. You were about to break the engagement with David."

Marissa nodded. "You're right, but I don't want to mess things up." She glanced up at the microwave clock. "We've got to go. After this is over, you and I are having a long overdue spa day. I need normal." Marissa hugged Kelly.

"Love you." Kelly whispered.

"Love you." Marissa smiled.

Ten minutes later, Justin and Marissa were back on the highway heading away from her friends' house.

"Thanks for swinging by to get Halo," Marissa said.

Justin nodded.

She allowed a few minutes to pass in silence. "You're not really comfortable with Craig, are you?" She'd seen Justin's slight bristle when Craig asked them where they were staying tonight.

"At this point, I'm suspicious of nearly everyone." Justin kept his gaze trained on the road.

"I've known Craig for years. Kelly and I were roommates in college. We met Craig our sophomore year. He's a great guy." Marissa hoped her words would ring true. She stared out of the window. Silly to think Craig could be involved in something like this. He'd never hurt her. Yet, hadn't she at one time thought the same about David?

Whipping through one suburban area to another, they headed

toward Walker's apartment. While the library held a certain measure of protection during normal operating hours, they'd now be entering Walker's private residence. Caution signs should have been flashing, however threatening vibes from Walker hadn't materialized in her.

Marissa angled her body toward Justin. "If David started all this by downloading data these people obviously didn't want him to have, then maybe we can end it if we find this data and give the information back."

Justin glanced her way. "You have a point. If we find this data, then we have a bargaining chip. We could give the information to the authorities, but we'd have to determine which agencies weren't in The Order's corner. Or, we could work out a deal with this Vivian person."

Marissa chewed her lip. "That's a dangerous game and may have been what led to David's murder."

Justin nodded. "I'm convinced David saw dollar signs when he discovered this data."

He pulled into the apartment's parking lot and cut the engine. "Trust me. When we get in here, if you sense something wrong, let me know." He leaned close and kissed her.

Walker's suburban apartment complex contained ten buildings, several of which were still under construction.

Marissa didn't take Walker for a guy who'd go for something this new. She pictured him living in an old house, or maybe a converted warehouse.

They located Building Six and made their way up to the second floor, Halo lumbering along with them.

Walker flung open the door and invited them inside with a sweep of his hand. "Whoa." He stopped and stared at Halo. "That's a huge animal."

Halo stared back and moved in front of Marissa.

"He's only lethal if you're a bad guy." Justin stepped inside the apartment.

Walker laughed a nervous chuckle. "Well, I-I guess I'll live."

Marissa placed a hand on Halo's head. "He's well behaved."

Walker relaxed his shoulders. "Come on in. I know what you're thinking. I don't look like I belong in a hip and swanky apartment. I'd prefer something more vintage, but here I don't have to worry about a sketchy Internet connection or clanging water pipes."

The "swanky" apartment's living room contained a hunter green leather couch, worn cracks snaking throughout, and a walnut coffee table stacked with books. Four bookshelves dominated the room, each filled to capacity.

He directed them to a room with a large worktable and two desks topped with several computers. On the table lay hundreds of photos some fanned out and some piled in stacks. "Welcome. I'm happy you're back after the disturbing incident yesterday. Marissa, how are you feeling?"

Walker wore a black Darth Vader T-shirt with dark jeans and blue Converse tennis shoes. He resembled a college student more than a post-graduate librarian. "I'm okay. Thanks. What's all this?" She eyed the pictures on the table as Halo remained at her side.

"All the photographs I could find associated with The Order. Many I took with a long-range zoom lens. I also wanted to show you a more detailed map of Babylon Hall. Not exactly to scale, but it's the best I could locate after researching state records. The property specifics on Google Earth are wiped out, so those kind of specifics are a no-go."

"How close did you get to the property?" Justin moved around the table, studying the photos.

"It's impossible to get too close. Guards are stationed all around the property. I hiked through the woods and came in from the east. I got within five hundred yards of the perimeter." Walker pointed to the aerial photo of the property. "During my research, I discovered a tunnel system under the estate. I can't be certain if it's still used, but one exit comes out into the woods, right about here." He tapped a spot on the map, near what appeared to be a deep ravine.

Marissa continued her tour of the photos on the table, and came to a stop. "That's her." Her heart jumped a beat as she pointed.

Walker leaned across the table to examine the picture. "That's Vivian Sinclair."

"I saw her in one of your pictures yesterday, and I've seen her up close." Marissa stared at the woman in the photo, posing in front of their enlarged heptagon logo. As she focused on the woman's eyes, she concluded both the woman at David's funeral and the woman in the bookstore were the same person.

Justin darted over to examine the photo. "There's the ring and the logo." He glanced up at Walker.

"Ah, yes, the emerald ring. Her father, Russell, gave her the ring to celebrate her coronation as head of The Order. Let's look at the seven-sided symbol, some say figures into numerology and deeper meanings." Walker stood at the head of the table and shoved his hands into his pockets. "The number seven plays a significant role in society and is important in religion. In the Bible, the seventh day is the Sabbath, there were seven plagues, and Jesus performed seven miracles. In Roman Catholicism, there are seven sacraments. The examples go on and on." He rotated his hands in a rolling motion "There are seven Wonders of the World, which may be part of why Vivian's estate is called Babylon Hall. The Statue of Liberty wears a crown of seven spikes, some say represents the seven continents and seven seas. By using the number seven, Russell Sinclair is elevating himself and The Order on par with important aspects of our history and religion. However, there isn't a lot of evidence to suggest The Order members are either religious or devil-worshipers, but they certainly have a dark side."

Justin leaned across the table, his jaw tight. "This is all very interesting, but Vivian Sinclair has been stalking Marissa. Yesterday's attack proved they are still after her. Vivian's people likely killed my patient, a student nurse, and David's girlfriend. I can't sit by and let Marissa be a sitting duck. I want to know everything. Now!"

Walker's head snapped up and his gaze widened. "I-I *have* been telling you all I know. Perhaps now's the time to call in the police."

"No. You just said last night the gun, I believe left intentionally, could be police issued. Vivian Sinclair likely has the police on her payroll. We can't be sure whom to trust. They obviously believe Marissa knows where this data is."

With his forefinger, Walker tapped his lip. "You said your patient, a student nurse, and David's girlfriend have all died or been killed?"

Justin nodded. "I'm certain Vivian had my patient killed because of the patch found in her room. A sniper near the hospital parking lot killed the student nurse who found the patch. Lastly, David's girlfriend, Tiffany, died after being run over by a black SUV who sped away."

Walker's eyes widened. "That's three people, four if you count David. There has to be three more."

Marissa stared at Walker. "Three more what?"

"Vivian believes in the symbolism of seven. I'm postulating she has developed a kill list of seven individuals somehow related to this situation."

Justin glanced around the room and took her hand. "Marissa and I have already been targeted. If there is a list, we're probably on it, but who is the last person?"

Marissa met Walker's gaze. "You have to take precautions."

Clearing his throat, Justin dropped Marissa's hand and placed an arm around her shoulders. "They think we know where the flash drive is. I think we all stay alive while the data is still missing."

"We have to find the flash drive before they do," Marissa said, staring at Vivian's picture.

Justin stalked to the other side of the table, his large body shadowing Walker's thin frame. "If you know where this information is, I suggest you tell us."

"I don't know where the data is. The last meeting with David, the meeting you kept for him, we planned to discuss how he'd share the data with me. He'd been afraid they were on to him. He had a flash drive hidden somewhere." Walker hung his head and whispered, "He said he hid the flash drive in a place only Marissa could find."

Walker and Justin stared at her—one with raised eyebrows, the other with a furrowed brow.

Marissa's mouth dropped open. "I don't know. I can't even think...

we didn't have a safe or a safety deposit box. No hidden floorboards at the condo or secret compartments."

"I don't think he meant you knew exactly where he hid the data. I think he expected you would be able to pinpoint a location. Perhaps some place special..." Walker took a step back from Justin.

With a prolonged stare, Justin's massive presence loomed over Walker before he turned to Marissa. "Are you sure you can't pinpoint one location he might have used as a hiding spot?"

Shrugging, Marissa shook her head. "The police have scoured the condo and both our cars."

"What about the studio?" Justin asked.

Marissa perked up and shifted her gaze between the men. "He did stop by a couple of weeks before I left for my business trip. I taught an evening class and forgot a CD. He brought me the CD and used my office to return a phone call before he left."

Justin moved toward the door. "Let's go. You too, Walker."

THREE HOURS LATER, Marissa leaned back against the headrest of Justin's SUV. Her head pounded like a jackhammer but she ignored the pain.

"I think you're scaring Walker." She turned to glimpse Walker following them in his car toward Timber Creek, a small town outside Babylon Hall.

Justin had insisted on two cars, just in case.

"I have this feeling he's holding something back." He shrugged. "I'm kind-of guarded after everything that's happened."

"I'm sorry the studio didn't reveal anything. Where could David have hidden the flash drive?" She'd been asking herself the same question over and over again without any answers.

Justin glanced at her, and then turned his attention back to the road. "Why don't you get some rest? I'll wake you when we arrive."

Marissa let her shoulders relax. "I'm too anxious to sleep. We're about to walk into the lion's den."

"We're not exactly walking in but just taking a look."

"We've been reacting to every move thrown at us. We need to get proactive. Gathering as much information as we can on Vivian, The Order, and Skies International will help us determine our next move. I'm afraid time is running out, and we're in for something huge." Marissa's pulse quickened. What more could they expect? The life-and-death consequences had never been more apparent.

Marissa glanced at Halo resting in the back seat and then stared out at the summer sky reminding her of peach and vanilla swirled ice cream. For the first time, in over a year, contentment swept over her, if only for a moment. Inside the cocoon of their SUV, with Halo in the back seat and Justin by her side, she could breathe, at little. A few seconds later, the little voice inside her whispered this feeling wouldn't last.

Evening had settled in when Justin pulled into the gravel driveway. Marissa stirred awake. She hadn't expected to fall asleep, but somewhere along the way she could no longer keep her eyes open. Glimpsing the rustic two-story house, she straightened in her seat. Steep roof pitches and huge windows framed the house. Giant fir trees surrounded the dwelling like watchmen on guard.

Justin followed the driveway to the side of the house. He jumped out of the SUV, punched in the garage code on the outer keypad the property rental agent had provided, and motioned for Walker to pull into the two-car garage. He kept the SUV outside.

Walker climbed out of his car, strolled to the driveway, and surveyed the house. "This is a spectacular timber-framed structure. Douglas fir or Sitka spruce are common options for wood, but there are others. If you examine the beams, you'll probably see the timbers are not fitted together with nails or screws, but instead the lattice design is completed with bricks or stones. Very often, construction like this means load-bearing walls aren't needed, giving way to large, open rooms."

"Feel free to inspect the exterior architecture, I'm going inside." Justin opened the SUV's back door for Halo then pulled out their bags. Extracting the keys from an envelope, Justin unlocked the back door.

Marissa stepped into the sunroom, filled with a gray overstuffed couch adorned with bright yellow pillows and another large gray-striped chair with a matching ottoman. The room screamed summer relaxation, and she craved a glass of iced tea and a good book.

Justin and Walker joined her and moved from the sunroom, through the kitchen, and into the cavernous living room. The brandy-colored wooden floors matched the exposed beams and created a seamless appearance. Wide, expansive windows on the back wall allowed stunning views of the lake. A path led from the house to a boat dock where a small fishing dinghy bobbed in the dark waters. On the other side of the lake, the forest rose opposing with dense summer foliage. In the distance, peaks from the Blue Ridge Mountains soared against the backdrop of a setting sun, capping off the picturesque view. "Beautiful," Marissa murmured.

Justin pulled her toward him. "Not nearly as beautiful as you." He ran a finger along her jaw before he walked to the door. "I'll take Halo out and then I'll be back."

"Just as I expected," Walker said, his gaze cast upward as he studied the living room ceiling.

Marissa ventured upstairs and chose a room decorated in various shades of purple, reminiscent of her childhood room. The large room contained a huge window seat overlooking the lake with the mountains in the background. Once again, she wanted to climb on the window seat and lose herself in the scenery, or in a book. She sighed, longing for the freedom of this carefree vacation house.

She placed her bag inside the room and leaned against the closed door. The house contained four bedrooms so she and Justin had no need to share a room. Tonight she'd be alone. They had spent all day, every day, together for over a week now. Outside of being hunted by an evil, crazy woman, she'd come to enjoy being with him. At least tonight, she'd have Halo to keep her company. She huffed a sigh. One moment she channeled her inner warrior by following a mad man onto a roof and firing a gun at a masked woman and the next she craved cuddling with Justin all night long. She cradled Halo's head. "I'm all over the place."

Halo licked her face, as if to soothe her teeter-totter emotions.

Once settled, she went back downstairs. Justin and Walker sat at the kitchen table, cans of soft drinks in their hands.

Justin rose as she entered. "Can I get you something? The pantry and fridge were already stocked."

"I'll help myself." Marissa waved him off, opened the refrigerator and pulled out a bottle of water. She cross the room to the table and slid into a chair in between Justin and Walker. "What's our next move?"

"We'll hike over to Babylon Hall in the morning, if the weather is good." Justin took a swig from his can.

"Forecast says we're in for a rainy period over the next few days. We'll have to play it by ear." Walker spread out one of his maps and explained the physical landscape of the area approaching Babylon Hall, the security checkpoints around the compound, and more about the compound itself.

"I think seeing Babylon Hall will give us perspective, but without the flash drive, I don't know how we will level the playing field." She clasped her hands around the cool bottle as Halo nudged his head onto her lap.

Justin nodded. "In order to play ball with them, we must have leverage." He turned to Walker. "You're sure David said Marissa would know the hiding place?"

"I'm positive." Walker stood and crossed the room.

Justin swiped a hand through his hair. "Make a list of places and things you did. Maybe writing things down will spark something."

"How am I supposed to know what David considered special? I didn't actually know the man. Yes, he could be charming and sweet, but I saw another side." She stood, the chair legs scraping across the floor and Halo stepped back. Through the window, she gazed at the mountain range, low clouds now impeding a full view. Just like her hazy view of the mountains, her view of David had been just as unfocused.

"I could go for a run but I'll settle for a nice soak in the tub." She inhaled and ambled out. After a long bath, Marissa stood in her room and stared out at the moon's reflection on the lake. Halo joined her, sitting at her feet. When she turned away and climbed into bed, Halo settled in next to her.

David had banned Halo from sleeping with them, so after many nights of sad stares, the dog got used to sleeping on the floor on Marissa's side of the bed. He seemed to understand the rule no longer applied.

An hour later, sleep still eluded her. Despite all her efforts, she couldn't relax. She focused on Halo's even breathing as her hand rested on his furry back. Sleeping anywhere must be nice.

She longed to speak with her parents, Vanessa, and Kelly. They represented her life, and a time when she didn't worry about fighting to stay alive. Now, she couldn't go anywhere without looking over her shoulder and wondering when the boogeyman would jump out of the shadows. They'd come so close to hurting or killing her. If not for Justin...

Why did every thought end with Justin? She'd always be thankful for him. He had risked his life.

She willed her brain not to ruminate over Justin, but his image pushed through. His strong hands and muscular chest flashed into her mind. She didn't want to miss his presence beside her, but she did. Although her heart ran toward Justin, her head considered a relationship a bad decision. She had many decisions to make. Selling the condo, finding a new place to live, getting on with her life. There would be no room for a relationship, but the thought of Justin not being around terrified her.

None of her plans mattered now. A madwoman hunted her. She had been lucky so far, but didn't luck always run out? Would they torture her before they killed her?

Vivian Sinclair's dress-up games served what point? Marissa

reviewed the encounter in the bookstore. Why didn't Vivian have her men take her then?

She reached over to the bedside table, switched on the light, and pulled a tablet from her purse. Perhaps listing various places around town she and David had enjoyed *would* stimulate her brain and pinpoint where he'd hidden the data. Anything to get this crazy woman off their backs.

Fifteen minutes later, she glared at the paltry list. If a compendium of happy memories spent doing mutually satisfying activities comprised the hallmark of a good relationship, she had written evidence she and David had been doomed.

David obviously worked out, but never bothered to go for a run with her, and couldn't even manage to tell her about his membership at Justin's training facility.

They frequently went out to dinner, but now Marissa concluded their meals were a result of necessity, rather than two people in love wanting to spend time together in nice restaurants.

She shoved the notepad back into her purse.

Memories of that night in the restaurant flooded back. She flipped off the light and wrapped her hands around her midsection. Sometimes, her womb still ached.

Chapter 34

A light knock on the door shook Marissa from runaway thoughts of masked men and women, Molotov cocktails, and killers on the loose in a hospital.

Halo's head popped up as his ears perked.

She relaxed when she opened the door to Justin. "Can't sleep either?"

He smiled and shook his head. "I have a nice room, but I'm kind of restless. Mind if I come in?"

At one point she would have attempted to cover herself, but Justin had already seen her in shorts, so the action appeared unnecessary and prudish. Besides, he'd dressed similarly.

Halo's tail beat a vigorous cadence in silent greeting.

Justin bent and scratched his head.

Marissa glimpsed a strip of moonlight shimmering on the lake, bookended by inky blackness on either side. "Beautiful night." She plopped down at the window seat.

"Are you okay?" Justin peered out then sat next to her.

Marissa shrugged and leaned against the wall. "I've been drawing blanks about the flash drive. I'm sickened I didn't know him well enough to figure this out."

"David could be complicated at times."

"I always thought of myself as a simple girl. I wanted a great career, security, honesty, and to find the love of my life." She threw her hands up. "Maybe I'm asking too much."

Justin stroked Halo's head. "You *can* be angry with him, you know."

Marissa pulled at her lip. "Do you believe in the possibility he downloaded this data for noble purposes?"

"No."

Marissa nodded. "He was a liar with a heartless personality." She wrung her hands and inhaled.

Justin angled toward her. "Talk to me."

Marissa remained quiet for a few seconds. When she spoke, she couldn't keep her voice from wavering, thick with emotion. "He was more than a liar." She gazed at the floor as she voiced the memories never been spoken to anyone.

The fresh aroma of bread and cheese had wafted through the air. Marissa and David had frequented the restaurant on several occasions. Tonight, however, Marissa could only stomach small pieces of food. Her pumpkin tortellini had almost gone untouched while David had almost devoured his sirloin with spinach gnocchi.

David sipped red wine after plopping another chunk of steak into his mouth. He glanced across the table. "Aren't you hungry?"

"Not really. I told you I wasn't feeling well." Marissa sipped water in an attempt to stave off a pounding headache on the horizon.

"Oh, right." David placed his fork against the plate and stared with bored eyes. "Look, I'll be straight with you. I'm not ready for a baby. The wedding is less than a year away, and I'm good with just you and I for now. I'm working hard to take my consulting business to the next level, and I need to give it every ounce of my attention. There's just no room for a baby."

Marissa clamped her fists under the table. How could he say he didn't want their baby? "It's not like we have a choice. Neither of us intended for this to happen, but it did. I'm pregnant, David. We're having a baby." She shifted in her seat. "I know our plans didn't include a baby right now, but it's ours and I'm happy about the pregnancy." She hoped declaring her delight at being pregnant with his child would make him see the light.

David expelled a loud sigh and gulped his wine. He finished the glass and signaled the waiter for another bottle. "I know you're probably all hopped up on the wedding planning and happily ever after shit, but now is not the time for a baby."

Marissa leaned across the table and lowered her voice. "David, do you hear what you're saying? We aren't just mulling over potentially having a baby, I'm already pregnant."

With his fork midway to his mouth, he clanked down his utensil louder than necessary. "Don't be so dense. It's a simple procedure." He pursed his lips.

Her mouth dropped open. She couldn't believe the man she had agreed to marry was the same man before her now.

Without an ounce of understanding or compassion, he shoved away his plate, knocking over a saltshaker. He appeared to seethe at her stupidity. Marissa had never seen this side of him. How could she marry a man like this? She understood him being blindsided by the news, but she'd never imagined he'd be this callous as to mention abortion.

"Excuse me." Marissa escaped from the table and made her way to the ladies' room. Slamming the door on the stall, she leaned over the commode and vomited. Even though her pregnancy measured two weeks shy of the three-month mark, she knew this nauseous feeling related to more than morning sickness. As her stomach released its contents, she allowed tears to fall. Her mind whirled with thoughts of her future. Regardless of what David wanted, she would have this baby. If he chose not to be part of their child's life, then she'd get by.

The weight of a thousand decisions plummeted down. Did she have the guts to cancel the wedding, move out, and have a baby on her own? With the wedding months away, she had time to grapple with the horrifying thought of telling everyone she'd called off the engagement. As she wrapped her arms around her belly, she'd never felt so alone. She hadn't told anyone about her pregnancy, hoping David would come around before she shared the news.

Leaning against the bathroom stall, she inhaled as the wave of nausea passed. *Before leaving the bathroom, she splashed water on her face, and returned to the table.*

David had finished his meal and had begun a conversation on his cell phone. His Rolex watch caught her attention in the soft lighting. David enjoyed expensive item, even if they weren't quite there financially. Another red flag? Had she been blinded by his charms? The recognition she might have been duped almost had her charging back to the toilet bowl. She'd worked too hard to be self-sustaining and in control to allow David to steamroll over her.

He continued his conversation for a few minutes more, then hung up. "Are you going to eat?"

Marissa glared at him. "I've lost my appetite."

"I'm just being honest." He pushed her glass of water closer. "Drink."

Marissa didn't want to comply, but with a parched throat she downed the entire glass, noting an odd taste but chalking her reaction up to her recent sickness. "Let's go. I'm not feeling well."

An hour later, she lay in the dark, her back to David. Sleep eluded her, but David's soft snoring, usually comforting, now served as a reminder of a heartless man.

What happened to him? After he proposed, something switched off and a new man emerged. One she didn't understand or even like. Could there be problems with his business? David never spoke much about his business, but nevertheless could she disregard the nastiness he spewed tonight? Tomorrow, she'd make him talk to her. Shutting her out didn't bode well for a successful marriage.

At the restaurant, she had been ready to call off the wedding, and now she pondered ways to save the relationship. Marissa pulled the blanket tighter around her, and a sharp pain shot through her abdomen. She gasped, but the discomfort dissipated.

Halo popped up and stared.

"I'm okay."

He seemed to nod, and lowered his head back to the floor.

She shifted in bed and glanced at the alarm clock, wanting sleep to take her away for a while.

Another shard of pain racked her and her heart started to race. This time, the pain didn't go away, but instead multiplied in intensity. Marissa sat up, beads of sweat forming on her face. She touched something wet and sticky on her leg. She stumbled to the bathroom for an inspection.

Bright blood greeted her as the pain continued.

Halo stood at the door, hesitated, then ventured farther into the bathroom. Soft licks were his way of comforting her.

"Go get David," Marissa said, grimacing as she doubled over in pain.

David stood at the door a few seconds later. "Oh, no."

Marissa lay on the floor as bright red blood and tissue burst out of her body. She held onto her stomach as if her hands could keep her baby inside. "I need to get to a hospital!" she yelled out as another round of pain shook her.

Once they arrived at the hospital and she'd been placed in a room, David mumbled something and left. She waited only mere minutes to hear a doctor pronounce what she'd already feared. She'd had a miscarriage. Having the word uttered aloud caused a mournful wail to escape. Shock registered with Marissa when she'd recognized she'd been the one emitting the pathetic moan.

A nurse rushed to her side and placed a warm arm across her shoulders. "Do you need me to call someone?"

Through clouded, tear-filled eyes, Marissa stared back at the young woman. "No, I-I... My fiancé brought me in." Where was David?

"I'll go out to the waiting area and see if he's there. What's his name?" Armed with David's full name, the nurse left the room.

Marissa collapsed back against the pillow.

The nurse wouldn't find him.

He'd abandoned her. Marissa ran a hand across her empty belly. "I'm sorry." She'd asked the doctor over and over again what she'd done wrong.

The doctor explained she'd done nothing to cause the miscarriage. It just happened. To make matters worse, the examination indicated remnants of fetal contents remained. She'd need a dilation and curettage to remove the balance. The news had been like salt dumped on an open wound.

She couldn't call her mother, Vanessa, or Kelly when she hadn't even told them about her pregnancy. Feeling like a fool, she'd have to get through this on her own.

Several hours later, with the D&C procedure completed and her obligatory time in the recovery room concluded, she'd been released. Morning had come, and David had not returned. Marissa called for a taxi.

The ride home flew by with a blur. She stared out the window, but the familiar scene didn't register. She stuffed cash into the driver's hand and ambled to the front door. Key in hand, she unlocked the door and stepped into an empty house.

She made her sick call into work, dumped food and water into Halo's bowls, and had crawled into bed. Sleep had been a welcome escape.

The warmth of another person shook her out of the memory.

Justin drew her close, engulfing her in his arms. "I'm so sorry," he whispered.

Marissa closed her eyes and leaned against his chest. Hearing his heartbeat through the thin layer of his shirt soothed her. "You're the only one who knows about this. David became so nasty I found myself pushing my hurt into a closet and locking the door. I couldn't discuss my feelings with him and he didn't appear interested." She paused. "I just wanted honesty, love, and a reliable partner in good times and bad."

Justin inhaled and stared.

Marissa's heart sped up. *Will Justin look at me in a different light?*

Justin sat straighter. "I knew about your miscarriage."

"David told you?" Her eyes widened. David hadn't talked about the baby or the miscarriage, so she assumed he hadn't spoken to anyone else.

"I was on duty down in Emergency, waiting for a trauma victim to arrive when I saw David leave. I tracked him down and he told me what happened. I called him an insensitive son of a bitch, and he stalked off. I stood outside your door when I heard you telling the nurse you didn't want to see or talk to anyone." He shrugged. "I thought I'd give you some time."

Marissa sat up and met his gaze. Her belly fluttered as she bit her lip. "You were there?"

Justin nodded. "You were going through a terrible shock. Then my trauma patient arrived, and surgery lasted for the next several hours. By the time I got to your room, you had left."

"I felt stupid. I'd accepted the marriage proposal of a man who couldn't stand by me when circumstances rocked my world. I didn't see him for days. Meanwhile, my mother and sister were excited about the wedding. I even had to try on wedding gowns that day. Pure torture, but I couldn't bring myself to cancel. I couldn't do anything."

Marissa recalled holding back tears during a time when she should have been steeped in happiness. Her mother floated on cloud nine, seeing her try on various wedding gowns. In the end, her mother and Vanessa had chosen the gown, and Marissa went along with their suggestion.

They'd never discussed the miscarriage. David wanted to pretend the baby never existed, and she'd been too mortified to allow her feelings out of the cage she'd built. In the end, their lives as a couple continued as if the baby had only been a blip on a screen, but for Marissa, pain became her daily companion.

"I know a lot about being paralyzed." He reached over and stroked her face. "Damn him. You are so beautiful, inside and out. How could he be so cruel?"

Her heart galloped, like she had no control. Pain from that time in her life grew fuzzy as she drifted into his arms.

"Marissa..." he said, as their lips met in an explosion.

Like a valve opening, Marissa allowed her emotions to flow freely. Shocked knocked her back as years of holding in emotions burst forth with a passion she didn't know lived in her.

Rising from the window seat, Justin pulled her up with him. He slowly turned her and then lowered her onto the bed.

With the glow of a full moon casting heavenly shadows in the room, Marissa lost all sense of time.

Chapter 35

Justin didn't want to leave the blissful cocoon he shared with Marissa. Although the rain pattering at the window dashed their plans for a hike this morning, lying here with her all day made for an even better option.

Marissa rested her head on his chest, and her thigh lay atop his. Last night obliterated not only years of resisting his feelings, but also the sense of loyalty to a friend who deserved none. This woman got under his skin, and in this moment, he'd do anything to keep her next to him.

Marissa stirred, but didn't open her eyes.

Soft brown hair tickled his chest, and although he didn't want to move, with reluctance he gently slid her head back onto the pillow and crept out of bed, pulling on his shorts and a shirt.

Halo's head popped up, and the dog tiptoed out of the room with him.

Half an hour later, Marissa padded into the kitchen wearing a tank top and sweats, her hair in a loose ponytail.

He smiled as he stared over the rim of his coffee cup. Sexy as hell. Setting his mug on the counter, he filled another cup.

"And you cook, too?" She grinned and accepted the full cup of coffee.

He leaned over and kissed her. "Last night was... fun." Pouring eggs into a skillet, Justin scrambled the mixture.

She laughed, tearing off a section of bacon and popping the meat into her mouth. "I agree."

Halo sauntered over and stared with longing eyes.

"You've been feeding him bacon, haven't you?"

"We like our meat." He winked at Halo.

Halo's tail flopped in response.

"Oh, I almost forgot." He glided across the kitchen and opened the refrigerator. Grabbing a tall glass of pink liquid, he turned and presented the drink. "Your smoothie, ma'am."

Marissa gave him a smile, which had him wanting to return to the cocoon. He loved making her smile.

"Justin..." Her voice caught, and she reached up on her tiptoes to kiss him.

"Wow, I'm making smoothies more often."

She placed the glass on the counter and stared out at the creamy orange tone of dawn awakening over the mountains. "I wish life could be this easy all the time. Thanks for the night off."

Justin returned to the stove, switched off the burner, and scooped the eggs into a serving bowl. "One day." He turned and gathered her into his arms, savoring the feel of her body against his once again. He didn't want to think about the future yet, choosing to enjoy the here and now instead.

What a new concept. He'd always been steeped in the past, reliving the horrors of war and death. Marissa had a point—a day off proved great.

The sound of a throat being cleared pulled them apart.

Walker entered the kitchen and Halo alerted. "Sorry to interrupt." He moved to the other side of the kitchen and sat at the table, keeping watch on the dog. "That animal hates me and by the looks of the weather we're going to be in close proximity for a while longer."

"Good morning." Marissa gathered three plates and deposited

them on the table. "Halo is just a bit overprotective when strangers are around."

Justin peered at Halo. Maybe the dog picked up on something. A vibe didn't ring right with Walker.

Marissa and Justin brought the rest of the food to the table. The three of them ate as Halo vacillated between his dog food and yearning glances at people food.

After they cleaned the kitchen, Walker pulled a map and several files from his messenger bag. With the large map smoothed out across the table, he pointed to certain landmarks along the way. "Before we go, I want to point out a few other things. Babylon Hall is approximately 5.3 miles from our current location. I suggest we take this route." He ran his forefinger along a path and stopped well away from the compound. "We can probably get about 500 yards from the perimeter. If we venture closer, we risk alerting security. A ridge is here, and if I'd remembered to bring my binoculars, we would have a much better view of the compound." Walker straightened and adjusted his red T-shirt emblazoned with the Coca-Cola logo.

Justin stared at Walker. Could he be trusted? Would he deliver them straight to Vivian? *He's not telling us everything.*

Justin studied the map for a few seconds more. "Tell me about Vivian's background."

Marissa refilled their coffee cups and took her seat as she sipped her smoothie.

Walker cleared his throat. "Vivian Sinclair is the only daughter of Russell and Mary Sinclair. At the time of Vivian's birth, The Order existed less than a year, with only a handful of members. Russell hadn't yet begun to rule with an iron fist. He wanted a son to carry on his name and by the time Mary got pregnant, two years after Vivian's birth, Russell had changed. Mary grew sickly and lost the baby boy. Russell blamed her and banished Mary to one of the cabins on the property."

"Wow, what a guy," Marissa commented.

"Yes, Russell Sinclair had quite a callous nature, even toward those you'd think he would care most about." Walker sipped his coffee. "I don't believe much has changed under Vivian's rule."

Marissa stroked Halo's head. "Did Mary ever conceive again?"

"Oh, yes. The next child ended in a stillbirth. This time, Russell had Mary beaten. About two years later, Mary again became pregnant, but by that time her mental and physical condition made carrying a child to term precarious. Miraculously, she delivered a son, at about twenty-six weeks' gestation. One theory is Mary didn't survive childbirth and Russell buried her in the Black Garden. I can't confirm the information nor can I find any records of what happened to the baby boy."

"The black garden?" Justin turned his attention away from the map and studied Walker. *These people are insane.* Once again he pondered whether Walker's allegiance.

"On the grounds of Babylon Hall, I've been told there is a large garden filled with black poppies. The Black Garden is actually a big graveyard inhabited by people Russell and Vivian have killed in the name of penance. No markers, just rows of dirt mounds topped with black flowers."

Marissa's head snapped up. "Penance! That's the word the woman used at the library. She said penance must be paid."

"We found the same word written on back of the patch from my patient's room," Justin said.

Walker nodded. "The woman has to be one of them."

Justin's jaw tightened. *What about you, Walker?* "And no one has investigated this organization?"

Walker drained his coffee cup then said, "There have been attempts, but the matter is either dropped, or those making the accusations disappear."

"How old was Vivian when her mother died, and who cared for her?" The effects of war and warped, sociopathic upbringing could have tragic consequences for children. Justin had seen the magnitude of such circumstances in Iraq. Young boys taught to shoot and blow up the enemy, to hate, had no chance at a normal childhood, critical for transformation into healthy-minded adults. Learned hatred grew roots in hardened hearts. Vivian appeared to walk the same path as her father.

"Various women living at the compound helped with Vivian. Russell apparently resigned himself to a female heir. When Vivian turned twenty-one Russell allowed her to sit in during certain meetings. She expressed the desire to take the helm of The Order, so Russell put her through a series of tests."

Walker refilled his coffee cup. He took a sip, grimaced, and then scooped more sugar into his cup. After smacking his lips together in dissatisfaction, he added a couple more teaspoons.

Ignoring Walker's apparent sugar addiction, Justin asked, "What types of tests?"

"At first, they were fairly benign. He'd make a decision without telling Vivian, then tested her to see if she came to the same conclusion. Then the tests progressed to firing people, killing small animals, and participating in his penance sessions."

"Penance sessions?" Marissa shifted in her seat as she shot a quick glance at Justin.

"Basically, the punishment for violating or challenging the rules of The Order, or even daring to think for oneself. The punishment involved demotion, imprisonment, or death. As Russell gained more power, he resorted almost exclusively to torture followed by death. There was no option to leave the organization, at least not alive."

Marissa leaned forward on the table. "I can't believe they've gotten away with this."

Walker shrugged. "Russell studied the business of running a syndicated mob and took their principles to heart. He demanded loyalty by threat of death or dismemberment. The right people in positions of influence and power held a key factor in managing The Order. He reached a level where no one bothered him, and everyone feared him."

"I'm guessing Vivian passed his tests with flying colors." Justin's voice hummed flat, his gaze trained on Walker.

"She had a couple of stumbles, I'm told, especially with the collection of the tokens."

Justin and Marissa stared at Walker, waiting for an explanation.

Walker finished off the last of his coffee and crossed the room to place the cup in the dishwasher. He paused to stare out the window before returning to the table.

Halo, who sat up on his haunches when Walker rose, relaxed again at Marissa's feet.

"Tokens are small pieces of a person's body, taken before they are killed at the request of the Grand Commander of The Order. Like I mentioned earlier, they took pieces of a finger, chopped off by an antique knife." Walker pulled the photo of Russell at his desk with a knife and pointed to the blade.

"That's barbaric!" Marissa gasped.

"The finger is preserved then the person is killed and buried in the Black Garden." Walker paused. "I'm told Vivian required a few tries to cut her first finger, but she's grown quite adept at the task now."

"Okay, so she proved to her old man her level of crazy matched his. How do we—"

Walker held up his hand. "We haven't gotten to her ultimate challenge. Remember her child? Russell wanted her to experience the pain of childbirth, so he allowed the pregnancy to continue. The day after she gave birth, he ordered her to kill the baby. After completion of this task, Russell vowed his full support."

"Killing your own child for the chance to run a cult is insane." Marissa caressed Halo's head and then strolled to the window.

Steady rain beat against the roof and low rain-soaked clouds concealed half of the mountain range. Justin inhaled the fresh scent of rain through an opened window. As his gaze swept over the lake a short distance from the house, Justin considered what he'd be doing now if David had lived and Marissa went ahead with the marriage. His plan had been to go fishing with Uncle Lou and to somehow forget about Marissa.

The first time he saw her he'd been enthralled but David moved in on her. Justin had no doubt he'd hurt her. Marissa's involvement with David set her on a track destined for destruction. Like witnessing bombs explode in Iraq with a powerless understanding he couldn't keep everyone safe, he stood by helpless to prevent the hell-fire he knew David would inflict upon her.

Plans could change in the blink of an eye, why couldn't pain dissipate with a snap of a finger?

Walker returned the photo to his file. He eyed Halo, who sprawled out by the window. "This way of life is all Vivian has known. She considered proving herself to Russell her ultimate goal, and she fulfilled every demand he made."

"I know you've said they have the police under their control, but what about contacting the FBI?" Marissa stared from Walker to Justin.

Walker shook his head. "Have you ever heard of J. Edgar Hoover? Russell befriended him and word is the hands off edict is still in effect today. However, I can't corroborate any of this so we could be looking at a myth."

Justin considered the information. In an emergency, he had little time to ponder the best course of action, but now he understood more about this woman and her evil organization, he needed to develop a concrete plan to keep Marissa safe. They couldn't continue to run, hide out, and hope they moved a couple steps ahead of the goons chasing them. One day they would be found. They had taken the time to gather data, and once they got a look at Babylon Hall, they needed to become proactive. Walker's information appeared believable and well researched, which bothered him. Could anything he said be trusted? "How did you get access to this information?" Justin stared at Walker, searching for signs of dishonesty.

Walker glanced from Marissa to Justin. "Most of the maps I procured from the state archives but the majority of this information comes straight from a former member. I promised the informant I would never reveal his, or her, identity."

With a sweep of her hand across the table, Marissa said, "This is a tremendous amount of information."

Walker nodded. "I've been researching The Order for several years now."

Halo arose from the corner of the room and ambled toward Justin, sitting at his feet.

Justin rubbed Halo's head before glancing up at Walker. "Based on what you've just told us, Vivian will not stop until she has what she wants. If she believes we have the data, then we won't be safe until we bring her down. Even if we find the information and hand it over, she will still want us dead. We've seen too much, even if we don't view one single word."

Damn. He didn't want to worry Marissa, but he wanted her to know the position they were in. He approached and placed his hands on her shoulders as he looked over her head through the window. "As I've told you before, we will get through this. We just need to be smart."

Marissa turned from the window and met his gaze. "I believe you."

The faith she displayed unnerved him. Laura had once looked at him with confidence, and he hadn't saved her. He blinked away the thought of failure. *Not an option.*

"Might as well make use of the down time. I'm going into town for binoculars and supplies before our hike," Justin said.

Walker opted to stay at the lake house.

Marissa couldn't leave a suspicious Halo alone with Walker, so they loaded the dog in the SUV and set out for town.

An hour later, Justin and Marissa had gathered everything they needed for the hike and dinner fixings. Although the rain had stopped, gray clouds continued to threaten.

So far, Marissa hadn't come up with any clues as to where David could have stashed the flash drive. Justin didn't want to suggest going back to the condo, but if she couldn't come up with anything else, they'd have no choice. Maybe they could spare another day here before heading back.

He kept a watchful eye for men in black SUVs and suspicious people in general, but at this point everyone appeared doubtful. He didn't have to remind Marissa to stay close as they headed back to the car, so when she tensed, he glanced her way. "What's wrong?"

Marissa stopped and squinted. "Is that...Justin, I think that's Neal and Susan up ahead."

He followed her gaze. "What the hell are they doing here?" Justin didn't believe in mere coincidences. Neal and Susan in the same Virginia town, within a few miles of Vivian set off alarms bells. His distrust of Neal rose to a new level.

Susan spotted them, nudged Neal, focused on his cellphone, and gave them a frantic wave as they rushed over.

"Well now, isn't this a huge surprise? What are you two doing here in Timber Creek?" Susan leaned to air-kiss Marissa and Justin.

"We rented a lake house not too far away. I guess I could ask the same?" Justin adjusted the bags in his arms.

Neal punched a button and lowered the phone. "Well, if it isn't the good doctor and the fair maiden Marissa."

Justin bristled at Neal's tone. Everything this guy said grated on his nerves.

"We have a house about ten miles north of here." Neal pointed with his thumb in hitchhiker fashion. "Susan needed time off the campaign trail, so I promised her a few days out in the sticks."

"By the looks of your bags, you will be here at least another day. You have to come over. We just had this gorgeous house built last year." Susan's hands gestured in wild emotion. "Our architect did a wonderful job. You know, he designed one of the Kennedy family mountain homes. Or maybe it was Tom Hanks? Oh well, I can't remember."

Neal sighed and glanced up at Susan, a couple inches taller. "Susan, can they get a word in? Maybe they have plans." He flashed a salacious grin as he reached to shake Justin's hand, but he held his gaze on Marissa.

"I'm not sure if we can...." Justin glanced at Marissa.

She gawked at Susan until he nudged her arm.

"Oh, umm. Your necklace is beautiful." Marissa stepped closer to inspect the diamond multi-point star with one green stone hanging from a silver chain.

Susan's hands fluttered to her neck. "Oh, well thank you. It's my something old. You know, from our wedding." She stepped back as her mouth dropped open. "Marissa, I'm sorry."

Justin didn't buy her oops-I-just-made-a-potentially-uncomfortable-comment. This woman appeared to be on a mission to prove herself superior.

Marissa smiled. "No worries." She glanced at Justin before stepping back.

"Why don't I give you a call about dinner? We need to get going. The dog is in the car and probably going insane." Justin took several steps away.

"Sure thing." Neal winked as his cellphone chirped. "Gotta get this." He turned from the group.

"Great! I'm glad you two are in town. Which house are you renting?" Susan placed a hand on her hip and cocked her head sideways.

"Not far. I'll give you a call." Justin gave a noncommittal wave as he and Marissa trotted off toward the car.

Once they were back in the SUV, Marissa tore through her purse.

Justin glanced sideways before he drove off. "What's wrong?"

She continued to rummage through her purse. "Utah. The day of the accident with the cab. The same day I came home and found David."

Justin kept his focus on the road ahead, with a few glances in the rear-view mirror. "What about the day you came home?"

Her eyes widened and her mouth gaped. "Someone took my laptop."

"Do you think your accident wasn't an accident, but an attempt by Vivian?"

Marissa nodded. "Yes, but there's more. An old woman on the shuttle, Mrs. Richey, from Ohio, had been in Utah visiting her first great-grandchild. At the airport, she dropped her purse, and so I bent down to pick up her things. A lady jumped out of the cab behind us. When I got to the curb, I saw her out of the corner of my eye. Something glinting in the sunlight caught my attention. Justin, I think the woman pushed me."

Justin's jaw clamped tight. "You could be right. We can't assume anything is a coincidence anymore."

"The thing is, now I recognize the woman who pushed me. I think." Marissa stared out the front window. "Susan."

"Susan Wingate? Are you sure?" He never had an issue with Susan and her power hungry motives didn't appeal to him, but was she capable of attempted murder?

"Sounds farfetched, but the necklace..." Her voice trailed off. "She wore the same necklace at the funeral. I noticed the little green stone at the top of the star."

"Okay, but the necklace doesn't look all that special, so maybe Susan just happens to have jewelry similar to the person in Utah." After hearing what he'd said, even Justin had a hard time believing the theory.

Too many coincidences. Neal and Susan happened to have a house within miles of the woman hell-bent on coming after them. Susan had the same necklace, or one very similar, to the person who pushed Marissa into the street. Neal may have introduced David to the CEO of Skies International, the same company with ties to Vivian Sinclair.

"Is there anything else causing you to believe the woman at the airport and Susan are the same?"

Marissa sighed. "No." She turned her attention back to her purse. "I know I didn't lose the paper."

"What are you looking for?"

"Her phone number." A few seconds later, she pulled out a folded piece of paper. "Yes! Mrs. Richey's address and phone number."

"Call her and see what she knows. We're in the same time zone as Ohio." Justin hoped Mrs. Richey could help shed some light on the situation. If Marissa's hunch proved correct and Susan had pushed her, Vivian and her crew already knew where they were.

Marissa put the phone on speaker and punched in the number. After several rings, they heard the click of the phone being answered.

"Hello, Mrs. Richey, this is Marissa Nash. We recently met on the shuttle bus in Utah."

"Oh, Marissa dear, of course I remember. How are you feeling?"

"I'm much better, thank you."

"How was your wedding? I've been anxiously awaiting those pictures of you in your gown."

Marissa took a deep breath. "My fiancé died unexpectedly before we could get married." She glanced at Justin and shrugged.

Justin nodded. He wouldn't have explained David had been murdered, either.

"Oh, my. I am truly sorry to hear such news. I'm sure being surrounded by your family and friends is a godsend."

"Absolutely." Marissa paused before continuing. "I guess with all the time I've had to sit and think, I've been remembering a detail about my accident at the airport. I thought maybe you could help me."

"Of course."

"Did you see a woman with blonde hair get out of the cab that hit me?"

"Why yes, I did. The woman flew by in an awful hurry. I don't mean to be rude, but I think she may have caused your accident. She moved so fast."

Marissa glanced at Justin. "You know, I thought something similar, too"

"I'm sure she made a terrible mistake," Mrs. Richey said.

"Did you happen to see her wearing a beautiful pendant, shaped almost like a star? I thought I saw the necklace just before the cab hit me."

"Hmm. A star pendant." Mrs. Richey remained quiet for a few moments. "No, I don't think I noticed a necklace. Would you hold on a minute, dear?"

"Sure."

A minute later, Mrs. Richey spoke. "Marissa, I did find something interesting after they put you in the ambulance and the woman disappeared into the airport. It's quite perplexing. I'm certain the blonde woman dropped an object. A green patch with the words, *Ordo Ortus*."

Chapter 36

Although the on and off downpour of rain the previous day spoiled their opportunity to see Babylon Hall, Justin considered the current weather ideal for hiking, limited sun with moderate temperatures. His internal barometer, however, measured Virginia conditions against the blazing hot deserts of Iraq. Despite little sleep, Justin awoke anxious to get the hike underway. They'd seen no sign of the black SUV in days. Sure they hadn't given up, Justin's mind spun with new possibilities of attack. After the hike, they needed to move. With Susan's possible involvement and both she and Neal aware of their general location, staying in one place had become too dangerous.

Even with his mind occupied by the men in black and Vivian Sinclair, he couldn't keep Marissa out of his thoughts. He hadn't intended to take their relationship to another level when he went to her room. Hell, maybe he did, but he couldn't haul back his actions, even if he wanted to.

He needed to forget. Forget his exploding feelings. Forget the night they'd spent together. Forget the hole boring into his heart with the understanding he had to let her go.

Their timing was off, and she wasn't ready. He didn't want to push her or she'd come to resent him. Once they eradicated the threat, he had to walk away. He cringed, not wanting to consider Marissa being out of his life.

Justin turned his focus to the hike as they began their trek to Babylon Hall.

Halo bounced along in apparent delight at the prospect of a long walk in the woods.

Marissa smiled at Justin and patted her side, showing him the gun glinting in the sun. They'd discussed carrying their weapons, just in case.

As they approached Babylon Hall, Walker began his commentary. "There are at least two guards manning security shacks around the perimeter of the property. Guardians also patrol the four-hundred-acre property, some on all terrain vehicles."

As they approached a hill, Justin extended his hand to help Marissa up.

She took his hand and trudged up the hill. After she reached the crest, she surveyed the scene.

Walker scrambled up the hill last, his green Marvin the Martian T-shirt matching the lush scenery. "Yes, this is the spot."

From their perch scattered with trees, Justin scanned the compound below. He pulled the new binoculars from his backpack. A large main house, surrounded by smaller ones, stood as the focal point. A large barn and attached stable sat at the edge of the property. Judging by the expansive barn, Justin expected to see several horses feeding in the pasture, yet only a single brown horse stood near the fence. "Impressive." He continued to survey the compound.

"Yes, this is an extraordinary facility, but extremely dangerous." Walker skimmed the surroundings.

Justin handed Marissa the binoculars. She examined the scene before returning them. "We got a look at the place. What now? We can't just sit around and wait to be attacked."

The three were quiet for a few seconds, and then Justin spoke. "We leave and go back to find the flash drive. I'm done with the history lessons and tours."

Walker shook his head. "The Order won't negotiate. However, I agree finding the data will get their attention." He turned and pointed in a different direction. "According to survey maps, I believe one of the tunnels comes out over there." He scrambled down the hill, moving parallel to the compound.

Tweeting birds, rustling leaves, and chirping crickets were the only noises emanating from the deep forest. Could there be hidden cameras stashed among the trees? Justin hadn't identified anything suspicious. He caught up to his hiking companions just as Walker uncovered a hidden door in the ground. The aged door had been covered in vegetation and dirt. A small numbered keypad belied the appearance of antiquity.

"I knew the door had to be here. The coordinates are perfect." Walker stared at a notebook.

"I don't think they were hiding this. Too easy to find." Justin squatted beside the door and looked up at Walker. "No offense."

"None taken. I agree. This door appeared on the map I got from the state."

"What does this mean? They want someone to find it and gain access to the compound?" Marissa asked.

"I don't know. Maybe they're confident in their security, should anyone dare trespass." Justin paused. "This could be a weak point. A way in. Or out."

"You aren't thinking about going in there?" Marissa pulled Halo closer and away from Walker, who gave the dog a skittish look.

"Not without insurance. We have nothing without the data. Plus, I'm sure if we manage to get the door open, alarm bells would trigger."

Marissa ran her hand along the door before looking back to Justin. "Even if we had the data, going in there seems like a suicide mission. Why would they allow us to waltz in, hand over the data, and leave?"

Walker rubbed his eyes. "Based on what I know, I don't believe Vivian would be so kind-hearted as to let you go. Even if she accepted you had nothing to do with the data breach, The Order preaches vengeance and penance, both judgments imposed by Vivian. The notion of going light on someone is not a concept she embraces."

"Aren't the people she kills ever reported missing?" Marissa pushed the vegetation back over the door while Halo sniffed a rotting log nearby.

"Some are, but remember, she has friends in high places. If she finds out someone is accusing her or The Order, or even thinking about infiltrating her organization, she sends out her minions to eliminate the problem." Walker pushed the last piece of vegetation over the door.

Justin stood with his hands on his hips. "We were working with the detectives, but at every move, they knew where to strike. Somehow, the men in the black SUV knew our hotel location, which floor we were on, and which room we were in. Hell yes, she has friends in the right places."

"Our situation can't be that hopeless." Marissa reached for Halo as the group started their journey back to the lake house. "We had nothing to do with the data breach. Up until David's murder and the discovery of the note leading to Walker, we had no idea who Vivian Sinclair, The Order, or even Skies International were."

Justin's gut clenched. "Walker, you knew about all this well before David's death. You were working with him. Why haven't you been on their target list?"

"David and I were careful when we met. We instituted the use of the surreptitious notes to avoid detection. They probably don't know about me."

Justin narrowed his gaze. "Are you telling me David held such a lax outlook, in terms of a potential threat, with everyone else but you? He didn't talk to his fiancée about the threat. He didn't get her out of town and he never said a word to me, his best friend, about any of this. But you, a stranger, he went out of his way to protect?" His voice rose, dripping with incredulity.

Walker continued in the direction of the house. "I can't d-defend David's actions, nor explain why he made his decisions."

Justin brought up the rear as the trio began the trek back. *Yet another thing off with this guy.* They'd gotten a peek at Babylon Hall, so tomorrow he and Marissa would put some distance between this place and Walker.

The cadence of crunching leaves under their feet cut through the silence and accompanied them back to the lake house.

DESPITE THE SERENE setting and the heart-fluttering excitement of her new closeness with Justin inside the lake house oasis, Marissa looked forward to getting far away from Babylon Hall. Living within yards of evil unnerved her, even with a gun tucked away.

Her escape plans were thwarted however, due to more impending storms. Walker had warned them after their hike to expect severe weather. He advised they leave in the morning. Even though the lake house stood on flat ground the route back, mountainous and prone to fog, could be treacherous.

After lunch, Walker pulled out his laptop and set up at the kitchen table. Marissa and Justin took Halo in the living room. They spent the next hour talking. To Marissa's pleasure they kept their conversation light, discussing everything from favorite movies and books to dream vacations. Halo snuggled up with them on the couch and after an hour and the conversation lapsed into comfortable silence, both he and Justin had fallen asleep.

Marissa crept into the kitchen, pulled a bottle of water from the refrigerator, and sat at the table across from Walker.

"How would you research a person's history?" Marissa took a sip of water.

Walker peered over the top of the screen. "Who do you want researched, and is there something more specific you want to know?"

"Can you research Susan Wingate?"

Walker gave her a prolonged stare. "Susan Wingate? Neal Wingate's wife? What do you want to know?"

Walker, always so quick to relay information, caused her to consider the request. "I don't know. We ran into Neal and Susan in town. Don't you think it's weird they have a place so close to Babylon Hall?"

Walker shrugged. "Candy?" He pushed a mound of various types of candy toward her.

"No thanks." Marissa glanced at the pile. The thought of ingesting all those sweets made her teeth hurt.

Walker turned back to the computer, the clicking of the keys more pronounced in the otherwise quiet room. Without moving his gaze off the screen Walker cleared his throat. "Susan Maynard Wingate is thirty-three years old from Bridgeport, Connecticut. Her parents are Cal and Donna Maynard. Mr. Maynard was a middle school principal, and Mrs. Maynard a former teacher. Both retired now. Susan is an only child who excelled in school." Walker went silent as his fingers flew across the keyboard. He nodded and began again. "She was on the track team, even won a state title in the 800-meter track event. She went to New York University and graduated with a B.S. in Business, and then received her MBA from Georgetown, two years later. She interned at Skies International and was offered a position after graduating from NYU. She moved to part-time status at Skies while in graduate school."

Walker sighed, but he continued to spew information. "After five years at Skies she married Neal Wingate in Bridgeport. Later, she left her job as director of Public Relations for Skies two months before Neal announced his run for the Senate."

He whipped around the computer and flashed a wedding photo.

Susan beamed in her strapless white gown while Neal gave a smug grin. They were meant for each other. Both driven and self-assured to the point Marissa marveled at their apparent one-track minds toward power and prestige. Perhaps they both needed each other to achieve their goals. They'd voiced their intention to one day occupy the White House. Marissa couldn't think of two less sincere people.

"Anything else you want to know?" Walker picked up a Tootsie Roll and unrolled the brown wrapper.

"I don't know. I wasn't sure what I was looking for." He didn't volunteer to dig deeper, so she decided to drop the quest. She probably could have come up with those facts on her own. However, a Google search resulting in an entry detailing how Susan Wingate tried to murder her at the request of the evil, villainous Vivian Sinclair didn't seem likely.

Marissa rose from the chair, opened the refrigerator and pulled out a package of chicken breasts. She decided on grilled chicken, broccoli, and baked potatoes for dinner. With the thunderstorm still raging, the inside grill on the gas stove would come in handy. She loved cooking, but had rarely cooked for David, as he preferred to go out.

With the chicken settled into a marinade, she sat across from Walker again.

His attention had returned to the computer screen.

"I get the impression you don't make any major moves without researching the subject. I'm betting you know a lot about David. What can you tell me?"

Walker pulled his gaze away from the screen and stared. "What can I tell you that you don't already know? You were about to marry him."

Marissa placed her elbows on the table. "I intended to break off the engagement, but I never got the chance. I don't think I really knew him." When she saw his hesitation, she added, "He's gone, so no sense of confidentiality remains."

Walker nodded and reached into his messenger bag. He rifled through several folders until he came to a plain red one and slid it across the table. "I'm sure you already know all this."

Marissa picked up the folder. Good or bad, she needed to know. She focused on various reports and files. Her breath caught with each revelation.

She read about David's honorable discharge from the Army, which should have been classified as dishonorable, but he lucked out. She couldn't believe he'd had an affair with his commanding officer's wife. Had he ever been faithful? If he could jeopardize his military career for a woman, what hope did she have he could have made a serious commitment to her?

The report continued into David's past. He had drug and gambling issues in college but managed to escape arrest.

She even read about a paternity claim, resulting in court action. The court documents, dated a year and a half ago, indicated DNA testing proved he fathered the child and owed the mother thousands of dollars in child support. The child, a boy, would be about three years old now. David had a child while they were together, while they lived together.

She waited for a stab of pain, but it never came. Pain had long ago given way to anger. Had she ever been happy with him? A quick scan of her memory resulted in very few fond memories. Instead, she remembered being shut out, his constant claims of having to work, and being abandoned at the one time she'd needed him most.

He'd been selfish, and had showed her time and time again he didn't really care. Yet, she'd stayed. Why? Didn't she share some fault in the hurt and anger she felt?

Even before her pregnancy, she'd been torn about staying with David. He had been difficult, but her life had been stable, and wasn't that what she wanted? Then, after the miscarriage, Marissa entered the unknown and her ability to make life decisions stalled. Doing nothing seemed the easiest decision. "Walker, where did you get all this information?" She stared at the court documents.

"Most of the data is in the public domain, and the rest... As long as you know who to talk to, there's not a lot you can't find. I ran a lot of this by Justin a few days ago."

Marissa's snapped up her head. Justin hadn't told her any of this information. Why? She'd specifically asked him to tell her about David. Didn't the fact he had a child register as something she should know?

Justin hadn't recently discovered the kind of person David had been. They went to college together. He had to know. His apparent lack of trust pierced her heart. "Thank you." She closed the file, slid the folder over to Walker, and marched back to the stove to finish dinner.

Walker glanced up from the computer screen. "Are you all right? I assumed you knew about David's background."

"I'm learning David had many titles: blackmailer, liar, and a fraud. He never told me about the child."

"I-I only knew David in the context of this situation, but I like you, and I'm glad you didn't marry him." Walker flashed a tight smile before turning back to the screen.

"What's going on?" Justin yawned and stretched at the doorway.

Marissa glared. What else had Justin kept from her?

MARISSA SAT in the sunroom facing the mountains and the lake. During a lull in the storms, Justin took Halo out while Walker escaped to his room. She watched from the window as Halo took off in hot pursuit of a squirrel. He'd circled back and slammed into the lake. Jumping out of the water, Halo had continued the chase into the woods. After the chase concluded, Halo trotted into the house ahead of Justin.

"He doesn't like squirrels, does he?"

"No, Halo and squirrels have a love-hate relationship. He hates them, but loves to taunt them." Marissa jumped out of her chair as the dog shook, tossing excess water in every direction. "Halo!" When he finished, pine needles and water droplets lay scattered about the shiny floor.

"Damn it!" Justin said.

"What happened?" Walker asked as he entered the room.

"Halo chased a squirrel, and now he has made a mess." Marissa accepted the broom from Justin and started sweeping errant pine needles into a pile.

"Squirrels are rodents, members of the *Sciuridae* family. Canines are natural hunters, similar to wolves, so Halo's inbred instinct is to hunt small, furry animals."

Justin stared at Walker. "Is there any subject you don't provide scientific or historical commentary for? I'll go search for a broom and mop."

Walker's mouth dropped open before he slammed his lips shut. "I'll be over there." He stalked off.

After Marissa swept up the pine needles, she announced, "I'm giving Halo a bath."

Holding Halo by his new collar, Marissa entered a bathroom off the garage, which contained a large tub. She filled the tub and pulled out the soap from his bag of dog supplies.

She lathered and rinsed his fur. Within minutes, dirt and more pine needles swirled down the drain.

"Why didn't he just talk to me?" Marissa dried Halo with a towel. "All I ever wanted was honesty."

Halo blinked and licked her face.

"Soon, I will find us a place." She reached into Halo's supply bag in search of his brush. Her hand swept against another bag. Marissa peeked inside the outer bag and scrunched her nose. She pulled out the smaller plain plastic bag. When she opened the bag, she felt her heart kick up as she spotted Halo's old collar.

Walker said David hid the flash drive in a place she'd find special. Could this be it?

She snapped open the leather pouch.

Inside, rested a shiny silver flash drive.

Chapter 37

Searching for cleaning supplies in the laundry room's closet, Justin froze when he heard Marissa's screams. He dropped the mop and sprinted out to the garage bathroom. "What's wrong?"

Before Marissa could answer, Walker appeared, but kept his distance from Halo.

Marissa stood and held up the flash drive. "I found it! Right here in the pouch on Halo's old collar. David placed the ring in this pouch when he proposed. He hid the flash drive inside. I also found this." She opened her other hand.

Justin approached her and picked up a piece of plastic. Turning the object over, he glanced up. "This is a fingerprint."

Walker moved closer and peered at the plastic fingerprint in Justin's hand. "A biometric secured flash drive. David is providing us with the key to examining the data."

"The flash drive has been right under my nose this whole time." Marissa wrung her hands.

"Let's go find out what's so important." He would have preferred to keep the flash drive away from Walker until they had time to review the information. *Too late.* He headed to the kitchen table where Walker's laptop sat, and within seconds, Walker had the flash drive inserted.

Justin placed the plastic fingerprint over his own finger and pressed into the flash drive pad.

Files appeared on the screen.

"What did you enter?" Marissa asked.

"Justin stood back and scanned the screen. Two files were on the drive.

Walker tried to copy both onto the computer's hard drive. The error sound on the computer indicated an unsuccessful task. Another attempted resulted in the same error sound. He tried to email the files without success.

"The USB drive is read only." Walker spoke up. "I think there is a way to disable the access level but I don't want jeopardize the information." He studied the screen. "David wanted to ensure this information remained protected. I'm no IT expert, but I believe we should concern ourselves with keeping this information secured."

Justin sighed. "Okay, let's review the information." He opened the file, and up popped seven memos, each document individually numbered and titled T.O. and Skies.

"The initials must refer to The Order," Marissa said.

The three of them huddled together as Walker opened memo one, signed by Vivian. They were silent as each came to the end of the missive.

"She's alluding to collusion in order to gain government contracts," Justin said. "Notice the seven memos."

Walker nodded. "Symbolism is a big thing with her. Skies International is a multi-billion dollar company. They have a huge government services division, which handles anything from database support, logistics, supply chain distribution, communication systems, to research and development. And that's just a sampling. They're also involved in pharmaceuticals, energy, food sciences, banking, transportation, and computer intelligence. You name it, Skies has a hand in it."

"This corporation has influence into virtually every aspect of human life." Marissa stared wide-eyed.

Justin turned back to the computer screen as Walker pulled up the next memo. "Skies has partnered with a major manufacturer of electronic voting machines." Justin huffed a breath. "She has access to affect election outcomes. This is insane."

They read all seven memos. The picture became clear. The Order, specifically Vivian, owned Skies, but her involvement had been cloaked via several layers of people and complicated legal maneuvers. The memos were proof Vivian ruled day-to-day operations at Skies. The memos discussed how their operatives had infiltrated the highest levels of government with plans to enact legislation in line with Vivian's edicts. The memos further indicated her plans were on track in several key gubernatorial and congressional races. She even boasted Skies had been the beneficiary of over a billion dollars in government contracts.

Justin reread the last memo. In plain language, Vivian wanted absolute power not only within the US, but the world at large. The last line of the memo stated, "Everyone will bow to the edicts of The Order". He glanced up from the computer. "This woman is delusional, like some crazed Lex Luthor out to rule the world."

Marissa shook her head. "This is surreal. Could people like this really exist?"

"If these documents are authentic, my suspicions are confirmed." Walker nodded. "David alluded to something of this magnitude, but this is quite a doozy."

"Do you think this is authentic?" Marissa glanced from Justin to Walker, her eyes focused and serious.

Justin turned his gaze to the screen. "Based on the number of recent deaths in their path and their relentless pursuit of us, I'd say either they know the information on the flash drive is legitimate, or they suspect we have something equally incriminating."

Walker nodded and wiped the sudden eruption of sweat from his brow. "David made himself a huge threat. Exposure of this information would jeopardize their entire network. I know she has friends in high places, but if the media got hold of this, Vivian would have trouble."

Justin now understood David's motives. Once he gained access to this document, he could name his price. He'd planned to blackmail Vivian into giving him millions in exchange for his silence. A crazy and suicidal move, considering the players, but not hard to believe David would try. David hadn't counted on Vivian being more ruthless than he.

Walker opened the other file. A spreadsheet materialized on the screen. He rubbed his eyes and leaned closer. "This is a list of names and agencies of people associated with The Order."

Justin recognized several names in government and big business. Were all these people really connected with Vivian and The Order?

"I think we should go to the police." Marissa rose and crossed the floor.

"We played straight with the police before and almost got killed." Justin raked his hands over his face. "We have no idea who to trust, so going to the authorities, whether local police, FBI, or some other agency, is risky. This information could save us. I don't want to gamble with the police, yet."

Walker continued reading through the documents.

"This information is also what got David killed." Marissa rubbed her forehead. "I'm sick of this game."

"What choice do we have? If even a drop of this is true, this organization needs to be investigated but you can bet they will come after us if we run to the wrong guys." Justin pointed to the computer screen.

"Everyone has choices, Justin." Marissa whistled to Halo and stalked out.

MARISSA CLOSED her bedroom door and clenched her fists. She stalked to the window and then remembered she shouldn't stand exposed. A jagged bolt of lightning flashed in the sky followed by the cymbal crashing sound of thunder. The angry weather mirrored Marissa's emotions.

Everything was wrong.

She sank into the oversized chair in the corner.

Halo curled up in front of her.

With her head leaned back, she closed her eyes. Paths to the resolution of all of her problems traipsed through her mind. Giving Vivian the flash drive probably wouldn't resolve anything. They couldn't unsee her plans and whether anyone believed them, they knew too much. Police involvement appeared to be their best option. Marissa understood Justin's position but they couldn't continue to deal with this situation in a vacuum.

Justin complicated matters. She'd mentioned several times how important she considered honesty. Her heart constricted with the realization her feelings for Justin ran deep. She'd told herself many times not to get involved. Now, she found herself sulking and in pain about the one thing she needed—trust—Justin hadn't given her.

Just as well, she couldn't handle a relationship now.

"I can always count on you, boy." Halo lumbered up, resting his head in her lap. She observed him, searching for any signs of distress in her dog. There were none. Did the sight of David's body replay in his memory, too?

Will either of us ever heal from these scars?

A knock caused Halo to perk his ears and he approached the door.

Marissa massaged her temples as she followed Halo and opened the door.

"We need to talk." Justin stood in the doorframe.

Halo's tail thumped from side to side in frenzied motion.

Traitor.

Marissa stepped away and motioned for Justin to enter.

"Walker told me you saw David's file." Justin stood with both hands on his hips. He had changed into shorts, showing off his well-defined legs.

She glared. "Yes, I *finally* got the truth about David."

He grimaced. "Marissa, I intended to tell you, but I thought you had enough hurt going on." He stepped closer.

She retreated and held up her hands. "Don't give me that. I'm not some weak woman who can't handle a little sting."

"You're more than capable of handling disappointment. But why should you? Nothing in that file, or what I know about David, will change anything. I thought I could wait and explain later." He massaged the middle of forehead. "Marissa, I just wanted to spare you more hurt."

"You don't get to decide when I hurt or feel anything." She stepped closer and jabbed her finger toward his chest. "I own that decision. After four years of David's bullshit, hasn't the time come I'm allowed to see him with clear lenses? Or are you too good of a friend to sully his memory?" She crossed her arms and met his gaze.

"None of this is about preserving David's memory." Justin paused, running a hand through his hair. "I should have warned you. I should have done a better job of pulling up David. I'm not making this about me, but I didn't want to share any blame with you."

"Is everything in the report true? David was some drug-addicted gambler who couldn't keep his pants on? Oh, I forgot the biggest one of all—a deadbeat dad." Her voice caught. She turned from Justin and studied the patterned floor. She didn't want him to make sensible arguments as to why he'd held back the information.

"I let him sleep off drug binges on my dorm room floor. I knew about David's gambling debts. In fact, I took part of the money I received after my parents' death and paid off a couple really bad people. I thought doing so would give him the opportunity to turn around. In the end, I'd just slapped a bandage on the situation."

"Did you know about the child?" Marissa still couldn't bring herself to look at him. How could she know there weren't more dark secrets in David's past? Sure, Walker produced thorough research, but he hadn't been there with David. He didn't know David like Justin did.

How ironic David had sworn he wasn't ready to be a father when he already had a son. Probably his most honest moment.

"I knew a few weeks before the child support hearing. He begged me to be there, then he asked me for money. I refused."

"Why would he ask you for money? He was making more than enough by then." New cars, thousand dollar suits, and Rolex watches were main staples in David's life. Why couldn't he provide for his own child?

Marissa glanced up at Justin as insight dawned. "He didn't want to use *his* money, did he? Even after DNA tests had proven he fathered the child. Selfish bastard."

"He told me the mother, Charlene, would bleed him dry if he started giving her money. The judge didn't see things his way and ordered monthly child support payments. The timing of the judgment probably landed right before he came across the information about The Order."

Marissa crossed her arms. "He saw blackmail as his ticket. He could pay off Charlene and still net a huge sum." All the secrecy and insistent demands for privacy now made sense. He'd even resorted to locking his home office, until the day he'd been in a hurry and forgot. The day she'd discovered the affair with Tiffany.

"I didn't know about the stolen data. At the time, he probably never thought, as the two people closest to him, our lives would become endangered if Skies or Vivian didn't play ball."

"It's one thing to be so callous with us, but to turn his back on his only living child? Did he even consider visitation?"

"Charlene offered, but he declined. In that moment, I saw his true nature. I tried talking him out of marrying you, but he wouldn't listen. I considered warning you, but I doubt you would have believed me." He paused. "For the record, I believe he did loved you, as much as he could."

"How could a person who would abandon his own child and then abandon his fiancée after she's miscarried, care about anyone but himself? His son will grow up with questions about his father, and why he didn't want to be a part of his life. My baby didn't even make it that far." Marissa paced the room.

Halo stood ready to go.

She stopped as tears began to flow. "Everything was so hard, and I didn't want to admit I had made such a horrible decision. Then I lost the baby, and I lost my way." Marissa sat on the edge of the bed and wiped her eyes with the back of her hand. With one exhale she reeled in her emotions.

"I know all this has been difficult, and I wanted to spare you more pain."

"I told you before I don't want your pity. I don't want anyone's pity. I can and will pick myself up and carry on. I've done so before." She stalked to the window, ripped back the curtains, and stared out into the stormy night.

After her miscarriage, she had lamented her empty womb, but she'd managed, even without the comfort of the man she intended to marry. The loss of the baby would always hurt, but she'd survived. And she'd do it again—on her own.

"This has nothing to do with pity. I wanted to protect you." Justin blew out a breath.

"Since when do I need protection from the truth?" She turned and glared.

Jaw tight, he returned her gaze. "Damn it, Marissa. We're being pursued by a bunch of homicidal maniacs. Stopping to discuss David's long, sordid past just didn't make the top of my priority list."

"Justin, for longer than I care to admit, David orchestrated my life." Marissa's voice grew higher as she stepped toward him. "I didn't get to choose whether I wanted to accept him for all his faults. He left me in this la-la-land where I ruled as queen of the clueless. Now I am on the receiving end of his last dastardly deed and you're telling me I don't have a right to know all there is about him?"

"I'm sorry, I..."

She stabbed her finger against his chest. "I told you about my miscarriage, and you were everything I needed. Everything David wasn't." She didn't bother to hide her tears. Her emotions were raw, like blood oozing from fresh wounds.

"I didn't tell you about David, but I won't apologize for caring about you." Justin pushed himself off the wall.

"Don't you get it? I appreciate all you've done for me, but what I wanted more than anything is to trust you and be viewed as an equal partner." She paused. "I want to contact the police or FBI and give them the data. Then Halo and I will go put our lives back together." Profoundly tired, her shoulders sagged and the pounding in her head wouldn't allow her to relax anytime soon. "After this is over please just leave me alone."

Justin placed his hands on her arms and held her with a firmness commanding her attention. "Don't *you* get it? I love you." After a long look into her eyes, he dropped his hands when a knock sounded at the door. "What?" Justin yelled.

Walker poked his head in. "Guys, I'm going to need you to look at this."

Chapter 38

Justin and Marissa followed Walker to the foyer.

Walker stopped two feet from the front door and rubbed his hands on his Thor T-shirt. "I heard a knock. I peeped out the window but didn't see anyone so I opened the door slowly." He glanced at Marissa. "I think this was for you."

"What are you talking about?" Marissa winkled her forehead.

Justin slipped his gun from his holster.

"Is-is that necessary?" Walker's eyes were huge as he stared at the firearm.

"Maybe." Using the tip of his gun, he moved the thin curtain from the long rectangular window next to the door. The portion of the driveway he could see appeared clear.

"Open the door," Walker said.

Justin allowed the curtain to fall back in place and shot Walker a quick glance. He hadn't heard the doorbell ring, but he hadn't been listening for visitors. He pulled the door with one hand and aimed the gun outward with the other.

Marissa gasped.

In the center of the doorway lay a box, inside a pair of ballet shoes covered with blood.

Justin shot a look around the driveway and front yard. Nothing except for driving rain, lightning zigzagging across the black sky, and thunder bellowing in accompaniment. He stepped around the grotesque shoes and made a quick perimeter check of the house. Not finding anything unusual, he returned to the front door.

Marissa, stooped over the shoes, glanced up. "There's a patch." She ripped the patch off the side of the box.

Justin wiped sweat from his brow and stepped closer to Marissa.

"Oh no!" Marissa turned the patch over in her hand. The back contained a picture of Sam.

Justin punched the door. "Damn!"

Before he could formulate another thought, he ducked when a window shattered and a shower of bullets slammed into the house.

MARISSA SCREAMED as Justin pushed her hard to the floor. Her brain scrambled to catch up with circumstances.

Bullets flew.

They were under siege.

"Stay down!" Justin shouted. He slammed the door and fired off shots through the broken window.

Walker crawled up behind her. "Wh-what do we do?" He shielded his head as debris rained down on them.

"Halo!" Through the smoke and dust Marissa spotted Halo in the great room barking and pacing at the chaos. The dog advanced toward her. "Crawl."

Halo obeyed, dropped to his belly, and scooted next to her in seconds.

"Get the flash drive!" Justin grimaced as he continued to fire at the unseen gunman.

Based on the number of shots volleying into the house, Marissa surmised there were at least two gunmen. Most likely Evil Eyes and his accomplice.

Her heart thundered. She ducked as a chunk of the wall splintered above her. They had to find a way out of the house—alive. "Walker, get to the kitchen and grab the flash drive. I'm going to help." She turned to Halo. "Stay." A second later, when a pause occurred in the action, she darted up the stairs and into her room. She yanked open her purse and whipped out her gun. She stopped. Could the police be trusted, especially this close to Babylon Hall? She hit 911 on her cell phone. Nothing. "Damn!" With spotty cell phone coverage and no landline, she couldn't call for help. She jammed the phone in her pocket and raced back to the front of the house.

"I told you to stay back." Justin bent low and slammed in a new magazine.

"You need help. I couldn't get a signal to call the police." Marissa rose and fired several shots. She had no idea where the bad guys were but shot into the dark driveway. The closest house was miles down the road so they couldn't count on outside help.

Justin rejoined the gun battle. After several back and forth shots, he pulled Marissa to the floor. "I should have gotten you out of here earlier. You and Walker get to his car. I'll hold them off. Go to Uncle Lou's. I'll meet you there."

Marissa's shook her head. "What about you?"

"I'll be right behind you." He glanced toward the kitchen. "Where the hell is Walker?" He paused. "Keep firing!" Justin raced off to the kitchen.

Marissa peered up just as another bullet pierced a nearby vase. She aimed and fired.

A few seconds later, Walker scuttled down the hall. "Let's go!"

Marissa scooted across the floor as Halo joined her. Just as she opened the garage door, she felt the breeze as a bullet whizzed by, lodging into the wall inches from her face. She screamed and scampered out into the dim coolness of the garage.

"They got Justin!" Walker said, stopping in the middle of the garage.

"What?" Marissa felt her heart drop. "Get in the car. Halo, too." She ran back toward the kitchen but slowed as she neared.

The gunshots had stopped.

She peered around the corner and almost screamed out loud. Justin stood facing her with hands raised while the other man held a gun at his head demanding the flash drive. *Should I get the flash drive from Walker?*

Justin gave a slight shake of his head.

Did he see her? Marissa slowed her breathing and raised her gun. When Justin stepped to the side, she fired.

The man yelled. The bullet entered his leg and he fell to the floor, scooting away.

Justin grabbed his gun just as Evil Eyes appeared from the sunroom at the back of the kitchen. "Go!" Justin yelled as he dove for cover behind the breakfast bar.

With a narrow miss of another bullet, Marissa ran back to the garage. She slammed on the button to raise the garage door and jumped into the passenger seat of Walker's Prius. "Drive!"

Walker nodded, throwing the flash drive in the console slot.

"Go!" Marissa glanced at Halo. His large girth occupied the entire back seat. He jerked as Walker gunned the car in reverse out of the garage.

Walker had to veer into the grass to avoid hitting Justin's SUV, parked with just enough room for the small car to slip out.

He threw the car in drive and they rocketed down the gravel driveway, spitting a trail of dust and stones.

With her heart booming in her chest, Marissa glanced back at the lake house. The absence of gunfire induced panic. *Justin has to be okay.* She stared at his SUV. *Please let him get out alive.*

"Where are we going?" Walker's eyes were wide and alert.

"Drive toward the city. Justin will call as soon as he can."

Halo whined and tried his best to stand despite being knocked around on the bumpy road.

"We'll be okay. We'll be okay." Marissa hoped repeating the mantra enough times would create the reality.

Walker squinted at the rear view mirror, and then groaned. "Oh, no."

Gasping, Marissa jerked her head toward the back window.

Despite the driving rain, she could see a black SUV barreling closer. "Faster!"

"I-I can't go any faster, or I'll lose control!" Walker's gaze fixated on the wet road and sweat erupted on his face, but he maintained a death grip on the steering wheel.

Marissa screamed as the black SUV made slight contact with the back of their car. At the speed they were traveling, the tiny bump jostled the vehicle. Walker's small car was no match for the behemoth SUV and the mad men inside.

Another tap sent them veering toward the edge of the road, but Walker managed to maneuver back onto the pavement.

Marissa picked up her phone and hit 911. This time an operator answered. "We need help!" She had no idea what road they were on. Why hadn't she paid better attention? Marissa described the setting as best she could. The monotone voice of the operator promised county sheriffs were on their way, but Marissa knew their best efforts might be too late.

This time, the SUV did more than tap.

Marissa's phone went flying, and the back window shattered.

Halo groaned as he fell against the back of her seat. He tried to shake off tiny glass fragments showering down on him.

"I can't control the car!" Walker's frantic efforts to bring the car under control failed as the SUV continued its assault.

After one last slam, the tiny car careened off the road and down an embankment.

Periodic lightning illuminated trees buzzing by. Marissa held on to the door handle and screamed, bracing for impact. Justin's face appeared in her mind. "Justin."

Then the small car slammed into a large tree.

Chapter 39

The long black robe trailed behind Vivian as she glided to a stop in front of the door at the end of the short hall. Vivian only visited this part of the main house on certain occasions.

With a quick punch of several numbers into a keypad, she heard a click, as the door unlocked. Automatic lighting came to life when the door opened, revealing five-foot shelves lining three walls. Jars of varying sizes occupied the shelves, and the odor of formaldehyde lingered in the air.

Turning to the right side of the room, Vivian stopped in front of several jars aligned along a single shelf. "Ahh." Vivian inhaled the telltale scent of this special room. "The babies. So pretty." Fingering the jars, she stared at the tiny, kidney-shaped fetuses, and then moved on to the unmistakable bodies of small, full-term babies.

The bodies, floating in the preservative, allowed her mind to wander. What would Babylon Hall have been like with the wail of a newborn, or the slapping of a toddler's feet on the wooden floors?

Another door occupied the fourth wall of the room. Using the keypad, she entered another code before stepping through the heavy door into a noiseless, windowless inner chamber. Gold walls and soft lights added to the subdued effect. Like the outer room, a slight odor of formaldehyde permeated the sterile, square space. She moved into the room, closed her eyes, and lowered her head.

Ahead of her stood an enormous golden altar with one large jar in the center. "Forgive me, Father. I've fallen off course, but soon all will be rectified." A small black pillow caught her knees as she knelt. "*Ordo Ortus, Ordo Ortus, Ordo Ortus.*" As Vivian repeated this chant, she sensed invisible warmth blanketing her, comforting her.

"You are wise, Father. My strength comes from you, from The Order. Some of our followers questioned my goals, but I am close. So close." She caressed the 16th century Cloisonné Ming Dynasty urn.

Russell had purchased the pear-shaped urn, decorated with dragons and blue lotus flowers, several years before his death.

Commissioned by Russell himself, this room served as an indoor memorial. Gold and crystal encrusted draperies matched a sparkling gold marble floor. Russell's favorite symphony, "Scottish Fantasy" by Max Bruch, played on a loop anytime Vivian visited. The classical piece had been Russell's ode to his Scottish roots.

Russell hated the idea of being interred in dirt, like the violators buried in his garden. The original Grand Commander deserved better. His will included specific instructions regarding his ashes, which were to remain in the memorial room inside the main house of Babylon Hall. Russell's rules restricted visitation to Vivian and only those she chose.

In her mind's eye, the image of her dear father floated before her, staring down at his lone heir. "Please forgive my temporary hitch. My fortitude to carry The Order and your name to the heights of glory has not been deterred. *Ordo Ortus.*"

Vivian kept her gaze at eye level, waiting to receive her father's blessing. She imagined what he'd say.

"*You will do as necessary to achieve our goals. I am with you, inside you, my daughter. I see your vision and approve your path. Go, enforce my will, your will. Enact penance in our name. Ordo Ortus.*"

Vivian nodded as tears snaked down her face. "Hail, Father. *Ordo Ortus.*"

After caressing the urn one last time, she stood and studied the glass jar below the urn. Russell's perfectly preserved right eye hung in suspension. Her long, red-tipped finger traced the front of the jar. "Hail, Father. Your all seeing eye guides us," she whispered, then drew in a long breath and backed from the altar, never turning her back on the original Grand Commander.

Chapter 40

When the gunfire ceased, the men made no attempt to track him down. They grabbed the laptop and with calm ease, exited through of the sunroom door.

Justin slammed his fists into a small area of wall undamaged by the bullet holes. He had emptied his gun on the men. Amazed he hadn't taken a bullet, Justin witnessed the men climb into the black SUV. A second later, the vehicle roared down the driveway.

Fumbling in his pocket, Justin pulled out the cell phone and punched in Marissa's number. Seconds elapsed and the call failed to connect. He needed to call Uncle Lou and Wendy. Had Vivian's people already nabbed Sam or was there still time to warn them? He raced through the house and grabbed Marissa's purse, hoping her cell was with her and not inside her bag. He locked up and jumped into his car. He'd have a hefty bill to pay for the damages, but he'd worry about the rental agency later. After he turned out of the driveway, he still couldn't get a call out.

He pulled on a week's worth of stubble, his stomach clenching. If he couldn't get coverage then maybe they were having difficulty too, but logic did little to assuage his growing concern.

Had Marissa and Walker taken the correct route? If the men in the black SUV went back to Babylon Hall, they should have gone the opposite direction. Fear of all the things, which might have gone wrong, settled into his bones.

Justin kept his eyes glued to the road, but saw nothing in the darkness. He approached one town after another with no sign of Walker and Marissa. They couldn't have been that far ahead of him. The towering peaks of the Blue Ridge Mountains held vigil to Justin's growing gnaw suggesting danger had once again shattered his world.

He resisted the urge to turn the car around, burst through the gates of Babylon Hall, and shoot his way to Sam. The number of guards surrounding the compound made his desire a stupid, compulsive move, destined to spur Vivian to speed up her plans, maybe even hurt Sam. He couldn't even be certain Vivian had Sam yet.

When he got closer to a larger city, Justin phoned Uncle Lou. Despite the late hour, Uncle Lou answered the phone with an alert hello. Justin gripped the phone. "Uncle Lou, I need you to check Sam's room right now."

"On my way. What's going on?"

Justin could hear his feet scuffling on the floor. "Nothing, I hope." Then he heard Wendy's voice. He clenched his jaw.

Wendy's scream provided the answer he hadn't wanted.

"Justin, Sam is gone. I found a green patch in her bed." Uncle Lou's voice boomed through the phone.

"Vivian Sinclair has her." Justin banged his hand against the steering wheel. "Call the police. Tell them I believe Sam has been taken to Babylon Hall. Has Marissa called?"

"No, I thought she was with you."

Justin didn't want to relay his concern Marissa and Walker were lost or worse. "Never mind. I'll be there in an hour."

Exactly an hour later Justin pulled into Uncle Lou's driveway, stopping next to two police cars. Justin jumped out and raced inside the house.

Wendy collapsed in his arms. "Why did this happen? We have to find her, Justin. I can't..." Tears flowed.

"Breathe." Justin held Wendy at arm's length, meeting her weepy gaze. "Just breathe." When her breathing normalized, Justin pulled her close. "I will find her."

"Justin." Aunt Iris touched his arm. "The police have some questions."

Wendy sat at the kitchen table wringing her hands, her nose red from crying. Justin hadn't witnessed Wendy this upset since their parents' death. Even her divorce hadn't yielded this kind of emotion. He'd hoped never to see her in anguish again, yet here they were.

He leaned against the wall as the officers launched into their questions. Why were they going through this? He knew who had Sam. He tried to speak up, but an officer hushed him indicating he needed baseline information first. As the police continued their questions, Justin surmised they were studying his family with suspicion. He couldn't blame them.

They collected a picture of Sam and implemented an Amber Alert.

"We are losing precious time! I know where she is." Justin stalked in front of the group.

They listened while he told them about Vivian and The Order. Justin even went to the car and pulled out Walker's maps, showing the location of Babylon Hall.

One of the officers left the room. After a few minutes, he returned and announced they'd dispatched a sheriff to Babylon Hall. Justin wanted to drive back to Babylon Hall and go in with the officers. If they found Sam and Marissa, he wanted to be a familiar face, but they shot down his idea. Instead, Justin paced...and waited.

"This woman sounds mad," Aunt Iris made coffee and pulled mugs from the cabinet.

With a shaking voice, Wendy asked, "Will she hurt Sam?"

Justin sat at the table. "I hope not. Right now, I don't think so. For whatever reason, she has enjoyed this cat-and-mouse game. Those guys had way more firepower than I alone could produce. They could have overpowered me and either killed or captured me, but they didn't."

"She's drawing you in," Uncle Lou surmised.

"I agree."

"Son, where is Marissa?" Uncle Lou led him out into the hall.

"When we were under attack I told her and Walker to get out. Walker is the guy who has performed extensive research on Vivian and The Order. They managed to take off in his car and I told Marissa to meet me here. I found no sign of them on the way here, and I can't get either one on their cells." Justin paused and leaned in closer. "On the drive in, I called in a few favors. My guys will be ready soon."

Uncle Lou nodded. "Exactly what your Dad would do. Me too, for that matter. Take anything you need from the shed. Don't let your emotions cause reckless decisions."

More officers arrived to comb the area, just in case anyone had seen Sam, or the girl herself had decided to take a walk. The actions were a waste of time, but since when did the police listen to him? Could these officers be on Vivian's payroll?

Justin glanced at his watch as he sat in the living room with the family. An hour went by with no communication. "Screw the police. I can't just sit and do nothing." Justin's impatience shattered as he jumped up.

Uncle Lou rose and placed a calming hand on his shoulder. "Just hold on, son. Give them a little more time."

Justin respected his uncle, but Lou hadn't seen the extent of this woman's vindictiveness. The longer they waited, the more danger Marissa and Sam were in. *I have to find them, soon.*

Wendy sniffled and clutched Aunt Iris's hand.

An officer returned. "I received an update." He consulted his phone. "The local sheriff and a couple of detectives were allowed entrance to Babylon Hall. They spoke with Vivian Sinclair herself. She denied knowing Samantha Hinton or Walker Mumfrey, but did admit to knowing the name Marissa Nash from a news account of her finding her fiancé murdered."

"Bullshit!" Justin threw up his hands. "Are you really just taking her word and packing it up?"

"Dr. Tanner, we have no reason to believe this woman has your niece or your friends. We don't even have enough for a warrant. She didn't have to allow the sheriff entrance to her home at all," the officer said, his voice calm.

"What about those patches, especially the one with Sam's picture?" Wendy asked.

The officer shook his head. "We need more and you haven't been able turn over those patches."

"Great! Let's award her citizen of the year." Justin curled his fists. The patch with Sam's picture had been lost when bullets started flying and he hadn't taken the time to search the rubble for it. Taking a few deep breaths, he hauled in his anger and put the finishing touches on a plan he'd been formulating. Turning to the officer, he asked, "Who were the detectives?"

The officer glanced at his phone. "Detectives Streeter and Kearns."

Chapter 41

Lost in a haze, she sensed her body floating, suspended in the atmosphere surrounded by fluffy clouds. Marissa attempted to open her eyes but met resistance, like her lids were too heavy to lift. Somewhere in her consciousness, a voice screamed, "Wake up!"

She strained to pull open her eyelids. With a flutter, they slid open, but only for a second. She heaved them open again to reveal a white, sterile room.

Where am I?

Lifting her head a few inches, she glanced down. *I'm in a bed. Somewhere.* Pain exploded against her skull, forcing her to drop back onto the pillow and seal shut her eyes.

Once the pain dimmed, she peered around the room as best she could without moving her head. The rectangular room contained no windows, clocks, or calendars to help orient her to time and place. A glance to her right brought an IV monitor into view. She scrambled her fingers and pinched plastic tubing tunneling into her arm, trickling a clear liquid into her body. Her gaze moved to her mid-section, taking in the tiny blue dots of an ugly hospital gown.

Okay, I'm in a hospital, but where? And where are Justin and Halo? Is Walker alive?

A door swooshed open, and a woman in robin's-egg blue scrubs entered. She smiled. "Hello, honey. I'm glad to see you awake." The woman stepped closer, examining the IV before moving on to her head. With gentle pressure, the woman peeled back what Marissa sensed was a bandage on the side of her forehead.

"The bleeding has stopped and I'm positive you'll heal nicely." The woman replaced the bandage and straightened. She placed her hands on her hips and stared down at Marissa.

A tall, slender build accented her authoritarian, demeanor as she hovered over Marissa. She had thin, wispy brown hair and a prominent, bony nose leading to meager lips. Warm brown eyes and the slight, feminine pink tinge to her lips were the only attributes to soften her appearance.

"Where am I?" Marissa said, her voice thick and gravelly.

The woman smiled and bent down. "Honey, you will be fine. I'm a nurse. My name is Nancy. Do you remember being in a car accident?"

The sensation of sliding downhill and then smashing into a tree, dripped through her memory like an old movie in slow motion. "Oh. Yes, I remember." Marissa shifted in the bed and braced for another onslaught of pain. She blew out a breath when the stab of pain diminished. "Another person was in the car. Where is Walker? And my dog, Halo?"

Nancy scrunched her nose. "I'm sorry, I don't know about anyone named Walker, and I haven't heard anything about a dog." She moved to a counter opposite the bed and filled a cup half full of water. "How are you feeling, Marissa?" she asked, approaching the bed.

"A little sore, and I have a monster headache." Every muscle in her body ached and she felt liked she'd just completed a marathon.

"I'm not surprised. You must be a little parched." Nancy patted her arm, and then held the cup with a bent straw for her to sip.

The cool water soothed her dry throat. Marissa took another sip and would have gone for a third but Nancy snatched away the cup, spraying tiny droplets of water.

"Not too much!" Nancy's eyes narrowed and her nostrils flared. After a second, she softened. "Now, honey, you rest. I'll bring in some crackers, but I don't want you eating too much yet."

Marissa nodded. She wiggled her fingers, and then moved her legs and toes under the thin white blanket. She sighed in relief. Her limbs were still working. "Umm, Nancy? Has anyone called my family? You obviously know my name so you must have my information."

Nancy smiled again. "Of course, I know who you are, Marissa."

She stared at the nurse, apprehension growing in the pit of her stomach. "How long have I been here?"

Nancy fluffed her pillow, and then stood staring into space. "You've been out for some time, but how long you've been here is immaterial."

"Immaterial!" Marissa sat upright, disregarding the pain.

"Relax, honey. You were very lucky, but you did sustain a concussion. You need rest." Nancy smiled and, with gentle hands, guided her back against the pillow. "In time, your family will be dealt with. Right now, get some rest."

My family will be dealt with. What the hell did she mean? Marissa sat up again. "I don't want to rest, I want to call my family. I can go home and rest there. I would like to see a doctor, please. In fact, can you contact Dr. Justin Tanner? He is a friend and more than qualified to care for me."

Again, Nancy smiled.

What's with all the smiling? If Nancy thought her smug smiles were calming bedside manner, she needed a refresher course in nursing. After two minutes, Marissa had grown sick of her condescending grin. Since when did a hospital refuse to allow a patient to contact their relatives? She turned to the bedside table. No phone.

"Marissa, you need to remain calm. In your state, getting emotional is not advisable."

"I don't give a damn what you think is advisable. Either you run out there and bring a doctor in here, or I'll go find one myself. In fact, never mind. I'll sign myself out against medical orders." Marissa swung her legs over the bed and braced against the frame to stand. She wrapped an arm around herself to hold the ugly gown in place.

Nancy stepped in front of her, hands on hips.

Marissa stared up at the woman towering over her like a huge brick wall.

"I can't allow you to leave the room. You're not stable enough. Now, get back in bed!"

Her voice boomed, her brown eyes morphing into daggers of flame as her lips pursed. Within seconds, her face melted back into a smile.

"I know you have a job to do, but you don't understand. I may be in danger, and I need to get out of here." Marissa glared at the bullying nurse with matched defiance.

Nancy sighed, her smile frozen in place. In a flash, she pulled out a syringe and jammed the needle into Marissa's arm.

Shock held her captive for a moment, then Marissa collapsed against the bed.

Chapter 42

A sensation of rigidity clashed with something soft in Marissa's consciousness. She sensed her body lying on a rock while a feather caressed her face, but the scene made no sense. She opened her eyes, but this time, the hospital setting had been replaced with a location much darker and more menacing. Iron bars dominated her field of vision. Marissa blinked. *Am I in a cell?*

"Marissa," a tiny voice whispered. "Marissa."

She blinked again, attempting to adjust the clarity of her vision and hearing. She inhaled a musty, earthy odor. *Could I be in a basement or even worse a grave?*

"Marissa."

The voice called again. Was the voice her imagination or a dream? She waited a few seconds more, but the iron bars remained in place, and the soft voice continued calling her name. Bolting upright, Marissa blinked, fear washing over her. "Sam?"

The little girl couldn't be in the cell with her. Could she?

"It's me. Sam. Are you sick? You've been sleeping for a long time. I rubbed your hair because you looked like you were hurt. My mom does that." The little girl smiled.

"Sam." Marissa's heart jumped. "What are you doing here?" She moved closer to the girl. "Are you okay?"

"A lady came through my window and made me go with her. She said you were sick and wanted to see me." She paused and glanced around. "I didn't know we were going to be put in jail."

Marissa followed her gaze. They were indeed in a jail cell. The cold, hard concrete floor and Sam's light touch explained her sensation, but little else. *Where were they?* A frightening answer surfaced.

"Sam, are you okay? Are you hurt?" Marissa pulled her close and inspected her. Aside from a small scratch on her cheek, she appeared unhurt.

"I'm okay, but I'm scared." Sam scooted even closer.

Marissa gathered her into her arms and hugged her. "We are sticking together, okay?"

"You mean like the buddy system? Like on field trips?"

"Yes, exactly like the buddy system." Marissa surveyed the small cell. Against one wall, a twin bed with thin sheets and one blanket sat in bleak misery. A toilet and sink were on the adjacent wall.

Marissa stood and braced against the wall as her vision tilted. After the dizziness subsided, she turned to Sam. "Why don't you have a seat on the bed?"

Sam nodded and scrambled up onto the mattress.

Marissa approached the bars and peered in each direction of the concrete hall in front of her. She suspected more cells were on either side. She moved to the end of her cell in an attempt to see farther down the hallway, but could discern little in the dim light.

They had to be at Babylon Hall, but she had no idea what Vivian had in mind. "How long have you been here?" Marissa asked, turning away from the bars.

Sam shrugged, her pig-tailed hair bounced in response. "A man came and gave me some lunch. You were still sleeping."

"Were you in your room at Uncle Lou's and Aunt Iris's last night?"

Sam nodded. "I think it was last night."

Sam couldn't have been here long, but even so, the family should have discovered her missing and alerted the police. Justin would know exactly where they were.

But the police were on Vivian's payroll. *Surely not all of them.*

Fear skirted through her. Sam had nothing to do with David's deeds, yet here she sat as part of Vivian's revenge. How did she figure in Vivian's plans?

A headache raged on as her stomach growled. She couldn't remember the last time she'd eaten, or even what day it was. The last several days were a muddled mess with snippets of scenes she couldn't be sure were even real.

Marissa rubbed her hands against her pants. Blue sweat pants and a white shirt draped her body. Someone had removed her hospital gown and redressed her. The thought of an unknown person seeing her naked unnerved her.

"Marissa, I'm scared." Sam's eyes were large with fear.

Marissa dropped onto the bed and pulled her into the crook of her arm. "Me too. I know your Uncle Justin is working hard to find us, so we have to be strong together." She inhaled, summoning the right words to calm the girl, even though her confidence waned in their rescue occurring before Vivian exacted her punishment. She placed her hand on her neck and sighed when she discovered her ballet necklace still intact.

"Uncle Justin has a lot of muscles, and he's smart, too. He will find us." The girl nodded.

When I was about your age, my grandmother gave me this necklace with the ballet shoe. The necklace always made me feel better when I was scared. I want you to wear it now." Marissa placed the necklace around the girl's neck.

Sam touched the tiny ballet shoe and glanced up at her. "Thanks Marissa. I feel better already." She smiled.

Marissa hugged her and prayed they'd find a way out soon.

The clanging of a heavy door swinging open and footsteps slapping against the concrete floor sent Marissa's heart into high gear. She pulled Sam closer as the footsteps slowed.

Vivian Sinclair stood in front of the cell, flanked by two grim-faced guards. With a blue top and matching pants, Vivian appeared the image of monochromatic evil. "Ahh, isn't this a picture? Marissa, we finally meet. Welcome to Babylon Hall."

Marissa steeled herself and held her head high. "You like to play dress up, but I suppose I'm looking at the real Vivian."

She threw her head back in laughter. "You figured me out."

"Not too hard." Marissa glanced at the huge emerald sitting on her witch-like claw.

"I hope you enjoyed my last present. I thought you could use a new pair of ballet shoes." Vivian grinned.

The memory of the bloody ballet shoes flashed in her mind. She'd had no time to process the sick gift before bullets started flying. "I didn't get a good look at the shoes. Too busy with uninvited guests."

"A pity." She paused, her expression serious. "Surveillance of the prey is an art. I like hunting alone, like the tiger. The tiger knows the characteristics of its prey, their seasonal migratory routes, when they are feeding, resting. This knowledge makes them a more efficient killing machine." She smiled, revealing a row of straight, white teeth, as her age-spotted, wrinkled hands remained clasped at her waist.

Marissa held on to Sam, the girl shivering in her arms. "Why don't you let this girl go back to her mother? She has nothing to do with this."

"Oh, but she does. This little tête-à-tête won't be complete without our hero. I am eagerly awaiting the good doctor's arrival." Vivian tilted her head, her hair remaining in place. "You remind me of a mother bear holding on to her cub. Do you feel safe, little one?" Vivian glared at Sam.

Sam dug her fingers into Marissa's arm.

"Speaking of animals, I see your motherly instincts are intact. A shame you never quite achieved bringing a live infant into the world."

Marissa stiffened and held Sam tighter.

"I know more about you than you think. I even know your former fiancé better than you ever did. You see, David took something from me, and in return, I took a lot of things from him." Vivian moved closer to the cell bars and, with one long, bony finger, summoned Marissa.

Not wanting Sam to hear, Marissa stepped up to the bars. "What do you want?"

"I'm a big proponent of knowledge, and the time has come for your enlightenment." Vivian moved even closer to her. "I supplied David with a vial of medical abortion pills. He slipped them to you without your knowledge." Vivian erupted in a loud cackle. "Beautiful."

Marissa clutched the bars for support. Her vision narrowed, but determination kept her from fainting. All this time, she wondered what she'd done wrong. All this time, she'd blamed herself for losing the baby. "You're a monster." Marissa whispered through gritted teeth.

"Stop with the melodrama. David would have been a sub-par father, anyway. He jumped at my offer of getting rid of your baby in exchange for me allowing him to live. Too bad he was stupid enough to believe I'd let him live after he stole from me." She paused. "By the way, I have tissue from your fetus preserved. Such a lovely addition to my collection. Maybe I'll let you tour my little museum before I enact my final deed."

"You were responsible for the miscarriage? My baby's death? Why?" Marissa, still cognizant of Sam sitting behind her, concentrated on keeping her anger from unleashing. As she held tight to the bars, she wanted to rip them away one by one. White-hot rage boiled inside her, just under the surface, like molten lava on the precipice of a volcano.

Vivian shrugged and flashed a sick grin. "Because I can."

Chapter 43

"That lady was mean and scary," Sam concluded after Vivian left.

"We're going to get away from the cruel lady." Marissa sat on her hands to keep them from shaking as Vivian's words replayed in her mind. She had to focus on Sam. "Uncle Justin is on his way to help, but we have to be ready to help ourselves, too."

Sam nodded. "Uncle Lou says I can run fast."

"Good." Marissa smiled. "Later, I may tell you to run as fast as you can. Why don't you take a nap now, so you can build up your strength?"

Sam reclined on the bed.

Marissa drew the thin blanket around her, and kissed her forehead. "I'm right here."

Fifteen minutes later, even breathing signaled she'd fallen asleep, her soft curls framing her face.

Marissa stared at a spot on the wall. She would never know if her baby had been a girl or a boy. She'd loved the tiny human once growing inside her, and David and Vivian were responsible for its death. Tears streamed from her eyes as she slunk to the other side of the cell to avoid disturbing Sam. Overwhelmed with emotion,

Marissa sank to the floor, wrapping her hands around bent knees. Sobs wracked her body and she mourned all she'd lost.

Her grandmother once told her heartache had a way of strengthening the soul. Like a ballerina builds her muscles and craft through continuous training, she would build newfound toughness and wisdom.

Marissa glanced at Sam. Why had this innocent child been involved in this madness? Her child had already been sacrificed; Marissa wouldn't allow another to suffer the same fate.

A knocking against the wall made her jump. She wiped her eyes, scrambling to the bars.

"Marissa," someone whispered.

"Who's there?" She didn't see any guards outside the cell. Besides, none of the guards had addressed her by name. She gripped the bars and waited for the unknown person to answer.

"Me. W-Walker." His voice whispered hoarse and strained.

"Walker? Are you in the next cell?" Marissa slid to the farthest corner of her cell, nearest the direction of the voice.

"I believe so. I've been in and out of consciousness, but I think I'm improving."

Marissa surveyed the hall. There were still no guards in sight. "Are you hurt?"

"Yes, but I'll live." Silence prevailed for several moments. "I heard a little of your conversation with Vivian. I'm sorry about your baby."

Marissa gripped the cell bars. "Thank you." She glanced at the sleeping child. "We have to find a way out of here. Samantha, Justin's niece, is here with me."

Walker cleared his throat. "I thought I heard a small child, but concluded my imagination had triggered the voice. Marissa, do me a favor and don't act like you're talking to me."

Her eyes widened. "They're watching us?" She moved to the side of the cell, her back to the common wall.

"I found a camera but no microphone, so they can't hear us." He cleared his throat again.

Marissa lowered her voice anyway. "Can you figure a way out of here?"

"Based on the last set of schematics I could find, circa 1974, this prison facility is below ground. A series of smaller tributary tunnels run directly behind this row of cells. They were once used for the guards to go back and forth with food and supplies." He coughed several times before continuing. "I have reason to believe the tunnel system is still intact.

"How do we get access to the tunnels?"

"Have you eaten a meal here yet?"

Confused, Marissa rubbed her head. "No, but Sam said someone bought her lunch."

"Go to the back of your cell, near the lavatory area, and hunt for a small door. I've been asleep every time my food has been delivered, so I've not seen a door open yet."

Mindful of possible cameras, Marissa stepped to the back of the cell. She washed her hands in the small aluminum sink, and then stooped to grab the paper towel roll underneath. While at ground level, she searched for a small door. After a few seconds, she spotted a row of hinges located between the end of the bed and the sink plumbing. She ran her hand over the rough edges. Could this be their way out? Maybe they could slip out of small square door. She scuttled back to her spot at the front of the cell. "Walker," she whispered. "I found the door."

"Affirmative. I found my door, too."

"What now?"

"If we can somehow get out through the delivery door, avoiding the cameras and the guards, then we might have a chance. I'm not certain of the route once we are in the tributary tunnels. We'll have wing it."

Marissa leaned her head against the wall. "How the hell can we pull this off?"

"First, we observe the guards. I think I've figured out who may be sympathetic. If we can get her to either become lackadaisical with her duties or sensitive to our plight, then we have a chance. Of course, I could have been dreaming, too."

"What? We are basing our survival on a woman you can't be sure exists? You just said you weren't sure if you heard a child, so how do you know you saw this guard?" Marissa shut her eyes against the throbbing headache jackhammering her skull.

"Valid point. My observation skills have been compromised, but I'm feeling better now. Let's think."

The cold concrete wall against her back and the dim lighting of the cell were visual reminders of the predicament Marissa found herself in. She shifted her gaze to Sam. Why had they involved Justin's niece?

Marissa rubbed her tired eyes. "Walker, are you sure you're up for this?"

"The way I see it, we have no choice." He paused then continued. "Justin doesn't trust me but I-I swear I'll do whatever I can to get you and Sam out of here. I promise."

Inhaling, Marissa breathed in the dank air. "Did you and David discuss what would happen after he showed you the data?"

"No. He didn't offer me a cut of any money he might have been able to finagle. I didn't get involved for money, and wouldn't have accepted any."

Marissa stared at the white tennis shoes on her feet, shivering as she recognized they weren't hers. "Why *did* you get involved?"

Walker sighed. "I'd already collected a lot of data on Vivian and The Order before I met David. The brutality and the all-encompassing evil of Russell, Vivian, and The Order members shocked me. I knew going to the police might be risky and, even if they believed me, I'd put my family and myself in danger. David's blackmail plan was dangerous and I told him so, but he ignored me." He paused. "I thought maybe if he could hurt them, even bring a little of their agenda to light, someone in law enforcement might become interested enough to investigate. Classmates and colleagues have tormented me off and on my entire life. What guy wants to be a librarian? Although I have no problem with the profession and have met lots of men librarians, I got to a point I needed to step out of my comfort zone and do something."

Even though Marissa couldn't see Walker's face, she sensed the sincerity in his words. Justin had been certain Walker had a hidden agenda, yet her intuition told her she could trust him. A wrong move and she and Sam would face certain death. She needed to know more about Walker. "You have an ability to analyze people and situations."

"I double majored in psychology and library sciences. I like research, and how people interact intrigues me. Lately, I've felt stifled, like life is passing me by. This situation is horrible, but by doing something, instead of hiding behind a computer and books, I'm taking action to right so many wrongs."

"Walker, we have to get out of here. Justin will try to find us but we can't wait to be rescued."

A full-fledged headache raged as Marissa's mind went back to the last conversation she'd had with Justin. She hadn't had time to dissect their discussion, but Justin professing his love, although unexpected, delighted her. Could she feel the same?

He had a way of pulling her into him, with a look or a touch. He made her feel comfortable and, despite the latest events, safe. She needed him, but maybe now wasn't their time.

A clanging of the heavy door sounded again. Now definitely wasn't the time.

The noise startled Sam awake. "Marissa?"

She darted across the floor to be next to Sam. "I'm right here."

Sam clung as they both waited for someone to materialize.

Footsteps clunked toward them. A few seconds later, a male guard stood in front of the cell. Without a hint of emotion, the guard approached a keypad and unlocked the door.

Marissa's heart knocked. What did he want?.

The guard entered the cell and stopped in front of them. He stared for longer than necessary then pointed. "Come with me."

His lips were set in a thin, grim line, almost disappearing into his skull. She suppressed a shudder. "Sam, we have to go." Marissa stood.

"No." The guard glared at Marissa. "Just you."

Sam clung even harder. "No, don't leave me."

Marisa hesitated, tightening her grip on the girl.

"This isn't a question." The guard stepped closer and moved his jacket aside to show his gun. "Ms. Sinclair has summoned you." He retreated toward the cell door.

Marissa would do all she could to shield Sam from any violence but had little confidence she'd succeed. The girl had already been yanked from her bed. She whispered, "My friend, Walker, is in the next cell. He will talk to you until I get back."

Sam's eyes grew large, but she held the ballet necklace and nodded.

Marissa hugged the child and followed the guard out of the cell. She held Sam's gaze until she rounded a corner. As they moved further away, the damp odor inside the facility became more prominent, reminding Marissa of her grandmother's basement.

The guard opened a heavy door at the end of the concrete hall and drew his weapon. He pushed her up a flight of stairs, and they emerged into a small beige anteroom. The guard grunted and pointed the gun at an outside door.

Marissa stepped out into a large garden. She shielded her eyes against the sudden sunlight, giving them time to adjust. Mounds of dirt rose in between rows of blooming black poppies. "The Black Garden," she said under her breath. Her heartbeat galloped inside her chest. Both beauty and death surrounded her. She wiped sweaty palms against her pants and followed the guard's instructions along a crisscross path through the middle of the garden. Marissa avoided stepping on the large mounds she assumed were the remains of those killed as penance.

A large statue stood in the middle of the garden. The inscription simply read: Russell Sinclair. Marissa squinted to survey the statue depicting a stone-faced man with his hand extended as if to welcome all the unfortunate souls to their resting place among the black poppies.

In front of her loomed a massive five-story hanging garden. Green leafy plants cascaded from the top two stories of the structure and flowed downward, converging into the field of black poppies. Marissa stopped, awed by the beauty. The ancient Hanging Gardens of Babylon, one of the Seven Wonders of the Ancient World, must have been the inspiration. The reference to seven brought her thoughts back to Vivian's kill list. Walker's theory certainly made sense. Marissa froze. With Vivian's capture of her, Walker and Sam, the list had been completed.

The guard nudged her with the gun. "Move."

They walked straight up to the hanging garden wall, and the guard opened a door camouflaged with green vines.

Marissa stepped through the vines into a long, wooden-floored connector hallway with windows on the garden side. A right turn and another long hallway deposited them into a large octagonal living room area with several doors. The ceiling, constructed of wooden beams, led to a domed point. The room resembled a hotel lobby with soft lighting and clusters of sofas and chairs grouped around coffee tables.

Two sides of the octagon contained floor-to-ceiling windows revealing a covered outdoor deck spanning half the circumference of the room. Through one window, Marissa spotted the stables and a large corral in the distance. A day earlier she'd observed the same scene from a tree-lined bluff.

"We meet again." Vivian swept into the room like a queen welcoming a long-lost friend.

"You sent for me." Marissa kept her voice even and controlled.

Dressed in all black with a pale yellow scarf around her neck, Vivian matched her black poppy garden.

The woman enjoyed symbolism. Marissa worked to determine the meaning of this meeting, the jaunt through the death garden, and Vivian's choice of clothing.

Vivian stepped closer. "Yes, I did." She extended her arm and caressed Marissa's hair. "So pretty."

Goose bumps rose on her skin, and Marissa yanked away her head.

"Don't worry, I'm not offended." Withdrawing her hand, Vivian stared at Marissa. "You're a guest here. I thought we should get to know each other better. Sit." She nodded to a nearby cluster of pale blue and beige sofas.

Marissa didn't move.

The guard poked her with the gun. "Sit."

Marissa sat on the edge of the sofa, her gaze darting about as she remained on alert. "What do you want?"

Vivian nodded at the guard.

He retreated to a far corner of the room just as another man in an impeccable gray suit entered.

The man appeared to be in his thirties, with dark hair and captivating blue eyes. He placed a serving tray on a nearby sideboard while he prepared two cups of tea. With soft footsteps and a gentleness rivaling a police bomb diffuser, he placed each teacup on the table without a single rattle. He turned to Marissa as he placed her cup in front of her.

His eyes peered into hers, but despite her head telling her to be afraid, she wasn't.

"That will be all, Edward." Vivian picked up her cup and sipped as Edward exited. "I have taken a liking to you, Marissa. Ever since your fiancé stole from me, I've had you on my radar."

"How nice. The tactic must be in the villainous bitch playbook. Evil tip number 5: know your enemy and everyone in their lives." Marissa narrowed her gaze.

Vivian chuckled. "Your sense of humor is a delicious surprise. I like your spunk."

Marissa had no idea where this defiant streak came from. Exhaustion, anger, and fear must have a way of upping her nerve. "Can we get on with this? Or better yet, why don't you deal with me and release Samantha?"

"No, and you should stop asking." She sat back against the sofa and crossed her legs. "My father was a driven man. He had certain ideas about life. As a young girl, I didn't understand. Time and age bred wisdom."

Marissa scanned the room. The guard who escorted her stood at the door they entered. Another guard manned a far door. She wanted to get back to Sam. Walker would do his best to help her, but... "I'm sure your men have retrieved David's flash drive they surely found in the car. I don't know anything about your organization or anyone who works for you, so I don't see why you are holding me captive."

"I have the flash drive but now I must attend to other plans." She paused before continuing. "My father, an intelligent man, taught me to value loyalty and punish those who threaten our ideas." Vivian smiled. "I'm sure you've probably discovered all kinds of horrible stories about me." She shrugged. "Some may even be true."

Marissa didn't touch her tea. She resisted the urge to wipe her sweaty palms or wring her hands. *Don't show fear. Remaining unemotional takes away some of the power from people like this.* Marissa read an article about handling bullies from a magazine in a waiting room, or maybe on an airplane. She hoped the advice worked, even though calling Vivian a bully seemed as ludicrous as calling a shark a cuddly animal.

"A strong woman is needed to lead a powerful organization. You see, men like David underestimate women like me." She rose from the sofa.

Marissa shifted to keep Vivian in her sight. When the mad woman moved behind her, Marissa's instinct urged her to run, but thoughts of armed guards kept her still.

With long, wrinkled fingers, Vivian twisted Marissa's hair and yanked back her head.

Marissa grabbed at Vivian's arm but her grip tightened. Tears threatened to erupt from the pain, but Marissa fought them back.

Vivian leaned over, her eyes glaring like daggers. "Now get up." She released her grip.

Marissa stood and stumbled around the sofa. They needed to find a way out of this sick place. Now. No time remained to monitor and observe people. They'd all end up in the Black Garden if they followed Walker's plan. Right now, she had to plan an escape from this madwoman's clutches.

One of the doors opened, and a different guard approached. He took hold of Marissa's arm and pulled her along as Vivian led. They followed several halls until they came to a large wooden door with elaborate carvings.

"This is a sacred room. Very few people are allowed access, but today is your lucky day." Vivian punched several numbers into a keypad and the door swung open.

Vivian entered and the guard pushed Marissa in after her.

Jars of various sizes lined the small room. *What is this place?* Marissa stepped closer to a jar, and jumped back. Round, floating grayed eyes stared back.

"Isn't my little museum beautiful? I'd like to think these are the best parts of people. Parts I extract and keep. Of course, I don't actually extract all of them myself."

Marissa counted jars of intestines, ears, feet, eyes, hearts, lungs, and anything else this demented woman wanted. Jars labeled with the name of its host represented almost every body part. When she got to the next shelf, she stopped. Her heart boomed inside her chest and her breath caught.

"Yes, move a little closer. Beautiful, aren't they?"

One step forward brought Marissa face-to-face with jars of fetuses. Two large jars contained almost full-term babies. With a sudden swoosh, Marissa felt like all the air had been sucked out of the room. The next jar was labeled Nash-Seybold. Half of a kidney-shaped fetus balanced in the yellowish solution. "No!" She clutched her middle and bent over as the room spun and droplets of sweat sprouted on her forehead.

Vivian whispered, "The night you miscarried and David took you to the hospital I had my men come and scoop up the fetal contents. We were lucky to find this little gem in all the blood." Grinning, she clapped her hands in delight.

"You're a monster."

"I know the feeling of having a baby ripped from you. Giving up the being growing inside of you, nurtured by you is torturous for some women who can't see the benefit. Your soul is ripped away, but like a cut, you bleed, a new epidermis grows, and you're better, stronger than before. A woman bleeds and suffers to spawn a new beginning. I sacrificed, but like Russell preached, I grew powerful, freed from the pull of a child." Her eyes glazed over. "Free to become the most powerful person on Earth."

Through clouded vision, Marissa stared at the tiny fetus that should have grown into a living child. Tears flowed and she fought to breathe.

"I will take my power to the next level. I have taken a rival's child. Harold's wife had a daughter. She needed to die. Now, I have a little girl forever entombed in my garden of black poppies. Harold's pretty wife had to die, too. However, I received a bonus. She was pregnant with another child." Vivian pointed to a jar with a small fetus. "Once I took your baby, I felt even more power coursing through my body."

The room continued to spin as Marissa clung to her stomach. *Why?* She knew the question would have no sane answer.

"Now, you know. You can die with the knowledge I control you. Just like I controlled David. Just like I will control everyone." Vivian bent toward her. "I thought I had the perfect place for little Samantha in my Black Garden, but I think the girl will go nicely inside a huge vessel, right next to your dead baby." She giggled. "I have my six and seven. How exciting."

"No! Don't touch her!" Marissa lurched toward Vivian. Rage coursed through her. Destroying the monster, her singular goal. She didn't care what happened to her. She only wanted to claw, scratch, do anything to keep this evil woman from hurting Sam or any other baby.

The guard slammed Marissa to the ground. He pinned her shoulders against the cool floor.

Marissa squirmed but when the guard trained his gun on her, she stilled.

Suddenly, the outside door opened.

"I apologize for the interruption, but you have an important call." Edward stepped into the room.

Vivian nodded and turned to leave. "Get her back to the cell."

Once her footsteps faded, Edward turned to the guard. "Is this level of force necessary?" He stooped next to Marissa. "It doesn't pay to attack Ms. Sinclair. You're lucky she didn't order your death on the spot." The crackle of a radio echoed in the room.

The stern guard released Marissa and holstered his gun as he turned to address the radio summons.

Edward helped Marissa up. In one quick motion, he slipped something into her hand. "Use it wisely," he whispered before turning toward the guard. "Ms. Sinclair instructed you to get her back to her cell."

Marissa quickly tucked the sheathed knife into her waistband. Now, she needed a plan.

Chapter 44

Justin and his team neared the outer perimeter of Babylon Hall in half the time the trek took with Walker and Marissa. Despite Justin's desire to get to the compound, he decided to wait until daylight broke when he could be assured of the right path.

Justin turned to the group. "Gabe, you're sure we have enough ammo?"

"Chopper, once again, we're good from beans to bullets." The ruddy-faced man smiled with a simultaneous pat of his artificial leg. "And don't worry about the walking stick, I've been working out." He paused and sucked in a big breath. "We'll find them, man."

In addition to Gabe, two retired Navy Seals, Rick 'Bobsled' Bobbin and Mario 'Cas' Castillo, had joined Justin's team. The men were regulars at GT, and Justin not only worked out with them, but also attended the same support group sessions. He'd fished bullets and shrapnel out of Gabe and Bobsled, and met Cas during his early field training exercises. They were excellent soldiers, and Justin had absolute faith in their commitment and abilities.

Before the point of no return, he cleared his throat. "This organization is very dangerous. I know you guys are a bunch of bad asses, but I'll hold no judgment or bad blood if you want to take off."

"Let's push on," Gabe said, gesturing toward the ground ahead.

Bobsled wiped the sweat from his forehead. "A couple of us wouldn't be here if it weren't for a certain bad-ass shrapnel picker. We got your six."

Justin nodded, thankful these guys vowed to have his back. Five minutes later, they were standing in front of the tunnel entrance Walker pointed out during their previous hike.

Justin squatted in front of the door and inspected the lock, which appeared the same since his last visit, rusted and untouched. He hadn't expected the door to be open and a welcome sign painted outside, but this portal represented most of the first-hand knowledge he had of Babylon Hall. "Based on the schematics, this portal is the farthest point to any possible location holding Sam, Marissa, and Walker. The lengthy distance would give them time to spot us. We're going in another way, but may need this as an escape route. Bobsled, can you pop the lock?"

"No problem." Bobsled pulled a tool out of his utility belt and, within seconds, had the lock opened.

Twenty minutes later, Justin slowed as the guard tower came into view. Through binoculars, he spotted the main gate, guarded by two men, but he focused on their proposed entry point—a tubular tunnel entrance large enough for trucks.

Justin lowered the binoculars, and a flash of a dirty white animal whipped past his line of sight.

"What was that?" A polar bear?" Gabe peered in the direction the animal ran.

Bobsled crinkled his nose. "Hey, genius, we're not in Antarctica."

"Couldn't be. Hold on." Justin disappeared around a large tree, coming face-to-face with a growl. "Halo!"

The dog's growls ceased. Halo stood on his hind legs, greeting Justin with two long, wet licks, like a painter making elongated strokes with a paintbrush.

Relief ran through him as he scratched the dog's head. "Where did you come from, boy?"

"You know this guy?" Cas kept his distance when Halo saluted him with a growl.

"He's a bit leery of strangers. This is a good sign, though. Halo belongs to Marissa, and if he's lurking around here, she has to be near."

Bobsled held his hands toward Halo in a sign of 'no threat'. "He's a Kuvasz, one of the best guard dogs out there. Marissa just won some major kudos with me."

As the dog returned to all fours, Justin spotted a large red-stained area on Halo's side. Blood. Justin bent to inspect the dog, running his hands through his thick, matted fur to the muscle beneath. "This isn't your blood. Where is Marissa?"

The dog barked and took off toward the compound's entrance. When they neared the gate, Halo stopped, both ears perked.

Justin nodded. "I know this is crazy, but Halo is freakishly smart. My gut tells me he saw something."

"I've heard crazier," Gabe said.

"How's our plan looking? Can we get in?" Justin reviewed the preliminary plan they'd designed on the drive up to Babylon Hall.

Cas scanned the area with his own set of high-powered binoculars. "The two guards at the gate are only focused on the street. Using the dense vegetation and some stealth moves, I think we could take out the tunnel guards and slip in."

Justin pulled Walker's papers from his backpack and displayed them on the ground. "I hope these old maps are still accurate. Walker said they have jail cells about here." He pointed to a location on the diagram. "This would be the logical place to start."

They gathered around the maps and studied the route inside the tunnel.

"Fellas, we still have to get across the street without detection." Cas pulled a small device from his pocket. "We are certain they have surveillance cameras, but we can take them out with a signal jammer."

Again, Justin viewed the estate entrance through binoculars. "Six guards—two each at the tower, the main gate, and in front of the tunnel."

Bobsled surveyed the guard tower. "I could take out the tower guards from here, but I'm betting that's bulletproof glass. A shot would alert the other guards, so that's a no-go. At some point, they'll realize they've been infiltrated. The trick is to get enough of a head start so we can make our escape."

Justin checked his watch. "According to Walker, at lunch time, in about fifteen, only one guard remains at each point. Guards enter and exit the interior compound through those side doors, which is great since they're well away from the tunnel entrance."

Cas nodded. "Bobsled, I'll wait until one of the tower guards leaves and then I'll activate the signal jammer. When I give you the go-ahead, you disable the remaining tower guard. I'll handle the gate guard."

Justin held tight to Halo's collar. "Gabe, you and I will deal with the tunnel guard."

"Affirmative."

Bobsled cleared his throat. "Only problem is, we're going in blind. We have no idea what, or who's, inside."

Cas shrugged. "We'll handle whatever happens on the fly. No choice."

"All right," Justin said. "Let's move."

Once the guards left for lunch and Cas gave the go-ahead signal, the men darted across at a bend in the road, out of view of the remaining guards.

About a hundred yards before the compound entrance, Justin pulled back on Halo's collar to stop the animal. He didn't want the dog barreling toward the guard, alerting him to their presence, or taking a stray bullet.

Each man knew their role and readied for action.

Justin instructed Halo to come and the dog trotted along beside him.

Cas gave the signal, doubled back a few yards, and jogged out into the street. He hailed the guard by pretending to be a lost hiker. In one quick motion he had the guard down and dragged the unconscious man behind the cover of trees.

The men and Halo entered the guard shack and slipped out the back door into the compound. The last tower guard had been napping and unaware of the disabled cameras, making Bobsled's job easy. He crept into the tower and knocked out the guard.

Halo stood at alert.

"Stay, boy," Justin whispered.

Within seconds, Gabe had crept up behind the tunnel guard and wrapped his large arms around his neck. The guard slithered to the ground. "He'll be out awhile." Gabe peered inside, gun drawn, waiting for guards to spot them. "Let's go."

Justin, Gabe, and Halo slipped inside the tunnel, followed seconds later by Cas and Bobsled.

The dank, earthy odor blasted Justin's nose. When his eyes adjusted to the dim light, he surveyed the area. They were inside an underground road and parking lot. Three luxury cars and two security vehicles were parked off to the side. The singular road came to a fork up ahead.

Gabe continued to scan their surroundings. "Which way, Chopper?"

Walker's maps didn't include the underground road. Justin cursed. Successful rescue missions weren't conducted on the fly.

THE ROUGH GUARD pushed Marissa back into her cell.

With haste, she pulled Sam into her arms. "Thank goodness, you're all right."

"I was really scared, but Walker told me a story about a guy named Luke Skywalker, and how he became a knight. I think Luke Skywalker and Walker are the same. They almost have the same name." Sam smiled, her small arms squeezing with surprising force.

"Walker?"

"Yes, I'm here."

"Thanks for taking care of Sam. We have to get out of here, now." Marissa moved to the front corner of her cell next to the shared wall with Walker's cell and lowered her voice. "Sam and I are six and seven. We can't wait any longer. Whatever happens, we need to get Sam out."

"The lunch trays were pushed through about fifteen minutes ago, which means someone will be coming back soon." Walker's voice sounded stronger. "Also, I think something is wrong with the camera in my cell. The tiny red light is out."

Marissa stared at the camera. "My light is out too. I hope that means help is coming. I've got a plan." She inhaled and held on to the cell bars. "If this works we'll escape through the tunnels but I'll need your help navigating our way out."

"Are you sure about this?"

"We have no choice." Marissa whispered her plan to Walker. Then she returned to Sam and said in a louder voice, "Everybody eat. We need them to come back."

Turkey sandwiches on white bread, small cups of red grapes, and two bottles of water sat untouched on the small tray in Marissa's cell. Silverware and condiments were obviously taboo.

"I don't like purple grapes, I like the green ones." Sam moved the cup of grapes to the side.

Marissa ate half of the sandwich and gulped half the water. "I don't like white bread either, but we need our strength." Unable to force down more, she moved to the bed. She had located the camera in a corner on the opposite side of the cell. With her back turned, she ripped several pieces of the sheet. She left them on the bed and covered the pile with the thin blanket.

After Sam had finished eating, Marissa pulled her closer. "We are getting out of here soon. When the time comes, I want you to stay close. I don't want to scare you, but I want to be honest. If someone tries to grab you, kick, scratch, and do whatever you can to get away. I hope we don't have to resort to fighting, but we need to be prepared for everything."

Sam's eyes widened, but she nodded and placed her hand in Marissa's.

"Walker?" Marissa asked. "Are you ready?"

"Yes. The trays should be picked up in the next ten minutes."

The little girl's grip tightened. "Isn't Uncle Justin coming?"

"I'm sure he is, honey, but we have to help ourselves." *I won't let us be sitting ducks, waiting for whatever insanity Vivian has in store.* She inhaled and allowed the air to release in slow measures.

Justin would be doing his best to get to them.

She hoped they could escape before he stepped into the trap. The bond they'd developed grew strong in her heart, despite their last argument. She needed him. Alive.

Chapter 45

V ivian placed the phone on the desk as Edward entered the office. "Our hero is here, and he's bringing extras." She clasped her hands together. "This will be fun." She closed her eyes. She hadn't imposed penance in this fashion in quite a while. She'd simultaneously be victorious, add a few more guests to her garden, and grow more powerful.

"Can I get you anything, ma'am?" Edward stood at attention near the door.

She shook her head, and Edward slipped away. Approaching the window, Vivian gazed out at the stables in the distance.

Titan grazed in the corral as if he had no cares in the world. Such behavior she took as a sign. *I'm on the right path.*

Vivian trailed a finger across the window, and then allowed her hand to fall upon her stomach. Once, a life grew inside. Why had her father been convinced when he said she couldn't be both a mother and a strong leader, capable of making hard decisions? Maybe other women couldn't but she could. *Father, do you see me now? I'm in total control.* She let out a high-pitched cackle.

Russell had been a pioneer, a visionary during his time. She'd appreciated his efforts, but times changed, and one couldn't expect

The Order to thrive under the same ancient thinking. Although in her sixties, Vivian liked to think of herself as a modern woman with one toe in the past and the rest headed toward the future.

Like babies were mistaken as weak and fragile, Vivian too represented resiliency and durability. Returning to her desk, she slid open the drawer and pulled out the knife. *I know what I'm doing, Father.*

The worn handle of the knife, smooth from years of use, had seen decades of enacting penance. While the handle had softened, the blade remained cold, sharp, and exact. Just as expected. Now the time had come to ensure an apprentice for the future.

Edward knocked on the door.

Vivian sighed and slipped the knife back into the drawer. "Come in."

"You have a visitor."

Vivian nodded.

A blonde, pony-tailed woman entered the room. "Hello Mother."

Chapter 46

The knife under her shirt pressed against her stomach, adding to the nerves twitching inside. She had no idea why Edward had chosen to help her, but she silently thanked him for the unexpected gift.

The small door loomed before her. She could only see in front of her. Anything or anyone behind the person collecting the tray represented an unknown factor. She made a mental list of what she needed to do, and possible responses to the guard's reaction. *Number one, think clearly and stay calm.*

Marissa and Sam sat on the bed.

The girl's hand shook in Marissa's grasp.

"I have an idea." Marissa kneeled in front of her. "Close your eyes and imagine you are back in your room."

Sam nodded. "Can Halo be in my room too?"

"Of course. What are you and Halo doing?"

Sam smiled and moved into a ballet first position. "We're practicing ballet!"

"Good. When you get scared remember the necklace and you and Halo dancing in your room. Once we're out of here, I'll make sure to ask your mom if you can join one of my ballet classes." Marissa hugged Sam.

Sam clung to her. "Thanks, Marissa."

At that moment, Walker banged against the wall, signaling his tray had been collected.

"Okay, it's time."

JUSTIN and his men took the right fork in the underground road. They stuck close to the walls, but had yet to spot any guards or vehicles.

"Are you sure this road will take us to the prison area?" Gabe slapped a new stick of gum in his mouth.

"Nope, but according to the maps, we're heading in the right direction. I know this isn't an ideal mission." Justin scanned the walls for signs of a door or something to indicate their position.

"Never been on a perfect mission," Bobsled said.

They walked in silence for another fifteen minutes before coming to an intersection. The tunnel they were in continued several more yards then dead-ended. To the right, the tunnel extended in both directions. With guns at the ready, the men examined the area before moving on.

After peering through night-vision goggles, Bobsled slid them off. "Clear."

As they moved further into the bowels of Babylon Hall, the danger magnified with each step. While so far they appeared to have escaped exposure, Justin had an uneasy feeling.

Gabe stopped and peered forward. "Door ahead."

Justin cocked his gun and, after the go-ahead nod from Bobsled, gently turned the knob. He relaxed at the sight of the storage closet. His senses were in overdrive. His eyes were in continuous motion, and his auditory perception stood on alert for signs of people, but so far he only registered the slapping of their footsteps on the tunnel floor. Most of all, he knew he had to trust his instincts—a skill these guys advised him to never discount. Random luck always ran out, but instinct cultivated and honed through years of experience, stuck.

Halo stopped, his ears pointed forward.

Justin pulled up. "Halo hears something."

"I don't hear anything." Cas, who'd been bringing up the rear, turned backward, scanning the tunnel with night-vision binoculars. "Nothing."

Bobsled brought his binoculars up and scanned in front and behind them. "Nothing."

They continued forward. Suddenly, something whizzed past Justin's head and slammed into the wall.

"Incoming!" Gabe yelled.

Four guards emerged from a door a few feet in front of them.

Justin pulled Halo against the wall as the rest of the crew followed suit.

Cas took out two of the guards.

Justin joined in a brief firefight. Bright muzzle flashes emitted from the firing guns in the darkened tunnel. Justin's ears rang with the deafening sounds reverberating against the tunnel walls, and he sniffed the growing odor of gunpowder with each fired shot.

Halo paced and growled at the influx of stimulation.

Justin's gaze shifted from the battle ahead to the dog's growing agitation. He couldn't allow Halo to get hurt.

After Bobsled and Gabe each handled the remaining guards and the gunfire ceased.

The men glanced at each other, and then scooped up the fallen guns and radios.

Halo sniffed at the guards, and sat off to the side.

Gabe searched through the pockets of the men. "Bingo."

"What?" Bobsled said, pointing to his ears.

"Bingo!" Gabe said, speaking louder to overcome the ringing in everyone's ears. They decided to forego earplugs to ensure they didn't miss important communication. Gabe held up a map.

Justin studied the map over Gabe's shoulder. "There." He pointed to a block of six cells. "According to this map, the cells should be up ahead. Check those guys for keys, and let's get moving. We've just announced our arrival."

Cas found one set of keys while Bobsled and Justin pulled the bodies back into the break room the guards had exited.

The team crept back into the hall and hurried toward the cells.

WHEN THE GUARD reached through the hatch for her tray, Marissa slammed the pocketknife into the outstretched hand.

The guard howled in pain.

She held on and pulled open the door as wide as she could. With all the strength she could muster, she slammed her foot right into the bridge of his nose. Blood splattered in every direction as the man screamed. Marissa called on her ballet skills and strong legs to continue kicking the guard's throat. She prayed another guard wouldn't find this guy, now unconscious, sticking halfway through the small door.

Leaning forward, Sam yanked the radio from the guard's pocket.

"Sam, get behind me!" Marissa didn't want the girl within arm's length of the guard. She grabbed the gun from the guard's side holster and pushed him back through the door into the guard's hall, at the same time taking aim. Marissa stuck her head through the door. No guards. Exhaling her long held breath, she pushed back into the cell and took hold of Sam's hands. "Remember what we talked about?"

The girl nodded, her wide eyes trained on Marissa. "I'll hurry." Sam sidled through the door and within seconds had the key in the lock.

Hearing the lock tumble, Marissa stepped back as the door swung open. She said a quick prayer; thankful the guards used keys on this side of the cellblock instead of a keypad. Marissa scooped up the radio and pulled Sam behind her. "Good girl."

Marissa surveyed their surroundings. Still no guards in sight. She continued to point the gun at the guard, as he began to stir. "Don't make a sound." She backed up to the next cell and unlocked the door.

Walker slipped through the door.

"Sam, give those ties to Walker." Marissa bent and pulled the knife out of the guard's hand.

Walker winced as he gagged the weakened guard's mouth before tying his limbs together. He stood and wiped sweat from his forehead. "This way."

Marissa wedged Sam between her and Walker, and the three of them crept out of the small service hall. The large door ahead would either present a chance to flee, or throw them deeper into peril. Holding her breath, she eased open the door, glanced in both directions, and nodded.

Walker raised his finger and gestured for them to go left.

In silence, they tiptoed along.

Marissa's heart pounded as she eyed the blind bend in the tunnel ahead. She hated being this vulnerable, but they had no other choice. Vivian not only had plans to kill her, but also Sam. She'd die before she allowed Vivian to carry out her plan.

They slowed as the bend neared. She raised the gun, now even more thankful for Uncle Lou's refresher course. *Clear and calm thoughts.* Marissa pushed Sam against the wall and inhaled. She and Walker made eye contact and nodded.

They turned the corner. A glint of something bright flashed in front of Marissa. Her breath caught as she faced the raised guns.

Chapter 47

"The doctor and his crew are close, along with the damn dog I should have killed." Roy Bane rubbed the bite wound on his lower leg as he waited in the doorway of the office.

"Good." Vivian clasped her hands together. "Now we can get this started."

Roy cleared his throat. "Also, Ms. Sinclair, the prisoners have escaped. They tied up a guard and mangled his hand pretty good. Seems our girl got her hands on a pocket knife, and now has a gun."

Scowling, Vivian whipped around in her office chair. "How did this happen? Who's responsible?"

Roy shifted in the doorway. "All surveillance cameras have been disabled. We're working to bring them back up."

Vivian stood. "I want every available guard to hunt them down and bring them back here. They can't be far." She leaned across her desk. "Do not kill them. I want the pleasure for myself."

"Yes, ma'am." Bane closed the door.

"Well, this should be fun." The blonde woman resumed filing her nails.

Vivian turned, her eyes blazing. "This is serious. You must prove yourself to The Order, and to me as Grand Commander, before I grant your ascension."

The woman put down the file and approached the desk. "I understand what's at stake." She yanked up her shirt, exposing a puckered red heptagon shape tattoo emblazoned on her lower stomach. "I understand The Order, and I've done everything you've asked. This tattoo shows you how committed I am." She allowed her shirt to fall back. "A time will come when you are the one who will have to trust me."

With her back rigid, Vivian glared at the woman. "My father demanded much. When the Freemasons disappointed him, he founded The Order. Of course, the Freemasons are well known and have a certain place in history, but they are a force of the past, fodder for conspiracy theorists and historians. We are the future."

Vivian scooped up the black-and-white photo of Russell and his men. "Father treated faithful followers well. When I assumed my position as Grand Commander, I took The Order to new heights. The Order will guide the world. I, and eventually you, if I desire, will control all."

The sound of Titan neighing in the pasture brought Vivian to the open window.

The horse bucked and jumped, throwing his brown head back in clear agitation. Titan came down with a thud and grew still, his large black eyes wild with fury, staring at Vivian.

She shuddered. "I need to go to the stables."

Chapter 48

Justin slapped his gun in the ready position as the smack of footsteps rounded the bend.

"Uncle Justin!" Sam screamed and ran toward him.

The sweet voice relaxed his stance. "Don't shoot!" He lowered his gun, and the men followed suit.

With a quick hug, Justin held Sam in front of him. "Are you okay?"

She nodded. Her eyes grew even larger when she spotted Halo.

The dog flapped his tail, and when Justin lowered Sam, the dog licked her face.

Stepping forward, Justin scooped Marissa into his arms. "Are you hurt?" With a light touch, he examined a cut on her face and prayed her injuries went no further. He pulled back, and a determined expression greeted him.

She carried a pocketknife stained with blood.

His heart walloped. Had they hurt her or Sam? He wanted to pull her close and ply her with kisses, but he held back.

"I'm okay. I'm glad you're here." Marissa said. "Halo." She bent to hug the dog, and he returned her affection with enthusiasm. "I thought they killed you."

"We found him just outside the compound." Justin turned and met Walker's gaze. "I'm glad you escaped."

Walker nodded. "Me too."

Justin's gaze moved between the knife and the gun.

Marissa straightened, glanced at her hands, and her mouth dropped open. "Not our blood." She folded the knife and slipped the blade under her sweatpants.

"Are you comfortable with the gun?" Justin stepped closer, eyeing the weapon in her hand.

Marissa nodded. "I'm good."

Her demeanor displayed focus and determination, like he'd never seen from her. His heart lurched at the thought of what might have happened. He swiped one finger along her cheek before pulling away. "I thought..."

She nodded and squeezed his hand.

Gabe stepped forward. "Glad to see you again, pretty lady." He turned to Sam. "And little, pretty lady."

Sam smiled, her hand stroking Halo's fur.

Walker cleared his throat. "We need to go. The guards can't be far. Besides, these tunnels are monitored. They know exactly where we are."

Bobsled checked his watch. "We jammed the signal, but only for two more hours."

"Genius." Walker pushed off the wall. "I believe the best route would be out through the stables. It's closest to the woods, and not as well guarded."

Cas peered ahead. "Let's move."

Justin rattled off introductions as they moved away from the injured guards. "Walker, are you hurt?" He eyed him. Walker winced, but could move, so an examination would have to wait.

"Shoulder injury, but I'm okay." He nodded and moved on.

"Uncle Justin, are we going home?" Sam stared upward with bright eyes.

"Yes, but we need to be as quiet as possible." Justin squeezed her hand. He wanted to phone Wendy to let her know he had Sam, but he couldn't stop to make a phone call.

Sam nodded and held his hand tighter before leaning in close. "Marissa and I were in jail together. We took care of each other."

Walking on the other side of Sam, Marissa whispered, "She was great. You should be proud."

"Thanks for taking care of her." Justin smiled.

Marissa nodded and wiped sweat from her forehead.

Justin unclipped a water bottle from his belt loop. "Drink this."

Instead of taking a sip, Marissa passed the water bottle to Sam. "Time for a water break." She winked as she placed her hand on Sam's shoulder.

As he witnessed the gesture, relief spread through him. Two of the most important people in his life were safe, for now. He glanced behind them. So far, no sign of guards. Fifteen minutes later, the radios Justin and Marissa swiped from the guards vibrated. "Damn." He stopped and held the radio near his ear. Three guards were headed their way.

"The door is just up ahead," Walker said.

"We need to pick up the pace, now."

Walker squinted and pointed. "I believe this door is for utilities. The next door should lead up to the main level. We should come out at, or near, the stables."

Justin recalled the map. "There's no cover from the stables to the woods. We'd be sitting ducks."

Marissa tugged Justin's shirtsleeve. "Whatever we do, we need to get Sam out of here. Vivian is going to kill her." Her strong posture matched her intense gaze.

Bobsled put down his binoculars. "We'll have company in about five minutes. Make a decision."

"I'm doubling back. I can draw them away." Cas checked his weapon and ammunition. "I can get back to the bend and then take the other route. They'll fall for the ruse."

Justin placed a hand on Cas's shoulder. "We need everyone to come out of this alive."

"I'm good." The man grinned. "Get them out of here. I got your six."

"Be careful, Cas," Marissa said. "Take Halo with you. I don't want him excited if we run into horses." She stooped in front of Halo and pointed toward the man. "Go with Cas."

Cas winked at her. Turning to Bobsled and Gabe, he smacked their hands and, with an obedient Halo in tow, took off in the opposite direction.

The group scrambled past the next door.

Justin arrived at the second door first. He turned the knob, but the door didn't budge.

"Keypad." Bobsled pointed.

Walker scooted past Marissa and Sam. "Let me." The first code he punched in elicited one beep. The red light remained.

"Come on, man, or we'll have to shoot our way out." Gabe cocked his gun.

"Walker, hurry." Marissa pulled Sam closer, wedging the girl in between her and Justin.

"Hold on." Walker tried another number.

The red light remained.

"You've got one more try before I blast the door." Bobsled scanned the tunnel.

Walker entered a new set of numbers. After a pause, two beeps sounded and the red light turned green. "We're in."

Justin stared at Walker.

"Somebody on the inside is friendly." Walker smiled.

Gunfire exploded farther down the tunnel.

Marissa stared wide-eyed.

Justin glanced in the direction of the sound. "Cas can handle himself."

With Justin in front and Bobsled in the back, the group rushed through the door and up the stairs. The outer door contained no keypad.

Justin had his gun ready as he slowly pushed open the door. He inhaled the strong odor of hay, wood, and manure. He didn't see anyone, so he opened the door wider, and the group crept into a nearby stall.

"We need to get our bearings before we move any further. What do you guys think?" Justin pulled Sam into a corner of the hay-covered floor. "Stay hidden."

The girl nodded and curled into a ball.

"I estimate the woods are 200 yards west of here. It's a straight shot, but we'd have to contend with open land." Walker peeped above the stall and pointed. "To the east is deeper into the compound —we don't want to go toward guesthouses and other buildings. While there is more cover if we stick closer to the buildings, we have no idea if the cottages are occupied. The main house is north of the stables with nothing but open land from here to there. The compound entrance is to the south, and you can be sure we'd run into guards. Don't forget the guard towers scattered around the perimeter." Walker collapsed against the gate, sweat spotting his Thor T-shirt.

"We either head farther into the witch's lair, or high-tail it through the open yard to the woods. Great." Bobsled peered up through the slits in the gate. "Right now, we're still good, but we can't stay here for long."

Justin huffed out a breath. "We need to get out of here, so I say we risk the open yard. Walker, are you okay to run?"

"My legs are fine."

"Mine, too," Gabe chimed in.

"Let's go." Bobsled ducked and ushered them out of the back gate.

Marissa seized Sam's hand and whispered, "Stay close, and don't make a sound."

Justin cocked his gun, his gaze taking in as much as possible. If he could just get them to the cover of the woods, then maybe they'd have a chance. His heart thundered. *No room for failure.*

For a moment, he was transported back to Iraq. Guns blasting, body parts tossed about, explosions, and decisions. Go left, go right, either way a toss-up. Faced with choosing the life of a child, or choosing the woman he cared deeply for, he'd weighed his options.

While in Iraq, he thought he could have both, but he chose to save the child first, and time ran out on Laura.

Justin exhaled. *Focus on the present.*

As the group neared a storage area filled with supplies at the far end of the barn, a bullet slammed into a nearby crate. Justin spotted guards aiming at them. "Get down!" He pulled Marissa and Sam to the floor.

Marissa pushed Sam into a corner. "Sam, wrap yourself into a ball and don't move!" Then she pulled out her gun and joined the firefight.

Justin, Gabe, and Bobsled traded fire, but they had nowhere to go as the men closed in on them.

After a few minutes, one of the guards screamed, "Hold your fire!" Quick to obey, the guards stopped firing.

Flanked by two more guards, Vivian glided into the stables. "Finally, we're all together."

MARISSA WENT RIGID, but her heart thundered in her chest as Vivian stopped several feet short of their group.

Three guards pounced from behind them, ripping their guns away.

Justin helped Marissa and, with a hand on her back, moved Sam behind them. He eyed Bobsled and Gabe as they closed ranks to shield Sam as well.

Walker, grimacing, stood last.

Marissa held her head high. No way would she give Vivian the satisfaction of seeing her fear. She reached for Justin's hand, and he responded with a squeeze. Behind her, Sam clutched the back of her shirt. Marissa glanced at the woods off in the distance, the towering black pines sturdy and inviting, yet just out of reach. They'd almost escaped, but now what?

"I'm so glad we can have this little reunion. I must admit, I didn't expect you here in my stables. I'm actually here on another mission, but I'm quite happy you've joined me. You will be my witnesses." Vivian smiled as she inched closer to the group before turning to Walker. "Welcome to Babylon Hall. Your involvement is way over your head. A librarian working with a common thief. Big mistake." She paused as she surveyed him. "I should have killed you earlier."

To Walker's credit, he remained still and matched Vivian's glare.

Next, she turned to Justin. "Dr. Tanner, I knew you wouldn't stay away. You've taken quite a liking to your best friend's fiancée. She is quite alluring." Vivian spun her attention to Marissa. "My dear, I know you had a shock. Seeing your baby, lifeless and frozen forever in my tomb." She flashed a smile, which didn't extend to her eyes.

Scratching her eyes out would have been a treat, but Marissa remained still.

Justin moved closer. "What is she talking about?"

Marissa glared at Vivian, her mind spinning back to those early days of pregnancy. Vivian had been ruthless but how easy had David's decision been to intentionally kill his own child? She couldn't forgive him.

"Tell him," Vivian said with a sneer.

Marissa closed her eyes for a moment, hoping she'd open them to a different reality. No luck. "Vivian and David drugged me so I would miscarry, and Vivian had someone take the fetus." She forced her voice to remain even and calm, her gaze never wavering from the evil being before her.

"What!" Justin turned to Marissa, eyes wide.

"I saw my baby in her sick museum." Marissa steeled her back.

Vivian moved closer, and a guard mirrored her steps. "I think you would have been an admirable mother. Too bad." Next, she peered at Sam, who peeked between Marissa and Justin. "I have plans for you, little one."

"Keep your hands off her." Marissa closed the gap between her and Justin, pushing Sam farther back.

"Your mothering instincts are on full display."

"My niece has nothing to do with this. Let her go. I know the cops have already been here, and you duped them into believing your lies.

They'll be back." Justin hated he'd been forced to throw crap against the wall.

"Doctor, you're wrong on several points. Your niece is very important. She will complete my collection, and she'll count as part of your penance. She's my number six. I don't think any of you understand the power I possess. As far as the police, I've got a few connections." She turned toward the open door and extended a hand. "Honey, why don't you come out and introduce yourself?"

Marissa gasped as April Kearns glided around the corner.

"Kearns," Justin said under his breath.

April stood before them, whipped her long hair back, and smiled. "You two stopped taking my calls. I didn't take offense, as I knew we'd meet again."

Justin's jaw tightened. "What do you have to gain from working with this psycho?"

"Now I'm offended." April laughed. "This psycho is my mother."

Even though they had suspected a mole in the police department, Marissa never imagined the spy would be Vivian's daughter.

"This reunion is wonderful, but we have a task to complete" Vivian nodded to her two guards. "Bring the two lovers. Leave the girl, the nerd, and the muscle under heavy guard."

"No." Sam cried out and clung to Marissa and Justin.

Justin leaned toward her. "We will be back. I promise you. Stay close to Walker, Gabe, and Bobsled." He winked, and then turned to Bobsled, pleading with him with his gaze.

Bobsled dipped his chin.

Marissa hugged Sam. "Remember your room."

With tears in her eyes, Sam gripped the necklace.

The guards pulled Justin and Marissa along. They were shuffled to the fence surrounding the corral.

Inside, a lone horse grazed.

Marissa's stomach rolled. How could a beautiful horse survive in such evil?

Vivian stood near the fence. "Titan."

The horse stared for several seconds then sauntered toward the fence.

When the horse reached the railing, Vivian grabbed his muzzle. "I saw the look. I am the all-powerful one. I won't tolerate dissent. Your mother died so you could live. How dare you question the power of Nyx—or me. Your use has expired."

Marissa moved her hand into Justin's.

He pulled her closer, despite the nudge from the guard behind them.

Marissa spotted Edward step out of the barn. His immaculate black suit appeared out of place for the dusty outdoor setting. He eyed Vivian, April, and the guards. "Ms. Sinclair, do you need anything here?" He moved closer until he stood two feet in front of Marissa and Justin.

"No, Edward. I'll be ready to travel back to the main house momentarily."

Marissa observed Edward, waiting for him to give her some type of sign but he never looked her way. *Why had he helped her?*

Edward turned, crossed his arms behind his back, and retreated into the barn.

"I'm not sure what will happen, but be ready." Justin squeezed her hand.

Marissa nodded. She trusted Justin's guys inside the barn would do everything they could to keep Sam safe. Outside, guards were everywhere, but she only counted three inside the barn.

"April, you've proven an excellent student. I have no doubt the next task will meet my approval." Vivian released the horse's reins and stepped away from the fence.

April's smile melted into grim determination. She accepted a rifle from a nearby guard and marched closer to the fence. Gun raised, she aimed at the horse's forehead.

Marissa screamed as a shot fired.

Chapter 49

Gunfire exploded as Justin pushed Marissa to the ground, scanning the immediate area.

April collapsed, and Titan galloped off in a wild panic. Chaos erupted.

Justin searched for Vivian. He spotted a guard rushing her toward one of their security vehicles. Another guard barreled toward Justin and he reared back, jamming an elbow backward, and knocked out the guard. He grabbed his gun and tugged Marissa toward the exterior of the barn.

Someone in an upper berth of the barn shot several guards.

Justin took out another guard, hoping the unexpected help continued, as he pulled Marissa as fast as he could without dragging her. They had to get to Sam. From the far end of the barn, he spotted Bobsled bursting through the back door carrying Sam, followed by Walker and Gabe. He ran toward the group.

Bobsled handed Sam off to Justin. "I'll cover you!"

Justin held Sam tight and pulled Marissa's hand. "Keep your heads down. Let's go." They sprinted toward the tree line with Walker close behind and Gabe bringing up the rear.

Bobsled and Gabe laid down cover fire, occupying the guards.

With the growing number of guards how long could they hold them back?

Walker lagged behind as they raced toward the cover of the trees. Before they reached their destination, Justin turned to assess their escape status.

Walker screamed and plummeted to the ground, blood spurting from a gunshot to his leg.

He moaned in pain, gripping his extremity.

Marissa slowed. "Walker!"

"Marissa, let's go." Justin tugged at her hand. "I'll come back for him!"

"I can't leave him." Marissa wriggled out of his grasp and turned back to Walker who had collapsed half way between the woods and the stables. "Get Sam to the woods!"

Justin spotted Cas returning fire from the forest's edge.

Bobsled, not far from the tree line, slowed, and sank to his knees as a bullet slammed into him.

Justin hesitated as memories of Iraq flooded in. Once again, decisions put him in the middle of two people. Go either direction and someone could be killed. The odor of gunfire, the smoke, and confusion added to the familiarity.

Sam wiggled in his arms, jolting him back to the present. He continued to hold her as he raced the last several yards, entering the darkened canopy of trees.

Cas ran toward him, Halo at his side.

Out of breath, Justin reached Cas and lowered Sam. "Walker and Bobsled have been hit. Cover Sam. I'll be right back."

Halo licked Sam's face, and then moved in front of her.

"Good boy." Justin yelled. "Watch Sam."

As Justin approached the tree line again, he met Bobsled moving slowly toward him.

"I'm hit, but it's not a killer. I'll live." Bobsled grimaced as Justin pulled him farther into the woods. He examined his wound. "I think the bullet went through my arm and missed all the important stuff."

Justin tore off a piece of his shirt and made a makeshift pressure bandage before turning to Cas. "It's not fatal. Take Sam, Bobsled, and Halo, and get the hell out of here. You know Uncle Lou. Call him." He sprinted back to the edge of the tree line, spotting Marissa struggling to support an injured Walker. Just as he took a step forward, a black SUV barreled past the stables and into the open field, cutting him off from Marissa and Walker. Guards surrounded the vehicle as Justin stared at the scene. Darkened windows prevented him from seeing into the SUV.

Gabe sprinted toward Justin, heaving to draw in air. "The fire-power was too much. I couldn't get to them. They've got Walker and Marissa in the SUV." He continued to fire at the few guards still shooting, and then all firing stopped. "They are calling back the guards."

A few seconds later, the SUV shot off towards the main house.

Marissa and Walker were gone.

Justin grabbed his binoculars and followed the vehicle as far as he could. The SUV turned left and headed for the main house.

He continued to track the vehicle, sure he spotted Marissa in the back. She turned and stared straight toward him. Letting go of the binoculars, he started toward the disappearing SUV.

Gabe grabbed his arm. "Running roughshod and getting yourself killed won't help them."

Justin nodded and huffed out a breath. He wanted to feel her eyes sweep over him, to feel her body next to his. Then, like a rocket taking off, she disappeared from sight.

Chapter 50

With a rough shove, Marissa stumbled into the large living room where she'd been earlier. She wanted to reach out to Walker, close behind her, but Evil Eyes stood in between them. Their hands were zip-tied behind them, and the pair slammed into chairs.

Walker scowled at the harsh treatment.

Marissa stared at the two men who'd abducted them from the field. The man accompanying Evil Eyes walked with a limp. Was he the guy she'd shot at the lake house?

Within minutes, Vivian entered, followed by Edward and two guards. "I'm growing quite tired of this game. I've played long enough. Other than Mr. Bane and a select few guards, my security team will be gutted. They have shown alarming ineptness." She turned to the maimed man. "Mr. Zogby got himself shot so his job is in question."

Zogby hung his head.

"Mr. Zogby should consider getting fired by a heartless bitch a great career move." Marissa lifted her head and met Vivian's gaze.

In three steps, Vivian reached Marissa, and the sound of her hand striking Marissa's face reverberated through the room.

Marissa slammed sideways to the floor, cheek stinging. Blood droplets littered the floor. Surmising Vivian's emerald ring caused the wound, she touched her face.

Vivian's eyes narrowed into slits. "Get up."

"Don't hurt her, Mother. I want her fully aware of what's about to happen." April entered the room with a slow gait, blood saturating her pants from a thigh wound. "Too bad my shooting arm is still intact, huh?"

Walker cleared his throat. "Loss of blood can affect muscle control and mind clarity. I contend you may have residual effects."

"Shut up. I'll get to you." Kearns slid a knife from her pocket and turned toward Marissa. "You and your boyfriend were astute enough to realize someone worked against you within the police department. Like your dead fiancé, your time has run out."

Was Vivian really her mother? Walker told them Vivian killed her child. Her heart thumped inside her chest. Whether these two women shared a genetic bond didn't matter, they were both psychotic.

Bane roughly tossed Marissa upright in her chair.

She tried pulling apart her hands, but the ties were tight and unmovable. A line of perspiration trailed down her back as she fought to control rising panic. She'd lost the knife Edward had given her which would be of little help now.

Bane and Zogby stepped away, but trained their guns on her and Walker.

Vivian sauntered to the window, staring out towards the woods. She spun and addressed one of the guards. "Escort our new guests in." She turned to Zogby. "Monitor the main door."

Marissa tensed. *Please don't let Justin, Sam or any of the guys walk in.*

Zogby and the guard nodded and exited through one of the doors.

Marissa stared at the multiple doors in the room. She recognized the door she'd entered earlier, and the door leading to Vivian's museum of horrors. The deck and the stables off in the distance were in Marissa's direct line of vision. If she managed to get free, her options for escape were dismal.

Vivian glided across the room stopping in front of April. "My daughter, your last task was interrupted, but we will continue. As you may one day take the helm of The Order, you must know danger is everywhere. There are those who lack the capacity to understand our edicts, and those who must pay for crossing us. You have been taught the ways of penance."

An expression of reverence floated over April. "I vow to bring our edicts to the world. Order, loyalty, willpower, and our justice will spread throughout the globe. Our followers will rise to the highest levels of government, business, and influence. From the throne of Babylon Hall, I will be the puppet master. *Ordo Ortus.*"

April's short monologue concluded Vivian nodded. "You are correct. You've learned well."

"Look who I found," Neal announced as he entered the room, followed by a guard holding Justin at gunpoint. "Hi, Marissa. Betcha didn't expect to see me." He beamed a campaign-wattage grin.

"Neal?" Marissa stared before turning to Justin, hoping to gauge whether he got Sam to safety.

"She's okay," Justin mouthed.

Marissa let out a breath before turning to Neal. "I thought you and David were friends."

Neal smirked. "Honey, nothing comes between me and my ambition. I hold The Order and Vivian in high regard."

"As a doctor, I'm amazed by this mass display of psychotic madness." Justin glanced back at Neal. "I never liked you, but I didn't take you for a nutty cult follower."

Neal laughed. "You were always so squeaky clean. I bet you allowed us to capture you, because your gut wouldn't permit you to let your lady love, and this other pathetic fellow, die without your gallant efforts to save them."

April sighed. "Why are we talking? Let's get on with this. I have fingers to collect." Strands of hair had separated from the ponytail and hung in a haphazard fashion around her oval face.

"Hold on." Neal raised his hand. "I'd like to get a few things off my chest before my good friend is executed. After all these years, you really didn't know David, or me, very well. Too busy saving the world."

"You have a promising political career, why get involved with these maniacs?" Justin scanned the room before making eye contact with Marissa.

She followed his gaze. *Did Justin have a plan?*

"These maniacs are *why* I have a promising political career. I interned for a subsidiary of Skies during college. I dazzled them so much, they chose me to ascend and do the work of The Order." Neal pressed a hand to his chest. "Yes, Neal Wingate, poor, average student, unable to get girls, everything the superstar stud here wasn't—and they wanted me. I even got the girl."

"You're nothing but a sellout." Justin flexed his fists.

Neal chuckled, his emerald cufflinks catching the sun. "As usual, Doctor, you're right. Sold to the highest bidder. I'm a cliché. I love money, power, and prestige, and Vivian gave me those treasures in exchange for my loyalty and determination to bring her vision to the world. Everyone has an agenda." Neal leaned toward Justin in a conspiratorial manner and softened his voice. "You wanna know something, Doc? The most powerful person in Washington isn't the president but who's behind the president. I agreed to be the front man, but the power nucleus lies right here." He punched at the air. "I have everything at my fingertips—wealth and growing power. So, hell yes, I'm a sellout."

Marissa struggled with her ties as Neal monopolized the room's attention. The ties didn't budge, and dug even deeper into her wrists. She glanced at Walker.

The right leg of his jeans had darkened from all the blood he'd lost. Though pale-faced and sweaty, Walker's gaze remained alert and focused.

"Then I guess the present company *is* your kind. You manipulated and sponged off David, but stupidity kept him from seeing the real you. I got tired of cleaning up his messes, and every single one of them could be traced back to you." Justin's biceps flexed but he remained still.

"Yes, I played manipulative games." Neal gave a hearty chortle. "Still do. I am where I am today due a ruthless attitude." He held up a finger. "But, David had been willing and eager as well." He reached out and ripped an Order patch off the nearest guard. "Don't you see?" He waved the patch in Justin's face.

Marissa gazed at Neal. Everything made sense now.

Neal stepped closer to Justin, staring upward due to their height difference. "David was a member of The Order. Part of our intelligence team, but he got too nosy. He hacked into a secured section of our server and stole highly confidential plans and associate lists. While I don't begrudge his entrepreneurial spirit, I draw the line when he intended to expose my wife and the people who gave me this fabulous life. No one will get in the way of my quest to 1600 Pennsylvania." He angled his head in Vivian's direction. "She concurred. He had to die."

Marissa shook with anger. How could David do this to her, to Justin? She placed her miscarriage, Sam's kidnapping, and all the other deaths, at his feet.

"Disloyalty is met with penance." April grinned.

Vivian waltzed across the room and stood next to Marissa. "My dear, only members of The Order and their families pay penance. I've had family members under my knife. I'm saddened I couldn't be there to collect David's finger but I decided the kill would be most effective in his home."

"Then why kill the nursing student, Justin's patient, or even Tiffany?" Marissa struggled to control her body's shaking. "Or us for that matter?" Witnessing true evil from one person had a terrifying effect, but observing such malice from an entire organization made for a mind-blowing experience.

Bane sighed. "They were used to make a point—you don't cross us. As for you, the doctor and the librarian—you know too much." He placed his hands on his hips.

Vivian exhaled. "Bane. I'll do the talking. "David, of course, had to be killed. Harold Silva's inattention to my company allowed the data to be accessed, so I had to terminate him." She glanced at April. "I had no choice. Your father had to die."

April shrugged, apparently nonplussed with the news of her father's death.

Vivian tapped the back of Marissa's chair. "Bane is right. I used the hospital patient, the nurse, and Tiffany to make a point. I think you received my message." She smiled. "You managed to sneak the child out so her life will have to be replaced in my lineup of seven. Marissa will be number six. The librarian hadn't initially been on my radar but since he played such an integral role in delivering the little girl to freedom, he will now be my lucky number seven."

Vivian smiled at Walker. "Welcome to your doom, Librarian." She turned to Justin. "Doctor, I considered you my number seven but I decided you should wallow in grief after the deaths of your friends.

Justin stepped forward, eyes blazing. "Your sick plan will never happen."

Vivian tossed her head back and laughed. "How cute you think you have a say in this."

Susan swept into the room and planted a kiss on Neal's lips. "Am I late for the party?"

"Who invited you?" April's question dripped with contempt.

"I have a place here, despite what you may think." Susan stood tall with hands on hips and glared from across the room.

Marissa's head pounded. Had she stepped into a demented soap opera?

"Susan, I chose you as Neal's mate, but at times, you've required limitations. However, your enthusiasm and support of our cause hasn't gone unnoticed. You've been an admirable recruit." Vivian's voice boomed throughout the room.

April's head snapped up. "An admirable recruit?"

Susan nodded, lowered her head, and spoke softly. "Vivian, I mean no disrespect. I am anxious to support Neal and usher in the goals of The Order. I believe my heart and my actions prove I'd be a worthy successor."

"Susan, you tried to kill me at the airport." Marissa shifted in her chair, her back ballet straight. "I saw your necklace."

Susan stared at Marissa, blinking slowly. "I wish I could take credit. I've been relegated to political wife and child kidnapper. The fun stuff like killing people has been deemed out of my realm of responsibilities, for now." She shrugged, and then slunk back to stand next to Neal.

"You were the one who took Sam?" Marissa longed to wipe the smug grin off Susan's face.

April advanced toward Marissa. "Never mind. Haven't you been listening? I've been in training." She pulled the necklace from behind her shirt and wiggled the green stone at the top.

The same necklace Susan wore.

"Yes, I'm a cop." April grinned. "But this is so much more. You've been slated for execution, however, prior to your placement on the kill list, you were my test. I wore a wig and I knocked you into the street, but the old lady got in my way. I couldn't risk another attempt. Fun times, but unfortunately the accident didn't result in your death."

"Enough! I'm growing tired of all this conversation." Vivian turned to a guard. "Untie them." She clasped her hands in front of her. "Father loathed meaningless talk. April, you will do well to understand. As a leader, you never admit your failures."

"Yes, Mother." April straightened and bowed her head.

The guard stepped forward and removed the zip ties.

Vivian turned to Susan. "Susan, don't allow your insecurities to rule your actions, especially in the face of opposition. You've disappointed me."

Susan stepped forward. "You know, April..."

Neal placed a hand on Susan's arm. "Now isn't the time."

Susan cut him a side-glance. "I've done everything you've asked of me, without fail, Grand Commander." She flashed a self-satisfied grin.

April's expression clouded as she placed the knife on the table next to Marissa. In one fluid motion, she yanked a gun from her pocket and aimed at Susan.

"April, I order you to stop!" Vivian screamed.

Susan cocked her head and smiled.

April licked her lips and fired.

Marissa's ears rang as the gunfire boomed throughout the huge room.

A tiny hole appeared in Susan's forehead. The smile on her face remained frozen for a second, then dissolved in confusion as she crumpled.

"Susan!" Neal yelled, catching his wife and sinking to the floor as she fell. "You didn't have to kill her." He glared at April.

Justin shook his head. He knelt next to Susan and examined her. "She's gone."

Rocking side to side, Neal screamed, "We were headed to the White House!"

April stood wide legged and grunted.

"April, you disappoint me." Vivian scooped up the knife and charged Marissa as April stood in stunned silence. She slammed Marissa's hand onto the table. "*Ordo Ortus.*" Her gaze wild, and a section of hair hung at a limp angle in front of her left eye.

Marissa writhed against Vivian's grip, but Bane held her arm in place.

Vivian raised the knife. Aiming for Marissa's pinkie finger, she held the blade with one hand.

Tensing, Marissa eyed the knife suspended in midair, her mind cluttered with inadequate escape routes. Her heart boomed inside her chest. "Justin!"

Just as the knife began a downward descent, Edward slammed into Vivian, knocking the weapon from her hand.

Vivian fell to the floor, eyes bulging as she stared at her disloyal assistant. "Edward."

He turned and shot the two guards in the room before they could react.

At the same time, Justin charged. He shoved Bane into the wall, knocking his holstered gun away.

Bane pushed off the wall and crashed into Justin, who withstood the onslaught and returned with a gut punch. Bane recoiled.

Justin turned just in time, but Bane's fist grazed his cheek. Justin staggered sideways then reared back and smashed his fist into Bane's temple.

Bane slammed to the floor, unconscious.

Justin picked up Bane's gun just before Zogby barreled into the room with his weapon aimed at Marissa. From a kneeling position, Justin turned and fired.

Zogby arched backward and fell to the floor, dead.

Another gunshot exploded.

On impulse, Marissa scrambled out of her seat, searching the room for a victim before realizing April had fired her gun into the air.

"I am in control. *Ordo Ortus.* I will be Grand Commander. I will take in the power of those who came before me: Russell Sinclair, Vivian Sinclair, and even the power of Nyx. I am the sole heir."

"No, you aren't." Walker stood and glanced down at Vivian, who still lay on the floor. "Hello, Mother."

Vivian's eyes widened. Without help, she managed to rise. "What? Who are you?"

Walker cleared his throat. "I-I'm the son you tossed away."

Marissa gasped. *Vivian was Walker's mother?*

Walker squared his shoulders. "Unlike April, I wasn't sent to live in luxury. I lived in foster care after being found abandoned on the side of the road. Eventually, a nice couple from Wisconsin adopted me. I once thought I drew the unlucky card, tossed away like an empty milk carton, but the Mumfreys loved me, and never kept my adoption secret. Eventually, I needed to find out who you were."

"I thought you died." Vivian held a hand to her throat. "When I had April, my father instructed me to kill her." Vivian eyed April. "I thought Harold loved me. I thought he'd marry me when I got pregnant, but his allegiance was to my father, not me." She turned to her daughter. "After you were born, I smuggled you out and to a friend. I knew you'd have a good life. I told my father I killed you and buried you in the Black Garden. Then I got pregnant again, and this time, my father wanted proof of a dead baby." Vivian paused and stared at Walker. "Another follower lived here on the grounds, pregnant with her fourth child. I forced an early birth, preserved the dead child, and presented it to my father after you were born. I only had time to toss you out on the road, but I intended to come back."

"You never bothered to find me." Walker's pained expression sliced through Marissa's heart.

Marissa's stomach lurched. Life meant nothing to Vivian, or her followers.

Justin sprinted across the room and grabbed Marissa's hand. "We're getting out of here."

April roared, "No one is leaving." She turned and shot Edward.

Edward yowled, cupping his injured hand as the gun fell.

Gun hand extended, April turned to Walker. "You think since you're my brother, you have a claim to all this?"

Rivers of sweat glided down Walker's face. "No, I want nothing of this insane ideology."

April laughed. "And you think I will allow *you* to live? I will not be bound by secrets." She glared at Vivian. "That's where you failed, Mother. Maybe Russell was right. Maybe you weren't capable of being a true leader. Mothers don't make good leaders, do they?" She aimed the gun. "Goodbye, Mother."

Marissa jumped as another gunshot echoed throughout the room.

A whimper escaped Vivian before she fell over, her eyes staring upward. Blood and brain tissue from the back of her head splattered the wall behind her.

Walker stepped forward and stared at his dead mother.

A wail sounded. April trembled, allowing the gun to tumble from her hand.

Neal rushed to pick up her gun.

"What have I done?" April rocked back and forth, then knelt beside her mother. She reached out to touch Vivian's face but withdrew her hand quickly. "She had to die, didn't she? To move The Order forward. *Ordo Ortus.*"

Neal massaged his forehead. "This needs to end. April is clearly insane." He turned, ignoring the gun in Justin's hand. "You and David had the looks and brains. Now is my time to shine." He puffed out his chest and nodded. "These women are out of my way, and Harold has been eliminated, my path to the top is clear."

Marissa glared at this pompous man. *He recovered from his wife's death quickly.*

Neal continued, "David and I were like brothers, kindred souls, but greed and recklessness took over. You don't piss off people with power and money. The only things standing in my way now are you people." He held the weapon steady and aimed the gun toward Edward, who cradled his bleeding hand. "Edward, you chose your allegiance, so sorry." Neal narrowed his eyes, but then in slow, deliberate motions, he shifted the gun from Walker to Justin to Marissa, and then back to Edward. "I think I'll start with...Marissa. There's always one girl who mucks things up."

"Don't, Neal." Justin pulled back on the trigger, and the gun clicked.

Marissa eyes widened. *The gun was out of ammo.*

Justin dropped the empty gun and lunged for the floor.

Neal raised his gun and fired just as Justin grabbed the rug and yanked, throwing Neal off balance.

The bullet wedged in a corner above Marissa's head, and she instinctively ducked.

Walker crawled next to her, breathing hard. "Bane!"

Edward kicked his gun toward Marissa.

Bane staggered up and charged toward her.

She raised the gun and fired, knocking Bane to the floor. He groaned in pain as Marissa fell back. When she scrambled up, she spotted April.

The blonde slid the emerald ring off Vivian's finger and picked up the knife but instead of advancing toward them April raced out of the room. Marissa jerked her head away from April's departure when she heard a crash.

Justin sprang again, pummeling Neal, who held on to the gun. They smashed through a table as Justin fought for the weapon.

Marissa aimed but hesitated. She couldn't risk hitting Justin.

A shot fired.

Within seconds, the police and people with FBI shirts invaded the room.

Justin and Neal lay entangled on the floor, a red pool of blood expanding beneath them.

Marissa stared at the intertwined bodies. *Please, not Justin.*

Chapter 51

Marissa sat in an uncomfortable hospital room chair and wrung her hands. Six hours had elapsed since the last shot was fired. She didn't know the last time she'd slept a full night, and after a three-hour interview with the FBI, they finally put her on their plane for the hour-long trip to Highland Memorial Hospital.

As she sat by the bedside, she'd phoned her parents and, after assuring them several times she hadn't been harmed, begged them not to come to the hospital. She had a mountain of events to process, but not tonight.

A few minutes later, Bobsled, Gabe, and Cas found her.

"I'm glad you're okay." Marissa stood and hugged each of them.

"It's nothing." Bobsled smiled and flashed the dollar bill-sized bandage covering the in-and-out bullet wound to his outer arm.

Marissa turned to Cas. "Thank you."

Grinning, he nodded.

Gabe patted her hand. "Can we do anything?"

Marissa smiled. "Sam is safe, thanks to you. She means everything to Justin."

"I think you do, too." Cas winked.

"Do you want us to stick around?" Bobsled asked.

"No, I'll tell him you stopped by."

Each man approached the bed and gave a light pat to the slumbering man's arm before leaving.

Once the door shut, Marissa turned and stared out the window. Night had fallen, and for once, hunting black SUVs didn't top her priorities list.

She exhaled, grateful Sam and Halo were safe with Wendy, Uncle Lou, and Aunt Iris.

"Do I still have two legs?" A hoarse voice emanated from the bed.

Marissa approached the bed. "In time your leg will work just like before. I called your family, and they will be here soon."

"Thank you." Walker patted Marissa's hand. "Where is my doctor?"

Justin sailed into the room, his blue scrubs molding to his tall, muscular body. He glanced at the monitors on the wall. "Walker, you will live to amass more useless data." He smiled and performed a quick exam of his injured leg.

Extending an arm, Walker shook Justin's hand. "Thank you."

Justin nodded. "This could have gone much worse. Thanks for taking care of Sam and Marissa. You're a good man. Rest."

Marissa leaned over and kissed Walker's cheek. "Thank you for everything. I'll be back later."

Walker nodded. He opened his mouth like he wanted to say something, but then clamped shut. Instead, he smiled up at Marissa.

FOUR WEEKS LATER, Halo bounced to the front door of Justin's house as a car door slammed outside. Marissa followed behind Halo as he waited for her to open the door.

Sam flew in and wrapped her arms around the excited dog. "I missed you, Halo." She stood to hug Marissa. "I missed you, too. California was fun." She grinned, displaying a new missing tooth.

"We're glad you're back." Marissa gave Sam an extra squeeze.

Even though weeks had passed, the thoughts and images of their terror continued to surface. On a much smaller level, she understood Justin's battle with PTSD.

Wendy strolled in and hugged Marissa. "I can't utter enough prayers of thanks."

Justin rounded the corner and scooped up Sam in his arms. "Who's this girl? She grew since I last saw her."

"I missed you, Uncle Justin."

Justin smiled as he set her down.

She scampered off to her room with Halo close behind.

He embraced Wendy. "Missed you, sis. I made coffee. Let's talk." He led the way to the kitchen.

The three sat at the kitchen table, coffee cups in hands, and Marissa and Justin explained the events of the last few weeks.

Now in physical therapy at the GT Training Center and back to work, Walker had finally gotten some answers. Years of research ended in him confronting his biological mother, with the added bonus of discovering his biological father, Harold Silva.

Edward, recovering from his own wound, had worked for Vivian for six years. He'd witnessed many of her atrocities and finally contacted the authorities. The FBI had opened a case on Vivian and The Order, but could never collect enough evidence for prosecution. Edward had become an FBI informant and now a key witness to all the misdeeds of Vivian, The Order, and Skies International. He'd even supplied Walker with the override codes allowing them to escape the tunnel.

"We were lucky Edward had been inside. Our escape would have been much harder had he not helped us." Marissa placed her hand over Wendy's. "I'm so thankful we got Sam out in time."

A tearful Wendy nodded. "I can't imagine the torture Vivian had in store. Thanks for keeping Sam safe." She turned to Justin. "What about April Kearns?"

Justin lowered his mug. "A body washed up on the riverbank ten miles from Babylon Hall. They're checking to see if it's April."

Neal and Susan Wingate were laid to rest together. Their involvement with Vivian and The Order hadn't been released to the public, yet. Neal probably would have won his campaign and Susan would have lapped up her new role.

With Carl Zogby and Vivian dead, Roy Bane was arrested for the murders of David, Tiffany, Emily, Mrs. Lambert, and Harold Silva.

The FBI had begun the long, arduous process of attempting to identify all of Russell and Vivian's victims, buried in the Black Garden and those preserved inside the museum of human remains.

The media coverage had been relentless for weeks. Marissa and Justin camped out in various locations to avoid the press. They'd been relieved the authorities kept Sam's name protected.

An hour later, Justin ushered Halo into the backseat and held the car door open for her. "Ready?"

Marissa nodded. Once inside the car, she pulled the engagement ring from her purse. "I'm selling the ring. The money will be split between the GT Training Center, David's son, and Mrs. Lambert's children."

He leaned over and kissed her. "You're amazing."

A short drive later, Justin pulled into the cemetery. Bright flowers lined the drive with dollops of trees emerging from a rug of lush green grass. The setting carried an uplifting, hopeful atmosphere, and by design Marissa chose a location far from David's burial site.

She stepped out of the car and took Justin's hand.

They snaked through several headstones, coming to a tiny, raised gray stone. Baby Nash had been laid to rest with respect and love. Halo settled at their feet. As tears fell, Marissa ran her hand over the sun-warmed stone.

"You'll never be forgotten." Marissa kissed the stone, and melted into Justin's arms.

After leaving the cemetery, Justin drove up to a small bungalow with a wide front porch and blue shutters.

Marissa climbed out of the car and stared at the house. "Perfect. Halo, we're home."

Halo followed and stood beside her, glancing upward with expressive brown eyes.

Justin wrapped his arms around her. "You know, my place is pretty great, too."

Marissa snaked her arms around his neck. "Good thing I negotiated a six-month lease."

"I love you." Justin caressed her face.

"I love you, too." Marissa sighed as contentment and peace swept over her.

Fear conquered, they were finally home.

THANK you for reading *Order of Fear*. I hope you enjoyed Marissa, Justin and the rest of the cast. Reviews are important to authors. Please consider leaving a review at the retailer of your choice. Thank you from the bottom of my heart!

PLEASE CONTINUE the Order Series with <u>Order of Malice</u> and Order of Rage.

INTERESTED IN GETTING up to the minute updates on new releases, sneak peeks, and sales? <u>Sign up for the Lisa Caviness newsletter here.</u>

NOW TURN the page for a sneak peek of Reid and Holly's story in the next thrilling book in the Order Series, <u>Order of Malice</u>.

THANK YOU!
Lisa Caviness

SNEAK PEEK

Sneak Peek of Order of Malice by Lisa Caviness

Working in the office of his Virginia home, Reid Patterson spent three hours organizing files and creating a timeline of activities associated with a new criminal trial. Reid stared at his chart. He hated never knowing for sure if their client had actually committed the crime for which they were accused, but he'd learned long ago his job was to ensure the client received fair and legal treatment through the justice system. The latest case—a man accused of bludgeoning his wife for the insurance money—sounded cliché, but Reid, as a jury consultant, had participated in four similar cases. In addition to other evidence, surveillance camera footage showed their client entering a hardware store where he purchased two hammers, one of which matched the victim's wounds. Reid groaned at the damning evidence, but he'd do his part in advising on the best jury possible. First, he needed to understand the specifics of the case in order to seat the right kind of jury.

Reid rubbed his eyes and wandered into the kitchen. He dumped milk and chocolate mix into a pot. While the mixture warmed, he stared out into the dark. Snow drifted down with furious intensity.

He'd be digging out from at least a foot by morning. He shivered, jogged over to the new thermostat, and punched up the temperature. His elderly landlord had allowed him to make a few modifications to the house. The first upgrade had been a new heater and air conditioner. As Reid heard the furnace click, he appreciated the hefty investment even more.

Before he could return to the kitchen, rapid hammering pounded on the front door. He glanced at his watch. 10 P.M. *Who could this be?* He angled his head and squinted through the peephole. A black-hooded figure with red-gloved hands stood on the porch. Reid stilled then peered through the peephole again. He raced to his lock box, placed his finger on the sensor, and retrieved his gun. As he ran back to the door, the knocking continued. This person was determined.

Sweat trickled down his back as Reid readied his gun. He inhaled and pulled open the door. "Can I help you?"

The hood tumbled back, revealing a young girl. Her hazel-eyed gaze burned into his.

"You tried to kill my mother."

ACKNOWLEDGMENTS

This book began on a few sheets of paper and traveled through many twists and revisions to end up here. Without the support, guidance, and shoulders to lean this book would have remained inside my notebook. I couldn't have done it without strong critique partners, dedicated beta readers, and many supportive authors I've met along the way. My heartfelt thanks to LaNora Mangano, Jillian Jacobs, T.C. Winters, Cheri Spell-Haase, Katherine Steinmeier, Arryn Harris, Donya Lynne, Anya Breton, and Ava Cuvay.

I would also like to acknowledge, Crossroads Romance Authors, Indiana RWA, Kiss of Death RWA Chapter, and Speed City Sisters in Crime Chapter for the wealth of information, support, and fellowship. And I can't forget The Juice Box. Thanks ladies!

A special thanks to Hank Phillippi Ryan for taking time to give a hand up to a new writer.

Thank you to Andrew Garrett, eDiscovery/Forensics Expert of Garrett Discovery, Inc (www.garrettdiscovery.com) for the wealth of information on investigations.

I would also like to thank:

Linda Carroll-Bradd, (www.lustreediting.com) Any mistakes are my own.

A.J. Corza (www.seeingstatic.com) for a genius cover design.

Lastly, thanks to DW, AT, NB, KA, and my Mom and Dad for their unwavering support.

ABOUT THE AUTHOR

As a lifelong reader of an eclectic pool of books from mystery/thrillers, science fiction, contemporary romance, and the classics, Lisa Caviness has never been without a book on the night-stand and a long to be read list. Although she began crafting stories as a child, she also held a deep interest in science. After college, she worked as a registered nurse before starting a career as a clinical project manager in pharmaceutical and medical device research. She has lived in Boston, Massachusetts and in the Midwest with her husband and kids.

Lisa writes romantic suspense and thrillers. She loves dreaming up story ideas where her characters are pushed to their limits during dangerous and blood-tingling adventures. Lisa is a member of Romance Writers of America (Crossroads Romance Writers, Indiana RWA, and Kiss of Death Chapters) and Sisters in Crime (Speed City Chapter).

For more information about Lisa, please see her website at: http://www.lisacavinessauthor.com

facebook.com/lisaCavinessWriter

twitter.com/LisaCaviness1

instagram.com/lisacaviness1

amazon.com/author/lisacaviness

ALSO BY LISA CAVINESS

The Order Series

Order of Fear

Order of Malice

Order of Rage

Anthologies

The Hope Chest

The Porch Swing

The Lake House

Order of Fear by Lisa Caviness

Published by Dream Theory Publishing, LLC

ISBN 978-0-9974132-0-5 (digital)

ISBN 978-0-9974132-1-2 (print)